WINNING THE Season

BETH BOLDEN

PROLOGUE

Asa's shirt was sticky and clung to his skin, a mixture of anxious sweat and the super-sweet Gatorade he'd been drenched in half an hour before.

He tried to tug it out of his khakis but it stuck, stubbornly, and suddenly, he couldn't help it—he started laughing and wasn't sure he could stop.

"You alright over there?" Scott asked, chuckling under his breath.

Asa glanced over and saw that he'd already managed to get his own shirt off, and his bare chest was smeared with green goo instead of the orange he was currently covered in.

"I see the defense got you," he said, watching as Scott tried to use his discarded shirt, already stained with neon-green patches, to clean off his chest. It wasn't working very well.

Scott's smile was wry. "Neither of us was quick enough."

"I think," Asa said, tugging his shirt up again, "we might've been distracted."

It wasn't surprising; winning a second national title in four years would be enough to distract anyone.

It was the first Scott was here to share with him.

Was that why the euphoria felt so much stronger this time? Because even more than the first time, he'd felt absolutely overwhelmed by the joy of it, the realization that they'd finally done it distracting him so much that even though he was normally nimble enough to avoid the quintessential Gatorade bath, he hadn't even noticed it coming today until he'd been soaked with it.

He'd been too busy staring at the scoreboard, somehow hoping that it wouldn't impossibly change in the last few seconds, and too busy staring at Scott, who was wearing a smile that Asa didn't think he'd ever seen on him before.

He thought he knew every smile Scott possessed. But he didn't know this one.

They'd known each other for over twenty years. And from the very beginning, when they'd played for Alabama, they'd always talked about this.

Coaching together.

Winning a National Championship together.

Asa finally got the shirt off. Beau would tell him he needed to stop wearing his polos so tight, but then Beau was seventeen and full of too many opinions about what he should and shouldn't be wearing.

Scott laughed, and suddenly he was right there, in Asa's face.

There was that smile again. The one that Asa didn't recognize.

It was lighting up Scott's eyes, like he'd been plugged into the nearest socket. "Here," he said, trying to wipe away some of the semi-dried orange goop with his shirt. "God knows how many interviews you'll be giving, and imagine the heart attack Beau's gonna have if you're still covered in Gatorade."

His hand paused on Asa's face.

Asa hadn't realized he was that close, until he was, and something funny churned in his stomach. Not happiness. Or exhilaration. He could identify those. He knew what they felt like. He'd felt them before.

This was different.

He could pick out every single different shade in Scott's eyes. Everyone might say they were gray, but they were actually green and blue and purple and a little tiny bit of light brown. You couldn't see that if you weren't close, like Asa was now.

"You did this," Scott said quietly. His voice, always so deep and resonant, with its Southern twang, was rough around the edges.

"*We* did this," Asa reminded him. "Together."

Scott kept wiping. It seemed impossible that Asa could still have fucking Gatorade on his face, but he hadn't stopped yet.

"We said we'd do it, didn't we?" Scott said, but it didn't sound particularly like a question. "Now damnit, stop squirming, I promised Beau I'd take care of you, and I'm gonna do it."

Asa looked ahead. Right into Scott's collarbone. It was tan from a summer of being outside and there was still plenty of corded muscle on either side of the bone.

He was taller than Asa by at least two inches. Back in college, he'd been a dynamite defensive end. Big and brawny with shoulders so broad that when they'd played together at Alabama, the regular shoulder pads hadn't fit him quite right.

It was funny, Asa knew all these things about Scott. Had known them for over twenty years. But today, for some reason, the knowledge of them settled weird and uncomfortable into the base of his stomach.

Asa swallowed hard. Hoped that Scott wouldn't notice and think he was uncomfortable. Especially when he knew Scott was gay, and he wasn't.

They'd changed together so many times he'd lost count, so none of this should have mattered.

But he'd never glanced down and seen the trail of golden hair leading down his flat stomach, ridged with muscle, and wondered if it would taste sweet.

Like Gatorade.

But he was thinking it now.

He cleared his throat. "You just about done?"

Scott chuckled low and soft. "Impatient much?"

He was. If only because suddenly this big bathroom, with its utilitarian blue tile walls and floor, suddenly felt too small and too tight, Scott too close.

You're just overwhelmed, Asa told himself. *That's all. You're crazy to be thinkin' that about Scott. He's been your best friend for at least twenty years.*

That's all they'd ever been. Best friends who worked together, off and on, sometimes on the same collegiate coaching staff, until Asa had gotten the break at Tennessee, and as soon as he could, when the longtime defensive coordinator had retired, he'd brought Scott on.

"I'm not patient, you know that," Asa said.

Scott chuckled again, and he glanced up, flashing that same grin. The one that Asa didn't quite recognize.

"I do know," he said. "Good thing I've got enough for both of us."

Finally, he took a step back and gave Asa an approving nod. "You'll do."

"Well, that's a relief," Asa retorted dryly.

He turned towards the mirror.

He looked flushed. Hair wild. Eyes even wilder.

He didn't look anything like himself.

What was that look on his face?

He didn't recognize it.

Kinda like that smile Scott was still wearing.

Scott's head hovered behind his own, and for a split, insane second, Asa nearly turned back and asked him the question that kept echoing through his head.

What are we doing?

But before he could do it, there was a knock on the bathroom door.

"It's just me," Beau said, letting himself in before either of them could say anything. "I've got some dry clothes. I'm sure everyone and their mother is gonna want to talk to you, so you might as well look presentable."

Beau barely glanced at him as he passed him the clothes, and then Scott another pile. So maybe it was just him. Maybe it was just leftover adrenaline, churning in his stomach, making him uneasy.

But it wasn't his stomach that had thought those things, was it?

Still, if Beau didn't notice—because Beau noticed *everything*—then it must not be anything.

But if it wasn't anything, why did the remembered knowledge of it keep fizzing under his skin long after they'd left the bathroom?

February

"So Beau's on a date, huh," Scott said, stretching out his long legs in front of him.

They were very long, and very bare, because they'd just gotten back from a run, and he was still wearing his shorts.

Asa nearly averted his eyes, because there was so much of them—golden skin dusted with blond hair—but then at the last second, he didn't, because that would be giving in to that weird, shaky feeling that he still hadn't managed to destroy completely.

The one that had started a month ago, and he hadn't quite been able to convince himself he was imagining.

Scott is your best friend. That's all he is.

He'd been repeating the same mantra over and over again, but it didn't seem to be having any effect.

Asa picked up his water bottle and chugged half of it. "It's Valentine's Day, of course he's on a date."

"You like this guy he's seein'?" Scott asked. He was Beau's godfather, so he had skin in the game too, but he wasn't Beau's father. And he didn't worry, the way Asa did, if he was ruining his son's life by dragging him along with him to every locker room, every conference room, through so many practices and games.

Beau seemed to enjoy it, and even said he wanted to be there, but Asa couldn't help but worry.

What kind of future was Beau settin' himself up for?

Would he be happy?

Would he stay in the closet for the next twenty years, like Scott had, just to be close to the game he loved?

"He's not a football player, so yes," Asa said wryly. "He's a guy in Beau's statistics class, and they're goin' to the Dairy Queen. I think it's gonna be just fine."

"You know, you can fool most anyone, but you can't fool me," Scott said. "You're worried about him."

"He's seventeen and probably making out and *worse* in the back of a 1998 Toyota Camry," Asa said. "'Course I'm fucking worried."

Scott's eyes twinkled. "Is it the 'worse' you're worried about?"

"*No*, you know I don't give a shit about that," Asa muttered. "At least I don't have to stress he's gonna get some girl pregnant."

"Like father, like son?" Scott asked unrepentantly, still grinning.

There was that smile he didn't recognize again.

Asa elbowed him in the side and didn't feel a single ounce of regret as Scott squawked. "That was unfair. Maybe we didn't plan for Beau, but I'm real glad we had him. And I wasn't *seventeen*."

"True, true," Scott said with a chuckle. "So Valentine's Day, and you're here with me. Where's your hot date?"

Asa wanted to tell him that he was *always* his favorite person to be with, but it was Valentine's Day, wasn't it? You were supposed to be indulging in romance.

Like Clay taking Beau to the Dairy Queen.

"You know I don't date," Asa said.

"Yeah, but the question is why? You're not old, Asa. You've still got it."

Asa almost asked him what he had, still.

But he didn't.

Instead, he asked, "What about you? You not doin' anything special either?"

Scott shook his head. "What am I gonna do? Head to the gay club and pick up a guy for the night? No, thanks. I'm good. Just sittin' here on your front porch and waiting for Beau to come home so we can scare the shit out of this new boyfriend."

The thing was, Scott didn't date either. Asa had never met a guy that he'd been with. Was it all just . . . hookups? Was that what they called it? He'd ask Beau, but Beau would moan helplessly at his incredible lack of coolness, and he didn't need that on top of everything else.

No, he wasn't cool.

Maybe he still had *it*, whatever *it* was, but he wasn't interested in using it. All he wanted was to sit on this porch, with Scott.

Truthfully, since Lynn had left—and even before that—he'd worked too much to have time for romance.

"I guess we're both a little pathetic," Asa said. "Single and uh . . . alone."

Scott shot him a sideways look. A hot look, that scorched him a little around the edges. What did that even *mean*? Asa didn't know. Asa wasn't sure he wanted to know, but he was drawn to the answer inexorably.

That was the danger of having a curious personality.

At least that was what he told himself.

"I won't tell," Scott said, "if you don't."

March

It was official; Asa wasn't getting over it.

It had been over two months now since the National Championship, and everything was both exactly the same and completely, radically different.

And not just because Beau was sitting up in his room now, ready to press the button on a social media post that would change everything about his life.

"Tell me he's not makin' a huge fuckin' mistake," Asa said to Scott, because he couldn't ask about the other thing.

The thing that haunted him at night.

I think I might be attracted to you, and I don't know what the fuck to do about it.

Scott sighed, toying with the label on his beer bottle.

"Beau's not me," Scott said.

"He's not *not* you," Asa said.

"Why, 'cause we're both gay and want to work in football?" Scott's voice was wry. They'd never lied to each other.

At least not til Asa had started carrying around this shameful secret.

He knew the parameters of it now, the way it was beginning to solidify around the edges and fill into the middle.

How he checked Scott out now, when he knew he wouldn't notice.

How he lay in bed late at night, skin damp and desperate, and he refused to touch himself and think about his best friend that way.

But he'd accepted, at least, that it wasn't momentary insanity, the product of a wild adrenaline surge, and that it was probably here to stay.

He'd learn to live with it. He'd learned to live with tougher.

Like the fact that his son was upstairs, about to change his whole life.

"I just don't want him hurt," Asa said. His voice sounded raw to his own ears.

He'd told Beau that it was his choice, that he loved him no matter what, that he'd protect him with every last molecule of himself.

He didn't know what Scott had told Beau, in the privacy of that room, before he'd come downstairs, but when he had, he'd headed straight to the fridge and pulled a pair of beers out, setting one in front of Asa after he'd chugged half of his own.

"Doesn't matter," Scott said. "World will chew you up and spit you out, no matter what. You just gotta be there to pick up the pieces after."

"How could I be anywhere else?"

"Yeah, but you realize the world's not gonna think you will, right?"

Asa stared at him.

There was a raw pain in Scott's eyes, in his face. "They're gonna think that you won't like it. College football coach in the South?"

Disgust flared through Asa. "What absolute assholes."

"I never thought it, you know *I* didn't," Scott said apologetically. Like he should fucking *apologize* for how homophobic the world was. New, hotter anger rushed through Asa. "'Course you'd support Beau."

"And I'll say so," Asa said. "Unequivocally."

Scott looked at him. Soft and vulnerable. The remnants of his pain still visible. "Never thought you'd do anything different," he said. "You're a good father. A good man."

Asa cleared his throat. "I'm a human," he said. "That's all. A decent fucking human."

"You're a human?"

Asa glanced up. There was Beau on the top of the stairs, shadows hiding half his face. But there was a freedom, a defiant *fuck you* there.

He'd done it, then. Gone and posted all his truths on social media. For any other kid about to graduate from high school, it would still have been a massive fucking deal personally, but nobody outside their circle would've cared.

But in Beau's case, everyone was going to give a shit because of Asa and the position he held.

As a result, he was both unbearably proud and also undeniably terrified.

How could he protect his son if he insisted on being so fucking brave?

He couldn't.

You can't, Scott had said, *you just gotta be there to pick up the pieces.*

And so he would.

April

It felt good to be back on the field again, back to someplace he could control.

After Beau had come out on social media last month, things had spiraled out of control. Lots of people assumed before Asa had even made a statement that he'd disowned his own son. Which, Asa thought, said a hell of a lot more about them than it said about him. Then he'd made a statement, and people seemed evenly split between not believing him and thinking he had some kind of ulterior motive for being so understanding.

Very few people just believed, like Scott did, that he was doing it because it was the goddamned right thing to do.

So after wading through all that fucking mess, Asa couldn't deny that he was real glad to be back where he belonged: on the sideline, not yelling, but making it real clear to a player that he needed to shape up. Or else.

"When the quarterback drops back," Asa said, trying to hold on to his temper, "that means he's gonna pass the goddamn ball. And that means what to you?"

The kid's face was sullen, sunken into difficult lines. Asa had worried about him when they'd recruited him out of Texas. He'd been the best player on his team—not necessarily the most skill, but the most raw athletic ability. It needed to be shaped and honed, but he'd resisted every step of the way.

"Blitz," the kid insisted.

Asa sighed.

Of course that was when Scott decided to show up. "What's up?" he asked, turning his attention to the kid in front of Asa—who, as far as he was concerned, was not nearly as afraid of him as he should be, considering his reputation.

"Marcus here thinks it's cool to blitz the quarterback every play."

"Marcus, we've discussed this." Scott shaded his eyes. "You're covering the middle. You know the plays."

"But he's right there," Marcus said, his stubborn chin jutting out even further. "If he can't throw the ball, then who cares who's in the middle."

That attitude, unfortunately, was going to doom him to third string for most of his football career at Tennessee, and ensure he was going to be labeled a huge bust.

And while he shouldn't take it personally, Asa *did*. Because he vouched for every single goddamn player on his team, and there was something he should be able to do to turn this train wreck around.

"He's gonna throw the ball. Allen's real mobile. He's gonna evade you, Marcus. And then he's gonna throw the ball, and because nobody's covering the middle, someone's gonna catch it and run forty yards."

Scott still sounded so patient.

Marcus did not look convinced.

Asa wasn't convinced either.

"Let's try it again, okay?" Scott said, patting him on the back. Marcus jogged back out to where the defense was convening in the huddle.

"Fucking hell," Asa huffed under his breath.

"He's gonna get it," Scott said.

"No, he's gonna be doing the same stupid shit every single play, I can feel it. We should move him to special teams coverage. Something. He can't go after the quarterback if he's coverin' the kickoff."

Scott turned to him, grinning. "Want to make it interesting?"

He didn't, not really, but the way Scott's smile lit up his insides—even when they shouldn't, even when he was trying so goddamn hard to ignore it—made him say, "Sure. Winner buys dinner after the spring game."

"Done," Scott said. He shoved his hands into his pockets. It was already warm, even though it was only April, and the wind ruffled through his light brown hair, the sun touching it with gold in spots.

He'd looked like this for twenty-plus years. A few less lines around his eyes, maybe. But the same.

And for twenty-three of those years, Asa couldn't have really told you anything about how he looked.

But in year twenty-four, he couldn't stop thinking about it.

The broadness of his shoulders in his t-shirt. The glints of gold in his hair. The heat in his cool eyes. The way his long stride ate up the field as he marched over to where the defense was gathering and then again as he walked back.

It was all a problem, and Asa didn't have a fucking clue what to do about it.

Scott was his best friend, and despite that he *knew* he was gay, there'd never been a moment where he thought that maybe Scott might feel the same about him. So he couldn't assume anything was mutual. He also couldn't jeopardize this team, and the future they were building. Because Beau's coming out had reminded him, brutally, that they were in the South, and football in the South was unforgiving, at best.

And what, was he going to just throw almost a thirty-year friendship away because he had a goddamn hard-on? No, he was not.

He was gonna ignore it.

"Okay, let's see how it goes," Scott said, eagerly.

Sure, Asa knew, that he was going to win the bet.

Scott had enough patience for ten thousand saints—or in this case, one bullheaded nineteen-year-old who thought they hung the fucking moon.

Asa blew the whistle, and the play unfolded, Allen dropping back, the ball in his hands, the deep receivers sprinting off the line, the corners shadowing them, there was Marcus, stance low, as he waited for the tight end to fall back into the slot, and the moment he caught the ball, a perfect spiral thrown by Allen, he had them on the turf.

He popped up, smiling ecstatically, like *he'd* just won a National Championship.

"Goddamn," Asa muttered. Not sure if he was happy he'd actually *done it* this time.

"Heeeeeyyyy," Scott crowed, turning towards Asa, clearly feeling good enough for both of them. "Guess you're buyin' me dinner."

Scott had never hesitated to touch him, and he didn't now, either, putting both hands on his shoulders and tugging him into a half-hug of triumph.

He was being pulled along this path, even though he didn't want to walk it, but every time Scott touched him, he realized he was a little further along. A little more desperate. A little less in control.

"Goddamn," Asa said again, as Scott walked away. "*Goddamn.*"

May

"You lookin' forward to going to college?" Scott asked Beau as they sat at one of the picnic tables dotted across the park. They were all full, because it was Memorial Day.

Asa had never been particularly good about celebrating holidays, but Memorial Day he could do, because it was technically before the football season started, and *after* the Spring Game.

Beau rolled his eyes. "Like I haven't been practically going to that school for years."

Asa ignored the twinge of guilt he felt. Sure, Beau had chosen to stay, when his mother had left, but he had really *chosen* to come to the office with his father every day?

Beau had probably decided he'd become a football coach because that was what he was surrounded by every single goddamn day.

"True, but now you're gonna get *paid* for all those brilliant contributions," Scott teased.

Asa scowled into his potato salad. "I paid him before," he said. "Beau's always had a very generous allowance."

Asa had told Beau that he could skip a year of being his assistant and working with the team, if he wanted to, to give himself a chance to adjust to college life. To find a life *outside* football, Asa had hoped, because he hadn't failed to notice that Beau was becoming just like him. Singularly focused to the exclusion of everything else.

But Beau had just laughed at him, and negotiated an even higher rate for his duties.

It wasn't that Beau didn't deserve the money; he did, 'cause he was fucking brilliant at analyzing film and breaking down plays. He could see the field better even than Asa. But there were some days when Asa thought, somewhat bitterly, that he'd doomed his son to the same lonely, isolated kind of life he led.

"It's all in the bank," Beau said.

Because of course it was. Where would he spend it? Besides semi-regular "dates" at the Dairy Queen with that guy from his statistics class, he didn't go out much.

Asa stabbed a chunk of potato with a lot of unnecessary force—and his plastic fork, unprepared for such vehemence, snapped right in half.

"Oh crap," Beau said, "let me grab you a new one. I think we have some in the car."

He jogged off before Asa could say that he wasn't very hungry anyway.

"You're worrying too much about him," Scott said as soon as Beau was out of hearing range.

"Can you blame me? I've pushed him into this."

Scott raised a golden-brown eyebrow. Asa was *almost* used to the flare of attraction now, and he'd stopped fighting it, mostly. It was easier to just accept that it happened. Of course, he wasn't *doing* anything about it, but he still felt it.

He'd have to be goddamned dead not to feel it.

"You didn't push him into football," Scott said. "He wants this."

"He says so, but what if he's just tryin' to impress me? You know, lots of people try to do that."

"Yeah, don't know why that is," Scott teased, elbowing him gently in the ribs. "You're not so hard to impress."

He was, and they both knew it.

"Seriously," Scott continued, "he wants this. It means something to him that he can be helpful to you. He's a good kid. Let him do what he wants."

"I hired him, didn't I?"

"Yeah, but every time it comes up, you scowl, scrunching up right between your eyebrows . . ." Scott trailed off, his fingers reaching up to brush Asa's forehead—and there it was again, that flare of attraction. "And if you're not careful, you're gonna get bad wrinkles."

"Nobody on earth gives a damn if I get wrinkles," Asa said.

But he knew that wasn't quite true.

Scott cared. It was shining in his eyes right now.

Un-fucking-missable.

Scott stroked the skin there, smoothing out the temporary creases. "You know that's not right. Beau gives a shit. I give a shit. Neither of us wants to hang out with some wrinkled old man."

Asa chuckled. How could Scott *always* pull him out of a bad mood? Maybe because he'd been doing it for so long, he always knew exactly what to say.

"That so?"

Scott nodded. His hand lingered though, and for a second, Asa was sure his heart skipped a beat. Breathing suddenly felt very labored.

It was just the touch of his fingertips to the side of his face, but it felt intimate. Real. A tangible touch to match the connection they'd always shared.

It doesn't mean that to him, it's just nice to him, that's all, Asa told himself, but he wasn't stupid enough to miss that the moment Beau approached, brandishing a new plastic fork, was when Scott dropped his hand.

He didn't want Beau to see.

It was just between him and me.

June

It was hot. Really goddamned hot.

And not just the temperature outside—though it was at least ninety still, even though the sun had nearly dropped behind the horizon.

Why had Asa suggested they stop at the Dairy Queen for ice cream?

It hadn't seemed stupid at the time, but it felt incredibly stupid now.

Because it seemed in the last five months, since he'd begun to realize he was attracted to Scott, he hadn't seen him eat an ice cream cone.

They'd ordered, just the same as always, grabbed some seats outside, their ice cream already beginning to drip down their hands. Asa had frozen, watching as Scott laughed, and licked a stripe up his hand, trying to gather as much melting milk into his mouth as possible.

Sweat trickled down Asa's spine, and not just because it was still hot as hell outside.

No, it was because he was more turned on than he could ever remember being, just watching Scott eat a goddamned ice cream cone.

His tongue seemed to curl around it, swiping the soft serve into a kind of submission that lit up every single one of Asa's nerves.

He'd tried so hard not to think of his best friend in such sexual terms—it was *unfair*, really, to both him and to Scott, who'd certainly never asked for it—but that ship was definitely in the middle of sailing.

Scott gestured with his cone. "You're drippin' everywhere, Asa." His voice was low and rough, and Asa shivered, even though it was so hot.

But the reminder did at least jerk him into action, licking up the cool ice cream as quickly as he could. Trying not to look over at Scott.

Trying as hard as he goddamned could not to think about what that tongue would feel like along his skin.

It's just been too long for you; you haven't had sex in . . . Asa couldn't actually remember the last time he'd had sex. It had been with his ex-wife, but even then, they hadn't really torn it up between the sheets. He'd always thought himself too busy, too focused, to really get lost in sex.

But he had a feeling if Scott leaned over and pressed his cool lips to his, they wouldn't just get lost, they'd disappear entirely.

It was why, late at night, long after he'd returned home, and gone to bed, he tentatively reached down his bare chest, down further, to where his cock pulsed and twitched against his leg. He was horny, that was all. Too long without stimulation. Wasn't it supposed to be a chemical thing?

But the image that instantaneously popped into his head—Scott, leaning over him, one of those irrepressible smiles on his handsome face, the muscles of his shoulders flexing, then his tongue flicking out, licking right along his skin, like he'd licked the ice cream—wasn't a chemical thing at all.

It was sheer, unadulterated *want*.

For the last person he should be thinking about.

He couldn't help it anymore. He'd fought against it long enough, and it felt sweet, like surrender, to wrap his hand around his cock and finally let himself think about Scott.

About Scott's tongue, and his shoulders, and his eyes and his hair.

About his friendship. His loyalty. The way he smiled. The way he laughed. The way he goddamned *smelled*.

His orgasm caught him by surprise, roaring through him with a power he'd never imagined.

Cleaning up with shaky fingers, Asa realized two things: 1) it was definitely not just a chemical thing, and 2) that ship wasn't just sailing, it had *sailed*.

July

The sky above them exploded in a million shards of light and color, the crowd oohing and aahing at the display.

Asa glanced around, uneasy, not for the first time, that it was just him and Scott.

How had he gotten to this point? They'd been hanging out together for over twenty years, but now? Now, he was shamefully holding his breath when he asked Beau if he wanted to tag along. Hoping, despite himself, that it would be just them.

Hoping, also, that it wouldn't.

"You okay?" Scott asked under his breath, nudging him with his shoulder. "You look distracted."

He was a lot of things. Distracted was the least of them.

His stomach felt like it existed in a perpetual clench, because every time Scott was around, it was like trying to contain a hurricane of butterflies. He might be a pro—had worked his ass off to be considered one of the best in the business—but he felt like a teenage boy whenever Scott looked at him.

Like Scott was looking at him now.

He felt hot everywhere Scott's gaze touched him—and there was no way to ignore that Scott was gazing at him pretty dang intently.

"I . . . uh . . ." Asa stammered over the words.

He didn't know if he was imagining but he swore . . . he *swore* . . . there was something in Scott's eyes now. Something intent. Something that felt like it resonated deep inside himself, that echoed all of his own jumbled feelings.

But he couldn't say so, because what if he was wrong?

There was so much he'd be risking: his job, *Scott's* job, their reputations, and a twenty-plus-year friendship he didn't know how he'd do without if it fell apart.

Asa had never considered himself particularly cowardly. He'd always gone after what he wanted.

But he'd never wanted anything like he wanted Scott.

The fireworks exploding above them reflected in Scott's eyes, and for a split second, he wanted so badly, Asa almost told the whole world to fuck off. Almost decided that all the risks didn't exist, that they were just roadblocks he'd thrown up because he was fucking terrified that he was falling for his best friend.

That he'd already fallen for him.

"You've been quiet." Scott's voice was rough. Asa could feel it sliding against his nerves, lighting them up. "Distracted."

Asa licked his lips. They weren't *alone* alone. There were probably thousands of people in this park, watching the fireworks.

But they were watching the fireworks.

They weren't watching them.

They were just two guys, heading into middle age, sitting together on this hillside.

Maybe in the dark, in the promise of anonymity, he could find his courage.

"You said that already." The tone of his voice shocked him. Low. Intimate. When was the last time he'd spoken to someone like this? Had he *ever* spoken to someone like this?

With Lynn, it had felt expected. They would date. They would fall into bed together. They would get married and have a child. Now, they'd done the last two out of order, but it had all felt very safe.

Scott was the safest person in the world, and yet, also, the most terrifying.

A smile tilted up the corner of Scott's mouth. God, he'd had dreams about that mouth.

Dreams where he pressed his own against it.

Dreams where it slid over his skin. Tasting him. Tormenting him.

His cock grew harder in his shorts—a side effect that he seemed to bring out these days, just by sitting next to Asa and fucking *breathing*—and Asa hoped that it was dark enough that Scott wouldn't see.

Because even though he might dream about it, he knew he wasn't ready to reach for it.

"I wouldn't have said it, if it wasn't true." Scott's voice grew teasing now, and had his head tilted down, closer to Asa's? It felt like it had. "You got something you want to tell me?"

Asa reached down, to the ground, trying to ground himself, and nearly gasped when his fingertips brushed the back of Scott's hand. He hadn't realized it was right there, so close, just lying innocently against the grass.

He should've apologized. Moved away. But he didn't. Maybe he wasn't brave enough to do everything he wanted, everything he dreamed about late at night, alone in his room, but there was nothing wrong about this.

He reached out, with a single fingertip, and just felt Scott's big hand, with its callouses and ridges and scars. Traced each inch of it, desperate to memorize all of it.

Maybe he wouldn't get everything he wanted, but he could have this.

Scott didn't move. Didn't blink. Just sat there and let him touch him.

Asa didn't answer the question. Couldn't answer it, because he wasn't wrong. There was something he desperately wanted to say, but it kept getting stuck in his throat.

So he said nothing, and touched Scott's hand, and hoped that was answer enough.

August

"Goddamn, that feels good."

It *looked* good.

Asa swallowed hard and watched as Scott lay back and let the water envelop his big body, his black boxer briefs soaking and clinging to his legs, to his waist, to . . . *goddamn*, Asa reminded himself, *you're not gonna think about his cock.*

But he was. Inevitably.

It had been Scott's idea to go to the quarry, to take a cool dip after practice.

He knew it wasn't possible, but it felt like this was the most bare skin of Scott's he'd seen since January, since the night they won the National Championship, and he'd been rocked on his heels by this crazy attraction he still couldn't explain.

"Uh, yeah, it does." Asa slipped his feet in, and then let the rest of him follow, hoping that the water might cool him down enough so he wouldn't feel like he was ten seconds away from exploring what Scott's slick, wet skin might feel like against his palms.

He stayed underwater for ten seconds, then twenty, and finally raised his head, spluttering and pushing his hair back as the water cascaded off his face.

It was August, so it was always busy here at the quarry, but it was a weeknight, so while there were a few pockets of what looked to be teenagers, they were mostly alone.

In his head, Asa imagined that was why Scott had suggested they come.

More and more it felt like they were both finding excuses to be alone.

Nothing happened, but Asa felt like they were teetering there, right on the brink.

Scott flipped onto his back and did a lazy backstroke around Asa. "You think the team's lookin' okay?"

"You know I think so." Asa had said it to them, even, after practice today. He wasn't stingy with praise—he'd found you could trap so many more flies with honey than with vinegar, a fact that many college and NFL coaches had yet to realize despite all the evidence to the contrary—but he did like to hold back, especially in the early parts of the season. Too much praise, and the kids wouldn't work hard enough.

And, someone might realize that all his gruff exterior was hiding was a bleeding heart.

Sure, he wanted to win.

But more than that, he wanted these kids to succeed at whatever they set their minds to. Maybe it was football. Maybe it wasn't. As the years went by, Asa discovered that it mattered less and less to him if it wasn't actually football.

Sure, the national titles felt good. The acclaim felt fucking wonderful. But now that he'd amassed all of those, he'd discovered the bragging rights didn't mean much.

"Yeah, I think Marcus is even gonna give up his dream of setting the sack record," Scott said, his smile glimmering in the dusk.

Asa rolled his eyes, kicking his legs to stay afloat. The quarry was deep. Even with their height, neither of them had any chance of touching the bottom.

"That kid is gonna be the death of me," he said. It was true though, with Scott's patience, and Asa's tenacity, they might actually convince the guy to play well enough to make the first team.

"It's always tough when there's that much potential," Scott said.

Half the time now, it felt like they were talking in double speak.

Were they talking about Marcus still? Or had they moved into deeper waters? Asa didn't know. If he asked, then it would be out in the open, and while he felt . . . less terrified . . . of that possibility, was he ready for it yet? Was the reward finally greater than the risk?

"A lot of risk. But then there's the upside, if it works out," Asa agreed quietly.

He didn't even know if he was talking about Marcus. Or about the connection that had bloomed between them, that seemed to lie just out of reach.

"I think I'm gonna play him, first game of the season." So he *was* talking about Marcus. Asa adjusted his thinking, considering what he'd said.

The first game was in a week. And truthfully, Asa had assumed Scott would start Marcus, as a test.

That was Scott's way.

He was a brilliant defensive mind, moving players around the field like chess pieces on a board, always trying to find the wiggle room that the other team hadn't anticipated or planned for.

When asked, that was why Asa had hired him as his defensive coordinator.

But truly, it might not have mattered, because he'd always wanted Scott next to him.

Lately, he couldn't help but wonder if this had actually been going on for a hell of a lot longer than he even realized. Maybe the catalyst had been January and that moment in the bathroom, but Asa hadn't ruled out that maybe these feelings had been brewing far longer than that.

"He's as ready as he'll ever be," Asa said, giving him a nod of approval.

"I worry about Allen's happy feet, though," Scott said, kicking up a spray of water that landed in tiny droplets against Asa's face. He scrubbed a hand over it and had zero compunction about splashing the other man right back.

"You let me worry about that," he said.

Scott kicked closer, until he was close enough Asa wondered how he didn't just drown in his gaze. His eyelashes were dark and wet, framing his light gray eyes. "You worry about enough," he said softly.

Asa almost told him that was his freaking job, he was the head coach, after all, but they both knew that.

"You sound like Beau."

Usually bringing up his son had the handy effect of ice water on whatever heat always seemed to be blooming between them. But today, it didn't. Scott didn't move. Didn't blink.

"Maybe," he said, roughly, "Beau got it from me. 'Cause I worry about you, too, Asa."

How easy would it be to just slide a little closer in the water? It was a quarry, and contained, without waves, but it would be so easy to just blame the nonexistent current.

Or he could blame nothing. He hadn't made up a single excuse for touching Scott's hand at the fireworks show last month. He'd just done it. And enjoyed every second of it.

Asa let himself drift closer. Put a hand on Scott's shoulder. The muscle tensed, and then relaxed. He didn't move an inch, but just stayed there like that, his fingertips sinking into Scott's slick skin.

Just when he thought they'd taken just about as much nearness as they could without inevitable combustion, Scott reached up and with a wet hand cupped Asa's chin. "I give a shit about you," he said. "Don't worry yourself into an early grave, okay?"

Asa's heartbeat tripled.

For a split second, he thought, *this is it, this is the moment,* but then Scott let go and slid away, his body moving through the water easily, the same way the intense expression on his face simply melted away.

Asa fought the compulsion to grab him back. It wasn't the right time. He knew it. But he still wanted it to be.

"No early graves," he added in a weak joking voice. "Got it."

"Promise," Scott said.

Asa rolled his eyes, but there was an insistence in his voice that he couldn't deny. "Fine, fine, I *promise*."

Scott glanced over at him, and their gazes met, and *goddamn*, the look in his eyes, it burned him, right down to the core. "Good," he said.

September

Asa felt like his equilibrium—shifting restlessly since last January—was finally evening out.

He could do this. He could live with all these goddamn emotions swirling inside him.

Looking out onto the field, as the time ticked down to halftime, he heard Scott call the play in to the defensive captain, and he nodded absently, pleased with his choice.

They were up fourteen points, and some coaches would start playing conservatively. But Scott wasn't a conservative kind of guy—and neither was he. Their coaching styles meshed well, an echo of how close their friendship had always been through the years.

And now you want to be even closer, a voice in his head added slyly. He pushed it away. This was game time. Focus time.

If they wanted to vie for another National Championship—and he did, they *both* did—then it was time to buckle down and stop thinking about all those tantalizing *what-ifs* that kept floating around his brain.

"Marcus looks good." He'd been instrumental in stopping two of Georgia's drives, tackling the receiver before they could get a first down.

And not once had he tried to rush the quarterback when he wasn't supposed to.

Whatever the hell Scott had said to him, it had worked.

Asa glanced over and saw that Scott had wandered over, in anticipation of the last minute before halftime.

"You knew better than me," Asa admitted. That wasn't usually easy for him to do, but it was surprisingly simple to do with Scott. He never worried when Scott was smarter than him, or could see things more clearly than he did.

It wasn't an embarrassment; it was an asset.

"You recruited him in the first place." Scott patted him on the back. With the last play of the half unfolding on the field, nobody was watching them. Nobody could see that Scott's hand lingered for just a second longer than necessary.

They were playing with fire, and instead of being terrified of it, instead of shying away from it, Asa found himself drawing even closer.

"We're a good team," Asa pointed out dryly. "I get the talent; you convince them they don't know shit, and that they should listen to you. Seems to work out pretty well."

Scott gazed over at him. That unspoken feeling was welling up inside him, spreading out, clogging the air between them. It happened all the time now.

Asa was pretty sure that it wasn't just him anymore. But Scott didn't make a move.

Well, you haven't either.

Not because he didn't want to. But because this wasn't just an itch he wanted to scratch. Scott was the second most important person in his life—second only to his son—and if they were going to do something about this thing blooming between them, it wasn't going to be just a hookup. It was going to be serious. Not just sex, but love.

And that, Asa believed, meant that they needed to walk carefully around it.

"Always wanted to do this with you," Scott said. "Just like this." He tugged his headset all the way off.

On the field, Georgia's quarterback threw the ball, and it landed right in Marcus' hands, as he jumped up to catch it. Ending the half with an interception.

"I think you just like being right," Asa pointed out, unable to help his smile.

It was so hard to want *more*, when just like Scott said, this was all he had ever dreamt of for his future. The thing he loved doing most, with the person he loved most at his side.

Was there more?

Could there be more?

Scott's eyes twinkled, and his stomach swooped, and *yes*, the answer seemed to be, *there's more, if you'll reach out and take it.*

October

"Some days," Scott drawled, as they sat on the hallway floor of the hotel the team was staying at before their game against LSU, "I really wonder how the hell we ended up here."

Scott couldn't know—though he might possibly have guessed—that was a question that Asa had been asking himself a hell of a lot recently.

How had he ended up here? Here, as in, *crazy in love with his best friend?*

Maybe he'd never been with a guy before. Maybe they'd not said a word to each other about it. Maybe they'd never even touched each other with romantic intent. But none of that mattered. Asa wasn't stupid. He knew what love felt like. He'd loved Scott before this. But now it was different.

It was still love, but it had an entirely unique flavor, and there was a part of Asa that wanted nothing more than to savor it.

"You mean, sittin' on the floor in the hallway of a hotel, hopin' that none of our players are gonna be goddamn stupid and try to sneak out on Halloween?" Asa shook his head. "I don't know, but we did somethin' bad, for sure."

Scott reached for the six-pack sitting on the floor between them and popped the cap off with an expert flick of his wrist. "I guess it's not so horrible," he said, shooting Asa a grin that would've made his knees incredibly weak—except he was already sitting down, thank *God*. "I'm here with you, aren't I?"

Asa nodded. Not sure he trusted himself to say more.

It felt like they'd been toeing this line.

They'd walk right up to it, right up to the "you're my friend, but you're something more, too" line, but they hadn't crossed it.

Someday, they were gonna cross it. Asa didn't know when or how, but he knew it would happen, because if Scott felt even a quarter of what he did, it was going to be inevitable.

He didn't worry about it anymore, because with that inevitability came certainty, and when it was right, he told himself, when he looked at Scott and the pressure became too great to bear, it would happen.

"Yeah, I suppose I've got a six-pack and you, so it can't be *too* bad," Asa teased, nudging him with his shoulder.

Even casual touches set him on fire now. He wondered, because he couldn't help it anymore, if they did the same to Scott.

"I guess we should be real glad that Beau hears all the rumors." Scott grinned, his teeth flashed in the fluorescent light of the hallway.

"Glad or disappointed? Hard to say, 'cause we could be tucked up in bed right now." The words fell off Asa's tongue before he considered them. Maybe the bottle and a half of beer he'd already drunk had filed his edges down, had loosened his brain.

Out of the corner of his eye, he saw Scott freeze, the bottle in his hand halfway to his mouth.

We could be tucked up in bed right now.

The *we* echoed through Asa's mind like a flashing neon light.

"Yeah." Scott's voice was somehow even deeper, rougher than normal. Like he'd thought about it too. Like Asa, he couldn't *stop* thinking about it. "Yeah, we could be."

Asa cleared his throat. If he was counting times when it was right to cross the line, it was definitely not this time, because they were supposed to be making sure nobody from the team did like they'd planned, which was sneak out to a big Halloween rager on the LSU campus.

Tonight, that was their job, not . . . not tucking themselves into the same bed.

Goddamn.

"We never did shit like this," Scott said, gesturing around the hallway and Asa knew he'd changed the subject deliberately.

"You kidding? We did worse. We snuck out all the time." They had. Regularly. They'd gone to every rickety, run-down bar from Carolina to Louisiana. They'd gotten into fights, they'd had each other's backs, they'd taken shots of moonshine and whiskey and laughed together until they couldn't stand up straight.

"Yeah, but we never made plans to hit a rival campus' party," Scott said dryly. "We made our own party."

There'd been others in their group, guys who'd come and gone as they'd joined the team and others who'd graduated. But at the heart of it had always been Scott and him.

"Not sure if that's better or worse," Asa pointed out.

"Better. I think. Still . . . might've been fun to really raise some hell."

Asa glanced over at him and realized Scott was staring at him.

Maybe . . . maybe he hadn't changed the subject after all.

"Is it too late?" Asa asked.

Scott considered this, his beer bottle dangling from his fingertips, between his legs, his elbows propped on his raised knees. "I dunno," he said. Not sounding like the confident Scott that Asa knew. That he was familiar with. And Asa knew, without being told, because *goddamn*, he knew this man, better than he knew himself, that he was thinking about what Beau had done earlier this year. How he'd come out.

How Scott never had.

"It's never too late," Asa said, trying to sound more certain than he felt.

Was it true? He didn't know, but he was going to *make* it true.

Scott shrugged. "Maybe. Maybe not."

A door down the hallway opened, and in a second, Scott was on his feet. "I've got this," he said, and as Asa watched him walk away, towards the open door, he couldn't help but feel that Scott wasn't just offering to deal with the problem, but actually running away.

He'd started the conversation, Asa thought moodily, staring at his beer, why did he keep refusing to finish it?

November

"You have a second?"

Asa looked up and saw Beau lingering in the doorway.

He didn't usually ask.

But he also didn't usually have that shadowed, hard look on his face either.

"Of course," Asa said, even though he had next week's practice plan to review and adjust still. Beau came first; he *always* came first.

To his surprise, Beau shut the door before walking in and flopping down on the seat opposite him.

"What's wrong?" Asa asked when Beau didn't say a word. "Do I need to surreptitiously kick some ass?"

"No," Beau said. He hesitated. "No. No, I handled it."

Asa leaned forward. He didn't like that look in Beau's eyes. "Handled what?"

Then, to his absolute horror, Beau's face crumpled, and he was crying.

His son might be eighteen and consider himself an adult, but there was zero hesitation; he shot up and in a second he was around his desk, tugging Beau into his arms.

He let Beau cry for a bit, alternatively steaming and worrying that something terrible had happened. Something terrible that he couldn't personally fix.

But he let Beau have his time, and finally, when his tears slowed, and then stopped, he lifted his head.

"Clay and I broke up," he said.

"The question still stands," Asa said steadily. "Do I need to kick his ass?"

"No, no, I . . . it's fine. He . . . he didn't care as much as I did. That's all. *God*, that's all."

That was exactly what Asa had been afraid of. Beau had tried to hide it, but a father knew. He'd realized, because he watched Beau, that while Clay had been perfectly content for their dates to be casual, and Beau had acted like he'd agreed, it was clear that his feelings ran deeper.

Beau shifted out of his arms, and back into the chair. He reached for a tissue and blew his nose. "I didn't even know I was so fucking upset until . . . well, you looked at me like that."

"Like what?" Asa settled his hip on the edge of the desk.

Beau shot him a look from reddened eyes. "Like you were worried about me."

"'Course I worry about you," Asa said.

"I knew it was coming, I knew we were growing apart, no matter how hard I tried to keep us together . . ." Beau trailed off. "I keep wondering if there's something I could have done, could have said, to prevent it. I keep feeling like there's something wrong with *me*."

"It wasn't right, and he wasn't the right man for you, Beau," Asa said with certainty. "The right man will fight for you. Always.

You're gonna meet him, and you're going to be more sure of him than anyone else—you know why? 'Cause he'll be sure of you."

Beau sighed. "I hate how smart you are. How do you know so much about this anyway?"

That was the real fucking question, wasn't it?

All Asa's knowledge was theoretical.

But his words hadn't just hit home with Beau, but with him, too.

What kind of love did he have if he didn't fight for Scott? Try to make him his?

Not a real or a strong love, that was for sure. Not the epic love he was convinced he could feel if he gave them half a chance.

He just shrugged. Maybe someday he would tell Beau. Maybe someday he and Scott would tell Beau together that they'd known and loved each other for all those years, and then they'd fallen in love.

"It's what everyone wants, isn't it?"

Beau gazed at him suspiciously. "You want it, too?"

"I'm a football coach, not a monk," he retorted dryly.

"You just . . . *don't* date, not at all."

Maybe not before, but maybe I will now.

He'd known that he was going to have to say something to Scott. But this incident had clarified it. He would wait until after the last game of the regular collegiate season. Their team was looking like a lock to make the playoffs, and they'd have several weeks to prepare. But there was no reason Asa couldn't take some of that time to finally make his feelings known.

Asa reached out and ruffled Beau's dark hair. "Despite this crazy smart brain," he teased, "you actually don't know everything."

"What?" Beau asked in faux shocked surprise.

There was the hint of a smile on his face now, even with the pain in his eyes.

It was his first heartbreak. It would hurt, Asa was sure of it, but he'd get over it.

His son was strong and brave. Stronger and braver maybe than his own father.

At least for now.

December

Asa didn't know if he was nervous or if he was something else entirely.

He'd sent Scott a text, asking him to stop by after dinner.

He'd sent Beau out.

He'd changed his shirt three times.

He'd stuck a six-pack of their favorite beer in the fridge.

Now there was nothing to do but wait.

He wasn't exactly the most romantic kind of guy, but Scott deserved his best effort, anyway. So he'd strung some of their old white Christmas lights up on the porch, hoping that might add a little bit of atmosphere.

With the main lights off, it nearly masked the fact that the porch could use a fresh coat of paint.

Asa watched, his heart rabbiting in his chest, as Scott pulled up in his truck, and jumped out. He was wearing jeans and a t-shirt, a flannel shirt thrown over, and in the dim light, he looked nearly as he had thirty years ago.

Asa curled his fingers into his own jeans. Hoping that he wasn't sweating all over everywhere.

"You actually decide to decorate for Christmas?" Scott sounded surprised as he walked up onto the porch. He took a seat, not next to Asa on the swing, but kitty-corner, on one of the big rattan chairs, the one that Beau usually liked to sit in.

Asa cleared his throat. "Somethin' like that."

"You said you wanted to talk?" Scott seemed completely unconcerned, his expression casual, his voice innocent of speculation. He had no idea what was coming.

You are going to do this, Asa told himself firmly, *and if he says no, then he says no, that's alright, your friendship's survived worse.*

But Asa wasn't entirely sure that was true.

"Yeah . . . uh . . ." Asa couldn't seem to tear his eyes away from Scott's. And maybe that was for the best. You couldn't really profess your eternal, undying love if you were staring at the floorboards. "It's been a year, hasn't it, since we won?"

"Twelve months," Scott said, leaning back, an amused smile tugging up one corner of his mouth.

There was no way to beat around the bush. He either had to say it or he didn't.

"Here's the thing . . . I realized somethin' that day, somethin' I didn't know before, but I know now, and I've spent the last twelve months realizing it." He took a deep breath. Plunged into the fire. "The thing is, I love you."

Scott didn't look even the slightest bit fazed. The problem was, he didn't look particularly overjoyed either. "I love you, too, Asa." He patted him on the shoulder, like they were just two freaking bros.

Asa wanted to scream. "No," he said, and before Scott could pull his hand away, he grabbed him by the forearm and tugged him over to the swing, so he landed right next to him, their thighs brushing together. "You're not listenin'. *I love you.*"

He reached up and cupped Scott's face. He'd shaved, his face smooth under his palm, and Asa's heart gave one big thump as recognition flared in Scott's eyes.

Heat and light and joy. For a second, that was all he could see, and it was too goddamned sweet, but then it faded. Turned to ash.

Then Scott was gone, turning away from him, his boots making staccato thumps on the porch boards as he paced back and forth. "I hoped . . ." His voice was wry, and full of pain. He chanced a glance towards Asa, who was frozen solid, something unpleasant and horrible unfurling inside him. "I hoped that we could just keep doing . . . this. Just this. Forever."

Asa heard what Scott was really saying.

I hoped that we'd stay just friends, forever.

"What?" The question felt wrenched out of Asa. "Why?"

"We can't do *more*, and do what we do, you know that, Asa."

He didn't know that. He didn't believe it. He'd known, of course, that it would be hard. It would be tough. But it wouldn't be impossible.

Nothing was impossible if he had the person he loved, the smartest, wiliest person he knew at his side. That was all that mattered.

"We just won a National Championship," Asa argued. "And I won another one, three years ago. I think we've proved we can do whatever the fuck we want."

"The world isn't what you want it to be, it's what it is," Scott said in a hard voice.

"Then we'll fucking make it the way we want it to be," Asa said. "Together. Goddamnit, I'm not . . ."

"They'll find a way to fire me, or fire you, or fire both of us. It's . . . it's not worth it. And if they don't fire us, they'll push us until we don't have a choice but to quit."

Asa just couldn't believe it, but at the same time . . . hadn't everyone questioned him over and over about Beau? They'd even questioned his statement, supporting him, sure he had some kind of ulterior motive.

"Are you just saying this because you don't feel . . ."

But Scott didn't even let him get the question out, in a second, he was back over, and somehow, impossibly, he was kneeling at Asa's feet. As wretched as Asa felt, it couldn't compare to the pain in Scott's eyes.

"No, no, *no*," Scott murmured, "I love you, I've loved you . . . *God*, don't make me tell you how long, it makes me look pathetic, and like a boy just followin' you around, 'cause he adored you, not because we were friends, though we *were*."

Asa reached down and took Scott's hand and squeezed it. "Can't we just . . . figure this out? Together? I don't want to do anything that isn't without you . . ."

But Scott didn't answer, just stared at him. It was the wrong time, Asa was still feeling that horrible panicked feeling squeezing his chest, the fear that Scott wouldn't change his mind swirling through in a nauseating lurch, but he nearly leaned down and just kissed him. Used the want that had bloomed so hard and fast between them this past year to convince him.

But he didn't want to *take* it, he wanted Scott's love and his desire freely given.

He'd never wanted anything else.

"I don't give a fuck where I coach," Asa tried again. "I don't care if I'm coaching the peewee team down the street. I don't care. I just want you. Next to me. That's it."

Scott still didn't speak. Like he wasn't sure he trusted himself to answer.

"And," Asa added, "who says anyone even has to know?"

That was the question that seemed to break him.

Scott shot to his feet, staring at Asa like he'd become a different person.

It was not how he'd believed this would go.

He'd believed it would either end happily, or bittersweet-ly—with Scott telling him he cared about him as a friend, but not as a lover.

He'd never imagined that Scott would feel the same, but would choose . . . well, *football*, instead of him.

"You want to hide it." Scott moistened his lips. Still staring at Asa.

"I'd do it, if that would convince you this is a good idea," Asa said, meaning it.

But Scott just shook his head, and said, "If you'd . . ." He cleared his throat, the emotion clogging it. "If you'd been closeted for the last twenty-plus years, you wouldn't say that. You wouldn't want it."

Asa knew some of how Scott felt. He knew he'd felt it deeply when Beau had come out.

Just once he'd suggested that maybe it wasn't too late for Scott to do it too, but he'd shut down the topic before it could even get started.

"It's not ideal," Asa said, and it wasn't. He wanted everyone to know who he loved. "But what's worse is not having you."

"You *have* me," Scott insisted. "We have *this*."

It was insane that he might believe it was enough.

"It's not enough," Asa said.

"It was enough for twelve months, for you," Scott said. "And it's been enough for me, for what feels like a fucking lifetime. I won't subject you to hidin', not you."

Asa stared at him.

"We can go back to the way we were," Scott said. "It'll have to be enough."

But Asa knew it wouldn't ever be. So what were they going to do?

He didn't know the answer to that, as he watched Scott walk away, and get in his truck to drive away.

He didn't know the answer to that when Beau came home, and asked him why his eyes were red. He lied to his son for the first time and said it was because he'd eaten something that was too hot and rubbed it in his eyes.

He didn't know the answer until the next Monday morning when he came into the Tennessee practice facility and Leonard Stubbins, the athletic director, dropped in to say that for the first time Scott had requested to be interviewed by other teams, and Tennessee had decided to let him.

He'd never wanted to before. He'd always turned down any requests, with a lighthearted laugh, like why would he want to be anywhere else.

And now, he was trying to be anywhere else.

A week later, when Scott came back to his house, late one Saturday night, Asa knew what he'd come to say.

"I'm takin' the job in Washington," he said, not even sitting down, and not meeting Asa's eyes. "I appreciate everything you've done for me, the knowledge you've given, the friendship we share."

"And that's it, then?" Asa asked in a hard voice. "You're pickin' a *job* over me and you, together?"

"I told you, it can't happen, they won't let it happen, and . . ." Asa watched as Scott hesitated, overcome with emotion. "And I won't do it to you. Make you choose like that. So I'm choosin'. This is a good job."

"It's three thousand miles away."

"Yeah, it is."

Asa dug his fingers into the wood of the swing bench and tried not to think about how much this hurt. How enormous the hole was going to be when Scott left his life, by his own fucking choice. "You're running away," he said.

"I'm not running . . ." Scott hesitated, then he glanced up, and maybe Asa hadn't believed it before, that he loved him too, because he'd still been hiding it—and how could he have even hidden it for so long? Asa hadn't even quite believed it—but he saw it now. Written plain as day on his face. Joy and devastation warred with him.

"I'm doin' this for you," Scott continued. "You're gonna fucking give it all up for me, and I can't, I just can't let you. I love you too much to let you. So I'm gonna go away, and maybe . . ." He glanced away, and the lump in Asa's throat grew. Probably matched Scott's own. "Maybe you'll understand how much I love you, if I do it. Maybe it'll make all of this worth it."

"I never asked you to sacrifice anything. Not for me."

"No," Scott said, and the look on his face was like a caress. Asa felt it like he'd actually touched him. "You remember the first day we met?"

Asa hadn't thought about it in years, and honestly didn't really remember it now. There were too many Scott memories crowding his brain. Picking one out was impossible. He shook his head.

"I do," Scott said. "I remember the first time I saw you, football orientation at Alabama. I knew I was gay. I'd known for awhile. But I saw you and you were laughing, putting some guy into his place, even though you were a freshman and he was a junior, a senior, maybe, but he didn't even give a shit. He just laughed, right along with you. Then you looked over at me, and you saw me, and I thought, maybe someone might really see me. I was fucking terrified. And I'd never been happier. Then we became friends, and that was better, and it was worse."

Asa swallowed hard. He didn't remember that day. He wished he could; but he didn't.

"I loved you every single day, every one of those years. When you met Lynn. When you had Beau. When you asked me to be Beau's godfather, I thought, well, at least I have a little piece of you."

"You've always had more than a little piece of me." Asa wasn't going to admit it, but the look in Scott's eyes was pure love, and pure, raw pain.

"Maybe. Maybe not. But this last year, you were right when you said things changed. They changed, and I still thought, this is better than anything I could have. Better than anything I could've imagined."

Asa had thought it wasn't enough, but Scott had lived with this for twenty-plus years.

"Then let's make it even better," Asa begged. "I don't give a shit where I'm coaching."

But Scott looked away. Didn't answer his plea. Not directly.

"I've given up a life. A chance to be really happy, though God knows who it was gonna be with, if it wasn't gonna be with you. All for a chance to do this, to play football and to coach, with you, and really, to prove to myself and to everyone else that I'm good at this. I gave it *all* up. Stayed in the closet. What was all that for if it wasn't to give us *this*? If it wasn't to give you the chance to keep doing it?"

Asa couldn't believe it.

"Are you really gonna let some homophobic assholes do this to us? Are you?" Asa demanded, and he stood, striding over to where Scott leaned against the front of the porch, like he couldn't bear to even get close.

But Asa got close. He pushed himself right into Scott's space, into his bubble, and pressed his whole body against Scott's—thigh to thigh, chest to chest, shoulder to shoulder. Felt, for that single glorious moment, what it might be like if Scott had chosen differently.

No, Asa thought, *he didn't choose. He didn't get the power to choose. He never chose. The world chose for him. For us.*

It would be so easy to just lean forward, press his mouth against Scott's. He'd finally know what it was like to taste him. It was torture being so goddamn close to what he wanted, to what he *needed,* but there was something shutting down behind Scott's gaze. An insurmountable pain.

"Not like this," he said quietly, and he raised a hand, pushing Asa's face away, while still cradling it like it was the most precious thing on earth. "I don't know how it ever happens, but not like this."

And as Asa watched him walk away for the last time, he knew that this was gonna hurt worse than anything else. Because that was the man he loved: honorable and real and honest. And loving. Scott believed he was walking away because he loved him that much.

Asa didn't think he could love him more if he'd let him, if he'd finally gotten that kiss.

But he never did.

CHAPTER ONE

Seven years later

December

Five minutes too late, Asa realized it was a mistake to face your boss, who also happened to be a respected pillar of the community as well as an enormously successful businessman, with your ass hanging out of your hospital gown.

"Rudy, please, we talked about this," Asa said, inserting as much persuasion as he could into his voice. He'd convinced plenty of people to do much harder things.

But Rudy was stubborn. Certain. Almost as certain as Asa himself, and it seemed he wasn't going to budge, and why? Because he just didn't want to.

He sighed, pushed his glasses up the bridge of his nose, and leaned against the wall next to Asa's hospital bed.

Heart palpitations. That was why he was here.

You had a heart attack, a voice inside Asa reminded him dryly. *You might not like that terminology but it happened. Even you can't change the facts.*

"Asa, you know I brought you here, to Miami, to win football games. And you're doing it, which is fucking fantastic. You've done everything you said you would. Season ticket sales are up

"

twenty percent. We're selling out the stadium every week. Everyone's talking about us. Which is what we wanted."

No, Asa thought, a little resentfully, *it was what you wanted.*

He'd come here, after his illustrious career as the head coach of Tennessee, to win football games. To win a Super Bowl.

That hadn't happened yet.

But Asa wasn't going to rule it out.

"But," Rudy continued, "if you're dead, none of this continues."

Trust Rudy to make the most dramatic argument possible.

Asa was developing a headache—not because he'd just had heart palpitations—but because he was still in this hospital, still in this room, in this bed, and his ass was *still* hanging out of his gown.

If he died, he wasn't going to do it exposed.

"I'm not going to die," Asa said. "The doctors said . . ."

"The doctors said you need to take it easy. Make some lifestyle changes."

Of course, Rudy's dire pronouncement was what got Beau into this conversation.

He loved his son.

He was brilliant and indomitable. But he was also a pain in his ass.

His bare, naked ass.

"Thank you, Beau, I was here for their lengthy lecture," Asa said dryly.

"Exactly," Rudy said, clamping onto Beau's argument with relish. "Lifestyle changes. You need to work less. Sleep more. Eat better. And that means . . . with the way this season is going, you need *help,* Asa."

"I don't want help. And if I did, I wouldn't want it from . . ." Asa couldn't quite bring himself to say his name.

Surely he'd said it in the last seven years. Hadn't he?

"Scott is eminently qualified to help you run this team. He helped you run the team at Tennessee. So what, he took another job?" Beau looked puzzled. He didn't know why Asa was so pissed that he and Rudy had cooked up this idea to bring Scott, newly unemployed, in as a consultant to help Asa coach the team.

Asa did not need help coaching the team.

He most definitely did not need Scott's help.

But then Beau also didn't know all their history, didn't know how much Asa did not want to see him again.

He wasn't . . . he'd never been angry.

Though that wasn't technically true either. He'd been furious at the world.

Ready to tear it all down, and rebuild it in a fundamentally different way.

It wasn't only that so many people had believed he'd turn his back on his own son. Or been surprised that he hadn't. It was that Scott believed that he needed to trade his chance at happiness for football.

He didn't know if he'd ever found it. Maybe he had, and in the end, it hadn't been Asa at all. But the point was, he didn't know. Not anymore.

It had been too hard, too painful, to open that door.

So for the last seven years, it had stayed closed.

Until now, when Beau was trying to open it with a fucking crowbar.

"I think Scott Callaway sounds like the perfect choice," Rudy said. "I never thought they gave him enough chances in Washington. But at least that means he's unemployed." He turned to Beau. "Let's get him on the phone, and then on the first flight out here."

Asa wasn't afraid of much, but he was afraid—fucking terrified, in fact—of the way joy and fear coalesced inside him into one ungainly, uncontrollable, nauseating ball.

"No," Asa said, and the word felt like it was choking him. "No, not him."

Beau's gaze swung to him, and there was shock in his eyes.

"What? What's wrong with Scott?"

"Asa," Rudy said, tapping his cane on the ground. He was seventy, and it was mostly an affectation, but it was a good one, "you know I respect you, so much, but you're going to have to find a way to work with Scott Callaway. I know you did once, and maybe things soured, but surely, you can fix them." He glanced over at Beau. "Beau certainly thinks you can. Hire him, and find a way to keep winning."

The door shut behind Rudy.

It was too much to ask that Beau would leave it alone.

He'd left it alone, a few months back, when Asa clearly hadn't wanted to talk about Scott—or *to* Scott.

But this was different.

"What's your problem with Scott?" Beau asked, coming nearer to Asa's bed. "That he took that other job? He needed to do that. He couldn't stay in Tennessee forever, not with how good he is."

"We need to get me out of here," Asa said, changing the subject. He didn't think he had a hope in hell of avoiding this conversation, but he could still try.

"What? They said they wanted you to stay overnight, to monitor . . ."

"No," Asa said, trying to untangle the monitoring wires surrounding him so he could undo them and get out of this goddamned bed. He wasn't an invalid; he wasn't even fucking sick.

"Dad," Beau said, and put a hand on his arm. Stopping him. "You've got to do what they say."

When Asa glanced up, he saw the fear in his son's eyes, the same fear that had paralyzed him, when he'd been afraid he might be dying.

"Fine, fine, but first thing tomorrow I'm getting out of here."

Beau nodded. "I'm going to call Scott. But then," he added, voice hardening, "I'm going to come back in here and we're going to talk about why you're so angry he's coming here."

"I'm not angry." But it sounded like anger. Even to Asa's ears.

He wasn't ready to tell Beau it was sheer fucking terror.

The only way he'd kept himself together without Scott Callaway was to live entirely without Scott Callaway.

He couldn't do half-measures. Not again.

Him showing up here, it was a half-measure, in the worst possible way.

Beau didn't say anything. Didn't even bother to argue. Just shot him a look, and turned and walked out.

He gave another half-hearted look to the wires surrounding him. Could he untangle them and somehow escape this room? Would they put out an APB on a runaway football coach, hospital gown flapping in the breeze?

Ugh, they totally would.

Asa flopped back against his bed and hoped that he might get something else to eat, now that they were making him stay overnight.

Maybe some hospital jello?

Though now that Beau was in charge, no doubt he was never getting jello again.

It took Beau fifteen minutes to come back.

During that fifteen minutes, Asa considered running away half a dozen times.

Each and every time, he decided it would be *more* embarrassing to be caught and brought back. Still didn't stop him from considering it.

"Hey, Scott's taking the first flight out in the morning," Beau said when he returned.

"Oh, I'm so relieved," Asa said sarcastically.

Sarcasm—always a welcome weapon against emotion.

"You gonna tell me what your problem with Scott is?" Beau demanded.

"It's nothing, I just don't like someone else comin' in and coachin' *my* team," Asa said.

It wasn't even a good excuse.

It was flimsy as hell.

Beau's gaze narrowed. "Of course he's not gonna be coaching the team. He's going to be a *consultant,* to help you. Like he did before. You two were inseparable. You won a National Championship together."

"I'm sure he still does real good work, and he will . . . I just don't want him around."

"Funny, he doesn't seem to have the same opinion about you."

Asa barely refrained from a biting retort that he'd sure experienced a change of heart in the last seven years.

Because, before, he hadn't seemed to be able to run away fast enough.

"He didn't say anything to you?" It was pathetic, that he was reduced to begging for scraps. But he did it anyway.

You could just call him yourself. That's always an option.

Except it wasn't.

Asa wasn't going to lose himself again. He had to stay strong. Stay in control. And Scott was the complete antithesis of control. He made Asa want to throw it away with both hands.

"He's damn worried about you," Beau said righteously. "So whatever issue you have with him, it's clearly one-sided. He was ready to jump on a plane tonight, but I said, get your shit together and come in the morning. You'll be out of the hospital then, and then . . ."

Not as one-sided as you might think, Asa thought rebelliously.

"And then what?" Asa snapped. "We play happy family again?"

"What the fuck is going on?" Beau asked flatly. "What is your problem with Scott? I can't believe you are actually pissed, *still*, that he took that job."

This was why he'd always been glad Beau hadn't picked up on the undercurrents between them. Why he'd been relieved that he'd never told Beau about his feelings. Or why Scott had really left.

In Beau's mind, Scott had left because he'd gotten a job offer from Washington that was too good to refuse.

He hadn't left Tennessee because he was trying to save Asa from himself.

"We . . . we had a difference of opinion when he left," Asa said, picking at the blanket and not quite meeting Beau's concerned, frustrated gaze. He hated lying to his son, but he didn't know what else to do.

He couldn't tell the truth. Not now. Especially not with Scott showing up tomorrow morning, apparently ready to pick right back up where they'd left off.

"What kind of difference of opinion? I never knew you guys to even *argue*, not seriously. Not about anything that actually mattered."

Maybe he could be honest enough. "I didn't want him to take the job."

"But it was a good job."

But he was mine, and I was his, and he threw it all away, because he felt like he should. Because he believed the world wanted him to.

It shouldn't still hurt. Asa knew it.

But it hurt as badly today as it had seven years ago.

And it's gonna hurt more tomorrow.

"Yeah, yeah, it was. Which is why he took it. I still didn't want him to." Asa took a deep breath. "I was selfish. Wanted him to stay in Tennessee, with me. With us."

"And *what*? He didn't? And you were pissed off at him because of it?" Beau looked confused, like he was still missing a piece of the puzzle.

He was.

It was a piece that Asa was going to fight tooth and nail not to disclose, because even though there was a part of him that wanted Beau to know the truth, too much time had gone by with him *not* admitting it.

"I guess, yeah. I said some things. He said some things." Asa moistened his lips. "We fought. Argued."

"Well," Beau said briskly. "Then you're just gonna have to apologize and get over it. You're both adults. You've known each other practically your whole lives. Maybe this is a blessing."

Asa barely refrained from rolling his eyes. "I'm lying here in the hospital, and my ass is hanging out the back of this gown. It's not a fucking blessing."

"Then make it one," Beau said pointedly. "I gotta get things straightened out. I thought he'd stay at my old place, for the time being."

It was another reminder that things had irrevocably changed. Beau was practically living with his boyfriend, Sebastian.

Or *actually* living with, if "old place," was any indication.

"Alright," Asa said. Though the way Beau was talking, it wasn't like he actually had any say in this.

He and Rudy had cooked this up, and were apparently determined to keep any of Asa's opinions out of it.

"And you," Beau said firmly, "are not going anywhere until tomorrow morning when I come pick you up."

"You've made that plenty clear," Asa said.

"And you're gonna fix things with Scott, okay? You guys were too close to just . . . let this silly, stupid fight about a job get between you."

Asa didn't say anything because what could he even say?

It wasn't a stupid fight; it was my life and he was my love?

Because he had been.

Any doubt in Asa's mind had disappeared after losing him, because it had hurt badly enough that there was no way it wasn't love.

"Don't be stubborn, okay?" Beau said softly. "I know you can let it go."

Except Asa didn't know if he could.

It wasn't like he hadn't spent plenty of sleepless nights contemplating the pathetic aloneness of his existence.

He had.

After Scott had left, taking hope with him, he'd lain here like this plenty of times.

But it hadn't been so terrifying because the thing he refused to use the official word for hadn't just happened to him.

Hadn't just reminded him of how ephemeral life really was.

Sleep was essentially impossible, despite the doctor's admonition that he needed to start getting more rest, so he didn't really *wake up early,* but when his watch hit six and the nurse appeared, he cajoled her into letting him shower and change, put his real clothes back on and unhook all the machines that had monitored him.

By the time Beau showed up at seven, he was impatient and ready to go.

"Come on," he said to Beau when he appeared in the doorway of his room. "It's Monday and I don't want to get behind. Let's get to the office and start breaking down the tape."

Beau shot him a look. "What about *take it easy* didn't get through to you?"

"I took it easy. Overnight. I . . ." He didn't want to lie and say he'd slept, because he hadn't. Not really. "I rested, quite a bit, and I'm feelin' good. Let's get breakfast and go to the office."

"I am going to drop you at home," Beau said. "And then I'm going to go meet Scott."

Asa definitely did *not* want to go meet Scott, but the idea of being left at home, the day after a game . . . when all the coaches would be in the office, going over the tape, making practice plans for the next week, shaping the game plan . . .

He balked.

"No," Asa said. "I'm gonna take it easy, okay? But you can't take me home. I'll . . ." He tried to think of something that Beau wouldn't want him to do. "I'll eat a pound of bacon if you try to take me home."

Beau rolled his eyes. "You are the most difficult man in the universe. And if you think you've still got bacon in your condo, think again."

The problem with being so stubborn himself was that Beau was just as stubborn. Maybe more.

He almost said that he could order anything he wanted in—but no doubt Beau had already considered that, too.

Asa sighed. "Fine, take me home, then, since you're so determined."

Beau smiled, like this was progress.

Except, when Beau dropped him off, he realized that the biggest problem with home was that it wasn't really home.

It wasn't the big rambling farmhouse he'd lived in with Beau and Lynn, and then just Beau, on the outskirts of Knoxville.

Home was currently a condo in one of Miami's high-rise buildings. It had come furnished, and Asa had spent so little time in it, he hadn't bothered to personalize it.

After Beau left, Asa tried to go to bed. He lay there, just the same as he had in the hospital, sleepless.

It wasn't just that Scott was here, though the fact that *Scott was here* was plenty, thank you very much. It was that Scott was here, and Scott was in *his* building, talking to *his* coaching staff, hanging out with *his* players, organizing *his* team.

After an hour of painfully circular thoughts, he got up. Opened his fridge. It wasn't like he'd ever kept much in it, but that hadn't stopped Beau from scrupulously going through it. The bacon and eggs he kept for breakfasts were gone, replaced by a carton of egg whites and a package of turkey bacon. Asa made a face.

His standard six-pack was also gone, not surprisingly.

It wasn't like his habits were *that* bad, Asa thought rebelliously.

He made himself a packet of oatmeal and resisted the urge to dump brown sugar and butter all over it—because he expected if he looked, the brown sugar and the butter would be gone, too.

The oatmeal tasted like glue in his mouth.

He ate half of it, and put the bowl in the sink, rinsing it out, staring out at the rest of the condo. It was gray and bland and didn't even feel like his. It felt like a hotel room, a place he slept—sometimes, anyway—and all he wanted was to be back in his office.

He made the decision fast, but then he made most of his decisions instinctively.

The Uber dropped him off at the corner of the practice facility, and just as Asa figured, there was nobody around, not mid-morning, and he was able to sneak in through the side door.

He'd spent enough time here, it was easy enough to know which busier hallways to avoid, and that the elevator was off-limits. Instead, he took the stairs, and told himself that Beau would even be proud that he was exercising.

He would, however, *not* be proud that Asa was here, but hopefully they wouldn't have to have that conversation.

He'd just sneak into his office, grab his laptop, and then find one of the barely used team rooms in the basement level to do his work in. It would be better, even, than normal. All this uninterrupted time to go over the film and make notes.

However, grabbing his laptop meant that he'd be going by potentially the busiest part of the building, especially on a Monday. If today was Tuesday, and they were having practice, the offices on this floor would be empty. But it was Monday—technically a day the players had off—and the coaches would all be in their offices, working on the tape from last night's game, and getting ready for the first meetings of the week.

Asa kept his head down, though he wasn't under any misconception that if he got spotted, his staff might actually mistake him for anyone else.

If he got spotted, it would be all over.

Beau would probably kill him. Or feed him turkey bacon for the rest of his life.

He slipped into his empty office and was pulling the power cord on his laptop when a rustling noise in the doorway made him look up.

Asa froze.

Scott, looking just as goddamned good as he had the day he left Tennessee, froze too.

For a moment, neither of them said a word. The silence drew out between them, thick with everything they hadn't said for the last seven years.

I missed you.

Why weren't you around?

Was leaving worth it?

Did you find some kinda vindication in all that goddamn pain?

"Asa." Scott spoke first. Apologetically.

It was hard, but Asa met his gaze head-on. Refused to flinch. He could do this. He'd faced down far tougher opponents in his life, but nobody he'd cared so deeply about.

That he *still* cared so deeply about. Because he'd wondered if those feelings, the ones that had bloomed so unexpectedly seven years ago, could have possibly lasted. And now he knew they could. They could, and they had.

"Beau said you were going to be at home," Scott continued. Still apologetic. Like he'd come in here, to Asa's domain, uninvited, because *one,* he had the right now and *two,* because he'd known Asa wouldn't be here.

"Beau was mistaken."

He'd gotten exactly three words out. That felt like a win.

"Here's the thing, though, Beau isn't often mistaken," Scott said. "Though, he does seem to be about us," he added wryly, almost as an afterthought.

Asa did not flinch at the *us,* but he had to fight against the inclination.

"I appreciate you coming all this way, and showing up at a moment's notice, but Beau was mistaken about that, too, thinkin' that we need help. We don't."

"Asa, you were in the *hospital.*" Scott's eyes were wide and concerned. Like he still had the right to give a shit about him.

Asa's fingers tightened on his laptop. "That was only a precautionary measure."

"According to Beau, you've been working like crazy. I shouldn't even be surprised . . . and I guess I'm not. But when he asked if I could come and help stop you, I didn't have any illusions about me convincin' you of anything. Not . . ." Scott cleared his throat. "Not anymore. But I did think that at least you might trust me to do the work. 'Cause you've got work that needs doing."

It was annoying, how well Beau knew him. He knew there was no one else on earth that Asa would trust to take over some of the work. Or, Asa supposed, to *share* the work.

But the problem with that was that sharing the work meant working together, and he couldn't work with Scott. Not again. Not without losing himself.

Not when some days he felt like a disintegrating tower, taped together and already listing, barely holding it together.

Scott was going to mow his composure right down, without even trying.

"You can't be here."

Sympathy—pure, unadulterated, obnoxious and unnecessary—flashed across Scott's face. "I know it's hard, but let me help. Just . . . let me do this."

"Don't you think you've done enough?" The words came out of Asa's mouth before he could snatch them back. He was trying to be cool and collected. He wasn't going to be that mess again, the one he'd been after Scott left.

The one who held it together during the days, and then cried at night.

"Yeah." Scott's voice was rough, and there was a damning look in his eyes, a look that Asa should've been happy he put there. But it turned out he wasn't. He only felt . . . *sad*. Full of regret. "Yeah. I've done enough. But who else are you gonna trust to run this football team? Beau? He can't do it all, and I know you, Asa, I know you aren't gonna put it all on him. You won't."

It was annoying.

Annoying that *one*, Scott was right, he didn't trust anyone else. And that *two*, he knew him, *knew* that he wouldn't be able to put everything on Beau's shoulders. He was too young, too inexperienced, and too . . . Asa inwardly sighed. Too full of potential to have a life that was just this. He hadn't thrown it all away yet, hadn't made those hard choices that guaranteed a regular life wasn't possible.

And Asa would be the last one to push him into that place. Goddamn it.

Asa sighed, and picked up his laptop. He didn't want to approach the door, not while Scott was still standing there, but he also didn't want him to know he didn't trust himself to get close.

You can do this.

Yet it was Scott who seemed to freeze when Asa skirted around the desk and headed towards the doorway.

Annoying, too, that Scott was still taller. He had to tilt his head back, and it reminded him, way too viscerally, of that last moment they'd shared before he'd left.

I don't know how it happens, but not like this.

Annoying that he'd made all the choices for them, and then taken that one away, too.

Asa stopped a good two feet away. Scott was still blocking the doorway, like he thought he could block Asa out.

"Still playin' unfair, Scott?" he asked mildly.

"Bringin' up Beau? Well . . ." Scott grinned, and it shouldn't have, but that smile, hitting him again in all those so-familiar places disarmed every weapon in Asa's arsenal. He didn't know how to fight against that feeling, that warmth, blooming in the base of his stomach. He didn't even want to.

That was the whole problem with Scott Callaway.

"I gotta do something to make you see reason, make sure . . ." Scott continued, and then paused, hesitating. "Make sure you don't end up a cautionary tale. Besides, you promised me. No early graves."

Maybe he still didn't remember the first time they'd ever met, but this was a memory that he definitely hadn't forgotten.

He *had* promised.

Asa cleared his throat. Changed the subject. "If you're gonna be runnin' the meeting later, just make sure that Beau addresses third down, on the defense."

"Did you think I wouldn't?"

That was the other annoying thing about Scott. He always knew. He always pushed back. He always brought his A game.

But those things were annoying in a whole different way.

In a *how do I possibly continue to resist you* way.

"I didn't know if you'd watched the tape," Asa said.

It was Scott's turn to roll his eyes. "You think you go to the NFL and I'm not picking apart every game you're playin'? You know me better than that, Asa." His voice went rough and hushed at the end.

Somehow he'd managed to hide his feelings from Asa for years. A whole lot of years.

But he wasn't hiding them now.

Asa could see them, plain as fucking day, right in his eyes.

That was a whole complication he wasn't prepared to deal with.

"Guess I should," Asa said. "I'll send my notes over."

"To me?"

"Of course to you," Asa retorted, "if I send them to Beau, I'll get lectured for working when I'm not supposed to be."

"You know, we're gonna talk about this," Scott said, moving out of the way as Asa started out through the door.

He stopped right in his tracks. He didn't want to talk about it; he didn't even want to *think* about it.

"I mean . . ." Scott's voice dropped again, hitting him right in the solar plexus. "Not about . . . not about *that*, but about you sneakin' in and workin' when you're not supposed to be."

"Sure," Asa said. It would be a very short conversation, consisting of exactly two words.

Fuck. Off.

Asa was nearly past him, had nearly escaped, when he spoke again.

"And about the other thing . . ." Scott sighed. Soft and inevitable. "I missed you."

He didn't run away.

A grownup, a fucking adult, *did not run away*.

But he hurried down the hallway at a faster than normal clip, and absolutely did not turn back around. Not to see Scott's face. Not to say anything back.

Because he was *this close* to telling him the whole truth.

I missed you, too.

Chapter Two

Scott's hands were still trembling.

It was like being plugged back into a socket, after so long without electricity, being in Asa's presence again.

Since he'd gotten the call from Beau, he hadn't really let himself consider what it would mean. What it would feel like.

He'd only allowed himself the worry.

Asa was sick; he was struggling and in the goddamn hospital. Beau had reassured him, more than once, that he'd be fine, that the doctors weren't particularly worried, they only wanted him to change his lifestyle.

Sleep more. Eat better. Work less.

That, Beau had said, was where he came in. He didn't know anyone else who'd be able to convince Asa to relax the reins.

Scott had agreed, because after how things had gone seven years ago, how could he not? How could he not be there for Asa when he needed him, more than anyone else?

But he didn't tell Beau that he wouldn't be able to convince him of jack shit now.

Asa was, understandably, still pissed.

Scott couldn't even blame him.

He was still pissed at himself.

He'd known the moment he landed in Washington that it was all wrong, that he'd made a mistake, that instead of trying to be so fucking noble, he should have just taken Asa's hand and kissed him and learned how to be happy.

No matter what that meant.

But he'd committed to leading Washington's program, and he'd done that, for six years.

Then a year ago, they'd let him go, and he'd gone home, not to Tennessee, because Asa was still there, and the whole damn state didn't feel big enough for the two of them, but back home to Alabama, to the small town he'd lived in before he'd gone to college.

"You alright?" Beau asked as they lingered at the front of the conference room, the rest of the coaching staff taking their seats, grumbling all the way.

It was deep into the season, it was the Monday after a game, and they were all tired.

Scott remembered exactly how it had felt, on those Mondays, even though he'd only ever coached in college, never in the NFL.

"Yeah, fine," Scott said automatically.

He was not fine.

Not even remotely.

He'd thought . . . well, he didn't know what he'd thought, exactly. But he hadn't imagined that he and Asa would meet again like this. He'd imagined running into him—sorta, kinda, on purpose—on the Tennessee campus. He'd imagined making things right.

The part of the imagining he'd purposefully forgotten was that Asa was going to be justifiably pissed at him.

"Alright," Beau said, raising his voice, "let's get this meeting started. Great team win yesterday." He began to clap his hands, and around the table, the rest of the coaches joined in immediately, like they knew it was coming.

That was something Scott recognized from Tennessee, and there was no doubt in his mind that Asa had started it here. Maybe the fact that this was the NFL wouldn't feel quite so strange—not if Asa had implemented his culture here in Miami.

"I think," Beau continued, the applause dying down, "if we continue to notch wins like these, we're going to exceed everyone's expectations. Maybe even our own."

The last time Scott had been around Beau, he'd been eighteen. Sure, they'd talked on the phone, and through text, a lot in the last seven years, but he hadn't been lucky enough to actually clap eyes on him and *see* the changes in him.

He'd grown up, of course, that was an inevitability, but now that Scott came to think about it, this natural leadership ability had always been present, even back then, when Beau had been only eighteen. He'd always been like Asa in that way. When he spoke, not everyone paid attention the first time, but by the second time around, they'd learned, and they were all listening. Asa had that quality, and Beau had it too, in spades.

"I'm gonna kick this meeting off by saying, Coach Dawson is sorry he can't be here today, but he *is* doing well."

"He out of the hospital yet?" Randy, who Beau had pointed out earlier was the passing coordinator, asked.

Beau nodded. "He is, and he's at home, resting. But I have a feeling that one day is all I'm gonna get out of him, before he comes back here. He's still going to be an incredibly involved presence on this team. Nobody, and certainly nothing, could stop him from being that. But to help cover some of the additional work, since the doctors have asked him to work more reasonable hours, we've brought in a consultant. This is Scott Callaway, who worked with Asa and me at Tennessee. We're real thankful he's offered to come here and help out."

Asa had clearly assembled a good, solid coaching staff, because as Scott met each set of eyes around the table, there was no hesitation, no concern, just complete acceptance. If Asa—and to an extent, Beau—said that he was needed, then he was needed. No questions asked.

Scott took his seat, next to a young-looking guy that he couldn't quite place at first, til he opened his mouth and then he realized he was sitting next to Davis Abernathy.

His mind automatically supplied, *the quarterback*, at the end of his name, but then he remembered that Davis wasn't playing anymore. He was *coaching*.

When Scott first started followed the way he was handling things in Miami, Asa hiring Davis Abernathy was the first indication that Asa was still going to be Asa.

He was still—*always*—going to be uniquely, perfectly himself.

The man he loved.

The man he'd follow to the ends of the earth and back.

Except you didn't. You let him go, and you told yourself it was the right thing, but you know it was shit.

It had been shit.

Asa had known it before he had, and he'd been furious. Scott couldn't even blame him for it.

But it didn't matter if Asa refused to ever give him the time of day, ever again, he'd still love him. Still do anything he could to help him now.

"How's this gonna work?" Davis asked. "Like the breakdown of work?"

Scott nearly spoke up, even though he wasn't the kind of guy who did that, typically. He was more the watch-and-wait type. But it was a tough question for Beau to handle right off the bat, and Scott couldn't help his first instinct, which was to cover for him.

But before he could speak up, Beau was already clicking a key on his laptop, and behind him, the screen lit up with a breakdown.

All the various tasks that had to be done. Most of which, Scott wouldn't be surprised to learn, Asa had done before today.

"I've divided up the work Coach Dawson was doing," Beau said, "and assigned it to various coaches. I don't care how you disseminate to your staff, just that the work gets done in a timely way."

"You mean, Coach isn't going to go through and make the defensive plan and then get *me* to sign off on it?" Brett sounded skeptical and Scott nearly laughed.

Of course Asa had been making the game plan for the defense, and then asking his coordinator to finalize and sign off on it.

If he had to guess, he'd been doing the same thing with the offense and the special teams.

Looking around the table, Scott wasn't surprised to see a few nods of agreement.

"No," Beau said. "It's going to be the other way around."

"You sure about that?" Brett asked. Not in a disrespectful way, but in a way that made it clear he didn't believe that Asa would actually let go enough for that to happen.

"Yes," Beau said crisply. "I'm planning practices, and with Scott's help, we'll implement the new plays and tweaks into the workload this week. Scott is also responsible for . . ." Beau hesitated. "Keeping Coach in check."

Scott nearly groaned out loud. That would've been impossible seven years ago, but now? He was one hundred percent certain that Asa was just going to tell him to fuck off.

"Notice you didn't give yourself the impossible job," Davis said, chuckling under his breath.

Beau shrugged. "Trust me, I'm gonna be doing enough, trying to get him to follow the doctor's orders. Scott just has to keep him distracted enough here to realize that he isn't doing all the work, still."

Oh, he'd be keeping Asa distracted alright.

And himself. Inevitably.

The situation had been fraught enough seven years ago, without knowing for sure that Asa returned his feelings, and without Asa being pissed as hell at him.

Now, it felt like there was a bomb ticking between them, just waiting to go off.

Would the explosion end in an argument? In a kiss?

Scott wasn't sure.

And Scott was always sure.

Beau continued on to the next page he'd prepared, breaking down some of the observations he'd made from yesterday's game.

Scott watched him and realized that he had a handle on this. They didn't even really *need* him, though he was sure he was somewhat of a safety blanket to Beau.

But Beau didn't really *need* him. He was grown up, an adult and a professional, running this meeting with the same surety and confidence of his father, but with a flair all his own.

He pulled his phone out of his pocket, and using the tablet Beau had given him earlier as cover, surreptitiously started filming Beau's breakdown of the game.

He was running film, pointing out some of the defensive guys out of position, and Brett kept blustering how that was acceptable, but Beau continued to shut him down.

From the looks of the film, Beau was right, and he knew it, and so did Brett, probably, but by the end of the short, terse conversation, Brett was the one making notes about positional alterations on the field.

It wasn't hard to find Asa's number in his phone. How many times had he pulled it up, too late at night, when he couldn't sleep, and the things they couldn't ever have had haunted him?

Too many times.

This time he pulled up their last conversation over text. It was seven years ago, when Asa had asked him to come over, to talk, just to *talk*, and he'd replied back and said he was on his way.

On my way. It was the last thing he'd ever sent.

It made him sound like such a pragmatic asshole.

In the last seven years, he should've said so many other things. About how much he regretted leaving Asa. About how much he missed him. About how wrong he'd been about so many goddamn things. How he didn't want to live without him anymore.

But he hadn't.

That was the thing about being the one who left; you didn't exactly have a lot of moral high ground to stand on.

Maybe he believed he didn't have the right to say any of those things, not anymore, but he could say this.

He attached the video he'd taken of Beau, so competent, so confident, leading the meeting, and putting Brett so perfectly in his place, so he wouldn't feel admonished or pissed off about it later, and he said, **He's gonna be a damn good coach. Just like his dad.**

Somehow, with an eerie kind of gut instinct, Asa knew that the text notification on his phone came from one person in particular.

Someone who hadn't texted him in seven years.

Sometimes, he'd still open that text window, and just read the last thing he'd sent to Scott.

Come see me tonight, if you've got time. Want to talk.

Scott hadn't said anything else, other than, **On my way.**

It felt so horribly normal. Like the resulting conversation hadn't destroyed him for years after.

Now, Scott had sent him something else.

For a single horrible moment, he worried that Scott would say something it was too late to say. An elaboration on *I missed you*.

But he hadn't.

Instead, there was a video, and when he clicked on it, the sound echoing in the abandoned equipment room he'd found, he realized that Scott had recorded Beau in the meeting. Beau, apparently convincing Brett to move his guys around slightly on the field.

He's gonna be a damn good coach. Just like his dad.

Asa knew all of this should make him less angry. No doubt that Scott had done it for that purpose. To try to bridge the gap. To remind him of the things they had in common—like Beau, and how much they both cared about him.

He was, undeniably, unrefutably, proud as hell of his son. He'd grown up in those last seven years, and he was proving it now, running the meeting just how Asa would've run it except . . . not quite. He'd have done it a little differently, and that was okay. Beau had a special touch all his own, and it made Asa want to text Scott back and agree.

He's gonna be the coach I hoped he might be, even when I didn't know if he should be.

Scott had always encouraged him to let Beau choose, even if Asa had been worried that he might be choosing the thing that would please Asa more than anything else.

This video right here was the answer to the questions Asa had been asking seven years ago. *Is this right? Should I push him harder? Or less? Or not at all? Is he doomed to become a football coach just because I'm always dragging him to football fields?*

No, Beau had become a football coach because he was born to be one.

Just the same as Asa was.

Asa leaned back in the chair and took a deep breath.

He knew Scott's text had been designed to take the sting out of his anger.

And it had.

But it also hadn't, all the same.

It also intensified his rage, til it felt like it was burning inside of him.

He composed and rejected several texts.

Yeah, he is gonna be, no thanks to you.

Think what he could've been, if you were around to mentor him.

Don't think you've got much room to talk, considering you've been MIA for seven years.

But as Asa deleted the last one, one agonizing letter at a time, even he could acknowledge it wasn't entirely true. Scott might have disappeared out of his life, but he'd never disappeared out of Beau's.

While he might've been around, he hadn't sat front and center to Beau's developing leadership skills either—and he was now.

Asa took one deep breath and then another. His heart was racing, not something that he'd ever worried about until now.

Wasn't he supposed to be dealing with less stress? Isn't that why Beau had brought Scott here?

That was fucking hilarious.

Finally, he replied, typing out carefully, **Yeah, he is. Proud of him.**

Scott texted back almost immediately. He'd always been a fast texter, something that Asa liked. There'd never been any game playing with Scott. What you saw was what you got, unless . . . of course . . . you were talking about how he'd apparently been in love with him for twenty-plus years and never said a goddamned word.

Not gonna take any personal responsibility for that, huh? Nothing about how he was smart enough to watch and learn?

Asa glanced back at his phone.

He knew what Scott was doing. Why did he *know* what Scott was doing and still manage to get sucked in?

It was not difficult to guess why. But he didn't have to like it.

You always thought I was some kind of legend. I'm just a man.

Scott replied so quickly that Asa nearly sent him another text, telling him to shut up, stop talking to him, and start paying attention to Beau's meeting.

But he didn't.

Maybe because of what Scott texted back.

Trust me, I've never forgotten that.

Asa thought he'd long grown out of feeling that flare of attraction sizzle up his spine.

It turned out, forty-nine was not too old to feel it.

Especially not when the guy causing it was Scott Callaway.

He set his phone aside. He wasn't going to answer that particular message. He didn't even know how.

If he knew Scott at all—and even though it had been seven long years since they'd talked, he knew he did, still—he wouldn't have expected him to answer.

He'd said it to disarm him. To remind him that even if they ignored it, those feelings hadn't just gone away.

Asa didn't need the reminder.

He didn't want it, either.

All he wanted was to get back to work.

An hour later, he finished up his notes, emailed them to Scott, without a single comment, and then slipped out of the lower level and back onto the street without anyone else seeing him.

He caught a cab back to his place, and by the time Beau swung by, around five, he was sitting on the couch, a glass of water on the coffee table in front of him, and ESPN playing on the TV.

"Have a nice relaxing day?" Beau asked.

Asa made a face. He'd worked for at least seventy-five percent of it, and he'd still hated it.

He was no good at taking time off. Which was why he never did.

"It probably wasn't *that* bad," Beau said as he unpacked sandwiches from a deli down the street onto the little table next to the kitchen. Asa didn't want to know what he'd ordered him. It wouldn't be his normal Italian cold cuts, he was sure about that.

"It was bad," Asa said, standing up and flipping off the TV. "I wasn't working, *and* you brought Scott here."

"Are you still on that? He took another job, Dad, and I know that sucks. I know you probably hated that he did it, but he had to look out for himself. You know that."

"Yeah, he sure had to look out for himself," Asa muttered.

Beau glanced over at him. "I knew you guys weren't as close as you used to be, but I thought that was just . . . I don't know . . . distance and that you were both crazy busy. But you gotta let that go."

"When you feel old and decrepit, I genuinely hope you have a son who lectures you on what you're supposed to let go of, and also cleans your house out of anything that's vaguely edible."

Beau didn't even look guilty, which was a bad sign.

"I signed you up for a meal delivery service today. It's supposed to be heart healthy, and they bring the food right to your door."

Asa sighed and glanced down at the sandwich. "What's this?"

Beau took a seat and opened his own sandwich. Was he really . . . yep, he was. He was going to eat salami and capicola in front of him, when his sandwich was probably all rabbit food.

"Turkey."

At least it was actually turkey and not some weird tofurkey thing. Asa unwrapped his sandwich and took a bite. It wasn't half bad actually, though it definitely would've been better if there'd been cheese and way less spinach piled on. But he could eat this.

"So," Beau said, leaning back in his chair after he'd demolished half of his sandwich, "Scott gave me your notes."

"He did *what*," Asa exclaimed.

"He gave me your notes. Well, not entirely true. At first, he tried to pretend all these detailed notes were his. But . . ." Beau narrowed his gaze. "Let's face it, he's not that good of a liar, and frankly he didn't try that hard, so I'm sure he knew I'd figure it out. So what, he's good enough to conspire with, but not good enough to forgive?"

"Something like that," Asa said.

"You weren't supposed to be working," Beau said.

"I'd like to know when you became so goddamn sanctimonious," Asa said. "I know it's not Sebastian."

"It's *you*, Dad," Beau said, his expression morphing into frustration. "I'm fucking terrified about you, about what might happen to you if you don't try to slow down."

"I only worked for a few hours. It was fine. I didn't feel . . ."

But he *had* felt anxious and excited. That hadn't been the work though, it was all Scott.

Too bad he couldn't admit that to Beau and convince him to send Scott back to Alabama.

"I felt fine. It was good. It was quiet and I enjoy the work, you know that," Asa finished softly.

He knew Beau was worried, and truthfully, he hated that for him. It was why he was eating this turkey sandwich with all its spinach and no provolone cheese with only a minor amount of bitching.

"The notes were good. But you had to know Scott wasn't gonna be able to pass them off as his."

He hadn't really thought about it. He'd only been thinking that *one*, the first meeting of the new week just couldn't happen without any of his input, and *two*, Scott cared enough about him that he'd do what he asked without questioning him.

Asa had apparently overestimated what Scott was willing to do for him.

"I'm going in tomorrow. It's the first practice of the week. I need to be there. And . . ." Asa hesitated. "Everyone needs to see me there. You know that."

Beau didn't look like he liked it, but he nodded. "But no more sixteen- or eighteen-hour days, okay? I will one hundred percent get security to carry you out."

"Eight to eight," Asa said, suddenly aware that this was a negotiation, and he wasn't going to go quietly.

"Twelve hours? No. Eight to five. Like a *normal person*."

Asa nearly rolled his eyes. Normal people didn't become coaches of NFL teams. He knew that. Beau even knew that.

But he could work with that. He could always bring his laptop back here, do a little more work in the evenings. Beau wasn't going to sit with him and monitor every second of his time. He wouldn't, because he knew Asa just wouldn't take it, and also because Sebastian wouldn't either.

"Fine," Asa said. "Fine. Eight to five. That's fair."

Beau looked suspicious. "That was way too easy."

"Listen, I spent the day contemplating the alternative, and it wasn't pretty." Asa picked up his sandwich. "So, I'm willing to concede the point."

"Alright," Beau said. "Eight to five. It's a deal."

CHAPTER THREE

SCOTT DIDN'T EXPECT THAT when Asa walked back onto the practice field, he'd acknowledge him.

He hadn't replied to his last text yesterday, and he had a feeling that Beau wouldn't be mincing words about Asa sending him notes yesterday.

He'd known the moment Asa sent them that they were way too detailed for him to possibly pass them off as his own—he'd come on board too late, with very little time to actually sit down and watch much game tape—but he supposed he could've faked it a little better.

Instead, after his very first suggestion, Beau had shot him a look and said, bluntly, "I guess my dad's gotten over being pissed at you."

Unfortunately that was not the case. And really, Scott hadn't expected any different.

Asa had sent him the notes because he hadn't had any other choice, and he'd probably thought that Scott would agree because of all those feelings they weren't talking about.

He watched as Asa walked onto the field, and everyone's eyes swiveled in his direction. Players went out of their way to jog over to him, to clap him on the back. It was easy to tell that he was beloved on this team, and even though Beau had told them he'd be okay, it was reassuring to see him in the flesh, *looking* okay.

The players did their joint warmup—and really, Scott hadn't even been surprised that he'd implemented the same kind of pre-practice and pre-game routine that they'd done at Tennessee; the man was brilliant and knew how to get the most out of his players—and when they were in the middle of it, Scott chose that moment to wander over to where Asa was standing.

He might look a little older, be a tiny bit more worn out around the edges, but he was still the man that Scott loved.

He wore his age well, with just a few smile lines, and a handful of gray hairs spreading out from his temples, through his dark hair. His blue eyes were just as intense as they'd been twenty years ago, or fifteen, or ten. When Asa's gaze swung his way, that blue still knocked the breath right out of his chest.

There'd been a time—and he'd been so goddamn sure, too—that he'd believed he'd grow out of these feelings. That over the years, with nothing else to sustain them but Asa's friendship, they'd fade.

But they never had.

Even the last seven years, Asa's anger, and now his cold shoulder, had done nothing to diminish them.

"You sold me out to Beau," was what Asa said, giving him that one single glance, as unaware as ever what just a look did to him.

Scott shoved his hands into his pockets. Watching the warmup on the field. Trying to even his breathing. It was a lot, being this close again. Learning to adjust to the inevitable avalanche of feelings washing over him. "I didn't, he actually guessed."

"You didn't really try to sell it," Asa pointed out.

"No. No, I didn't. You know why I'm here? Why I'm really here?"

"Ostensibly to help me coach a team I don't need help coaching," Asa retorted.

Yep, he was definitely still mad.

Turned out it didn't matter whether he'd expected it or not, or whether he thought he deserved it or not—the anger still stung.

"Your owner thinks I'm here to do that, and I can't say I *won't* help, because even you know, more minds set on a task is better than less. But Beau didn't put me on football. He put me on *you*."

Asa turned to him then. "Are you fucking kidding me? He made you the Asa monitor?"

Scott had told himself that if he was going to do this, if he was going to come to Miami and be there for Asa and for Beau, he was going to do it with complete honesty. He hadn't expected the first test to crop up so quickly, but it had.

"He'd probably call it something else. But he legitimately divided up your duties. There was even a spreadsheet."

A smile crept across Asa's face, and it shouldn't have affected him so strongly, still—but it did. "Of course there was," Asa muttered.

"You," Scott said, "were doin' way too much, by the way. Stuff you should've left to your coordinators. They're qualified. Let them do their goddamned jobs, Asa."

Asa shot him a wry look. It was like the last seven years hadn't passed, like those years of hard work and misery and loneliness in Washington hadn't happened. He erased them with a single fucking look.

Was it any wonder that when Asa needed him, he'd come running?

You didn't just do it for him, you did it because you're just as fucking damaged as he is. Your ailments just didn't land you in a goddamn hospital.

"It's not that easy, there's a lot of egos to manage, to control, and if I let one of them get too cocky, get too sure of themselves, let them draw up the game plan with their own future in mind instead of *our* future . . ."

"You don't trust them." Scott shouldn't have been surprised. Asa was a tough nut to crack. Possibly because anyone who managed it learned that inside, he was soft and sweet and gooey. Utterly trusting, even. So over the years, he'd grown this hard-ass shell, and this fuck-off exterior, and he'd used them both to protect himself.

But Scott had only ever seen others get caught by Asa's walls. He'd always been inside of them, from the very beginning.

"How can I?" Asa said it matter-of-factly. "I barely know them. The last person I trusted . . ."

He didn't need to finish that sentence.

Scott knew it was him.

Asa had trusted him, completely, and he'd blown it, not only by taking another job, but because of *why* he'd taken it.

"Beau was right, you do need the help," Scott said.

Asa rolled his eyes. "Yeah, we're nine and three. We're in line to win the division. We're going to the playoffs. We really *don't* need the help."

Scott was silent for a moment. He knew Asa bluster when he heard it.

"What did you always say? The only game that matters is the next one?" Scott pointed this out quietly. Asa made a face, but he didn't reply.

They watched, silently, as the warmup ended, and the team broke into their positional groups.

Scott's natural inclination was to head to where Brett was gathering the defense together, probably to run some drills. But Asa was heading the opposite direction, towards where Paxton, the young quarterback, had circled up the offense.

Both Davis and Randy, the passing coordinator, glanced over at Asa as he approached.

Randy resumed his talk about progressions, about Pax making sure to work through options two through four, when the first option wasn't immediately available. Pax was nodding, Davis was making notes, and when Randy finished up, even looking over at Asa, no doubt expecting him to add his two cents in, he didn't say a word about the progressions Pax was taking.

But he did have something else to say. "I want us to focus on third downs again this week," he said, "especially in the scrimmage at the end of practice. Defense needs more work on stopping third down, and y'all need more work breaking through and getting the first."

Randy nodded, agreeing with what Asa had suggested. "That's a great idea," he said. "Come on," he added. "Let's run the short third down package."

Asa turned away and headed back to the sideline, Scott trailing after him.

"Are you really gonna follow me around like a lost puppy?" Asa asked, annoyance rich in his voice.

"I'm gettin' a handle on how you handle your practices, first off," Scott said mildly. "And second, yeah, that's sorta my job, according to Beau."

"Ugh," Asa groaned. "Please don't. Just don't."

"I'm supposed to be assisting you, that's what Beau assigned to me. So right now, I'm just kinda . . . I guess . . . gettin' a feel for how you coach this team. Though, it's not much different than how you coached before."

"No shit," Asa said sarcastically.

"You're angry." Scott stated it cautiously. Specifically didn't ask. Because he didn't want to hear the answer.

Asa turned to him, shading his eyes with his notepad. "Yeah, I'm angry." He hesitated. "And if you tell me to just get over it like Beau told me, I'm gonna get angrier."

Of course Beau chose that moment to pop up next to his father.

"Everything going good?"

Scott shot him a baleful look. "No."

Beau looked resigned, but not exactly surprised. "Again?"

"*Still*," Asa hissed under his breath. "He's fucking following me around, like a bad memory."

Beau chuckled, and Asa glared harder.

"It's not funny," Asa retorted.

"He's supposed to be assisting you. He's got to follow you around, you know, to be the kind of good assistant I know he wants to be," Beau said reasonably. "The kind of good assistant I *know* you want him to be, if you could get over this."

Scott almost told him to stop, because nothing Beau was saying was helping his situation. Not that Scott thought there was much he *could* do. Asa was mad. *Legitimately* mad.

Asa stared at Beau in disbelief, and then tucking his notepad under his arm, stomped off towards where the defense was facing off against each other, working on improving their first step off the line.

Scott went to follow, even though he knew what kind of anger he was going to get pointed his direction if he did, but Beau stopped him by putting a hand on his arm. "Maybe give him a minute to cool off," he suggested.

"I think he's gonna need more than a minute," Scott pointed out dryly.

Not for the first time, he was tempted to tell Beau what had *really* happened, seven years ago, and why Asa wasn't going to just "get over it" anytime soon. But it wasn't his place to say, it was his father's, and he'd clearly decided that he didn't want Beau to know the truth.

"This is gonna be fine," Beau said confidently, but Scott knew him so well, it was hard to miss the hint of panic in his tone.

"Maybe, maybe not," Scott said.

It hurt to think that maybe they couldn't get past this.

But that's why you didn't bother reaching out, not once, because you were afraid you'd made your bed and Asa was going to make you lie in it.

He was such a stubborn son of a bitch, and God help him, Scott loved him for it.

"We need you here," Beau said. "Whether he realizes it or not."

Scott heard, *I need you here, we both need you here, whether he realizes it or not,* so, he nodded. "Alright," he said.

Beau turned to check in with the special teams coordinator, but before he did, he glanced back at Scott. "Dinner tonight?"

"Sure." He didn't have much to do, except go through the practice footage and compile his notes on past games, which he could easily do after dinner. Beau had told him that Asa wasn't allowed to work past five, so he'd have a whole empty evening ahead of him to catch up.

"Great. I'll text you the address," Beau said.

"Is this dinner thing something we're going to be doing every night now?" Asa asked as he watched Beau unpack the food he'd had delivered. "And if it is, why isn't Sebastian here?"

"Not a regular thing, I just thought you'd like to talk about how practice is going, now that you're taking a step back."

"What? I thought I wasn't allowed to talk about football after five PM," Asa said sarcastically.

Beau rolled his eyes, so quick he might've missed it, but while Asa might be getting older and might have a slightly bum ticker, his eyes were just fine.

"If I thought I could actually stop you thinking about it, I'd consider it, but I know better."

Asa didn't want to admit it—and he definitely wasn't going to admit it to Beau—but he hadn't been spending as much time thinking about football as he usually did. And that was all Scott Callaway's fault.

He'd been undeniably distracted, by the painful rush of awareness and returning feelings, after being numb for so long. *For too long.*

He didn't necessarily agree with that inner voice; the numbness had worked, hadn't it? He didn't need it to go away.

But now it was, inevitably, because of Scott's presence.

There was a knock on the door.

"I'll get it," Asa said. "Since you're so busy preparing dinner."

"Sarcasm is not a valid argument," Beau called out as Asa headed towards the front door.

He pulled it open, and then nearly shut it again.

"Of course it's you," Scott said.

Echoing just how Asa felt.

"Naturally," Asa said with resignation. He opened the door wider. "You might as well come in, because I'm sure you got invited to dinner."

Scott shot him an apologetic look as he crossed the threshold. "Yeah, but I wasn't told this place was yours."

"Why would you be?" Was he still mad? Oh, he was still plenty mad.

But Scott must've showered after practice, maybe even after they'd left the practice complex, because when he passed by Asa, nearer than probably either of them were completely comfortable with, due to the miniscule foyer, he smelled like soap and sunshine and fresh grass. Asa wanted to bury his head in his chest and feel the solid warmth of it. To let himself get carried away by his feelings.

The one thing being numb had guaranteed was that he didn't have these kinds of thoughts.

"Beau," Scott said dryly as he walked into the kitchen. "I'm here, as summoned."

"Good," Beau said, his tone brisk. "Dinner's heating. I hope you enjoy it."

A suspicion bloomed in the back of Asa's brain. "You hope *we* enjoy it? Aren't you?"

"No," Beau said unrepentantly. "I'm going to eat with my boyfriend. And the two of you are going to hash this out and stop fighting on the sideline of the practice field. We're nine and three.

But there's still work to do. Work that needs to be done not *just* by you, Dad, no matter how much you refuse to acknowledge it. So you either work things out with Scott now, or you don't, and we find someone else, someone you'll trust even less."

Beau turned and headed towards the door. Asa stared at the retreating back of his son with disbelief. The door shut behind him. He was speechless.

The disbelief was a good alternative to the anger, at least.

"Well," Scott said, breaking the silence, "I guess he didn't have a handy closet to lock us in."

Asa shot him a look, uncomfortable and more than a little terrified of the fact that they were here, *alone*, in his condo. He didn't want to be alone with Scott.

He didn't quite trust himself to keep shoving him away.

Not when all he wanted was to pull him close.

Closer than they'd ever been.

"He doesn't know," Asa argued, even though with his current—and limited—scope of knowledge, Beau could have totally justifiably shoved them into a closet.

"We're not playin' seven minutes in heaven, Asa, we're trying not to kill each other," Scott said, so reasonably.

Now, he was fucking thinking of seven minutes in a closet, pressed up against Scott.

Fucking hell.

"I know that," Asa said testily.

"Well, let's eat so we can at least give Beau the satisfaction of doing that." Scott skirted around him and pulled the casserole dish out of the microwave, which hadn't stopped beeping in the last minute.

They might as well eat, Asa finally reasoned. The food was here. Scott was here. It wouldn't kill him to break bread with him.

Maybe Scott was right and it would get Beau off their backs.

Personally, he didn't buy it, because Beau was more like him than he liked to acknowledge.

"What *is* this?" Scott asked as he dished up whatever Beau had heated up.

Asa grabbed plates and peered into the casserole dish. "Meatloaf? Of some form?"

Scott looked at it skeptically. "It doesn't *feel* like meatloaf."

"Beau said he was ordering in some kind of healthy meal service. God only knows what it is. But . . ." If he declared the meal inedible, then the "breaking bread" portion of the evening would be over, and he already knew the making-up part wasn't going to be happening, which meant Scott wouldn't have a reason to stay.

It was funny; Scott being here, in his condo, was terrifying.

But the thought of watching him walk away again burned.

"But we'll have to give Beau the benefit of the doubt," Asa finished, trying for optimism. The sandwich hadn't been all bad yesterday, had it?

Scott dished up the meatloaf, and the sides, which according to the package were mashed cauliflower and sautéed green beans, and Asa took one plate and led the way to the table he and Beau had eaten at yesterday.

It hadn't seemed so goddamn tiny yesterday, but it did today, with Asa contorting his legs around one of the chair legs so that it wouldn't end up brushing one of Scott's feet.

Why was he so tall? Why did he always have to stretch his legs out?

Half-heartedly, he pushed the cauliflower around his plate, wishing that even though it looked like mashed potatoes, it *tasted* like mashed potatoes.

Scott hadn't looked up at him, and was eating mechanically—and that hit Asa right where it hurt. How many times had he seen Scott eat just this way, like food was fuel, and he was just trying to get enough to push him into the next thing? How many hundreds of meals had they shared?

More than he could even hope to count.

It was easy to miss someone. It was so much harder to get them back—especially when Asa didn't know how to bridge this distance between them.

Distance you put there, distance you insisted on, that uncooperative voice reminded him.

He had every right to be angry, Asa told himself. But, glancing up at Scott from under his lashes, he had a feeling that he hadn't been the only miserable one.

There was something hungry about Scott now. Hungrier than before. Like he'd take every bit of Asa he was allowed, even if it was only Asa's anger.

He took a bite of meatloaf and cringed.

"I can't believe you're actually eating this," Asa said, setting his fork down.

Scott's smile was sheepish. "I'm trying not to be rude. Beau got this for . . . well, for you, and he invited me."

"Yeah, would've been nice if he'd bothered to get something goddamned edible. This tastes like . . ."

"Cardboard? Old, wet cardboard?" Scott finished for him.

Asa nodded, shuddering. He stared at his plate. "I don't get it. I'm *fine*. Isn't there a way to do this without sacrificing eating anything edible ever again?"

Scott glanced up. Their eyes met. For a second, it was like the past seven years had never existed, like they'd never missed each other.

Love pulsed hot and heavy inside him. It was everything he'd feared he'd feel, when Scott came, and everything he'd missed.

"I think . . ." Scott said slowly, "that Beau's just trying to do the right thing. And you know him, he . . . he can go overboard? Trying to do what he thinks is right?" He hesitated. "Kinda like someone else I know."

Asa knew it was his best trait—and also his worst. Just like it was Beau's.

"Yeah," he said with a sigh.

"Here," Scott said, "I have an idea."

"What is it?"

"Just . . . trust me."

Asa raised an eyebrow. "Really?" he asked dryly.

"Okay, I know you don't, not anymore, I can't really blame you for that, but you can for this. For an edible meal you don't want to immediately chuck into a trash can, anyway."

"Something decent-tasting that Beau isn't going to kill you for? Lead the way."

Scott looked surprised, but nodded, looking something up on his phone.

"Alright," he said. "We can even walk there."

The worst part of it all, Asa thought as he got up and followed Scott out the door, was that he didn't *not* trust Scott. Trusting him felt as natural as breathing, and even as angry as he'd been—even as hurt and numb as he'd made himself—that had never changed.

Dusk was falling in downtown Miami, and as they walked down the sidewalk, neither of them said a word.

Maybe, Asa thought, they'd already said too much to each other.

Then Scott turned the corner, and to Asa's surprise, he didn't walk right past the Burger King, but instead, pulled open the door.

Asa eyed him with trepidation. "You do realize that Beau is gonna kill you, right? Real slow."

"Are you sayin' you'd feel bad about that?" Scott asked, grinning.

Couldn't be any tougher than living without you for the last seven years.

"Might, a little," Asa admitted.

"No need to worry. They've got something you can eat that Beau will hundred percent not kill me over. I know what you like, I'll order for us, if you grab a table."

"Alright," Asa said dubiously.

He found them a table in the back, and was only sitting there a few minutes, scrolling through email on his phone, despite Beau's insistence on not working past five, when Scott walked up with a tray.

He eyed the two burgers on the tray as he set it down on the table.

"You know I can't eat that."

It was the first time he'd actually acknowledged it to himself, and he couldn't help it, he winced.

"Yeah, you can," Scott said with a smile that would've thawed Antarctica. "It's called the Impossible Burger. It's not meat, but it tastes like meat. And it's sure a hell of a lot better than whatever that meatloaf was supposed to be."

"It is?" Asa was surprised, because the Scott he'd known forever was definitely a meat-eater. He didn't think anything about Scott could surprise him anymore—but this did.

"Actually went vegetarian for a few years, when I was in Washington," Scott said. "Cholesterol is a bitch. Which is something you're about to discover."

"Huh," Asa said and reached for one of the burgers in the chain's typical wrapper. He unwrapped it, and took a bite. And to his shock, it *did* taste just like the burgers he'd always enjoyed.

"This is actually . . . really, really good," he said, after chewing and swallowing. He hesitated. "Thanks for the suggestion, and for bringing me here."

Scott's gaze was soft. Understanding. "'Course," he said. "Things didn't get so bad with me, but then I was never under the stress you were, either, Asa."

"You mean," Asa said, "the stress you and Beau think I put myself under."

Scott nodded.

Asa took another few bites of his burger. He talked to Beau, sure, and he even talked to Lynn still, occasionally. He had other friends that he'd made in this community, but he'd never been close to anyone like he'd been close to Scott—before or since.

That must be why he wanted, so fucking badly, to just *talk* to someone.

To Scott.

"I worked so hard 'cause I wanted it so badly," Asa finally said. "Not just because we all want to succeed, because of course I do, I always have, but because I knew what that success would mean."

"For Beau."

Of course, Asa didn't have to explain in full—Scott already knew.

Even all these years later, Scott knew him better than he knew himself.

"Yes, for Beau. I thought, comin' here, to Miami, makes a strange kind of sense. It's where O'Connor came out, and revolutionized the sport. And the opportunity to rebuild? To build a team the way *I* wanted? It was too good to pass up, but unless I get the results Rudy wants, it's all over."

"Makes sense." Scott hesitated. "But, Asa, you're doin' too much work. Beau knows it. Your coordinators know it. *You* know it. You've got to delegate."

"That why you agreed to eat with me? You wanted me to see your side of things? Tell me I'm wrong about how I've handled things here?" Asa knew he was still challenging him, still pushing back. They'd always done that for each other, he and Scott, but this felt different. Everything felt different after that fateful conversation seven years ago and now, after Asa had made it clear he wasn't welcome here.

"Asa, you gotta stop fightin' me on this," Scott said. "If I go, maybe they bring someone else in, someone maybe you don't know, or maybe they just saddle Beau with everything. You want to do that to him?"

Asa hated the truth in Scott's eyes. He didn't want him to be right. And he didn't want him to use Beau to make the argument.

But whether he used his son or not—that didn't change the logic of it.

"You know I don't."

"Can't we just . . . I don't know . . ." Scott leaned back and pushed his fingers through his hair. It had more gray in it than when he'd left Knoxville, but it was still soft and wavy and Asa was still jealous that he got to touch it and he never had. "Call a truce?"

Asa shot him a look.

"Okay, it's not that simple, I know it's not. You don't want me here, because it hurts. I get it." Scott set down his burger, like he'd just lost his appetite. "It hurts me too."

"I thought we weren't talkin' about that."

"We aren't, we *can't*, because . . ." Scott sighed. "Even if I was wrong, even if I wish I could make a different call than I did, I didn't. It happened. I left. I can't change that."

"And now you're back," Asa said, hearing the resentful edge to his voice.

"Because you need me. I know you hate that, but it's true."

"It's the worst when you use such unassailable logic that I can't argue with you," Asa retorted.

"I know." Scott smiled. "So, how about it? Truce?"

"No."

Scott looked surprised.

Probably because he thought he'd had it in the bag.

"It's not a truce," Asa continued, "because you weren't ever angry at me. I was only angry at you."

Scott sighed. "Yeah. That's true. Sort of. I was plenty angry at myself, for awhile. And," he added, the corner of his mouth twisting, "at everyone. At everything."

It felt so much like what Asa had experienced. That burning pain, just underneath the breastbone, aching with the injustice, with the acceptance that he might never be happy again. Not really happy. Not like he'd been, those twelve months with Scott, when his eyes had finally opened and he'd seen the truth of what existed between them.

Maybe it was the logic of Scott's argument.

Maybe it was the Whopper, sitting in his stomach, hard evidence that Scott not only gave a shit about him, but that he *knew* him, better than anyone else.

Or maybe it was the fact that Scott had suffered just as much as he had, for the choices he'd made.

"That's fair, then. Truce." Asa stuck out his hand. He knew it was coming. The force of Scott touching him, his hand curling into his. It felt like lightning, the feel of that calloused palm, brushing up against his. Once, it had felt nearly as familiar as his own.

Today, it just felt like coming home.

Asa saw the echo of everything he felt in Scott's eyes.

"Truce," Scott said.

Chapter Four

It was Wednesday. A practice day. And the first day of their truce.

Scott didn't know what to expect from Asa, after he'd agreed to laying down their arms. But he'd shown up at the practice facility early, getting his workout in, and was just heading towards his makeshift office, just next to Asa's, when he heard the man's voice bellowing.

Scott poked his head into Asa's doorway, and nearly laughed—which certainly would have blown the truce to pieces.

Asa was standing in his office, facing one corner, that was currently occupied by a very large Christmas tree, decorated with little hanging footballs and brightly colored tropical fish, all dusted in a not-inconsiderable amount of glitter.

Unsurprisingly, he was frowning.

"Beau!" Asa bellowed again.

He must have heard Scott in the doorway because he looked over, no doubt expecting that his son had come when called.

"You're not Beau," Asa said.

"Not the last time I checked," Scott said, walking into the office. It was certainly a *lot* of Christmas tree.

And he knew—remembered so well, in fact—how Asa had never been the biggest fan of holidays. How many times had he heard Asa say you could have Thanksgiving and Christmas or the football season?

It was one of the few things they'd ever disagreed on.

Nothing much seemed to have changed.

"Please tell me you're not responsible for this abomination," Asa said in a disgruntled tone, gesturing at the tree.

Scott raised an eyebrow.

"I know you love all this kind of shit. All this . . . *holiday cheer*," Asa continued. "It's not a crazy assumption, considering *you* showed up, and then this . . . this . . . *thing* appeared."

"It's a Christmas tree, Asa," Scott said, unable to help the laugh that escaped him. "It's just a Christmas tree."

Asa shot the tree a glare, clearly daring it to question his judgement.

"And it's covered in *glitter*," Asa said.

"I think it's cute," Scott said, ignoring Asa's eye roll as he walked closer, looking at all the ornaments. They were surprisingly clever, all the little tropical fish, interspersed with the footballs. It was an elaborate enough presentation that it was clear this wasn't the first year the Piranhas had decorated for the holidays.

"You would," Asa said with resignation.

"You know, considering your reputation, it's kinda shocking you're this much of a Grinch," Scott teased.

A crease appeared between Asa's brows. "My son's boyfriend was convinced I was going to have him killed and buried under my football field. Is that the kind of reputation you're talkin' about?"

"No, no, no," Scott said, shaking his head. "I'm not talkin' about the one you *think* you have, the one that everyone who doesn't really know you believes in. I'm talkin' about the one where you're an absolute fucking bleeding heart. The one everyone figures out after they get to know you better."

Asa harrumphed, shooting the tree one last glare, before he retreated behind his big desk.

"Speakin' of that . . ." Asa set his elbows on the edge of his desk and sighed. "I'm sure you've heard about all our . . . relationships on the team."

Scott took the opportunity—the *truce*, he told himself, it was just the truce—to sit down in one of the chairs in front of Asa's desk. He wasn't being forcibly kicked out, and he was gonna take all the advantages he could.

As much as Asa would give him, he'd take.

He'd been too long without him and it had fucking hurt.

"Oh, I heard," Scott said with amusement. He'd avidly followed every piece of Piranhas news he could, after Asa and Beau had taken the job. Plus, since Beau and he still chatted semi-regularly, he'd gotten plenty of insider info, too.

"Started with Beau and Howard, yeah?" he added.

Asa shook his head. "It started at *training camp*. With two of the rookies, and I will tell you right now, if you ever have to go into the wide receiver room, *knock*. If you ever have to go into any unoccupied closet, *knock twice*."

Scott chuckled. "Oh, to be young and insatiable, again."

"Then, it was Beau and Sebastian, and I do like him, you know? He's good for Beau. Gets him out of the office. Gets him out of his own head, which you know, can be a real challenge."

"I do know," Scott said, nodding. Asa didn't see it, of course, but he was the exact same way. "What was up with that guy who got outed? He's your center, right?"

"Logan. He's great. And yeah . . ." Asa sighed heavily with resignation. "Dylan is his boyfriend, and our kicker. Not at first, though, but who knows what really happened there. Probably only them. I should be grateful, at least, that I don't know *every blasted detail* of their relationship."

Scott raised an eyebrow. "You runnin' a football team or a matchmaking service, Asa?"

Asa groaned. "That wasn't even the worst of it. Davis came to me last week, and well . . . this is really why I'm tellin' you this whole story, because even though it's not open knowledge, I do not doubt you're gonna see some things and wonder. He and Pax are dating."

Scott's jaw dropped open. "Your . . . your quarterback coach is dating the quarterback?"

Asa shook his head. "I genuinely don't know what's in the fucking water in Miami. A truckload of Viagra, maybe?"

"And you just . . . *let* them do this?"

"Listen, we're nine and three. Paxton is a big part of that. Davis is a big part of that. What was I supposed to do? Forbid them from seeing each other? They see each other for twelve hours or so a day just doing their regular work." Asa looked exasperated and Scott couldn't blame him.

Scott also thought he understood why this was all happening—and it wasn't because a bunch of Viagra had gotten dumped into the Gatorade.

It was because Asa was secretly, deeply, a romantic.

He wanted happiness for everyone around him—even if he didn't think he'd ever have it for himself.

"You don't see what you did here?" Scott asked casually.

"Apparently not," Asa retorted without much heat. "Why don't you tell me?"

"You came here and proved me wrong," Scott said.

"I don't know what you mean," Asa said, a crease forming between his brows.

God, it would be so easy to just walk around the desk and press him into the chair. Kiss him.

Scott wasn't supposed to be thinking about doing it—he wasn't supposed to be thinking about it at *all*, he'd come here to work, and to help Asa out when he needed it—but how was he supposed to *not* think about it when Asa had come to Miami and created a culture opposite to the one Scott had always believed would keep them apart?

He used to be a lot better at compartmentalizing. How else could he have been in love with his best friend for twenty years and never been found out?

But the pain of the separation—and the pain of knowing that he *could've* had Asa, if he'd just reached out and taken him—had worn him down until it was hard to pretend that he didn't want it.

That he hadn't always wanted it.

"I told you there was no room in football for queer relationships. And you came here and proved me wrong. One couple at a time."

Asa stared at him, eyes wide.

The hair on Scott's arms rose, the silence becoming thick with all the things they weren't saying.

I still want you. I want you, more than anything else. Nothing is more important to me than you.

Asa finally looked away, breaking their eye contact. "I didn't *do* anything," he said, sounding flustered.

"You didn't fire Davis when he told you he was with your quarterback," Scott said quietly. "You didn't bury Beau's boyfriend under the field."

"Funny thing about being a head coach in the NFL," Asa retorted dryly, "they sorta look down on you murdering people and using your field as a graveyard."

"You know what I mean," Scott said, shooting him a look. It should've been a friendly, teasing look. But instead, the moment their eyes met, it felt like the temperature in the room spiked.

"I'm still not sure I'm following," Asa said, but his voice had dropped, and gone rough around the edges, and *goddamn*, how were they going to do this and not fall all over each other?

Maybe he shouldn't have asked for a truce. Maybe Asa shouldn't have granted it.

But it was a little too late for that.

"I mean . . ." Scott found his voice dropping, and he discovered he was leaning closer, before he could stop himself. "I mean that I told you two guys couldn't be together, openly, on a football team, and you made a place where it could happen. Proved me really fucking wrong."

Asa stared at him.

Scott stared right back, even though a voice in the back of his head was screaming *danger*. Not that he was listening. Not that he'd ever really listened. Not the way he should.

If he'd listened, he'd have put more space between them ages ago, left the first time he'd gotten a decent job offer. Maybe never come to Tennessee at all. But he'd done it, because when Asa had called, how could he possibly resist?

"Hey," a voice said from the doorway, "did I hear you bellowing my name? Like I'm still five and you're trying to get me to come down for dinner?"

Scott straightened instinctively as Beau walked into the office.

"Uh . . ." Asa stammered.

Beau leaned a hip against the side of the desk. "You know," he said, "that we have an intercom system so that you *don't* have to bellow my name to get my attention."

For someone who was so smart and so usually observant, Scott thought it was odd how Beau hadn't really caught on to the undercurrents going on between him and his father.

But if he didn't sense them—or didn't want to bring them up—then Scott definitely wasn't going to call attention to them.

"Oh yeah, the intercom . . ." Asa trailed off. He still looked distracted, and Scott decided that the truce meant he should save him.

"Your dad's upset about the Christmas tree," Scott said to Beau.

Beau rolled his eyes. "Of course he is."

"I'm gone for not even twenty-four hours," Asa said, and Scott, who knew him better than anyone else did, *still*, could see him gathering up his focus, ready to deploy one of his arguments, "and you tell the staff to decorate for *Christmas*."

"It's a standard thing they do, Dad," Beau said reasonably. But he was grinning. "I didn't have anything to do with it, but it's nice. I like it. So does everyone else."

Asa sighed. Loudly.

Because he *was* a bleeding heart, deep inside, Scott knew he wouldn't argue. Wouldn't insist that anything be taken down. He'd glare at that tree in the corner, but he'd tolerate it, because everyone else loved it.

"And," Beau added, "Tristan is putting together a team-wide Secret Santa, which you're gonna allow, *and* you're gonna participate in."

"I was gone for *less than twenty-four hours*," Asa ground out.

"It's the holidays, Dad. You know it'll be good for morale." Beau looked amused.

"Morale is just fine." He turned to Scott. "Don't you think?"

Beau was outright grinning now. "Oh, I see that the truce worked out just fine, you're even voluntarily bringing Scott into the discussion now."

"He's here, isn't he?" Asa said with a sniff.

But Scott knew—the way Beau did—what it really meant.

"Morale's fine, but it could always be better, and you know that, Asa." He said it gently, but Asa still made a face, clearly annoyed he'd been overruled.

Of course, that didn't mean that he wouldn't allow the Secret Santa or refuse to participate. Because he would. That was just the kind of guy, the kind of *coach*, Asa was.

"See?" Beau said, and pushed off the desk. "I'll see you two in a few for the coaches' meeting."

Asa watched as Beau sauntered off. He shook his head with resignation.

"Goddamn," Asa said. "How did this happen?"

"You mean, how did you raise a son who's unbelievably stubborn and does exactly what he thinks is right?" Scott paused. "I have no fucking clue."

"You're not helping," Asa countered.

"Come on, not even a little? I even sent you that text about that third down defensive configuration." It was impossible not to tease Asa a little, not when his words always seemed to smooth out the wrinkle between his brows—even still.

"You did." Asa's voice was grudging. "It was a good setup. I sent it on to Brett, he can work on it in practice today."

"See, you're at least a little glad I'm here," Scott teased.

But the look that Asa shot him back wasn't teasing at all, but incredibly serious.

"Yeah," he said. "Yeah, I think I am."

"Really?" Scott couldn't help the question that escaped out of him—or the disbelief in his voice.

Asa shot him a look. It was hot, singeing him around the edges, but it was sweet, too, and warmed him up inside. Made him feel, for the first time in a long time, like he'd actually done the right thing by Asa.

"You were right," Asa said. "If it wasn't you, it would be someone else, someone else I didn't trust, who'd interfere and piss me off. Or it would just be Beau, and we both know I don't want that."

It was the exact same argument that Scott had made last night. The logic he'd deployed to get Asa on board with him helping out. It shouldn't have hurt that Asa had agreed with it, or admitted it was why he was glad Scott was here after all.

Whatever you might have had together, that chance is over, he told himself firmly.

He'd known it.

He'd told himself before he even came to Miami.

But that didn't mean he hadn't secretly, deep down, wanted more.

So much more.

Asa was proud of himself.

He'd made nice with Scott.

He hadn't immediately demanded that the dang Christmas tree in his office be taken down.

But this whole Secret Santa thing?

There were limits.

And this was his.

He walked into the conference room for the coaches' meeting carrying a whole pile of notes and his tablet, and nearly ran right into Tristan.

It took him a moment—Scott *was* a distraction, no matter how he kept claiming he wasn't—to realize that the rookie wide receiver really shouldn't have been here.

"Oh shit, Coach, sorry," Tristan exclaimed, reaching out to steady him and catch his tablet, which threatened to slide right off the top of the pile.

"Tristan," Asa said, "you know, you have a meeting right now."

"Oh, I know," Tristan said cheerfully, "and I'm gonna get there in a minute, but I wanted to stop by here first and make sure the coaching staff drew their Secret Santa."

Asa had to give Tristan full points. He didn't quail even when faced with a trademark Asa Dawson staredown.

Too much holiday fucking spirit, Asa thought as Tristan shook the paper bag he was holding. "And you've got to pick, too, Coach."

"Do I have to?" he asked dryly.

"Absolutely," Tristan said. "It wouldn't be a team Secret Santa if you weren't in it."

"Oh, damn," Asa said. "Wouldn't that just suck?"

He could feel Beau watching him from the other side of the room, where he'd been chatting with Randy and Davis.

Scott wasn't present—he'd gone to get coffee before the meeting started—but it didn't matter at all that he wasn't there, because Asa already knew what he'd be thinking. And the kind of look he'd be giving him.

"Come on, Coach, pick a name," Tristan said, extending the bag, shaking it a little.

"Fine, fine," Asa said. He reached in and pulled a piece of paper out and stuck it on top of his pile, maneuvering his way to the seat at the top of the table.

"You know, Coach," Tristan said earnestly as he followed him with his tablet, and handed it over after he'd set the rest of his notes down, "you're supposed to actually *look* at the name."

"Oh, I will, don't you worry about that," Asa said.

Tristan's face broke into a big smile. "I'm so glad you're doing this."

"Me too, son, me too."

Apparently Tristan—despite having quite a capacity for it himself—didn't recognize sarcasm. Or maybe he just didn't acknowledge it in relation to holiday cheer.

In any case, Tristan clearly felt like he'd accomplished his goal, because he left the conference room with a huge-ass grin on his face.

Scott slid into the seat next to Asa's less than a minute later, like it had been made to be his, and nudged him, waving an identical slip of paper to Asa's.

"Tristan caught me in the hall," he murmured, tucking his head way too close to Asa's, making his heart skip a beat in an entirely different way than it had on the sideline less than a week ago. "Please tell me you didn't destroy that boy's love of Christmas."

"He's a grown man, not a boy," Asa said with a sniff. "And one of the best new wide receivers in the league, as well as practically a lock for Rookie Offensive Player of the Year."

"Still, tell me you took one," Scott said in a low voice.

Asa rolled his eyes, and pointed to his own slip of paper, sitting on top of his notes. "I took one. You happy now?"

"You know, there's room for both?"

Asa shot him an uncomprehending look. "Room for what?"

"Room for football and for a real life," Scott said reasonably. "It's what you want for Beau, isn't it? Why can't you have it?"

"Maybe I just don't like Christmas."

"No, what you don't like is *distractions*," Scott said conspiratorially.

That was one hundred and ten percent the truth—but what Scott must not realize was that on the scale of distractibility, he was so much worse than any Secret Santa or Christmas tree in his office.

He was the most tantalizing and tempting possibility of a real life, dangling out there.

You tried it once, and he shut you down.

Even if Asa wanted to go there again—and he wasn't sure he did, even as his heart leapt at the possibility—who was to say that Scott wouldn't just turn him down again?

Because you know he wouldn't. He sat in your office not even half an hour ago and told you that you made a space for two queer men to be together. Who was he talkin' about if he wasn't talking about you and him?

"Coach?"

Asa looked up, realizing that Beau was trying to get his attention.

Goddamn.

He'd been so distracted, he'd not even begun the meeting.

If he needed proof that it was a bad idea to even try to get involved with Scott again, this was it.

"Right, yes, let's get started," Asa said, clearing his throat and raising his voice as he stood up at the head of the table.

But the whole time he was going over his notes, some of which he knew Scott had already shared and he had zero compunction sharing again, because as far as he could see, the practice schedule Beau had compiled didn't adequately address the issues, he was thinking about what Scott had said.

You came here, and you proved me wrong. One pair at a time.

That wasn't why he'd done anything he had while he'd been here. Did he want a more equitable playing field for Beau and for every other queer person who wanted to be involved in the game they loved but didn't feel like there was a place for them? Of course he did. He was a fair and just man. He believed that everyone should get a chance, and should be judged on their capability and their skill, not on who they loved or what color their skin was.

Besides, what was he going to do? Tell Tristan and Wade they couldn't be together, when they were so obviously into each other that Kelly, the traveling coordinator, had to make sure nobody else roomed next to them the night before a game? Could he really have informed Davis that he wasn't taking his deal, and fired him, even though he'd been instrumental in completely turning Pax's career around?

No way. That would've been a dumbass move, and he wasn't a dumbass coach.

All he'd done, Asa told himself firmly, was the right thing.

That was all.

Except then, when he returned to his seat and as Randy, the passing coordinator, broke down some practice film from yesterday, showing a new shift he wanted to try for the offensive line, he looked at the slip of paper that he'd pulled from Tristan's bag.

Written there, in stark black letters, was a name: *Scott Callaway*.

Fuck me sideways, Asa thought with heat.

Had Tristan done this? Why would he? He didn't know. *Nobody knew*. Not even Beau, though he found it difficult to believe that his son, usually so observant, could have completely missed the undercurrents in his relationship with Scott—no matter how he'd tried to hide them.

Maybe Beau just didn't see it because he didn't want to.

But if Beau was oblivious, then everyone else had to be, too.

It wasn't like when Dylan and Logan had pretended to be dating, and everyone on earth had realized that they were *really* dating. Or when Beau and Sebastian had been sneaking around, and it was appallingly obvious to everyone what they were actually doing.

Nope, his secret was safe.

This was just fate fucking with him. Yet again.

The meeting ended an hour later, and Asa headed back to his office. He'd eat some lunch, hopefully without Beau supervising every calorie he ingested, and he'd go over the rest of his notes, and check them against the practice plan for the afternoon.

But when he got back into his office, there was Scott.

And there was another fucking desk.

"What are you doing?" Asa asked testily as he set his load of notes and tablet on *his* desk. Not the desk currently kitty-corner to his that had not been there a mere hour before. The scrap of paper with Scott's name burned in his pocket, full of unbearable temptation.

How could he forget it existed when Scott was *right there*, apparently moving in?

"Settin' up my workstation," Scott said nonchalantly as he plugged his tablet in.

"I'm sorry, I think you misread the name plate outside the door. This is *my* office, not yours."

"Oh," Scott said with a wild grin that set all of Asa's insides alight in both an extremely pleasant and extremely annoying way, "you mean that little closet that we both know wasn't really an office?"

"Yes," Asa said, grinding his teeth. "We can find you a better one if that one's too small."

"No need. Already found one."

"You mean, you found *mine*," Asa retorted.

"Well, yeah, but it only makes sense, right? We're supposed to be workin' together, right? I'm supposed to be assisting you. Best way for me to do it is to be right here."

Asa stared balefully at the other desk. First the Christmas tree. Then Secret Santa. And now this.

"Am I gonna walk in tomorrow and discover a sprig of mistletoe hanging in every doorway of this goddamn building?" Asa questioned.

Scott's smile turned sly.

He'd been seeing that kind of smile on Scott's handsome face for twenty-plus years. It shouldn't still be so sexy. It shouldn't affect him so viscerally.

But it did.

Still.

Always.

"You want some mistletoe, huh? Want an excuse to get close?" Scott teased.

Nobody else had ever teased him the way Scott did. Knew how to unwind him and then wind him back up again the same way. He'd never allowed anyone else, but Scott? Scott didn't do it because Asa allowed it or not. He did it because it was as easy to him as goddamn breathing.

"No," Asa said gruffly, lying through his teeth. "I'm just saying, you get an inch, you take a mile."

Scott didn't look even the tiniest bit guilty about this.

"You're annoyed that I just moved in."

No, he was annoyed that he couldn't seem to take a deep breath near Scott and it seemed like he was constantly around.

And now he was going to be around even more.

"I'm annoyed that you didn't ask," Asa finally said, because the truth was a lot thornier to explain.

"Sorry," Scott said. And *now*, he was meek. "You left early for the meeting, and I ran into that gal that manages the facilities? And she asked me how the office was, and well . . ." Scott hesitated. "You know how crappy that office was, you know it because you gave it to me."

"Did I?" Asa pretended innocence but they both knew better. He'd absolutely sent Kelly an email, asking her to assign Scott what *had* been a closet as a "personal favor to him." She'd done it, because she was loyal, bless her, but it had been kind of a shitty move. Petty *and* shitty, and yet, undeniably satisfying.

"She said you did," Scott said, his expression turning stern. "She offered something better, but I said, no need, I had an idea."

"Moving in here," Asa said flatly.

"You've got plenty of space, and I just needed an extra desk. Kelly said she'd take care of it while we were in the meeting."

Of course she had. She wasn't going to move a desk in here in front of Asa. She wasn't that stupid.

"I won't make a peep, I promise," Scott said, and even though it was the last thing Asa wanted to deal with, the hope in his voice and in his eyes was unmistakable. Scott *wanted* to be here, with him, even if they weren't speaking. Even if they were just sitting in the same room, side by side. "But," he added, clearly taking Asa's silence for disapproval, "if it's too much, or you're uncomfortable . . ."

"No, no, it's fine, it's really fine," Asa said, before he could change his mind. Maybe if he acted like it wasn't a big deal, it wouldn't *be* a big deal.

Scott's expression softened. "Well, forget I'm here, alright?"

Like that was ever going to be possible.

Chapter Five

"Hey."

Scott looked up and saw Beau jogging over. Practice had just about ended, and Asa had already taken off for the weekly press briefing, and he was just finishing up here on the field.

Supposedly Asa was going home after he met with the reporters, but Scott hadn't any idea how Beau hoped to make that a reality.

Even with dividing up the work, there was still stuff left on Asa's plate. Scott knew, because he'd spent a few hours before practice in Asa's office—now *his* office, too—watching him work through an additional set of notes. The man could make notes on notes. It was one of the reasons why he was such a damn good football coach, and probably also why he'd worked himself into a heart attack.

"What's up?" he asked Beau when he stopped by the bench he was currently leaning against.

"You know my dad's supposed to leave at five."

Scott thought it was interesting how the way Beau named Asa changed based on the circumstances. Sometimes he was *Coach*, and sometimes he was *Dad*.

Now, he was clearly worried about him, so it was obviously *Dad*.

"I did hear that." Scott didn't mention that he knew it because Asa had been bitching about it as they'd come down to the field for practice.

"He means well, but he's drivin' me up a freaking wall," Asa had said about his son. "Watching me like a freaking hawk. Putting me on a work timer. Monitoring every single thing I put in my mouth."

Scott had been in the middle of drinking out of a water bottle and he'd ended up laughing so hard he nearly choked.

"Oh, please, get your mind out of the goddamn gutter," Asa had retorted fiercely, but he'd not been able to hide the amusement in his eyes or the smile twitching up the corner of his lips.

"I want you to go home with him," Beau said, and if Scott had been drinking, he'd have choked again. "Make sure he doesn't work."

"He's not gonna want to have me around underfoot," Scott argued reasonably. "Just . . . trust he's gonna make good choices, yeah?"

Beau shot him a look. "This is Asa we're talking about, right? After all, I heard that you moved into his office, so I don't think you've got much room to talk."

"That was . . ." *An excuse to get close, even if Asa didn't want me to. An excuse to get as much of him as I can, before I lose him again.* "Expedient, considering how closely we're working together."

Beau did not look convinced. "Just hang out with him for a few hours. Watch ESPN or something, or maybe, God forbid, do something that *isn't* work related, if you can swing it."

"Right," Scott said, not bothering to tell Beau how impossible of a task this was, because he *knew*. There was a reason he was giving it to Scott instead of taking it himself.

If he didn't know better, he'd guess that Beau had figured out what was *really* going on between them, and had decided, between the surprise dinner and now this request, that he was trying to push them together. But no, Scott was almost a hundred percent certain that Beau did not know.

It hadn't been his choice to tell him—that was all Asa—but really, what was there to even tell? Nothing had ever happened.

Son, I'm in love with your father, and I've been goddamn pining for him for over twenty years now.

Yeah, that was not a conversation he wanted to have with Beau.

"So you'll do it?"

Scott sighed. "You know he's gonna hate it."

"Yep," Beau said without regret. "But he's already semi-pissed off at you, so no harm, no foul."

Yeah, there was no way Beau knew.

"Fine," Scott said. It wasn't like he *didn't* want to spend the evening with Asa. He just had a pretty good feeling that Asa didn't want to spend it with him.

Beau had the nerve to look grateful. "Thanks," he said. He paused. "I'm real glad you're here."

Scott raised an eyebrow. "To do all the dirty work with Asa?"

He wasn't thinking about it like that. *He wasn't.*

But who was he kidding? He'd been thinking about Asa like that forever. Nothing had ever changed.

If Asa ever invited him to his bed—not that Scott expected it to happen, because he'd had that chance, and he'd blown it, and now Asa was probably over him, or too angry to even consider it—he'd not hesitate.

But that was definitely not going to be happening tonight, or any other night soon.

"Not just because of that," Beau said, and suddenly he looked so young again, like he'd looked, eighteen and vulnerable, right before Scott had left for Washington. "It's just good to have you back."

He wasn't going to lie, not to Beau. At least not about this. "Yeah, it's real good to be back," he said, patting Beau on the back.

"He said he's headin' home after grabbing a salad from the cafeteria," Beau said. "But there's plenty of meal kits in his fridge, if you want something to eat when you get to his place."

"I think I can manage to feed myself," Scott said dryly. Because if the meal kits were anything like that "meatloaf" and "mashed potatoes" Beau had foisted on his father last night, he was going to pass.

Davis appeared and grabbed Beau, apparently needing him to see something he and Pax were working on.

And wasn't *that* something?

Scott had known that Asa was forging his own direction here in Miami, but allowing the quarterback and the quarterback coach to be together? That confession had been totally unexpected, and for a moment, he'd thought, *maybe it's not over for us, after all, if this is what Asa's been doin'.* But then he'd realized that Asa hadn't been trying to make a space for them—hadn't been thinking about him, and longing for him, the way he'd been longing for Asa—he'd been angry at Scott's rejection and trying to prove him wrong.

Which was, unfortunately, not the same thing at all.

After practice ended, Scott grabbed a quick workout in the gym. If he was going to spend the whole evening with Asa, he needed to work off some of all this additional . . . tension. But it didn't help, because after he showered and dressed, grabbing something out of their office, before heading out of the building, he realized that he was still just as keyed up as ever.

He used to manage his feelings better, used to be more adept at keeping them compartmentalized, but he'd missed Asa too much. Wanted him too much. It was impossible to shove all these emotions back into the box, because just being near him was overwhelming in the best kind of way.

It felt like the very beginning, all over again, when they'd first become friends, and Scott had been sick with love, terrified that Asa would figure it out and terrified that he'd never get over it, that he'd pine like this forever.

He had, but over the years he'd made his peace with it.

Then Asa had blown it all up by falling in love, too, and now, after so long without him, it was hard to re-adjust back to that semi-comfortable state of acceptance.

After so long apart, his feelings wouldn't be placated; they tore at him fiercely, with sharp claws, demanding to be heard and seen and acknowledged.

It's not happening, even if you want it more than you've ever wanted anythin', Scott reminded himself as he walked through the Miami dusk towards the building Asa's apartment was in—and his own, that he was temporarily borrowing from Beau.

He took the elevator up to Asa's floor and, after heading down the hallway, took a deep breath and knocked on his door.

As he waited, he could hear Asa grumping as he walked into the foyer, right before he pulled open the door.

"Of course it's you," he said, staring Scott down. "Did Beau send you to check up on me?"

"He means well," Scott said. Noticing that Asa very deliberately had not invited him in, or opened the door any further.

"He's a goddamn pain in my ass," Asa retorted. "And he knows it, which is why he sent you instead of coming himself."

It was not only logical, it was true, which meant that Scott couldn't really argue with it.

"Yeah," he admitted. "But," he added, holding up a flash drive in his hand, "I got the footage from the scrimmage at practice, and I thought you might want to go over it instead of flipping through two hundred channels that you don't give a shit about, tryin' to find something else to watch."

Asa's eyes narrowed. "You're gonna break Beau's rule?"

"I thought of it as more a guideline," Scott said. "Besides, you're an adult. You know where the line is. Might've ignored it forever, but you know where it is."

Still, Asa didn't open the door any further.

Scott hadn't really anticipated Asa refusing to let him in.

After all, he'd given in pretty easily about the office to-day—considering how stubborn Scott knew he was.

"Why don't you just give me the footage and we'll say you watched me like a good little boy?" Asa said.

It wasn't the first time Asa had ever flirted with him, but it was the first time he'd done it after he *knew* that his feelings weren't just his own.

It shouldn't have made any difference, but Scott felt it deep down, felt the pulse of longing surge through him. How easy would it be to just lean in and see if Asa was willing to cash those checks he kept writing?

He might be angry, still, but that didn't mean he didn't feel the same nearly irresistible pull as Scott.

"Here I thought you didn't really want me to be *good*," Scott said, lowering his voice and leaning in just a fraction.

For a second, it seemed like Asa leaned in too, and the realization hit, Scott's heart racing with the knowledge of it, that their first kiss might take place in an apartment building hallway in Miami.

He'd told Asa once, *I don't know how it happens, but not like this*. Would it be like this? Would it end up being just sex, an itch that Asa had always wanted to scratch, and now could?

Scott wasn't stupid; he'd take any scrap of Asa that he could get. Even if it hurt. Even if it was impossible, in the end.

But then instead of closing the distance between them, Asa turned his head, and it took Scott a moment to realize that he was opening the door wider. "Come on, then," Asa said gruffly, the rough edge to his voice the only evidence that they'd edged right up to the line.

As Scott followed him deeper into the apartment, leading him to the living room, he realized it felt just like that summer, right before everything had gone to shit. When they'd played with the line between *we're friends* and *we're something more*, and it had felt both exhilarating and terrifying. Because what if Asa tried to cross it?

He had, in the end, and it had ruined everything.

No, Scott reminded himself, *you ruined everything, by listening to what Asa offered and turning him down because of some stupid, goddamned misplaced idea that you were being noble.*

He'd come here, to Miami, and that was the beginning and the end of him being noble this time around.

"Here," Asa said, holding his hand out for the drive, and Scott dropped it into his palm, not taking the risk of touching him.

There was only so far his self-control could stretch, and it was already thin enough.

He settled on the couch as Asa cued up the footage, making sure he scrupulously kept to the right side.

"You want anything to drink?"

"I don't suppose you have any beer?"

Asa shot him a look. "If you wanted any beer that Beau didn't clear out of here, you should've brought it."

"What, am I gonna be your contraband dealer now?"

"That's actually not a bad idea," Asa said, as he headed into the kitchen. Scott heard the fridge opening and closing, and then he reappeared with two glasses full of what looked to be iced tea.

"It's not sweet," Asa said mournfully. "But it's something."

Scott took the glass that Asa held out to him. "You know, you're not in bad shape."

Asa's glare could have cut steel. "Oh, thank you. I'm touched."

"I mean . . . Beau's goin' a little overboard here. You had too much stress. You worked too hard. Not enough sleep. But you're . . ." Scott realized as he glanced over at Asa, who'd taken the left side of the couch, that he was in real trouble. Not only because Asa's pride was significant, and it was also currently bruised, but because he was gonna have to admit to checking him out *plenty* of times over the years. "You're not . . . uh . . . well, you look like you've been usin' the gym plenty in the last couple of years."

Asa's smile wasn't so much a grin as a baring of his teeth. "What a gentleman," he said sarcastically. "Should I strip down for you, let you look your fill?"

He'd been playing with fire, and he knew it. Should've known, too, that Asa was the kind of guy who'd never blinked. He'd send them right into the blaze, if Scott pushed hard enough.

Isn't that what you want? To burn all the way up?

But it wasn't his choice. Asa had offered once, and he'd turned him down, flat. So, no, it wasn't up to him now. No matter how hard he pushed both of them.

"Uh, well, I'm not exactly gonna turn you down but . . ."

"I get it," Asa said flatly, and picked up the remote, clicking over to the footage he'd plugged into the TV. The first play began, and Scott tried to drag his attention—and his uncooperative cock, harder than he'd been in ages, just at the thought of Asa stripping down and letting him look . . . and letting him *touch*—back to football.

Scott frankly didn't think Asa got it at all. But he wasn't going to argue.

They watched the first play in silence.

Then Asa did his normal thing, rewinding the footage and watching it again, and then again.

He always watched every play three times. First time, he liked to say, was to get acquainted. Second time was to form a friendship. Third time, to dig in and *understand* just how it ticked.

But this time, he didn't just watch it three times. He watched it a fourth too.

It hit Scott like a bolt of lightning as he glanced over, nearly saying something to Asa about how he'd changed his routine, when he realized, from Asa's blank expression, and the way his fingers were trembling while gripping the remote like a lifeline, that he wasn't really watching.

But while he was debating whether he was going to say something, make it a *thing*, Asa tossed the remote onto the couch between them and turned, the expression on his face an undeniable challenge.

"Was it always like this for you?" Asa demanded rather than asked.

"Yes and no," Scott said. He was not going to laugh, he was *not* going to laugh. Because really, it wasn't funny. Except it was, a little. *Ironic*, Beau would've called it.

"Well, by all means don't elaborate, Scott," Asa said, the sarcasm rich in his voice. He didn't sound very happy about it.

Scott supposed he didn't blame him for that. But he'd given up on gettin' over this ages ago.

"No, not at first. 'Cause it was real obvious that you weren't into me like that, and it was a lot easier to pretend that I wasn't, too. Could kinda bury it away, not think about it. But that last summer?" Scott sighed. "I knew everything was changin' and it was real hard, almost impossible to focus on anything, not when I thought you might feel the same way about me that I felt about you."

Asa didn't say anything for a long time, but his gaze just *burned*, right into Scott.

"Okay," he finally said. Then he picked up the remote again, and rewound back to the beginning of the first play again.

This time, Scott actually focused on the play unfolding on the screen, and when it finished, Asa paused it, scribbling down a few notes.

They were through three plays when Scott felt compelled to speak up.

"Who's that corner you've got?" he asked, pointing to the screen. "It's not Sebastian, he's not playing corner anymore."

"That's Rose. Micah Rose. He's a rookie."

"Plays like a rookie," Scott said.

Asa rolled his eyes. "He's having a bit of trouble adjusting."

"How so?"

Asa gestured to the screen with his pen. "You saw. And there've been a few other things . . ."

It was unlike Asa not to give all the information when someone asked. Usually you had to get him to shut up.

"What other things?"

"Just . . . you don't wanna deal with Rose, just trust me on this one, alright?"

"Why don't I?"

Asa made a frustrated noise. "You can't just let things go, can you?"

"No, not really," Scott said. "It's why I'm good. It's why you didn't tell me to fuck off the first week of practice at Alabama. And why we're still . . . well, not *friends*, but well, you trust me not to screw this up. What's up with Rose?"

"Fifth game of the season, we were up in Foxborough."

"I remember that one."

"Well, he melted down in the locker room at halftime. Said . . ." Asa cleared his throat. He looked more uncomfortable than Scott could remember seeing him in a *long* time. Maybe ever. "He said some shit. Beau's convinced he's not . . . like that, he's just dealin' with a lot. Got a lot on his plate."

"You're not convinced." Scott stated it rather than asked.

"We're buildin' something here, something good, and I'm not sure he's part of it. He's not done anything since, but I don't trust him. And I . . ." Asa wet his lips. "I don't trust him around you, alright? What if he says some shit, again, and you kill him? I can't be responsible for that."

Scott was surprised—and that longing surged through him again. Asa still cared about him. It was buried under about a shit ton of anger and resentment, but it was still there. He hadn't killed it dead, which as far as Scott was concerned, was a minor fucking miracle.

"You're not worried about me killin' him, you're worried that *you're* gonna kill him if he says shit," Scott guessed.

Asa shot him a baleful glare. "I hate you."

"No, you just hate that you can fool everyone else on this team, but you've never been able to fool me, Asa."

Asa didn't answer that.

"He's slightly off," Scott said, dragging the topic back to Micah Rose. "He needs some work. I could help him."

"What did I *just* say about him saying shit?" Asa sounded frustrated.

Scott shrugged. "So he calls me a fag. It's happened before. It'll happen again. I sort of take it as it comes, these days."

"How did you . . ." Asa swore under his breath. "Beau told you."

"Besides, I'm still deep in the closet, aren't I?"

He was, even though he didn't intend to be for much longer. He'd already started telling some people in his hometown. If Beau hadn't called, he'd have been essentially out in a few months.

It had been time.

Long past time.

Asa didn't answer that one either. Just took a deep breath and turned to Scott with a serious expression on his face. "Just leave it alone, okay? Are you capable of doing that?"

Scott was surprised at how adamant Asa was being about this. "Yeah, sure, of course. I *can* do that." He didn't say that he would; only that he *could*.

Because now his curiosity was piqued. He'd made projects of lots of defensive players over the years. It was why he'd decided, after he'd been let go in Washington, that he wouldn't take another head coaching job. He'd stick to being a defensive coordinator. But then Beau had called, just when he'd started to consider taking a few offers.

"Good," Asa said gruffly. "Now do you want to hear my thoughts?"

"Like you're not going to give them to me anyway," Scott said, amused.

Asa rolled his eyes, but he couldn't hide the smile on his face.

Scott had been used to the sweltering heat of an Alabama summer. The humidity of Tennessee that could stretch easily from April to October.

But he was not used to sweating through a t-shirt in December.

"This fucking weather," Beau muttered as he wiped his face, the sun shining onto the practice field, the thick, muggy air raising the heat index a half dozen degrees.

"It's unnatural," Scott agreed.

"They're callin' for a lot of rain this afternoon, hopefully we can get through practice, before the weather breaks."

"Fingers crossed," Scott said dryly.

Asa was off on the smaller second field, observing special teams coverage practice, because according to him, he'd seen a gap in their punt return package, and he wanted to close it up before any other teams found it.

Scott had stayed on, to watch the defense, and to . . . well, he wasn't going to prevaricate. If he saw a chance to approach Micah Rose, he was going to take it.

No matter what Asa thought.

Sure, they'd brought him here to be a glorified babysitter, but he could still contribute. He still had the background and the knowledge to make a difference here, and frankly, it was unlike Asa to reject that expertise.

Despite the heat, he jogged down to where the defense was working against the second team offense. They were working on deep ball coverage today, and it was the perfect opportunity to watch Rose in action.

Sebastian was covering through the middle, deeper than most safeties would be, and Scott had a feeling that was because he didn't really trust Micah to take care of his assignment.

Truthfully, Scott wasn't sure he blamed him. If someone had used that word with Asa, he'd have been absolutely unforgiving about it.

He stood on the sideline and watched for a few minutes. The defense ran one play, and then another.

And yeah, everyone ignored Rose, and his misplaced positioning. The defense, clearly, had gotten used to compensating for his lack of effective coverage.

Could it work? Sure. Had it been working? Basically, so far.

But this was the kind of thing, Scott believed, that could come back and bite the Piranhas in the ass during their run-up to the playoffs and in a playoff run. Some brilliant offensive mind was going to realize what Sebastian was doing, and they were going to design a play to expose that weakness, and nobody would be able to stop it.

The best choice was to fix the origin of the problem.

After the third play, Scott jogged onto the field, coming to a stop next to Brett, the defensive coordinator. He'd done a good job with what he had, but he didn't have the kind of time or attention to fix every problem.

But Scott could.

"What's up?" Brett asked, not sounding particularly pleased that Scott had decided to join them.

"Hey, before you run it again," Scott said, "I want to try a different formation."

Brett tilted his head. "What kind of formation?"

"I want Howard in the middle, closer to the linebackers," Scott said. *Where he's supposed to be.*

Sebastian shot him a look, inclining his head just enough that Scott had a feeling he knew where this was going. "But . . ." he said.

"No, we're going to see what that looks like," Scott said, layering a bit more authority into his voice. He was a special consultant sure, and not really in the main coaching hierarchy, but he knew his reputation preceded him.

Every single one of these players—and definitely Brett—knew what he'd accomplished. Knew what he was capable of.

"Alright," Brett said with resignation.

Scott fell back, with Brett, and they watched together in silence as the play unfolded. And sure enough, without the pressure of Sebastian further up the field, the wide receiver slid right into the soft part of the zone, and caught a pass for twenty-three yards.

Brett sighed audibly. "See?" he said. "I'm doin' the best with what I've got, Callaway."

"Your problem is Rose."

"Yep," Brett said. "And don't think I haven't told Asa that. He told me to make it work, and I made it work."

Asa hadn't known what to do with the problem. It was unlike him. But considering what had happened with Beau, Scott wasn't all that surprised.

He'd left off dealing with Rose himself, and shoved the problem into Brett's lap, who'd done the best he could with it.

But Scott was here now, and he was going to address it, *personally*.

"Hey, Rose," Scott said, jogging over to where Rose was standing by the bench, taking a water break. No doubt he was tired, after having to track that wideout down after letting him catch the pass.

The guy looked up with suspicion in his gaze.

He was young, yeah, so young. But not as young as some of the players that Scott had coached over the years.

After going back to his own apartment last night, Scott had looked up Micah Rose.

A solid second round pick, from Wisconsin. He had all the athletic gifts he'd need to be an exceptional shut-down corner. He had pretty decent vision. Good speed. And on top of that, he had one of the all-time best corners to teach him how to be better, in Sebastian. But not surprisingly, that mentoring hadn't really happened—and Scott couldn't blame Sebastian for that after what he'd said to Beau.

"Who're you?" Micah asked, a little belligerently.

"Scott Callaway." He'd learned, the hard way, that players would respect you, if you respected them. He put out his hand.

Micah shook it briefly. His grip was firm, but his eyes were hesitant. Nervous.

He was wondering, Scott realized, what he'd heard about him. That was the thing, football players had long memories.

"You're here to help out Coach," Micah said.

"Yep, I sure am," Scott replied.

"He tell you to come over here?"

Scott shook his head. "I came over here because I saw some stuff in the practice tape that I thought I could help you with. First year, yeah?"

"Yeah," Micah said.

"Tough year, the rookie year."

"You ever been a rookie?" Micah challenged.

There was that edge to him again, and Scott wasn't surprised that everyone had decided to just let this guy go.

But Scott wasn't so easily dissuaded.

"Yeah, actually," he said, even though Micah should know this. "For a year or two. Played in a few games for the Falcons. Then I became a coach. For Alabama. Clemson. Tennessee. Then Washington."

His credibility established, Scott continued. "I could help, if you wanted."

"Help me do what?" Micah asked suspiciously.

"Be better," Scott said.

"I'm gonna be the top corner in the NFL," Micah said after a long pause. He spat into the ground. "I don't need any goddamn help."

"Yeah, yeah, you do. You're lettin' guys get behind you, in front of you. Howard's havin' to work further back in the zone, leavin' you guys vulnerable, because you can't handle your assignments. And you might not want to admit it, but it's true. You know it's true."

Micah stared at him.

It was just as Scott had figured; nobody *talked* about it. They'd just made the adjustments. They hadn't made Micah face what his lack of preparation and practice had resulted in.

The first step was to make him face it.

The second? To fix it, once he was willing to go there.

"I think it's bullshit," Micah said.

Nope, not there yet.

"Well, you think about it," Scott said mildly. "And let me know if you'd like my help to become that corner. The top corner."

He was five steps away, nearly about to take his sixth step when a voice behind him called. "What would you even teach me? You ain't never been a corner in your goddamn life."

"Nope," Scott said, turning around. "I was a defensive end."

"Built like it," Micah muttered.

"Didn't come easy, I had to work at it," Scott pointed out.

That was the problem with the NFL. Guys came in, and they'd been the best player on their high school team, then maybe one of the best players on their college team, merely by showing up and doing the reps and playing in the games. Then they were drafted into the NFL and everyone was fucking amazing. It wasn't enough to be the fastest or the quickest or to have the best instincts. Some guys never learned the humility necessary to hit that next level.

Maybe Micah would. Maybe he wouldn't.

But Scott wasn't going to let him coast anymore, and possibly cost the defense—and the whole team—wins that they should've had.

"I can cover," Micah said, sticking out his chin. "I can cover damn good."

"You cover Nicholson in practice?"

"Sometimes," Micah said.

"Next time, I want you to cover Lewis."

"What? Why? He's just a tight end."

"Nicholson's the easier assignment. He's still learnin' how to run the best routes. He's just goddamn fast. He'll get craftier, then he'll be tougher, but Wade? He's big and he's fast and he's sneaky."

"Yeah, he is," Micah admitted.

"You gotta cover everyone like you're coverin' Wade," Scott said. "That's a place to start."

Then he walked away because this was more about a change of attitude and a willingness to learn than it was real skill right now.

But as he headed back to where Beau stood, watching over the starting offense, he realized that Asa was back, and he was frowning as he watched Scott leave Micah behind.

Well, shit.

Chapter Six

Was it too fucking much to ask Scott to do *one* thing and have him goddamn listen?

Asa's temper grew from a simmer to a boil as practice came to an end.

He'd asked Scott to stay away from Micah Rose, and instead of listening, instead of doing what he'd *said* he'd do, which was keep his distance, he'd gone right over there the moment Asa's back was turned, the moment he was distracted with something else.

Was Scott technically in the closet? Yes, he was. Rose might not say a word to him, but ever since that shit had gone down with Beau, Asa *hadn't* trusted him. Not to keep his mouth shut when it mattered.

What if he'd said it again? What if he'd said it to *Scott*?

Asa fucking hated that Scott had been right about his reaction. Because yeah, he'd absolutely kill him, if he said that word to Scott. It had taken immense self-control not to unleash hell on Rose for saying it to Beau.

He didn't think he could control himself a second time.

Scott was going to need to listen to him now, but the last thing Asa needed was anyone overhearing and reporting back to Beau.

So, he waited, lingering at the doorway, in the muggy late-afternoon sunshine, watching as some ominous, dark-looking clouds began to roll in. Near the end of practice, Randy had mentioned that there was possibly going to be a big storm this afternoon, and it looked like it was heading their way.

Maybe, Asa mused, as he leaned against the side of the building, he should've called a car. Maybe Scott had, and that's why he hadn't shown up yet.

Twenty minutes later, he was just about to give up, and confront Scott later, when the door opened and there he was, filling the doorway with his wide shoulders.

"So, you wanna do this now, huh?" Scott asked, before Asa could say a word.

"You used to listen to me," Asa said, before he could snatch the words back. That hadn't been what he'd wanted to say at all, but in the end, maybe that was why he was so goddamn angry. He'd told Scott to listen to him, and Scott had immediately done whatever the hell he wanted.

Scott leaned back against the wall, right next to Asa, and chuckled under his breath. Which only pissed Asa off more. This wasn't funny. It wasn't funny at all.

"What, you think I deferred to you, like a good little boy?"

"Not that again," Asa snapped back. "Don't flirt with me when I'm angry with you."

"Hey, you started it," Scott said, raising his hands in mock defeat. "All I'm sayin' is you *think* I listened to you every single time—and I'm not saying I didn't, I've always taken what you say real serious, because I know how smart you are, how much insight you've got—but you still saw what you wanted to see, Asa."

"What are you saying?" he demanded.

"I'm sayin' . . . you're damn good at gettin' everyone to do what you want, and all I did was learn from the best." And there was that little grin again. That infuriating smile. Asa wanted to wipe it off his face with his fist—or his mouth.

That was the whole problem, wasn't it?

These feelings that had never gone away, they'd been buried, deep, hibernating, but now they weren't buried at all anymore, they were right there on the surface, and they just kept growing and growing. Asa didn't know how to contain them anymore, didn't know how to do anything but stand here and let them make him absolutely crazy.

Let them demolish his self-control brick by brick.

"So what, you used all my tricks on me?" Asa was not happy.

But Scott just shrugged casually, like it wasn't a big deal—and didn't answer the question. "I think he feels real isolated."

"Who?"

Scott rolled his eyes. "Rose. That's who we're talkin' about, right? The one you're pissed off that I approached. You know, I'm a grown man, I can take care of myself. I been doin' it a long-ass time. You have a problem that needs fixed, that I can *fix*, even if you keep pretending that you don't."

Thunder rumbled in the distance. Asa pushed off from the wall. If he wanted to get home before the skies opened, he needed to leave now.

Besides, this whole conversation was pointless. Scott was right, and Asa hated that Scott was right. They didn't need to break it down any further.

It was true; the biggest reason he'd been pissed off was that Scott hadn't listened.

He heard footsteps behind him, and knew that Scott had followed. Well, that wasn't all that surprising, considering they were heading to the same place.

Maybe he would just let it go. Or not talk at all. That would be good, too.

"You know, he's not the only one who's fucked things up. Who made a mistake and regretted it," Scott said, the moment that thought crossed Asa's mind.

"Save me your apologies," Asa said through clenched teeth.

He felt a raindrop hit his neck, and as the wind picked up, he started walking faster.

The streets, usually bustling around this time, were mostly empty, because everyone else had been smart enough to stay out of the oncoming storm.

Not you, a voice inside Asa whispered, *you wanna embrace the storm.*

Another drop of rain, and then another hit his head, and Asa just managed to duck under the overhang of a near building before the clouds opened up, rain beginning to fall down in sheets.

Scott hit the wall next to him with a huff. It was not a very big overhang. Scott's arm brushed his and Asa wanted to scream.

Demand to know why he didn't just leave him alone.

You know why he won't.

You don't even want him to. Not really.

"Not interested in any of my regrets, huh?" Scott asked. He sounded tired. Frustrated.

"Because they don't change a goddamn thing," Asa retorted. "Okay, you regret taking that job, but you still did it. You still *disappeared* for seven years."

"You're still mad."

"No *shit*," Asa yelled. Nobody else ever made him lose his composure. Nobody but Scott.

"I was tryin' to do the right thing, the . . ." Scott sighed. "The noble thing, I guess. Leave you alone. Save you from your own terrible impulses." His voice turned wry. "I guess you don't know anythin' about that."

Wasn't it enough that he'd rejected Asa and then left and now was back, even though Asa didn't want him to be? Did he need to be goddamned right, *too*?

Asa didn't trust himself to say anything he wouldn't regret later—and that included everything from just how much he'd missed Scott to how pissed off he was that he never just *stopped*—and instead, just stared out at the rain.

Scott must've sensed how far he'd pushed Asa, because he didn't say another word.

Maybe it would have been enough to finally get his goddamned silence, but he was so close, his big body crowding into Asa's, and suddenly, having Scott in his space was just intolerable. He only hesitated for a split second, before pushing off and heading right into the heart of the storm.

Rain drenched him almost instantly, and he heard the footsteps behind him. Chasing after him, because even though Scott apparently didn't really want him, he wouldn't let him go, either.

A hand grabbed his arm, and pulled him around.

Rain meandered in rivulets down Scott's face, his hair plastered to his skull. "What the fuck are you doin'?" he demanded.

"Leaving," Asa said. "You've done it, you should recognize the gesture."

Scott shook his head. "Okay, you're not just mad. You're angry."

Asa swallowed hard. "Yeah. Yeah. I am. I'm fucking angry. Angry that you left. Angry that you stole that choice from me. Angry that you thought I could ever be happy without you. Angry that I didn't follow you. Angry that I had to pretend like nothing was wrong. Angry that I had to come here and do this *without you*, when you were supposed to be next to me, by my side, this whole time. So yeah, I'm angry. But maybe . . ." He could barely catch his breath. "Maybe I'm angry that I goddamned missed you, too."

Scott didn't say anything for a long moment, just stared. The rain was coming down in sheets now, but Asa couldn't feel it. He was lost in the way Scott was staring at him, at the intent look in his eyes.

He knew that look; because he'd seen it in his own eyes seven years ago, the night he'd told Scott he'd fallen in love with him.

"You done?" he asked in a low voice.

Asa's breath caught in his lungs, in his throat, and he couldn't speak. He nodded.

Scott reached for him, his big hand cupping his wet cheek, and was he shaking because it was pouring on them?

Or because Scott was taking a step closer and then another, until he could feel the heat of him through his soaked clothes?

How long had Scott wanted to kiss him?

How long had Asa wanted Scott to just forget all the reasons why he shouldn't kiss him?

Scott leaned in, his lips cool and wet on his, but it was barely a brush. Barely a kiss.

For a split second, Asa felt it all. The press of his muscular leg, warm and damp against his own, the miniscule scratch of his stubble against his cheek, his heart pounding in his chest, that wave of longing reaching up and grabbing him hard, shaking him, until he couldn't resist it anymore. He reached up, and threading his fingers through Scott's hair, pulled him down and kissed him back.

Scott had yearned for this for so long, he'd nearly given up on ever having it, ever getting to *feel* it, but he'd been wrong.

Kissing Asa wasn't an impossibility; it was an inevitability.

He hadn't known what to expect—he'd had so many dreams and hopes and fantasies, and maybe all that fire lying dormant inside Asa, maybe a kiss wouldn't set it alight after all, because it wasn't like Asa had gone around kissing guys, or kissing *anyone*, really.

But he'd hoped anyway, because what was life if you didn't harbor even the tiniest little bit of hope?

He shouldn't have worried.

Asa was clinging to him, fingers digging into his scalp, his mouth pressed firmly to Scott's own, like he couldn't even bear to take a breath, and then his tongue was there, and no matter how cold and wet Scott was, the brush of it against his own was enough to light him up.

They stumbled backwards a few steps and it took Scott a few moments to realize why the rain wasn't falling on them anymore. Asa, he discovered, had pulled them back under the overhang that they'd been hiding underneath before.

Scott opened his mouth to say something, though *what*, he wasn't quite sure, because this was an occasion he hadn't prepared for.

Maybe he should say he was sorry, again?

Or ask if Asa was still angry?

Perhaps it would be better if he just told Asa he loved him, again? 'Cause the last time he had, it hadn't exactly gone over well—though heading out the door right after tended to have that effect on a love confession.

But before he could decide which was the right path, Asa pushed him back against the brick, and for a second, just stared at him.

Then he licked his lips, and leaned in, and swiped his tongue right across Scott's mouth.

Heat blasted right through him.

"I guess . . ." Scott stammered. "I guess you're not angry anymore."

"I was. And then I wasn't. Now I'm just . . ."

Scott raised an eyebrow, surprised at how flustered Asa was. Surprised at how much it was flustering *him*.

"I don't know how this is supposed to work," Asa finally explained. "How does this work?"

"How does what work?" Scott was having difficulty even forming complete sentences; all he was thinking was how much he wanted to kiss Asa again. How easy it would be to wrap his hand around Asa's waist and drag him close.

So he did, pulling Asa tight against him. It was amazing how warm it was between them, even when they were soaking wet.

"I mean . . ." Asa's voice dropped to a low, sexy growl that Scott hadn't ever imagined he possessed. "I don't know how . . ." He waved between them. "This whole thing works."

He was *allowed* now, or at the very least Asa hadn't yelled at him again, so he ran his hand up Asa's side and then back down again, cradling it against his hip. "What 'whole thing'?"

Asa shot him a deliciously hot look. Challenging and full of the fire that Scott knew lurked underneath his good-ol'-boy exterior. "Sex, Scott. *Sex.*"

Scott told himself he shouldn't be surprised. After all, they'd definitely been kissing, and that was absolutely Asa's erection pressing into his thigh, even though he'd tried to ignore it.

He didn't want to push. Asa was the most important person in the world to him, and the last thing he wanted was to lose him again. If that meant all they did was kiss forever, well, Scott was gonna get a monumental case of blue balls, but he'd deal with it. He'd endure whatever gladly, relieved that at the very least, he could touch Asa.

But apparently Asa wanted more.

A hell of a lot more.

He swallowed hard.

"You want to have sex?"

"For God's sake, Scott, *yes*, what possibly gave it away?" Asa thrust his hips crudely—and terrifically—against Scott. He hadn't thought it was possible, but somehow his cock grew even harder. This was the man he loved, and he was *asking* Scott to touch him. And wanting to touch him in return. "I'm not such a prude that I imagine that's a roll of quarters in your pocket."

"Uh, it's not," Scott admitted ruefully. "I just didn't know what was . . . well, what this was."

"*You* kissed *me*," Asa reminded him.

He had. He had because he didn't think he could take another minute of the tension pulling tight inside him, drawing him closer and closer to Asa.

"Yes, uh, I did, but I thought . . ." There was nothing to say but the truth. "I sorta thought you might hie off and slap me or something after. Or tell me you were angry again."

"No." Asa's expression softened. "No. Not at all." Then he leaned in, and God, their mouths were brushing again, and it was everything, everything Scott had ever dreamt of. It was sweet and dirty and he could *feel* Asa's passion and his love, a physical manifestation of all that heat and light streaking through him.

Asa broke the kiss, moving away a fraction. Scott nearly caught him and dragged him right back. Even though, *yeah*, they were on a public street and there was the small matter of the question that Asa had asked.

Sex.

Just the word was echoing in Scott's head, amplifying and repeating, until he felt just about as hungry as he'd been as a teenager.

"So?" Asa asked, impatience in his voice.

"So?" Scott repeated dumbly. He used to be good at this. Or at least he'd imagined that he was, but apparently any suave charm he possessed went right out the window when it really mattered.

"For God's sake, Scott. *Sex.*"

Scott heard the rawness in his own voice. "If I'd known you were this eager . . ."

Asa shot him a look. "Am I the only one that's so eager?"

"No." Scott reached down and took Asa's hand and squeezed it. "I guess . . ." He cleared his throat. "I guess we should go get out of these wet clothes."

Asa grinned. "Guess we should."

Asa told himself that he wasn't going to overthink the situation, but the moment he let himself into his place, Scott right behind him, and they both started dripping onto the carpeting, he couldn't help it.

He'd only been thinking about doing this for a year—and then for seven years after that—but by his own admission, Scott had wanted him, in one way or another, since they were nineteen years old.

That was a lot of expectation to live up to and Asa would be the first to admit that while he'd watched and wanted and even spent more than his share of time fantasizing, he had zero practical experience.

He turned to Scott, but there was already resignation on his face. Acceptance, yes, but resignation. And that fucking stung.

"We don't have to do anything you're not ready for," Scott said in a low voice. "I'd be happy to just do this forever." He leaned in and kissed him, and it was so sweet. But it was *just* sweet, like Scott was afraid that he'd change his mind, or that passion might be their undoing.

The thing was, Asa was convinced that if anything could be their undoing, it would've been the last twenty-plus years. And it hadn't worked. Their feelings hadn't died. They still wanted each other—still loved each other—as much as they had before.

Was he really going to let a little thing like a lack of experience stop him?

Asa nipped at Scott's bottom lip, tongue delving deeply into his mouth, and pressed against him, letting him feel all of his arousal. Then let his hands wander, the way he'd imagined so many times, that summer, seven years ago.

"No," Asa said firmly. "I want to do this. I want *you*."

"Then . . ." Scott smiled, and toed off his shoes, which made squelching noises as he kicked them to the side.

Oh God, he's getting naked. Scott . . . naked.

How long had he thought about Scott's big, broad body? It was easier to forget he was taller than Asa, and broader, with these shoulders, and those big beefy arms, and *goddamn*, Asa was going to not only get to see his body in its full and uninterrupted glory, he was going to get to *touch it*.

But Scott didn't remove any more clothing. Instead, he stepped closer to Asa, and backed him up, caging him in with that big body, and his fingers began to nimbly thumb open the buttons on Asa's shirt. He was slow and methodical, and with each one that popped open, Asa felt his heartbeat accelerate. The doctor at the hospital had told him to avoid stressful or high-intensity situations. It had seemed funny at the time, because he was a coach in the National Football League and his whole life seemed made up of stressful and high-intensity situations, but what he hadn't taken into consideration was Scott's arrival and the possibility they might do *this*.

Because nothing was more stressful and high intensity than Scott Callaway stripping him down.

His fingers flicked open the last button and Scott's eyes grew impossibly darker as he reached in between the two halves of Asa's shirt and placed a palm flat against his bare skin.

It was just a touch, a hand against his chest, but Asa sucked in a breath and felt his pulse rabbit even harder.

That was even before Scott's fingers ventured further south, sliding down his stomach, and ending at the button on his jeans. "You still good?" he asked in a low, deep voice, rough around the edges.

Asa nodded, wordlessly. His cock was pulsing just a few inches from where Scott's hand had stopped and he wanted, more than he'd ever imagined possible, for it to keep going, to relieve some of the pressure building inside him.

He'd thought the moment would be too momentous to worry about what Scott saw when he looked at him—he was middle aged, and things weren't quite as taut as they'd been once, and there were a few gray hairs threaded through the dark ones, leading down to where his stomach met his pants. But Scott was looking and there was no hesitancy in his gaze, none whatsoever, only a starstruck worship like he'd been wanting to do this forever—and he *had*, Asa realized—and it was finally happening, and there was no way he could ever be disappointed.

He flicked open the button on the jeans, and it took a little maneuvering to get the fly down and then he was pushing the wet material down Asa's legs, following them down. Asa couldn't stop staring, could barely force his eyes to blink normally, because the sight of Scott on his knees was absolutely mesmerizing.

"Good?" Scott asked, which was actually a wild understatement.

Asa was so much better than just *good*; he was fucking phenomenal.

"Yes. You don't have to keep asking, you know," Asa pointed out, his voice cracking when Scott tucked a pair of fingers under the waistband of his black boxer briefs. His cock twitched, as hard as it had ever been in his whole damn life, desperate not to just be touched, but to be touched by *Scott*.

"Yes, I do," Scott said in that rough, gravelly tone. "I love you." He glanced up and their gazes met. "I've loved you every single goddamn day for too many years to remember. I'm not gonna fuck this up now."

Asa cupped his cheek with a hand. "Trust me, you couldn't possibly."

"I did once . . ."

But Asa didn't let him continue. "No," he said firmly. With conviction. "No, we're not going to talk about that right now, or even think about it. We're here, we're together now, and that is all that matters."

Scott didn't say anything, but the wildness of his grin was answer enough, and Asa's pulse hammered at the sight of it. He tugged down Asa's briefs, and Asa inhaled sharply when he ducked his head close.

He hadn't even touched him yet, and he felt like he was right on the edge, too many years of wanting this and never having it, having to use his hand and his imagination.

He didn't beg. Not ever. He'd never felt the need before.

Asa felt the need now. "Scott . . . *please.*"

Then Scott's tongue flicked out and that was all the warning he got before it was curling around the head of his cock, so hot and so perfect, as unbelievably good as he'd always dreamt it would be.

There were too many things to focus on at once.

Scott's hand, scorching as a brand, holding his bare hip in place.

The groan he made, deep in his throat, when he tasted Asa for the first time.

His broad shoulders, as they trembled.

And then there was the white-hot heat as Scott's mouth enveloped him, swallowing him down like he'd been born to do it.

Asa's fingers curled into Scott's hair, and he tugged, without even meaning to. Mindlessly he just wanted more, and more, and more. Never in his life had it ever felt like this, like he was grabbing on to a live electric wire, with both hands. It was achingly perfect and also way too much, all at the same time.

Someone was panting into the air between them, and Asa realized it was him, he was making those keening, smug noises as Scott sucked him.

He was so goddamn eager, Asa could barely stand it, could barely brush the thought with his consciousness, because if he really thought about how much Scott wanted it, wanted *him*, he was going to lose the last little bit of self-control he had left, and then it would be over, and while *yes*, he knew it was probably going to happen again, it would never happen again for the very first time.

And he wanted to remember every single second of the first time.

He wanted it emblazoned on his brain, so if he ever had to live without Scott again, he could relive it, one incredible moment at a time.

Scott groaned again, and then nudged Asa's knees apart, and his palm was suddenly warm and wet against the sensitive skin of his balls, and Asa wasn't proud of it, but he moaned garbled nonsense. Praise and pleading and promises. All mixed up, until he didn't know one from the other, and it didn't matter, because it was all so goddamned perfect.

Then Scott's fingers slid further back, and his thumb merely slid over his hole. Not even dipping in, not even teasing, just the touch of it, had Asa's head hitting the back of the wall as he groaned through the spike of pleasure. He wanted to come, so badly, wanted to lose himself to it, but then it would be over, and they would never do it like this again, not for the first time, and the last thing he wanted was for the dirty joy of it to end.

"Come on, come for me," Scott ground out as he took a breath, "give it to me, Asa."

It was just his name, in that deep, low, desperate voice, that sent him over the edge.

He barely had time to squeeze Scott's hair hard, to warn him, and then he was lost, pulsing with what felt like endless ecstasy as he emptied out.

Finally, the pleasure finally petered out, but even then, the last few throbs of it still felt better than anything he'd ever experienced in his life.

He thought he'd had sex before, but it had never been like this before.

"Goddamn," Asa muttered.

"My thoughts exactly," Scott said with a guttural laugh.

The remnants were still fizzing through him when he reached down and tugged Scott back up to his feet with a groan.

It felt like the most natural thing in the world to kiss him, this man he loved, who'd given him something he'd never imagined he'd have.

Scott framed his face with those big hands and they kissed and kissed, even as Asa felt the hot, undeniable pressure of Scott's hard cock against his bare thigh, even through the material of his shorts.

Asa didn't think he was even aware of how he was rubbing against him, desperately, unconsciously trying to find the right pressure to relieve him.

And was it really fair to Scott to have to rub off against him, without Asa really giving any effort?

It wasn't, even if Asa didn't have any practical experience.

Even if he couldn't make Scott feel the same way he had.

When Asa broke the kiss, Scott was panting, breathing hard, like he'd just been sprinting.

"Come on," Asa said softly, and took his hands and led him down the hall, into his bedroom.

The room was so impersonal, so not *his*, it felt wrong to push Scott down onto the edge of the bed. But maybe after Scott's scent, and his own, were imprinted here, it would feel a little more like he belonged here.

Would feel a little less lonely when he lay down by himself next.

Asa reached over and tugged up Scott's t-shirt. *God*, he was just as big and broad as he remembered, his muscles just as strong, and now he could actually touch them.

So he did, tracing patterns down Scott's arms, to his chest, and then lower. Then lower still, until his fingers hesitated on the waistband of his shorts.

"I . . ." Asa's breath stuttered.

"Whatever you want. Whatever you're comfortable with." Scott hesitated. "If it's nothing, then . . . it's fine." He could see the force of will it took for Scott to say it. The tremor in his body as he gave in to the possibility that he might not receive what he'd given so freely to Asa.

Wasn't this why he loved this man, though? His selflessness? His loyalty? His friendship?

But it was more than that too, a bone-deep appreciation of who he was as a person.

Scott might not be a perfect person, but he was the perfect person for Asa.

"That's not what I meant," Asa said sternly, and he tugged Scott's shorts down. "I *meant*, it's hard to decide what I want to do with you. You're . . ." He brushed the front of Scott's bulge, leaking into his briefs, with the back of his knuckles, and Scott shuddered. "You're so gorgeous. I've wanted to touch you for so long, I feel . . ."

"Feel what?" Scott's voice was so rough. So desperate.

Asa tucked his hand into his briefs, and felt his cock twitch in his grip.

"I feel *you*," Asa said with a hushed kind of awe as Scott strained against his touch.

"God, feel me some more," Scott said, and if that was as close as he'd ever get to begging, Asa would take it.

With his other hand, he pushed Scott's briefs down and re-gripped. He was bigger than he'd imagined, in all those late-night fantasies, and thicker, and Asa gave one experimental stroke, and Scott's cut-off expletive was all the answer he needed.

He could do this. He could make his man—because there was no question about it now, Scott was *his man*, and had been *his man* for years now—feel good.

"You like this?" Asa asked, even though it was obvious Scott did. His head was thrown back, there was sweat dotting his forehead, and every muscle in that incredible body was straining. Fighting it and loving it all at the same time.

"Yes," Scott said. "More. Please."

Asa worked him a little harder, a little rougher, learning how a thumb smoothed over the head of him, made him jump, made him twitch, made him swear.

It was incredible to watch him like this, expression full of pleasure, eyes squeezed shut. This was a Scott that was for Asa's enjoyment and Asa's alone. Nobody else was ever going to see him like this again.

All the past? It wasn't like it didn't matter—because it had, it had forged them into the two people who stood here today—but it was the past.

Asa leaned forward and brushed a kiss across his lips, and Scott shuddered, leaning in, wanting more, and Asa couldn't do anything else but give it to him. He tilted his head, tongue sliding between Scott's lips, and kissed him hard, with all the pent-up longing and desire he'd been feeling not just since he'd come to Miami, but since that day in the locker room, the day they'd won the National Championship.

Scott groaned and then, suddenly, he was pulsing between them with his orgasm.

Asa had never seen anything more beautiful than Scott in the throes of pleasure. Or felt anything more spectacular than Scott's cock twitching against his palm as he worked the last little bit of satisfaction out of him.

When it was over, Scott's eyes opened. He didn't say anything, but Asa discovered that he didn't need to. The happiness in his eyes, the softness of his gray gaze, that was all he needed.

He didn't want to, but he needed to clean up, so he detoured really quickly into the bathroom, grabbed a washcloth, and rinsed off, coming back to find Scott, still gloriously naked, but now lounging on his bed.

Asa cleaned him the rest of the way off, and tossing the used cloth into the bin, settled onto the bed next to him.

"Well," Scott said, turning to him, looking like a big satiated lion, "you still angry with me?"

Asa felt a pulse of guilt. He'd unleashed some of the anger he'd felt—well, *most* of the anger he'd felt—at Scott earlier. And while maybe he'd deserved some of it, he hadn't deserved all of it.

Some of it was just fury at the situation, at the way the world had conspired to keep them apart, and some of it was anger at himself.

Why had he let things go on so long? He could've called Scott. He could have fixed things. At least returned to their normal friendship.

Would it have been tough? Absolutely. It hadn't been a walk in the park since Scott had come to Miami, even, but they'd figured it out.

And then they'd *figured it out.*

Maybe they could've been doing this years earlier.

"No," Asa said with a sigh. "No. Not even a little. I wasn't even . . . I wasn't even that angry with you before."

"You sure seemed angry." Scott was still grinning.

"Maybe I was angry that I wanted you so much, still," Asa pointed out dryly. "Or angry that you kept pushing me to want you more."

"Maybe," Scott said. He paused. "I regret it, you know. More than anything I've ever done in my whole goddamn life, leaving you. Leaving you *and* leaving Beau, though don't tell him it's mostly you. I knew it was a mistake the moment my truck turned down your drive. And *God*, when I got to Washington, all I wanted was to come back to Tennessee."

"And I should've stopped you, should've come after you, not let you make that sacrifice," Asa said quietly, and it seemed natural, and totally inevitable, for him to move closer to Scott, to lean his head on his shoulder.

There'd always been a feeling of self-consciousness after sex, like he'd just let someone in that he didn't want there, but there was none of that with Scott. He wanted all of him, as close as he could get him, for as long as he could have him.

"You couldn't have," Scott said wryly. "I was on a mission to be as noble—and as miserable—as fucking possible."

"Not anymore, I think," Asa said.

"Doesn't mean I'm not sorry that I did it then," Scott said with resignation. "'Cause I am. Real sorry."

Asa hadn't wanted his apology before. He'd run from it.

But now he turned it over in his head, feeling all the facets of it, and then accepted it. "I'm sorry, too," he said. He put his hand on Scott's chest, right where his heart beat. "I love you, too, you know. Maybe not for as long as you, but long enough."

"It's not a competition." Scott's voice was amused.

For a long time, neither of them said anything; they just lay there. Enjoying the feel of each other and the realization that they could do this now. Asa could reach out and touch Scott's chest, feel his heart beating just under his rib cage. He was allowed to do this now.

You've been allowed to do it forever, you just didn't. You stupid, stupid man.

But even then, Asa couldn't really feel bad about it, because they were here now.

He supposed something he should have asked was, *what are we going to do about this now?* But he didn't, because the answer was plain as day, as obvious as any answer he'd ever acknowledged in his whole goddamn life: now, they were going to do whatever they wanted. He didn't know what that was, but this was a good place to start.

CHAPTER SEVEN

OF COURSE, DOING WHATEVER the hell they wanted now did not mean that they were ever going to agree on everything.

"Come on," Scott said in the most persuasive tone he could deploy—Asa was familiar with all of his voices, every single one of his tactics, and he knew, he *knew*, what Scott was trying to do and he wasn't going to give in. Nope, not today, not ever.

"I am not going to help you go Christmas shopping for your Secret Santa," Asa said firmly.

Sure, he hadn't kicked Scott out of bed last night. Sure, he'd not been able to stop himself from a nice, lazy makeout session against the bathroom door when confronted with a wet Scott right out of the shower, but he was not giving in now and being forced to indulge in more holiday bullshit.

Holiday bullshit was firmly off-limits, even when he was in the best mood he'd been in . . . well, in forever.

He couldn't even remember the last time he'd felt this light.

"I don't even know this guy," Scott rationalized as they sat in Asa's office—now Asa-and-Scott's office, a development he'd hated yesterday, but now he could see the positive. "How am I supposed to buy him something?"

"I don't know, ask Tristan, since it was his fucking idea," Asa muttered. "Besides, I'm not even supposed to know who your Secret Santa person is. It's called *Secret* Santa for a reason."

"You're really not going to tell me your Secret Santa?" Scott leaned back in his chair, tucking his arms underneath his head. Asa felt a jolt of awareness deep. He'd kinda hoped that after they'd officially crossed from unrequited to *requited,* that he might find Scott slightly less distracting.

Maybe he'd actually be able to put his head down and get some work done.

"Of course not," Asa retorted. There was no way that Scott could know about the crumpled little piece of paper that was currently sitting in his kitchen trash.

Speaking of that, Asa realized that drawing Scott's name really wasn't the end of the world it had been only two days ago. He could *do* something about his feelings now, maybe even something big and wonderful. Something that showed Scott just how important he was to Asa—something that showed him just how much he loved him.

Of course he had no idea what that might be, but it was something to keep in the back of his mind and to slowly consider as the weeks to Christmas ticked by.

"All I need is a few ideas. What do you know about him?"

"Him?" Asa asked, distracted, still, even though what he'd *meant* to do this morning was to analyze some of the past weeks' defensive tape. To try to see what Scott kept arguing needed to be fixed.

"Kenyon. That's who I got."

"Oh, uh, well, he's a bit of a mystery," Asa admitted.

Scott shot him a look.

"I'm not even sayin' that because I don't want to help you go *Christmas shopping*," Asa said. "I'm sayin' that because it's true."

"I googled him last night," Scott said. "Didn't find much. Just a lot about a foundation he runs."

"The We Read Foundation," Asa said. He rewound the video on his laptop and rewatched it again—for the third time. He was beginning to be afraid that not only did Scott have a point; he didn't know how they were going to fix this. "Like it says, it's about literacy . . . of some kind."

Scott raised an eyebrow. "You donated a signed football, it was listed right there on their site, and you don't even know what they really do?"

"That was just the right move, considering I was the new coach and I wanted to win him over . . . wait a minute." Asa dropped his voice. "When exactly 'last night' were you *googling* Kenyon?"

"Oh, you know, after you fell asleep on my chest," Scott said, grinning like he'd just won the lottery.

Asa wanted to argue that it hadn't happened—but it had—and it wasn't like he hadn't enjoyed some of the best sleep he'd gotten in years, just because he was finally wrapped up in the man he loved.

"Tristan said we needed to give a few small gifts, working up to the big party, so I thought I should get started," Scott said. "Now that I wasn't so distracted."

"What . . . *small* gifts?" Asa was incredulous. Why hadn't he just told Tristan to shove it when he'd waved that paper bag under his nose?

He knew why. It was the same reason he'd donated that signed football to Kenyon's charity, even if he didn't know exactly what they did.

He was always trying to do right by his players, by *his guys*. Because they were his, no question about it.

"Did you even listen to what Tristan was saying?" Scott was laughing openly now, and Asa hated everything.

Especially Christmas.

Goddamn.

"I might've tuned him partially out, but if you know Tristan at all, that's kind of *necessary*. You gotta apply a filter or you're gonna get way more information than you ever bargained for, like the way Wade . . . well, a lot more stuff about Wade than you ever wanted to know."

"And this has to do with the Secret Santa how?" Scott asked mildly.

Asa rolled his eyes. "I'm just sayin', I had a damn good reason to tune him out, and so I did. We're supposed to be giving *what*?"

"Smaller gifts, like running up to the big party," Scott explained. "How do you not know about Secret Santa?" He paused. "Wait, don't answer that. It's only gonna depress me that you've been working straight through the last seven holidays."

"I worked straight through all the others, too, long before you left," Asa said.

Scott's stern look told Asa all he needed to know about how that was going to work going forward.

Wait until he found out that Asa had skipped Thanksgiving with Beau and Sebastian to put a long night of film study in.

"You're gonna enjoy this holiday now, this year," Scott said. And it was a vow and a promise, and well, from Asa's point of view, also a threat.

"We have a lot to do."

"Yeah, we do, but there's two of us now," Scott reminded him. "I can handle some of it. And you're not doing your coordinator's work anymore."

And speaking of that . . . Asa had taken his foot, just a little, off the accelerator and look what Brett had done to the defense. He'd given in, and cobbled together a half-assed solution, instead of dealing with the root of the issue.

Asa refocused on the play on his screen. He was definitely beginning to see what Scott had seen—and it annoyed him that Scott had seen it first, had recognized the problem, even *diagnosed it*, before Asa had ever identified that a problem existed—but the real question was going to be what the hell was he going to do about it?

He was going to need to call Brett in, and discuss why this had happened, and what they could do about it. If anything.

At least, Asa thought, trying to be optimistic, none of their opponents had figured out this particular gap in their coverage yet.

It was so subtle you might miss it . . . unless you were looking for it.

And Scott was always looking for it.

He had his back, even if Asa was being difficult. Even if he was refusing to listen and warning him off.

That was Scott, and why Asa loved him.

"You see it," Scott said, his voice right in his ear. He hadn't even realized that Scott had come over, and was leaning right over the desk, all big and brawny and right in his personal bubble. Asa jerked, surprised. Surprised, but *pleased*.

He sighed with resignation. "I see it. I just don't know how we're gonna fix it. You talked to Rose, I'm sure he wasn't any more forthcoming about his issues than he's been with me or Brett."

"Brett's basically lettin' Sebastian run the defense." Scott paused, and then held up a hand. "Don't argue with me, I saw it, and yeah, it's workin' now, but when some other team sees this . . ."

"We're gonna give up forty-plus points, easy," Asa said heavily. That was the kind of game they couldn't afford to play, because the offense could sputter out sometimes. That was something else he was working on—and Beau and Davis, too—but he knew they couldn't push too hard, too fast, because Pax was still getting his feet under him, and if they rushed him too much . . . well, he'd start to make a lot of catastrophic mistakes.

Asa knew they'd been relying on their defense to keep the scores manageable. But if this got out . . . if they were exposed . . . it would be a nightmare, and they could kiss any hopes of going deep into the playoffs goodbye.

"Easy," Scott agreed.

"Well, shit," Asa said.

"Rose wasn't . . . entirely intractable yesterday. I could do some more work with him today."

"It's confidence. The guy lacks confidence. Trust in his own instincts."

"He doesn't *have* instincts, yet, and nobody's developin' them, because they all think he's a piece of shit." Scott summarized the situation succinctly.

The blunt honesty didn't make Asa feel any better, but at least it was the whole truth, laid out clearly. You could only fix the things that you could see.

"Let me guess, he's not further endeared himself to anyone since the incident, either," Asa said.

Scott shook his head. "He's sulking. No question about it. But no, I didn't get the impression he's a bad guy, just . . . lost. I felt out Beau, a bit, and he said he'd talk to Sebastian."

"Sebastian is not going to like this. Not at all."

"Beau's crafty. He can talk him around."

Asa was not convinced of that, though. Yes, Sebastian cared a lot about what Beau thought, especially when it came to football, but Sebastian was also in love with Beau, and as a result was still justifiably pissed off at Micah. There was a strong possibility one of those would overrule the other. Asa could already guess which it would be.

"I think . . . I think it would actually be better if you did it."

Asa hated that he was suggesting this, and hated even more that he was fairly certain that this was what Scott had intended from the beginning.

He'd just wanted Asa to work around to it himself, because that was always easier than arguing with him.

"I'll do it, then," Scott said with a nod.

"You don't have to be so *smug* about it," Asa retorted, leaning back in his chair. Scott had his hip propped on the desk next to him, and if anyone walked by the open door, they'd see them having a discussion, but they wouldn't see how they were looking at each other.

Asa knew that nobody could know about him and Scott—especially not now, because he had yet to figure out how he was going to tell Beau about it—but it was only the first day. It had been hard enough to keep his hands to himself the moment they'd headed into the practice facility, to say nothing of the desire he had to just walk out the door and yell to the sky that he was in love with Scott Callaway and they'd finally, *finally*, had sex and it had been so goddamned good, he didn't know how they'd waited all this time.

"You haven't seen smug yet," Scott murmured, and *God*, it would be so easy to just reach up and curl his fingers around his neck and tug him down, right where Asa wanted him. The last kiss they'd shared, with Scott pressed up against the bathroom door, leaving them both panting, had been too long ago.

He'd gone twenty-plus years without kissing him, and now two hours seemed impossible.

You are dead gone, Asa thought with his own sense of smugness. *Absolutely dead gone.*

"You got a lunch meeting?" Asa asked, even though *he* had one, he'd started scheduling them in an effort to compensate for the early quit-time he'd agreed on with Beau.

"I do now," Scott said and he sounded regretful. "I'm going to go find Sebastian and talk to him."

"Well, that sounds a hell of a lot less fun than what I'd had in mind," Asa said.

"Yeah, but . . . I keep thinkin' . . . we're flying to Kansas City tomorrow, and Chicago the week after that. Those teams . . . they can lay some points down. I don't want to get caught out with our pants down."

"You really think you can fix the problem that fast?" Asa shouldn't have been surprised; this was Scott he was talking to, who was brilliant and could intuitively organize a defense like nobody's business. But then, he wasn't going to get full power here, Brett was still their defensive coordinator, and fixing a problem months in the making? Not that simple, either. Even if this was Scott they were talking about.

"No, but I'm sure gonna try to stick some Band-Aids on it," Scott said ruefully.

Scott was halfway to the cafeteria to discuss the defensive scheme issue with Sebastian when he realized that Asa had deftly stepped around not only the Christmas shopping question, but the question of who he'd gotten for his Secret Santa.

He'd distracted him by flirting with him, and *goddamn*, it had worked.

Better than it had even worked before, now that Scott knew what he tasted like and smelled like, and the way his eyes went blurry and sweet when he came.

Asa didn't give two shits about being festive or keeping to tradition, so there must be another reason he hadn't wanted to tell him.

Scott decided, as he approached the table where Sebastian and, *of course*, Beau were sitting, he would have to bring it up later tonight. Figure out exactly why Asa had been so uncharacteristically reticent.

And, while he was at it, he was going to have to find a few additional ways to make sure that Asa slowed down and actually *enjoyed* this holiday, unlike any of the others they'd lived through together.

"Hey," he said, sitting down next to Beau, across from Sebastian, who glanced up with a suspicious look in his eye. Clearly he'd noticed Scott's attempted intervention with Micah yesterday and had accurately assessed that his appearance today had something to do with that.

"Hey," Beau said. "Don't usually see you down here, slumming with the players."

"Sebastian knows why I'm here," Scott said.

Beau looked surprised. And not much surprised him. "Really?"

After all, this morning, Beau had said he'd deal with it. But Scott knew he was right; involving Beau was tricky. Too tricky for the sure success he was looking for.

"Rose isn't any of your business," Sebastian said stubbornly.

"And he hasn't been much of yours, either."

"I've tried to help the guy," Sebastian said. "We dropped me back a little, just to give him a bit more coverage, a bit more help."

"He doesn't need help. Well, not help that way. Help developing his instincts? His confidence? The right moves to stop a play by himself? Yeah, he needs those."

"We tried that. He wasn't exactly . . . open to our suggestions," Sebastian said.

Beau interceded. "I told you what happened."

"Yeah, but he's still here on this team, so he must have tried to fix it."

"He did. He's not . . ." Beau hesitated, and Scott could see the conundrum in his eyes. Should he agree with Scott and piss Sebastian off or brush it off so he could make peace with the man he loved? Scott knew Beau, but he didn't know this *new* Beau, in and out. This Beau that was in a committed, loving relationship.

He shouldn't have worried.

"He's not the homophobe everyone thinks he is," Beau finally continued. "He's not a bad guy. Got a bad rap, yeah, made some enemies, especially Sebastian over here. Got a bad attitude, but no, not a bad guy."

Sebastian shot him a hot glare. "He said . . . well, you know what he said."

"I know what he said," Beau said calmly. "He didn't mean it. It was convenient, the first insult he could think of. He's not a bone-deep asshole like that. He's just not. He's lost." Beau shot Sebastian a look right back. "Sure, we don't know anyone else that's been lost, huh? Tryin' to find his way? Trying to figure out how to play football the best way he can?"

Sebastian muttered under his breath, and to Scott's shock, Beau stood up. He patted Scott on the shoulder. "I've got meetings," he said, "and it'd probably be easier if you reasoned with him without me here, anyway. He sees my face, all he remembers is how much he wanted to blacken both of Micah's eyes."

"How true is that?" Scott asked once Beau had walked away.

Sebastian eyed him suspiciously. "Not as untrue as you'd probably like it to be."

"I wanna show you something," Scott said. He whipped out his tablet and set it up, right there on the cafeteria table, even though Sebastian wasn't done with his pot roast yet.

He pushed play, but didn't watch the screen as it played, just Sebastian's face. And like he'd expected, he saw the realization dawn.

"There's a soft spot in our zone," he said, leaning back and tossing his napkin on the table. "Real soft."

"It's a miracle nobody's seen it yet."

"Brett should've seen it," Sebastian said. "*I* should've seen it . . . I've been . . ." He trailed off without finishing his sentence.

"Practically running the defense? Adjusting the schemes to work with what you have? And that includes Rose in the state he's currently in? Yeah, I know."

Sebastian didn't say anything for a moment. He appeared to be picking his words very carefully. "When Beau tells me someone else is brilliant, it has weight," he finally said, "I know it does. But you've been here less than a week."

"I've been following from a distance, we'll say," Scott said.

"Because you're close with Coach?" Sebastian asked.

Now *that* was an even thornier topic than Rose's history with the Piranhas.

"Yes and no," Scott said carefully.

He certainly had no intention of revealing anything about his past history or his feelings to Sebastian, who would no doubt race off first thing to tell his boyfriend.

And the only one who should be telling Beau about them was his father. Though when that was going to happen, Scott wasn't sure. He wasn't going to be stupid enough to bring it up *now*, not when they'd finally settled at least some of their baggage.

There was time to get the rest of it figured out.

"I'm a student of defense," Scott continued. "I watch a lot of games. I didn't think I wanted to go back to a head coaching slot, so I've been watching, gettin' ready for defensive coordinator interviews."

"Coach should've hired you. Nothing against Brett," Sebastian added hurriedly. "He's fine, he's good, and I know Coach really trusts him, but you . . . you saw this and nobody else did."

"We can hope that nobody else did," Scott said.

Sebastian frowned, realizing the repercussions. "You think someone's gonna see and try to expose us."

"I want you to talk to Rose. I think . . ." Scott hesitated. He thought he'd read Sebastian right, that he wouldn't set the situation back even further. "I think you might get through to him the best."

"He doesn't listen. It's like trying to squeeze water from a rock."

"I think if you show him this, he's gonna listen. He's not stupid."

"He just *acts* stupid."

Scott crossed his arms across his chest. "Wasn't it a little stupid to think you could keep up with Nicholson and the rest of those crazy-fast wide receivers?"

Sebastian's lips compressed together. "You do not fuck around. Beau didn't mention that."

That was because he normally took a more subtle approach—he had the *time* to do it—but with two big games coming up on the Piranhas' schedule, he needed to be much more direct.

Though, frankly, Sebastian was the kind of player, and the kind of man, who probably appreciated frankness over Scott blowing smoke up his ass anyway.

"That's apparently the rumor," Scott said with a quick grin. "Now, about practice today . . . I want you to approach Rose. I want you to work with him. And two things, okay? I want you to not take no for an answer, and I want you to not get pissed off when he doesn't listen."

Sebastian eyed him with trepidation. "You have a lot of expectations."

"That's *also* the rumor," Scott said, trying to find humor in the situation. But the truth was, he was nervous.

He might be doing all this too late.

"So, nobody punched anyone in practice today? A good sign," Asa said as he lifted the dish out of the microwave.

Scott sighed. "I told Sebastian not to lose his temper if he didn't get through to Micah immediately. I could tell he tried. He did yell a bit. But . . . we're going to take that as a success."

"I talked to Brett. He's going to run Sebastian further up in the Chiefs game Sunday on a couple of plays, but he wasn't happy about it."

"How not happy is *wasn't happy*?"

"He yelled. Told me the defense scheme was working and we were tilting at windmills. Had a few choice things to say about you, too."

Scott didn't regret that he'd missed that conversation. But he'd known it would be worse if he was there. If Brett had a face to direct all his frustration towards.

"I'm sure he did."

"By the end of practice, I do think Micah looked a touch more comfortable. But that's practice. Game's a whole different story."

"Hmmm," Asa said, setting the hot dish down on the table.

They hadn't discussed it specifically, but Scott had counted on that coming back to Asa's place after practice, and they'd spend the evening together again—and, he wasn't going to lie, he was *really* hoping they'd end up in bed again, but even if all they did was hang out on the couch, Scott couldn't say it wouldn't be one of the better evenings of his whole goddamn life.

"This looks . . ."

"It looks like shit," Asa said, and to Scott's surprise, he leaned in against him. Asa didn't lean on people—literally or metaphorically—but he would with him. In private. When it was just the two of them.

Scott pressed a kiss to the side of Asa's head.

"Beau would be real proud you're eating the food he got you," Scott said, tucking an arm around Asa's waist. How was it possible they fit together so well like this, even though they'd never done it before? And he'd eat so much worse, if it meant he could keep doing it. "Even if it does look . . . well, questionable."

This was supposed to be a shepherd's pie, but instead of being topped with mashed potatoes, there was an unappealing-looking layer of quinoa.

"Well, nothing to do but dig in, I suppose," Asa said, but didn't move. Like he too, didn't want to stop touching now that they'd started again.

Then, unexpectedly, he shifted, but instead of moving further away, towards the table, Asa curled tighter into Scott's arms, and tilted his head back. Brushing Scott's mouth with his own once, and then twice. Scott groaned and gave in and kissed him hard and fast, devouring him like he'd been thinking about doing all day.

They broke apart with a breathless laugh. "I've thought about that all day," Asa admitted, echoing Scott's thoughts almost exactly.

"Me too. Maybe we just spent too much time only thinking about it . . ." Scott didn't even get the whole sentence out before they were stumbling backwards, hitting the wall, and Asa was kissing him again.

On the edge all day, he was worked up in a second, cock hard and pressing against his fly, already imagining the bliss that he'd feel the moment he could get his hands on the man he loved.

He let himself get lost, not giving a shit about defenses, about the Chiefs, about Sebastian's near-inability to not punch Micah Rose in the face, not even about quinoa-topped casseroles, but then . . . there was a noise.

At first he didn't quite recognize the weird rapping echo of it, until Asa pulled off, breathing hard, and headed towards the front door.

And of course, opened it, to Beau, who was smiling, and Sebastian, who was not.

"Oh, uh, wasn't expecting you tonight," Asa stammered.

Scott tried to rearrange his erection as subtly as possible, but he thought Sebastian might've gotten a glimpse.

"Clearly," Beau said. "I sent you a text, saying we were coming over for dinner."

Scott saw the panic that streaked across Asa's face before he quickly buried it. "I was talkin' with Scott and didn't notice," Asa said.

Sebastian raised an eyebrow. *God*, maybe he *had* seen. If only he could be convinced to keep his mouth shut until Asa worked his way around to telling Beau.

"Well, as you can see, we've got plenty of food. A lovely quinoa-topped casserole," Scott said.

Sebastian looked unimpressed. Beau's expression was similar, even though he was clearly trying to hide it.

"I thought we'd also stick in a fun holiday movie," Beau said. "Try to wrestle up some Christmas spirit."

Asa shot his son a glare. "You thought we'd do *what*?"

"Yeah," Beau said. "We always pass it by, you know, but not for any good reason. And now Scott's here, and he loves Christmas movies."

Asa's glare shifted from Beau to Scott quicker than he'd dreamt could be possible.

"I do," Scott said weakly. Though if he had to pick between watching a Christmas movie and making out with Asa on the couch . . . there was absolutely no question which he'd prefer.

"See?" Beau said to Sebastian. "Told you this was a good idea."

Sebastian looked increasingly skeptical even as Asa brought two more sets of silverware and plates to the table.

"Especially," Beau continued, "because you told me you wouldn't be able to make our regular pre-game day dinner date."

"Uh," Asa said, looking guilty. Had he told Beau he wouldn't have dinner with him because he wanted to spend time with Scott?

To Scott's eyes, that was how it was looking.

Maybe he'd been wrong before; maybe what Asa needed to do was tell Beau ASAP so they could get some freaking privacy.

Beau not knowing—and Beau not being happy for them—was definitely going to be a problem.

"Last-minute meetings," Scott said, chiming in. "You know how it is."

"I'm glad we could make it tonight, then," Beau said, and gestured at Scott. "And you're already here, too. We stopped by your apartment, but you weren't home. Sebastian thought you might be here, and you were!"

"Surprise," Scott said weakly.

They all settled around the table, and Asa began to dish up casserole for everyone, followed by the salad that Scott had thrown together, with the roasted butternut squash and dried cranberries he'd grabbed from the gourmet market around the corner.

"This looks really good," Beau said cheerfully, clearly trying to put a positive spin on things.

"Sure does," Sebastian echoed with a mournful note in his voice as he took his first forkful of casserole. Scott thought the two of them might understand each other better than anyone might think. No lie, he'd planned on enduring the casserole because of the payoff he'd be getting later. That had felt like a no-brainer trade-off. But now, there'd be no payoff, and even when they were watching the movie, he couldn't exactly put his arm around Asa like he wanted to, or distract him from all that inherent holiday sappiness by seducing him.

It was funny how keeping his hands to himself before had never been particularly difficult, he'd done it for so many years it should've felt natural, but instead, all Scott craved was the freedom of the previous evening, when he could touch Asa just because he wanted to.

"Offense looked good today," Scott said, inserting himself into the awkward silence that had fallen around the table as everyone tried to eat what was on their plates without grimacing.

"They're movin' the ball well," Asa agreed, and Beau nodded enthusiastically.

"Pax has come so far," Beau said. "His confidence is just . . . heads and tails above where it used to be. Davis has been an invaluable add to the team. I wasn't sure about it, but you know, Dad, sometimes you really get it right."

"Sometimes I do," Asa said dryly.

"Couldn't have anything to do with the fact that he's wildly in love with Davis," Sebastian said with a sly glance over at his boyfriend. "At least that couldn't hurt."

Beau shot him a look. "It's not *why*, but no, I'm sure that they're on . . . well, ahem, the *same page*, doesn't hurt."

"I'm sure it doesn't," Scott said.

He could attest to that, personally. But so could Beau and Sebastian. Asa had told him, late last night—or had it been early this morning?—that he'd worried about this big plan of Beau's to convert Sebastian over to a safety, and maybe that was the problem with the defensive scheme? That Sebastian wasn't playing well as a safety?

But no, Scott had watched the tape. The man had been a born corner, and now he was transitioning into a born safety.

It had been the right call. A call that Beau had made, and then convinced Sebastian of. As for the convincing, Scott was pretty sure that not all of it had happened on the field, and that most of it hadn't exactly been platonic.

"The new scheme . . ." Sebastian said, and then hesitated.

"What about it?" Scott asked.

Sebastian sighed, like he didn't want to say it. "I think it's good."

"See, told you that you'd come around," Beau said lightly.

Sebastian glowered at him.

"That's why I brought Scott here," Asa said.

"Excuse me?" Beau retorted. "*You* brought Scott here? You fought me every step of the way and now you're apparently sharing dinners and all buddy-buddy, and it's *you* brought Scott in."

"Alright, I *allowed* you to bring Scott in," Asa corrected, grinning.

Beau rolled his eyes. "I'm not sure what happened, and maybe I don't want to know."

You don't want to know.

"Yeah, I just bet you don't," Sebastian muttered to his half-eaten casserole.

Scott was becoming more and more sure that Sebastian had guessed the truth. He just had to hope that either Beau was too sure of his own to believe him, or that he wouldn't share it. At least not yet.

"What movie are we watching?" Scott asked, in a semi-desperate bid to change the subject. He'd thought the one he'd picked about the offense had been an easy, not-awkward gambit, but apparently, there weren't a lot of those remaining.

"*Elf,*" Beau said. "I know my dad's never seen it . . ."

"There's a reason for that," Asa inserted.

"And I think it'll be good to watch something that doesn't take place on a football field and that he can't analyze incessantly for two hours."

Before Beau had shown up with his boyfriend in tow, Scott had been pretty dang sure that he could've distracted Asa from football for *at least* two hours. Maybe even more.

He even liked *Elf*, but he knew what Beau had planned wouldn't be nearly as much fun as what he'd envisioned.

Too bad. Maybe it was good Asa had preemptively canceled dinner last night, because that might be their only time to be alone.

Dinner didn't drag out too much, because Scott had a feeling that everyone was hoping to find a midnight snack to eat later, to compensate.

Beau helped Asa clear the table as Sebastian and Scott headed into the living room to get the movie going.

Sebastian shot him a knowing look when he attempted to take the couch—hoping, at least, that he could be *next* to Asa during the next two hours—and so Scott retreated, annoyed, to the chair.

Asa took the other one, leaving the couch to Beau and Sebastian, who immediately glued themselves together like they didn't know how to do anything else.

Scott was not only disappointed that he didn't get to sit close enough to Asa to touch him whenever he felt like it, but also that he could barely hear all those half-audible comments Asa kept muttering under his breath.

"Santa took a baby."

"What an idiot, he thinks he's actually an elf."

"Best coffee?" That was followed by a scoff loud enough that Beau actually turned his head and shot his father a lazy glare.

"Someone better lock this guy up before he accidentally hurts himself."

And then the most annoyed muttering of all, *"What an absolute shit father."*

Asa would know, Scott figured, because he'd always been the best father he knew—not just the best father to Beau that he could be, but the guys on the team? He'd always been their surrogate father, too, and he'd tried his best to do right by them, even when they gave him fits and frustrated the hell out of him.

"This freaking guy," Asa murmured when Buddy piled his plate high with spaghetti and candy and syrup.

It continued, with comments about the girl, and how she didn't know what she was signing up for, and the wretched way the publishing house had treated basically every single goddamn character, until the very end, when everyone was singing, trying to get Santa's sleigh off the ground. When Scott looked over, it was obvious that Asa was trying to hide his enjoyment.

The credits started rolling, and Beau reached over and flipped off the TV. "So," he said, turning towards Asa, "what did you think?"

Asa raised a dubious eyebrow. "A complete waste of an hour and a half. The guy actually thought he was an elf. He ate spaghetti with maple syrup and candy. He decorated way too many things. It was . . . interestin', I guess, from a sociological perspective . . ."

Beau burst out laughing. "You are full of such shit," he said.

"You liked it," Scott said.

Asa shrugged. "It was *fine*. A little strong on the spirit of Christmas and all that jazz, but yeah, it was fine."

"You're welcome," Beau said.

When he and Sebastian went to leave, the latter turned towards Asa. "This whole Grinch thing? It might fool a lot of people but it doesn't fool me."

Without waiting for a response, Sebastian followed Beau towards the door.

"Hey, Scott, I gotta pick some stuff up at my place, so I thought I'd follow you down," Beau said as he grabbed his coat.

Well, shit. There went his brilliant idea of lingering behind, so at *least* he could get a goodnight kiss.

Asa was going to need to tell Beau. There was no way around it.

"Uh, sure, okay," Scott said, mentally scrambling for an excuse so he could stay.

But Beau was looking at him impatiently, and Sebastian was looking at him knowingly, like he understood exactly what he was trying to do, so there was nothing to do but follow them to the door.

"Thanks for dinner," Scott said, leaning a bit nearer to Asa. But this was as close as he was gonna get, because then Beau turned around again. A few days ago, Asa had been mad as hell at him and had wanted him to leave Miami. It would be weird for them to hug, it *would*, but Scott almost did it anyway.

"It was horrible, but you're welcome," Asa said, the corner of his mouth quirking up.

"You know," Beau said as they headed towards the elevator, "I think my dad might be warming to you, a little, again."

"Nobody's more surprised than me," Scott said, almost managing to keep a straight face.

"Uh-huh," Sebastian grumbled under his breath. "Surprised, my ass."

"What was that?" Beau asked.

"Nothing, nothing, not a damn thing," Sebastian said.

It took Beau less than a minute to grab what he wanted from the apartment, but then he was gone, and in less than sixty seconds, Scott's evening was ruined.

He sighed and flopped down on the couch, too keyed up to think about sleeping, and too frustrated to do anything else.

He pulled his phone out of his pocket and saw that Asa had sent him a text. **I love my son, but he's an interfering ass.**

Scott cackled out loud as he typed out his reply. **You could tell him and then he'd accidentally interfere less.**

Asa's response came through almost instantly. **One problem with that solution: the actual "telling him" part.**

Before Scott could agree, because that *was* clearly an issue, at least in Asa's mind, he sent another text. **You could always come back up here. Finish what we started . . .**

It wasn't that Scott didn't feel tempted. He did. But a glance at his watch told him it was after ten, and Asa was supposed to be getting more sleep—and he definitely hadn't *last* night.

Cute you thought that was starting. I'd show you what starting looks like, but it's late and I'm tired. Rain check?

There was a long pause and for a second, for one horrible moment, Scott was afraid he'd fucked this up again. But then Asa sent a last message just when he'd pulled himself off the couch, heading into the bathroom to brush his teeth: **Cute you think I'd be fooled for a second. Yes, I'll go to sleep like a good little boy.**

Scott fell asleep with a wide-ass grin on his face.

Chapter Eight

The team was scheduled to fly to Kansas City in the early afternoon, but Asa hoped to get a few hours of solid work in on refining the game plan in the morning, so he showed up at the office at eight AM sharp, holding two coffees.

One, he set on his own desk.

The other, he set on Scott's, and after a long internal debate with himself, he pulled open the bottom drawer in his desk, and pulled out one of the bows he'd stowed in there in preparation for this moment.

He stuck the bright, jaunty red bow on the lid of the coffee, and had just settled back in his desk when Scott appeared, a light mist covering him as he walked into the office. He'd walked, then. Asa had taken one look at the rain and had called a car. Considering, more than once, if he should ask Scott to join him.

But he hadn't, because even though he'd wanted Scott here, with him, all the time, how could he stage the coffee properly if he was present the whole time?

"Hey," Scott said, and the look in his eyes as he approached their desks was almost as good as a kiss.

Almost.

"Hey," Asa said, keeping his expression neutral as Scott pulled his jacket off, exposing his brawny forearms and biceps, accentuated by a way-too-tight t-shirt. Not that Asa was complaining. No way.

"Oh, look, what's this?" Scott asked as he settled down in his desk. "Did my Secret Santa do this?"

"I don't know, Scott, it's a coffee with a bow on it, what do you think?"

Scott grinned. "Did you see them come in?"

"For the thousandth time, it's called *Secret* Santa," Asa said.

"So you're just not gonna tell me." Scott sounded amused by this. "Can I guess?"

"Of course not," Asa said. But he was watching as Scott pulled the bow off, and stuck it on the corner of his laptop screen, and then took a hesitant sip of the coffee.

It wasn't a shock that realization dawned across his face.

Not that many people could know Scott's coffee order—or at least the way he'd taken it for the twenty-plus years they'd gotten coffee together.

"Asa," Scott said and his voice was like a caress against his cheek.

"Yes?" he tried for innocence, but it was probably too late. He'd known it would be, the moment he'd decided to gift Scott his favorite cup of coffee.

But Scott just leaned back in his chair. "Never mind," he said, still smiling. "I just think my Secret Santa knows me pretty damn well, that's all."

"Oh?"

"Loves me a lot, too," Scott teased.

"I'd imagine."

Scott's shit-eating expression was totally worth the hassle of calling for the car and then convincing the driver to detour to a nearby coffee shop and wait while Asa ran in and grabbed a pair of coffees.

Totally worth painstakingly repeating Scott's old coffee order to the baristas and having them think that it was *his* coffee. Even worth signing half a dozen autographs and listening to twice as many suggestions for how they might beat the Chiefs on Sunday.

It had all been worth it, just to see Scott's smile.

"Whatcha working on?" Scott asked, leaning over and taking a peek at his laptop.

"Final game plan for the walkthrough," Asa said. "Beau emailed me over the final last night, and I'm just now taking a look at it, making some tweaks."

"Is it really the final if you make changes after?" Scott teased.

"I'm the head coach of this football team," Asa said. "It's my responsibility if we win or we lose, so yeah, I'm takin' a hard look at it. I let . . . I let Brett do whatever for weeks 'cause I was too busy trying to get the offense moving, scoring some points. And look where that landed us."

"It's not Brett's fault. He did the best he could with what he had."

Asa grunted. He supposed Scott wasn't wrong, but he was still worried.

Scott had walked in and seen the problem almost immediately. They'd been lucky that no offense coordinator had seen it yet, and figured out how to expose them.

And if one did, every team they played for the rest of the year would, and if they couldn't adjust, all the hazy, beautiful possibilities of this season would end up flushed down the goddamn toilet.

"I actually had a thought last night."

Asa shot him a questioning look.

"Yeah," Scott said, still grinning, "I wasn't sleeping either."

"I told you . . ." Asa trailed off, lowering his voice. "You should've come back up."

He'd asked and Scott had turned him down, and at the time, Asa had seen the intelligence of the decision. But at two in the morning, when he'd been staring at the dark ceiling above the bed, it had seemed like total bullshit. Sleeping with Scott for one night was enough to make him want to do it every single night going forward.

"Maybe I wouldn't have come up with this idea, then," Scott said, clearly trying to put a positive spin on it.

They'd be in Kansas City tonight, the night before the game, and no matter what Asa wanted, he couldn't imagine sneaking out of his room to visit Scott in his own.

But maybe he would anyway. It wasn't like him spending one night with Scott in Kansas City would change the way the team was going to play.

"Let's see it, then," Asa said.

Scott pulled out his tablet and sketched it out, Asa watching and humming under his breath. It was good, like almost all of Scott's ideas, and he added it to the walkthrough.

"You get all situated with Kelly?" Asa asked innocently. "You make sure to tell her she can't put you next to or above or anywhere near Wade and Tristan?"

Scott's lips quirked up into a wry smile. "Are they really that bad?"

"I pray to God," Asa said, with humor, "that you never find out."

"Then I guess it's good I talked to her. She's got me all set up on the staff floor at the hotel."

"Good," Asa said. And he thought, but didn't say, *that makes you even easier to get to, after curfew hits.*

Scott had been around a lot of teams in his life.

Teams he'd played on and teams he'd coached.

But he'd never seen a walkthrough like this one before.

Logan, the center, was wearing a Santa hat, *proudly*, and a t-shirt that proclaimed, *Ho, Ho, Ho, Hold my Beer*, and Tristan kept singing snippets of Christmas songs every time, *loudly*, someone mentioned his name or asked him a question.

He'd already seen some presents being exchanged, gifts left in the locker room, on seats on planes, and the low-level chatter among every group of players he passed was all about who had gotten who for Secret Santa.

He'd been working with the defensive folks again, during the walkthrough, and the good news was, Scott thought as he pressed the elevator button to go up to his room, they'd come up with a scheme that would close the gap that other teams could exploit. The bad news was that Micah didn't seem too confident in the new scheme. They were only going to partially implement it, because it was too soon to really overhaul the whole thing, in time for this game. Scott just had to hope that the Chiefs' offensive minds hadn't spotted the problem as quickly as he had.

Would this end up burning them so badly they were going to wish they'd left it as is?

Scott really hoped not.

When he'd left the room where the defense was huddled, Sebastian had been walking Micah through play-by-play, giving him tips, and miracle of all Christmas miracles, it seemed as though Micah was actually listening.

Maybe this wouldn't be a disaster after all.

Maybe something good would come of it.

Seven years ago, Scott wouldn't have touched Rose with a ten-foot pole. He'd have avoided him, afraid, even though he'd never have admitted it to anyone, or even to himself, that Rose would find out his secret and expose him.

Or even worse—that he'd judge him.

But Scott was trying something new, had been working on it since he'd been in Washington a few years: not giving a shit what other people thought of him or his sexuality.

When he'd gotten Beau's call, he'd been in the middle of a plan to slowly come out to the people in his hometown.

When that was accomplished, he'd planned to come out publicly, in some understated way—at least he'd hoped that was possible. He didn't want to make his sexuality reveal a big deal; but it was also who he was, a part of him that he'd hidden for way too long, thinking that nobody really wanted the *real* Scott Callaway.

It had taken him too many years to dismiss what other people thought. But, he reminded himself as he got off the elevator onto the staff floor, just because he'd been wrong, just because he'd struggled with this, didn't mean that he couldn't change his course now.

And truthfully, the best place to do it was always going to be here, in Miami. Or even in Los Angeles, with the Riptide. Or with a handful of college programs that he knew didn't care who he loved.

Even if he'd ended up coaching kid football, the way that Asa had said he'd be willing to do, seven years back, Scott had made his peace with it.

Honesty, he'd discovered, was more important than anything else.

He inserted his card key into the door lock and pushed his way in.

It was a hotel room like so many other hotel rooms he'd stayed in over his career. He pulled out his toiletry bag, hung up his pants for tomorrow, so they wouldn't be creased, and after stripping down to just his boxers, flopped down on the bed, reaching for the remote to flip the TV on.

He'd turn on ESPN, maybe even catch some of the scores of the college games.

For a split second, he considered texting Asa, asking him what he was doing.

Asking him to come over to his room.

But Asa wasn't the kind of guy willing to sneak around after curfew. He'd always been a stickler for it, in fact.

Scott hadn't asked—and still didn't want to ask—because he didn't want Asa to turn him down.

You're okay on your own, you've been on your own for long enough now, you should be used to it.

But he wasn't. Less than a week basking in the warmth of Asa's presence, and now he wanted it all the time.

Scott tossed the remote down onto the bed with a frustrated grunt, and he was just about to reach for his phone anyway, damn

Asa and his irresistible self to hell, when a knock on the door stopped him.

It could be anyone at the door—Beau with a last-minute idea, even Sebastian, wanting to rant about how difficult Micah was—but Scott knew who he wanted it to be. He groaned as he pulled himself up, and on the way to the door threw on the t-shirt he'd just taken off.

He'd just finished dragging it over his head when he reached the door.

When he opened it, Asa was standing there, hand poised to knock again.

Pleasure swept through Scott in a giddy, warm wave. "Hey," he said, leaning against the doorjamb. "I didn't expect you."

Asa looked vaguely worried-slash-guilty, which meant that he was here for precisely the reason that Scott hoped he was—and that meant the reason wasn't even remotely football related.

"Can I come in?"

Scott grinned. "Can you?"

"Scott," Asa admonished as he finally held the door open wider so Asa could get out of the hallway. "Someone was gonna see."

"Someone was gonna see you come into my room, your *assistant head coach's* room, and think what? That we were gonna get down and dirty over some play diagrams?" It was too much fun to tease Asa, he'd not gotten to do it for too long, and now he was going to enjoy making Asa work for this a little.

Asa shot him a look of pure frustration. "It's after curfew, Scott."

"You know, that doesn't actually apply to coaching staff," Scott said, not moving from the little entryway opposite the bathroom. It was just so amusing to watch Asa's annoyance mount. He knew what he wanted, but maybe . . . just maybe . . . he wanted him to actually ask for it.

"And you *know* I never ask my players to do something I wouldn't do myself," Asa retorted.

Scott knew it. It was one of the reasons he'd always admired Asa so much. He'd never make a rule he wasn't prepared to follow himself.

"Is this you saying you condone them sneaking into their lover's room after curfew?" Scott teased softly.

"I don't know," Asa said, "is that what this is?"

The other thing he absolutely fucking adored about Asa was his ability to take it and then dish it right back.

"Is it?" Scott asked, because suddenly he wasn't sure. Maybe Asa *had* come here for a football thing, and he'd read this whole thing wrong.

He knew what answer he was hoping for.

Asa didn't answer the question with words; he reached out and settled into Scott's arms like he'd always been there, like they'd never missed their chances, like they'd never been separated.

Like they'd been doing this the whole goddamned time.

"You know exactly what this is," Asa murmured in that rough sexy growl, and kissed him.

Yesterday, he'd only gotten that brief taste of Asa before they'd been interrupted by Beau and Sebastian. It hadn't been enough, not nearly enough, and he'd known that, but feeling the hunger come roaring back, like it had never been satisfied, was an entirely different thing.

"God," Scott moaned into Asa's mouth as they stumbled towards the bed. He pulled Asa down on top of him, and his pulse rabbited as Asa took to that like a duck took to water, grinding down on him like he wasn't just chasing his own orgasm but searching for Scott's, too.

"I . . . could . . . *barely* . . . make it through the goddamned walkthrough," Asa said, panting as he reached over and began to tug Scott's shirt off.

Scott was surprised. Asa always seemed so cool and collected, and tonight hadn't been any different. He knew there was fire buried deep underneath all that unflappable exterior, but he'd still never guessed that he was this hot, this eager.

And now he wasn't going to be able to forget it.

"Were you thinkin' about this?" Scott asked, pulling Asa's shirt off and tossing it to the side. He'd worn soft, loose sweatpants like he was going to be relaxing in his room, and it was so easy to push those down, a groan rumbling in the back of his throat as he discovered that not only was Asa's cock already hard, he'd been wearing nothing underneath them.

"You fuckin' were," Scott continued, in complete awe and more in love than he'd ever imagined he could be. "You came here thinkin' just about this."

Asa's kiss was his answer: hot and messy and so goddamned perfect.

He *knew* of course that it wasn't just him who was in this—he'd known that for seven years, and even for a few months before that, when it had been impossible to miss that Asa's feelings were changing—but he'd still never imagined it would be like this.

That Asa would not only be there every dirty step of the way, but that he'd be the one holding out his hand, shooting Scott a look of pure impatience.

Just like the one he was giving him now.

"Come on," Asa panted as Scott worked his cock nice and slow—slow because he wanted to prolong this as much as possible, and they were both so worked up, it definitely wasn't going to take very long.

"You don't like this?" Scott teased, swiping a thumb across the head, gathering moisture and then jerking him leisurely, like they had all night.

Asa bit off a muttered oath. He was already twitching in his fist, muscles tensing, and Scott went even slower, anticipating that Asa, so fucking worked up, was going to come like a goddamn rocket.

But instead of spilling into his hand, Asa suddenly pushed him backwards, divesting him of his own boxers, and then he was climbing back on top of him.

Scott groaned as he felt Asa's cock, slick with his precome, rubbing against his own.

"It's funny," Asa crooned, his accent growing thicker as he leaned over Scott's chest, face hovering only an inch from Scott's own, "you keep thinkin' you can dictate how these things go."

Scott wanted him to lean down and kiss him more than he wanted to take his next breath. He shifted his hips, feeling the white-hot burst of pleasure roll through him as Asa's cock nudged his own.

"I did last time, didn't I?" Scott said. "You even said, *I don't know how this works.*"

Asa rolled his eyes. "I know how it works. I've got eyes and a computer, don't I?"

God, he was not gonna be able to control himself much longer if he thought *anymore* about Asa watching porn and getting himself off.

"I *meant*," Asa continued, "that I didn't know how to . . . like if there were rules about suggesting it or how we go about it or . . ."

"You wanted a game plan for sex?"

"I thought that might be nice, but." Asa paused and swiveled *his* hips, leaving Scott breathless with desire. "I think we can improvise."

"Can we?" Scott challenged.

"Oh, we *can*," Asa said and then he was lining himself up right against Scott, callouses on his hands brushing right against all his sensitive spots. Then Asa leaned forward that last inch, and maybe Scott should've been embarrassed at how fast he reached the edge, but suddenly it was all heat and movement and lips and tongue and Scott lost himself in the sensation of Asa all around him, mouth working against his own, body thrusting so perfectly he didn't even think—he just lost himself.

He wanted to hold on, to make it last, to pull Asa along with him, but then he felt Asa tense up, shuddering against him, liquid splashing against his lower abs, up his chest, and he came before he could even hope to stop himself.

Asa slid a little down his chest and, for a second, just lay there, his own rapid breathing echoing Scott's.

"Well," Scott said, feeling—and sounding—a little stupid. "I think you did just fine without a diagram."

Asa elbowed him in the side, and Scott couldn't help it, he laughed.

"I guess I shouldn't have expected sex with you to be different than everything else with you," Asa ruminated.

Scott's heart clenched. He couldn't really breathe—and not just because Asa was currently perched on top of his diaphragm.

"Frustrating and challenging and amazing," Asa continued in a murmur.

Scott's fingers tightened against Asa's bare hips. "Yeah?"

"And perfect, too, did I forget to add that?" Asa sounded very amused.

"Well, it must be pretty damn good, considering how eager you were."

"I shouldn't have, but I suppose I should have." Asa sighed. "Gotta take something for myself, isn't that what y'all are always tellin' me to do?"

"I don't think this is what Beau had in mind," Scott said, chuckling.

"Yeah, but it still counts." Asa was quiet for a moment. "I suppose I'm gonna have to tell him."

"At some point, yes," Scott said. "But that timeline is yours." His hand trailed up Asa's bare spine. The happy sigh Asa gave at his touch made him hope that maybe he'd never move. Even though they'd made a real mess on the top of Scott's sheets.

His eyes had closed, but when he opened them, Asa was staring right at him, the love in his gaze unmistakable. "That's why this works, you know," Asa said quietly. "Why I love you. Why I trust you. Why I'd do anything for you. Why I'd give up my career for you."

"Because I don't want to tell you what to do with your own son?"

"No, because you're . . ." Asa hesitated. "Because you're *you*. You're Scott. Nobody else knows me as well as you do. There's nobody else that could."

Scott's hand drifted lower, to the still-amazing curves of Asa's ass. "It's a privilege to know you," he said in a hushed voice, his heart in his throat. "In every possible way."

Asa made a happy, content sound in the back of his throat. "Officially," he said, "new favorite way to spend the night before a game."

"This means you're gonna be sneaking into my room every week?" Scott couldn't help the hopefulness that bled into his voice.

"You gonna make me feel like that every time?" Asa cleared his throat. "Absofuckinglutely."

Scott chuckled. "There's more, so much more, I want to do it all with you . . . everything I've ever thought . . . everything I've ever fantasized about . . . it's all there."

"How about we start with a shower?" Asa said wryly. "I think we're beginning to . . . uh . . . stick together."

It sucked to move, but then only a few minutes later, Asa was following him into the hot water.

"This shower," Asa said, as Scott laughed, trying to maneuver them away from the spray, "is not really big enough."

"No," Scott agreed.

Asa leaned back against the tile wall. His blue eyes were smoky and seductive, and there was nothing Scott regretted more than only getting around to doing this now, when there was no way he could get it up again so soon after such a strong orgasm.

"Next time, I'll get a suite," Asa said as Scott grabbed the soap and began to clean himself up.

"How're you gonna explain that? *Sorry, Kelly, but I gotta have a big-ass shower so I can get my guy off without accidentally sucking down a liter of water?*"

Asa laughed as Scott ducked himself under the spray, rinsing off the soap.

"Maybe not like that," Asa said. "But I'll think of something." He reached out and tugged Scott closer, fingers digging into his shoulders. "'Cause I gotta tell you, seeing you wet, it . . ." Asa's tongue flicked out, licking his bottom lip, sending a spike of desire through Scott. "It gets me hot, Scott. *Real* hot."

He knew he took care of his body. It had always been a tool for him. First because of football, and then, he'd continued to work out because it was an easy—or *easier*—way to work out all the frustration he felt.

All that excess sexual tension he'd never been able to manage.

But hearing that Asa was attracted to him, like that, looking at him like this, gaze burning into his skin, every desperate workout felt worth it.

"You make me wish I was young again," Asa said with a wry smile.

"Same," Scott said and dipped his head, kissing him. This they could do. They could do this all goddamn night, and he wouldn't even be disappointed.

Asa's mouth opened under his, and it was funny, because every time it happened, every time he let Scott in like he was meant to be there, it felt amazing, like a miracle.

They kissed lazily against the shower wall for what could've been minutes or maybe even longer. Til the water began to grow cooler, and Scott's hands were touching Asa everywhere, tracing the lines of his muscles, then working down, fingers digging into his ass and then slipping lower.

"God, Scott," Asa gasped, as he panted into the air they shared.

It took Scott a second to realize that he was definitely getting harder, and desire was swimming through his veins hot and strong again, and that Asa was in the same position, eyes unfocused and glassy as he clung to him.

"Is that something you want?" Scott asked, his normal brain-to-mouth filter completely incinerated by the heat between them.

"You inside me? Yes, *yes*, and . . ." Asa hesitated. "But I don't care if we don't, or you want me to . . ."

"I told you before," Scott said, hearing his voice shake, "I want you all kinds of ways. It doesn't matter to me. Just what you feel comfortable with. What you want."

"What I want . . ." Asa trembled against him. "What I want is you."

"Next time," Scott promised. "I don't have . . . I wanna be careful with you, alright? I'll take you out to dinner next week, romance you properly, then . . ."

Asa grinned. "Fuck me properly?"

"*Yes*," Scott vowed.

"It's a date, then," Asa said and then to Scott's shock, he slid down, to his knees, his breath hot against his dick.

"You don't have to . . ." Scott said, and then trailed off, because Asa shot him a look. The kind of look that promised retribution, and it was silly to provoke this man, especially not when he was *this man* and he was that close to his cock.

"I *want* to," Asa said, and then shut him up entirely by trailing his tongue along the underside of his dick. He hummed under his breath, Scott's hands clenched into fists, as he realized that he was experimenting. Trying it out. Seeing how he liked it. Seeing how Scott tasted.

Then he was enveloped by Asa's hot, wet mouth and thinking . . . well, it was goddamn overrated. He just sank into the steam surrounding them and the tentative brushes of Asa's mouth, growing more confident by the moment.

Asa had never needed a scheme for sex.

He never needed a scheme for anything. He was always at his best when he was improvising.

Scott made a note to remind him of that, but then when he glanced down, the thought went up in smoke. The fantasy he'd carried for so goddamn long, better than he ever could've imagined: Asa on his knees, his dark head between his thighs, his own hand working his hard cock as he pleasured Scott.

"Jesus," Scott exhaled, tipping his head back and hitting the tile wall. "Keep doing that, just that."

Asa's hand replaced his mouth and it was warm from the water and tight and he was just rough enough, and then there was the undeniable pleasure in his own eyes, blurring as he reached his own orgasm.

It hit Scott like a freight train, overwhelming him.

He'd had sex in his life. He'd hardly been a monk.

But it had never been like this before.

He'd never barely finished coming and was already thinking about when he could get Asa alone again. Get him naked. Make him his.

CHAPTER NINE

ASA FELT LIKE HE'D been scooped out and all his insides replaced with someone else.

Someone who took risks. Someone who did exactly whatever the fuck he wanted. Someone who fell in love and *reveled* in it, instead of trying to pretend it had never happened.

As Asa stood on the sideline, waiting for the kickoff and the game to begin, it seemed unbelievable that Scott had only been here in Miami a week.

One week, and everything had changed.

"You good?" Beau asked, walking up next to him.

"Yes, Beau, I'm not going to collapse on the sideline. I feel good." *Better than I have in ages. Happier, too.*

But he couldn't tell Beau any of the reasons why. It wasn't just more sleep and better food and working less. It was reuniting with the other half of his heart; it was having Scott back in his life again. As a friend. As something more, *finally*.

The thing was, he *wanted* to tell Beau. He wanted Beau to be happy that he was happy, but the problem was that he'd kept it all a secret before. If he'd had any idea that it would turn out like this, he'd have told Beau the truth that December night, seven years ago. He'd have told him exactly why he was crying, and why Scott was leaving.

But that ship had sailed a long fucking time ago—and now he was going to be stuck not only admitting to Beau that he'd lied, but that he'd lied for *years*.

It was not going to be a pleasant conversation, and even though Beau was a reasonable person and loved both of them, Asa knew he wasn't going to take the news well, if only because of how he was hearing it.

When he was hearing it.

"You look good." Beau's tone sounded suspicious. "Really good, in fact."

"Amazing what sleep will do for a man," Asa said. *And a half dozen orgasms in the last few days.*

"I'm surprised that you were okay with Scott up in the booth," Beau said. "I'd have thought you'd have wanted him down here, with you. You're practically inseparable these days."

Oh, if *only* he knew. Asa regretted a lot of things, but nothing more than lying to his son. And that he *kept* lying to his son.

"Uh, well . . ." Asa hesitated. "He can see the field better from up there, and call in adjustments as needed. Besides, Brett's down here.

"If there's gonna be a problem," Asa continued, because he could see that Beau wasn't convinced, "he'll be the first person to see it."

"I mean, *yeah*, there's a bit of a gap in the coverage," Beau said, "but I doubt it's going to be an issue. Nobody else has seen it before now."

"Doesn't mean nobody will," Asa said. "We've gotten lucky. You know what I like to say about luck."

"It never lasts, and you'd better be prepared when it runs out," Beau said wryly.

"That's right," Asa said.

The offense jogged onto the field and Beau left, heading over to the other side of the sideline, where Davis was standing, watching as Pax led his team onto the field.

He'd been spending more and more time with Davis, getting Pax ready for every game, and it was an excellent use of his time and his brain.

But Scott had been right, there was no way they could survive a team laying forty-plus points on them.

The game started out decently enough.

The offense drove down the field, all the way from the twenty-yard line to past mid-field, mixing in a good combination of Kenyon runs and short passes. Then Pax threw an absolute dart to Wade, who muscled the ball down to the Chiefs' twenty-five-yard line.

Asa had been pleased with Randy's game plan for the offense, and he'd felt it would match up well against the Chiefs' defense, and it was looking like that was the case.

Randy called a run play and Asa saw the issue immediately, even before the flag came out of the official's pocket.

Rob, the left tackle, was supposed to pull to the left, but instead of just pulling his assigned defensive lineman, he yanked on his jersey, which he *knew* was not allowed, but that didn't stop him.

Or the referee from throwing the flag.

"Goddamn it," Asa muttered.

"He knows better than that," Randy said over their radio channel.

"Yeah, well, *tell him that*," Asa griped.

He knew the stats and what they said; if the offense racked up a holding penalty on a drive, they were far less likely to score.

Beau muttered a bad word into his headset as Kenyon got the ball and was tackled behind the line of scrimmage.

Now what had seemed like an extremely promising drive came to a screaming halt, and after two incomplete passes in a row, Dylan jogged onto the field to kick the field goal.

After nailing it right between the uprights, Asa decided that while they'd stopped themselves with a stupid mistake, it wasn't a terrible start to the game.

"Pax lookin' sharp," Asa heard over the radio channel, Scott's deep drawl unmistakable.

It shouldn't send shivers up his spine. Shouldn't make him think about last night. Shouldn't make him think about this morning.

But apparently while his focus was notorious for being un-shakeable, Scott could derail it pretty damn easily.

"That pass to Wade was fuckin' sweet," Davis agreed.

Up three to zero, Asa felt pretty good about their start. And, of course, that was when everything went to hell.

From the first play the Chiefs' offense ran, it was obvious to Asa, even from down here on the field, that they'd seen the gap in their defensive coverage.

"Shit, shit, shit." That was Beau. He'd seen it too.

"Brett, you gotta move Sebastian back over. He's gotta cover the middle." Asa could hear the frustration in Scott's voice, hear how impotent he felt, because the final call came down to Brett.

But Asa saw Brett shake his head. "We're gonna give up a long-ass pass to Kelce, Micah can't cover him by himself."

"He's *gotta*," Scott said.

But Brett didn't respond.

Asa told himself that maybe it was just coincidence. But when the next three passes all fell right in that soft spot in their coverage, and the Chiefs were moving the ball at will, heading right down the field, like the defense wasn't even on the field, he knew it wasn't.

He sighed. This was going to be a long game.

That was the Chiefs' first touchdown.

By the second, Scott was swearing over the radio channel.

By the third, Asa decided that he couldn't let Brett kill them like this. Even if they could keep up—and they *couldn't*, it just wasn't in their makeup, and like clockwork he could see the pressure piling on Pax's shoulders, every single time he took the field—this was just foolish.

"You gotta try the new scheme." Asa pulled off his headset before he told Brett this. None of the other coaches needed to hear him pull rank on his defensive coordinator.

Brett's jaw clenched. "It's not gonna improve the situation."

"We're down twenty-one to ten, and they're scoring at will. If we want to be in this game, we've got to try *something*." Maybe it wouldn't work, but then they'd know, and if Scott and Beau could spend the next week working with Micah . . . surely it would be an improvement.

"Give Micah a chance."

"We've tried that. Remember the Patriots game?"

Asa did.

It would be hard to forget it.

Micah had given up three touchdowns—but they'd won, anyway.

"Yeah, I do," Asa said. "And history isn't gonna repeat itself, we're going to lose this game badly. You wanna answer for that?

'Cause I don't." He kept his voice neutral, but he let the steel of his resolve show in his expression.

Brett had to know if he flouted him here, then he'd be the first coach that Asa fired.

Scott could step into his job in a second.

Up to this point, Brett had done well enough, but if he was going to be stubborn, going to ignore Asa's directives, then that didn't matter.

"No," Brett muttered.

"Good," Asa said crisply. He reached up, to lift his headset back onto his head, but Brett's words stopped him.

"Everything was goddamned fine, til your friend showed up. Started fucking with things."

Asa kept his temper. The worst place to lose it was the sideline, in the middle of a game.

"This has nothing to do with Scott. He just pointed out the problem. The problem that the Chiefs just exploited."

"Yeah, funny 'bout that timing," Brett said bitterly. "'Cause it was *working*."

Anger spiked through Asa. He'd hoped that Brett wouldn't go there, or at least if he did, he'd at least save it.

"You trust him?" Brett continued to dig himself an early grave. "You really trust him?"

"With my life. Definitely with my football team." Asa turned and walked away. His heart was pumping, his blood hot, his pulse rabbiting. He could feel it. Knew he wasn't supposed to be getting angry. Was supposed to be keeping his temper.

But what Brett had vaguely accused Scott of was infuriating.

Scott would never betray him. *Never*.

He pulled his headset back on, and watched, seeing, but not really seeing, as the offense had to kick another field goal.

Twenty-one to thirteen, as they headed into the locker room for halftime.

It could've been worse; and it could've been a damn sight better, too.

Something had gone down between Asa and Brett during the second quarter. Scott could sense Asa's towering fury, could sense Brett's resentment, as he entered the locker room, heading over to where the defense was loosely gathered together.

Asa was giving one of his pep talks that wasn't really a pep talk. It was more of an exhortation to not let the Chiefs just go down the field like they weren't even there.

Sebastian looked pissed off and Micah looked despondent. The rest of the defense seemed a mix of the two.

Not ideal.

"You've got the skill, it's just a matter of effort," Asa said, and he sounded like he believed his own words. But Scott knew him better than that. Could see through him, even when nobody else could. Deep down, he was frustrated and furious and *not* sure that they could pull this off. "So reach down, find that drive, that need to succeed, and let's get this done, alright?"

There was a chorus of responses. Most of them seemed enthusiastic, but Scott had coached enough defenses to know this whole unit was floundering, and suddenly at that. They'd been exposed, and that wasn't ever an easy thing to take.

Brett said a few words, and then Scott decided he'd had enough say, because whatever exchange he and Asa had had, he'd seen from the booth, had been enough to seriously piss Asa off. Designing a questionable scheme . . . well, that happened. Shit happened. But pissing Asa off? Scott was way less likely to forgive whatever Brett had said when he'd shot his mouth off.

"So," Scott said, dropping to his knee in front of where Micah sat on the bench. "Not a great start, huh?"

Micah shot him a belligerent look.

"This game isn't over," Scott pointed out. "You can still go out there, play your ass off, make your mark. Prove to all those people who don't think you can cover that you *can*."

"Nobody here thinks I can."

"Then prove them fucking wrong," Scott said.

There was a flash of something in Micah's eyes. A challenge, maybe? Maybe that was what Micah needed.

Not only a whole world to think he couldn't do it, but one person who did.

"You think so?"

"Yeah, I think so. I've watched tons of film of you, kid," Scott said. "You've got it. You just need to elevate it. This is the NFL now. Not college. You listenin' to what Howard has to say?"

Micah nodded, then regret creased his features. "Well, not as much as I could have, probably."

"Then *listen*," Scott said. He stood, and patted Micah on the shoulder. "You got this."

Scott exchanged a glance with Asa, and he felt the weight of it even as halftime ended and he took the stairs back up to the booth for the remainder of the game.

"So, am I gonna have to figure out how to keep up with the Chiefs scoring a touchdown every drive in the second half?" Randy asked him wryly as he took his seat next to him and pulled his headset on.

Scott glanced over. He liked Randy a lot, and he'd done a lot with the offense.

"Uh, not sure. Maybe," he hedged. "We're tryin' something new. Well, continuing to try something new."

"Got it," Randy said. "Well, Pax has got the capacity, unless he gets in his own way. Too deep into his own head."

"Don't you have Davis to stop him from doing that?"

Randy's expression was amused. "You ever met Paxton Kelly? He's stubborn as hell. Maybe Davis could drag him out of it, but the guy's determined to take every ounce of the blame when things go wrong."

Scott knew someone else like that.

"Yeah," Scott said. "Yeah. That could get tough."

"Hopefully your 'something new' works better than it did in the first half," Randy said, flipping open his playbook.

They wouldn't have to wait long to know, because the Chiefs had the ball first to kick off the third quarter.

Right away, Scott liked the way the defense laid out on the first play of their drive. Sebastian positioned the way he needed to be, stifling any potential run game and helping to cover anything short.

But of course that left Micah to cover one of the wide receivers. He had the speed. He shot off the line, trailing really well, and at just the right time took a great angle, shifting his body, throwing up an arm in the air, deflecting the ball just as it sailed towards the player he was covering.

"Yes!" Scott yelled, pumping his fist. It was just one play. But it was one play that could build on another, that could change a game. That could change a defense. That could completely alter a team's fate.

"He's gotta keep it up," Asa said into his ear.

There were at least a dozen coaching staff on the same frequency, exchanging quick notes about the game, about plays, so he *knew* Asa's words weren't only for him.

But instead, it felt like Asa was lying next to him, sharing a pillow, sharing their bed, and he'd murmured those words just for him.

He'd always felt that intimate connection with Asa, but it had never felt stronger. More immediate. More real.

He pushed the thought away, because he wasn't going to let this distract him during a game. Especially a game as important as this one.

He could focus, right? He was a professional, and had been doing this long enough that there were no excuses.

The offense set up for the next play.

Scott leaned forward, watching closely, and this time they tried a run, cutting back past the blocks, the running back dodging past one defender, then two, then he faced off against Howard. Howard made a split-second decision, and then went, but it was the wrong way, and Scott made an involuntary and completely horrified sound as he raced down the sideline and scored.

"You were sayin'?" Asa asked ruefully into the headset.

"It's gonna be fine, it's really gonna be fine," Scott repeated. Trying to will that belief into life.

But he couldn't deny, as the third quarter ticked down, and the fourth started, that he was losing his grip.

They were down 34 to 20, hadn't managed to get as much moving on offense as Scott knew Randy had hoped they could, and now, the Chiefs were driving again, probably hoping to eat up much of the fourth quarter clock and also . . . incidentally . . . get themselves to that magic forty points.

God, he regretted ever telling Asa that it could happen.

That some team could face off against the Piranhas and lay forty points on them. He felt like the harbinger of the worst luck, even though he knew it wasn't him. He'd merely been the messenger.

Micah had done better on his coverage assignments, but it wasn't perfect, and it seemed like a bad situation brewing on this drive, when they went to him again and again, and Scott found himself clenching his teeth, waiting for the inevitable.

It didn't happen.

Micah shadowed Kelce, going toe-to-toe with the big wide receiver, and in the end, it was damn good coverage. Good enough that Mahomes threw the ball away, and the Chiefs settled for a three-point try.

Even though they were losing by seventeen points, Scott could see Micah's face-splitting grin as he made his way back to the sideline.

Was it perfect? No. The defense had been beat up and battered during this game, and Scott could see Randy scrambling, trying to figure out a way for the Piranhas' offense to keep up.

In the end, they just couldn't.

They lost, 45 to 27, two scores short of what they'd needed to tie the game.

Pax had thrown a Hail Mary pass deep into coverage and it had gotten picked off, resulting in a touchdown going the other way. It hadn't mattered, but it was the nail in the coffin for the day. The final indignity, Scott decided, proud that instead of throwing his headset, which he kinda wanted to do, like Randy had done *twice*, he set it down on the desk in front of him.

The flight home was going to be a bitch.

No question about it.

Asa felt like hot garbage.

Funny how last week's game had ended in him going to the hospital for mysterious chest pains, and somehow that had still felt like a better finale than this week's game.

"I really thought we were gonna pull that one out," Beau said glumly.

Asa hadn't coached many total disasters, but from the beginning, this had felt like one of them. So, he *hadn't* expected that they might actually figure out how to pull out a win, but would it have been nice?

Yeah, because he wouldn't be feeling like this right now. While keeping the worst of his panic out of his face, because the last thing they needed right now was for the players to realize just how much of an epic fail their play had been.

"I'm gonna go deal with the reporters," Asa said, not answering Beau's unspoken question. It wasn't that he didn't trust Beau not to give the truth away—he was too smart, and he knew better—but there was a confused bewilderment on his face that hurt more than even seeing the screens around the stadium lit up with the final score.

He'd let Beau down.

He'd let the team down.

He'd let the players down.

And even worse, he'd sent Pax out to win a game he couldn't possibly win.

Guilt crawled through him in a nauseating wave.

Facing the reporters would be easier than facing Pax, but he was who he needed to talk to first.

The Chiefs' media room was in the basement, nearly in the same area as the Piranhas'. He found Pax in a hallway a few dozen yards away, just like he'd expected he would.

And also like he'd expected, Pax wasn't alone.

Davis was leaning against the wall, he hadn't changed from the game yet, and his dark hair was pushed back, still damp with sweat.

Pax leaned against him, his forehead tipped against Davis', and they weren't speaking.

Asa knew they were in love. He'd known for awhile, and Davis had flat-out told him they were.

But this was a painfully intimate moment.

You did this, you paired them up, like you hoped this would happen.

In fact, he really hadn't. He'd hoped they'd be good for each other. Not that they'd be crazy about each other.

He cleared his throat and Pax glanced over.

"Sorry, Coach," he mumbled, and as wretched as Asa felt, it was reflected in the misery in Pax's eyes.

It was one thing to hate losing. Asa hated losing, too. But it was entirely another to internalize it the way Pax was starting to.

Which was why he was here.

He couldn't possibly let Pax take full responsibility for what had happened today.

"Hey, it's alright," Asa said, meaning it. If he'd thought he could get away with sneaking off and spending even five minutes with Scott, he'd have done it. But he was the head coach of this football team, and he had responsibilities.

Starting with this one.

"I need to talk to him, for a second, if you don't mind, Davis," Asa continued, directing the comment at the tall, dark-haired man.

Reluctantly, Pax broke away from his boyfriend.

Davis *didn't* shoot Asa a look that promised retribution if he made Pax feel worse, but Asa supposed that he wouldn't blame him much if he had.

"I'll see you on the bus," Davis said. The glance Pax shot him as he turned the corner was as good as a kiss.

Asa had to wonder if he and Scott were that obvious. Surely not.

But *oh God,* what if they were?

That, his brain reminded him, was a problem for a different day.

"I just wanted to tell you, I thought you played real good today, Pax," Asa said, all too aware that Pax was currently bracing for the worst.

"What?" Pax sounded startled. "But we . . . we *lost.*"

"Yes, we did. But that loss, that loss is entirely on me. Not on you. You put us in a position to win."

"Not enough, not in the third quarter," Pax muttered. "Definitely not enough in the fourth."

"Bullshit," Asa said succinctly. "You didn't turn the ball over except at the very end. You drove the team down the field more than once. Nobody is ever expectin' you to score forty-plus points, Pax. Nobody. Not even me."

Asa watched as Pax absorbed this. His back straightened a little, and he looked less haunted. Less totally absorbed by the loss.

Did Asa feel any better? Not really, but this was his job. His burden that he'd agreed to carry.

And he'd carry it when it became too great for his players to bear.

"Alright," Pax said. He hesitated. "You know just about anyone else would've blamed me."

Asa knew.

It made him angry enough to want to scream. Burn it all down. What gave those men the right to grind these men below their heels, like they were expendable? Like their bodies and their hearts were merely fodder for the machine of football?

Asa didn't know, but he wasn't ever going to be that kind of coach.

"I'm not that kind of coach, Pax. You know that."

"I do." Pax met his gaze, and his own didn't waver. "Thank God for that."

Maybe he did feel a little better as he headed towards the media room, where Helen was waiting for him in the hallway, by the door that led to where everyone waited, ready to feast on his mistakes.

"Tough loss," she said.

Asa rolled his eyes.

"Okay, that's a gross understatement," she said briskly. "But I was trying to be nice."

"I'll try to remember that when these vultures try to tear me apart," Asa said wryly.

Helen shrugged. "You never let them own you. Just keep doing that."

Asa didn't think he'd ever get used to the cascade of blinding bulb flashes as he took the podium.

Sometimes he took questions first. Sometimes he talked a bit first.

Today, it was a no-brainer which he was going to do.

"First, y'all, I want to start with a quick statement. I take full and personal responsibility for today's loss. The defensive decision that led to all those touchdowns in the first half, that's on me."

"Not on Brett Jackson?" Julian Anderson, the most annoying reporter of the bunch, called out, naming the defensive coordinator.

"No, it's on me," Asa said. "I help put together the defensive scheme. I finalize it." It was a little white lie. He hadn't helped Brett put it together, but he'd approved it. He'd not spent the time he should've, making sure it was sound.

He should've seen what Scott had seen in an instant.

What the Chiefs had clearly seen.

"This loss is on me. Pax and the offense aren't designed to score forty points. Would it be great if they could? I think they've got that ceiling, and more, but they're still gelling, still gettin' their feet under them, and I won't ask that of them. Pax did the best job in a shit position, playing from behind the whole game. He had some great throws. Some really excellent reads. He stretched the field, gave Kenyon some room to run. I was really pleased with the offensive game plan and how it worked."

Helen stepped forward. "We have time for a few questions before Coach has to grab his ride back to Miami."

"What happened with the defensive scheme? Looks like you tried to adjust it a bit, move Howard into a different position, leaving Rose to handle some of the coverages by himself."

Of course Julian was the first and the loudest.

Asa supposed he should've admired his fortitude and his obvious drive.

He didn't. At all.

"We tried some adjustments at halftime," Asa acknowledged. "We'll be fine-tunin' those, during this week's practices."

"Do you think the Bears watched this game?" It was another reporter this time, but Asa mentally ground his teeth together at the question.

"I'm sure the Bears and all the remaining opponents on our schedule will pick this one apart," Asa said. "But, and I stress this, we take this game and *every* game real serious. We're going to find ways to win. I know we will. We've got the talent and the skill, on the field and off. I trust the guys. We'll find a way."

"Speaking of that," it was Julian again, because of course it was, "I saw a new guy with you guys, tall, with blond hair. Is that Scott Callaway? Did you add him to the coaching roster? Why make that kind of change mid-season?"

The blessing, Helen had said, in their first meeting after Asa's heart attack, was that the press had seemingly not gotten wind of the situation. They still didn't know what had happened, and Asa hoped that was the way it would stay.

But if they didn't know about his enforced hospital stay, of course they wouldn't know why he'd brought Scott on.

"We added Scott to the coaching staff because he brings a unique perspective to the defensive side of the ball," Asa said.

"That's it?" Julian questioned. "Didn't seem like he brought much this Sunday."

Asa had to stop himself from *actually* grinding his teeth together. "He had less than a week to prepare. He's already got plans for next week. Expect big things."

He stood up then, cutting the conference off, because he had no intention of listening to any more of this crap, and even less intention of answering it.

"Big plans?"

Asa looked up as he walked into his dark office, and he supposed he shouldn't be surprised that Scott was in here.

After all, he'd adopted this office as his own, and then there was the way they'd not gotten even a moment to talk.

On the plane ride home, he'd not been anywhere visible, not in the staff section of the plane anyway, and Asa had been afraid of looking a little too desperate as he searched for him.

Instead, he'd sat back in his seat, and tried to even out his breathing, using the meditation app that the doctor at the hospital had recommended.

"It seemed like a good thing to say at the time," Asa said flippantly. He didn't turn the light on, just approached his desk where Scott was leaning against it.

"No, you were pissed off and thought it might distract everyone to start making promises."

It was annoying how well Scott knew him.

"Yeah?" Asa challenged.

"Yeah," Scott agreed, the corner of his mouth tilting up into a smile. "Come 'ere." He reached for him and Asa had a brief debate with himself before he let himself be pulled into the warm, relaxing circle of Scott's arms.

"You're gonna be just fine," Scott said, his hand drawing broad sweeps up and down his back, both reassuring and distracting. "Just fine."

"I just hate it," Asa said, his voice cracking.

"I know."

He would.

He'd know just how much.

Which was why he was here. Why he'd known that somehow Asa would elude Beau's determined efforts to get him to go home, and he'd come here anyway.

Asa took one shuddering, deep breath, and then another. And another.

It helped.

Finally, he pulled away and took a step back from Scott. Because if he kept close, he was gonna want to get all the way close, and that was not gonna happen in his office, of all goddamned places.

"What are we doin', Scott?" Asa asked.

The question he'd been trying to shut out during all his meditation, but hadn't been able to silence entirely.

Then he'd seen Scott and it had all come rushing back, just as insistent as it had been, sitting in front of those reporters, taking responsibility for getting blown out.

Scott's forehead creased. "Tonight? Well, I'm here, and the generic plan was to try to convince you to go home and get some sleep, come back early in the morning and we'd tear it all apart. Put it back together again."

"I mean, what are we doin' with *us*," Asa said, hating how stupidly plaintive he sounded. How pathetic. How absolutely lovesick.

"Oh. *Oh.* Well . . ." Scott rubbed his chin. "I sorta thought we were doin' what we should've done seven years ago. Maybe we did it in a weird order, fallin' in love and *then* being together, but does it matter how it happens, long as it happens?"

Asa wanted to say no, it didn't matter.

Because to his heart, mending itself back together after so long fractured and broken, it didn't in the least.

"And," Scott said, his tone growing all firm and certain and, Asa couldn't deny it any longer, *dead fucking sexy*, "don't you dare say this has anything to do with the loss today. You know it doesn't. You're just panicking, looking for patterns. And this, this right here"—Scott was suddenly right there in front of him again, and it felt so natural to just touch him, to dig his fingers into his muscular shoulder—"this right here is the best thing that ever happened to me, and I'm gonna go out on a limb and say the best thing that ever happened to you too. We can have both. We *should* have both."

"Football and a life?"

"Yeah," Scott said.

Asa didn't say anything. He knew, in the logical part of his brain, that Scott was right. The two things were not connected. They'd reconnected, and the Piranhas had lost to the Chiefs.

Maybe without Scott to at least give them a heads-up, it would've been even worse.

They'd have been unprepared, unable to even attempt implementing a new scheme.

"Actually, I was thinkin' . . . I was thinkin' how glad I was that you were here today."

Scott looked floored. "Really?"

Asa nodded. "How much worse this would've been without you." He paused. "And," he added wryly, "how shitty it would've been to go home alone to my empty place."

"I can help with that, for sure," Scott said, reaching out and tangling his fingers with Asa's, squeezing them.

"Thought you might."

It hurt to let go of Scott's hand, but there might still be people in the building. Asa might not have been the only one who'd taken the loss hard and was working tonight.

He might have accepted that Scott was in his life to stay. But he knew neither of them knew how to tell anyone else—and if he *was* going to tell anyone, he was going to have to start with Beau.

"Also thought you should know, Micah's on board," Scott said as they headed down the stairs towards the ground floor.

Asa was surprised. But not really. Not when he really thought about it. "That's where you were on the ride home. With Micah."

"We broke the coverage down, play by play, and I can't believe I'm even sayin' this, but he sounds . . . I don't know, *invigorated* almost, like he can suddenly see a different vision of himself, and he wants that."

It wasn't surprising to hear Scott tell him about the new-and-hopefully-improved Micah Rose, because the truth was, Scott was a freaking miracle worker.

He could turn any player into the better, and sometimes even the best, version of themselves.

He'd done it, too, with Asa.

Turned him from a cold, lonely shadow of his former self, back into a flesh-and-blood man.

A man who felt and loved and *wanted*.

"Thank you," Asa said, interrupting Scott's impassioned declaration of how much Micah had grasped during their film session.

"For helpin' him, of course. You know that's partly what I'm here for," Scott said, glancing over at him.

"For that, yeah, but for being here. With me."

Scott smiled slow and sweet. Asa's stomach somersaulted, plain and simple. "Asa," he said seriously, "I mean it when I say it's absolutely my pleasure."

Chapter Ten

"If you're too tired, we can just . . ."

"No," Asa didn't even let Scott finish his sentence. "Absolutely fucking not. You told me you were takin' me on a date and you're takin' me on a date. Unless . . ." He shot Scott a firm glance. "Unless you're backing out?"

"I'm not backing out, I just wanted to make sure you still wanted to go. Trust me, I'd much rather go out with you than sit here in this office and work," Scott said, clearly amused as he leaned back in his chair.

For as long as he'd known him, Scott hadn't shirked work. In fact, if something needed to be done, he'd usually be first in line to get it done.

But as hard as he worked, he played hard too. That was something Asa wished he could learn.

Maybe he could ask Scott to teach him.

Or maybe Scott was planning on teaching him, no matter if he asked for it or not.

"Besides," Scott continued with a smug grin, "I made some pretty great plans, and I'd hate to cancel them."

"You gonna tell me what these great plans are?" Asa wondered as he shut his computer down. It had been a long-ass day of meetings, and like Scott had promised they'd do, they'd gotten here early this morning, and started breaking down yesterday's game film.

Normally, he'd follow up all those meetings with some additional work, but even if Scott hadn't arrived here, even if Beau hadn't made all his threats, Asa had known the time was coming where he didn't have a choice but to slow down.

"Nope," Scott said, still grinning.

Still looking very satisfied with himself.

"Alright. Do we need to change or can I go in this?" He was in khakis and a Piranhas polo, though Scott was in his own normal uniform of jeans and a t-shirt, and somehow making even that casual attire look hot as hell.

It defied logic.

"Nope, you look fine," Scott said, standing up. Asa followed suit. "You ready to go?"

Asa nodded, but he couldn't deny his heart beat a little bit faster as they walked down the hall towards the elevator together, even as he tried to mentally get over the guilt he felt at leaving early.

It's not early, it's normal time, it's almost five, Asa reminded himself.

"You breakin' out in hives yet?" Scott teased as the elevator carrying them moved towards the ground floor.

Asa rolled his eyes. "'Course not," he insisted. Even though he was lying, and they both knew it.

"Leavin' at five on a Monday. Hell must've frozen over."

"You must think you're real cute," Asa retorted.

Scott just smiled. "Yeah, actually, I do. Or maybe it's this guy I'm seeing. He keeps telling me how gorgeous I am."

It was like every time Scott's shirt came off, Asa lost his brain-to-mouth filter.

That was the only reason for it.

Asa nudged him with his hip, right before the door opened. "Maybe 'cause you are," he murmured, and the look in Scott's eyes—affectionate and warm and so loving—nearly made him open his mouth and say, "Forget the date, let's just go to my place and you can do that thing I wanted you to do Saturday."

Nearly.

But the truth was, as much as Asa wanted to drag him home by his teeth, he also wanted a chance to do this too. A date with Scott, something he'd never imagined he'd have, ever.

Even seven years ago, that had been a pipe dream.

Now it was a reality.

The door dinged open, and there was Sebastian, waiting to take the elevator.

"Coach, Coach," he said formally, nodding acknowledgement. But Asa was sure there was some kind of twinkle of knowledge in his eyes. Did he know? Had he told Beau?

No, at least he hadn't told Beau, because if he had, Asa would know—because Beau would've read him the riot act instead of sitting next to him just an hour ago, nodding along to one of his suggestions during their last meeting.

It was Monday—technically a day the players had off, and though Sebastian was in his workout gear, Asa knew he'd come to see Beau.

Especially when he spied the takeout bag he was carrying.

"You two off?" Sebastian asked.

"Yeah, leaving at five. What a novel concept," Scott said.

"I'm just bringing Beau some dinner 'cause he won't see sense and do the same as y'all," Sebastian said.

Asa nodded to his son's partner, heart in his throat as they headed out the front door.

They were in the cab, on their way to an address Asa didn't recognize, when Scott spoke up.

"I think Sebastian might know." His voice was guarded.

"What?" Asa wasn't proud, he might've half screeched that question. He'd thought he was the only one who suspected that his son's partner knew, but if Scott did too . . .

Well, shit.

"You didn't see his face the other night? He's guessed."

"And he hasn't told Beau."

"One point in his favor," Scott said wryly.

"We're only givin' him one point for that? How 'bout a hundred?"

Scott chuckled under his breath, like this was funny. It wasn't.

He wasn't ready to tell Beau yet. He didn't know how he'd even start.

Son, when a man loves a man and . . . And well, *something*. It wasn't like Asa had to even explain that part of it to his son.

It was the "I'm not straight, either" part.

It was the "Scott is who made me realize I wasn't" part.

Those were the damning parts—which was probably why Sebastian hadn't said anything yet. He knew just how damning they were gonna be.

"I don't think he's going to tell Beau," Scott pointed out. "And I don't see Beau figuring it out either, in case you were worried about that."

"Of course I'm worried about that," Asa said. "Beau sees me on a pedestal. He'd never imagine I'd keep this from him. Because I gotta be the one to tell him. But how? I don't even know where to begin."

"I have to ask . . ." Scott hesitated. "Why didn't you tell him before?"

"You mean, when you left?" When Scott nodded, Asa sighed and flopped back against the ratty cab seat. "Because I thought it was over. And honestly I didn't have the words then, *especially* then, to tell him how it felt, what it meant. So I didn't, and then there never seemed to be the right time, or maybe I never had the right words, and then I decided it didn't matter after all, because the chance of you coming back into our lives was slim to none . . ."

Scott's expression was horribly sympathetic. It galled Asa. He *should* have found a way then, and he was going to pay for it now.

And telling Beau that he regretted it wasn't going to make a damn bit of difference in his reaction.

"Guess you were wrong about that," Scott said.

"I'm glad I was," Asa said. "In case I haven't said so. Though, I'm assumin' you got the gist of how I felt about it."

Scott grinned. "Sure did."

The cab pulled up, Scott pulled a couple of bills from his wallet, and they got out.

Asa hadn't realized it, but they'd driven all the way to the water, almost.

He could smell the salt in the air, and feel it on the breeze.

"We're just over here, at this cute little place," Scott said, gesturing towards one of the smaller buildings lining the harbor.

The sun was just beginning to set, as they walked into the restaurant.

"Two for Callaway," Scott said to the hostess standing up at the greeting station.

"Sure thing, it says here you wanted harbor view?" she asked.

"Yep, please, if it's possible."

The hostess smiled, shooting Asa a knowing look. "Of course. Only the best for our hometown coach."

Well, Asa supposed the two of them going out to dinner wasn't automatically a date. And if people talked? So what. He didn't have to confirm anything. He just worried about what people might say and how that might affect Scott. He'd never wanted to be out, and Asa didn't know if that had changed.

The table was by one of the big plate glass windows that overlooked the bay, and as they examined their menus, darkness began to fall.

"This is really nice," Asa said as he looked over the menu. The food seemed to be mostly vegetarian or even vegan, but to his surprise, a lot of the dishes sounded delicious. Creative and interesting, even.

"It came highly recommended, and extra bonus," Scott added with a knowing grin, "it's got a great view."

"Too bad we missed most of the sunset," Asa said.

"Oh," Scott said, "that wasn't the view I was talkin' about."

"What view, then?"

"Back at Tennessee, how often did I tell you to slow down and smell the roses?" Scott asked, leaning back in his chair. Looking like they had all the time in the world.

"Way too often, even though I don't much like the scent of roses," Asa said dryly.

"Well, think of tonight as slowin' down to see the lights, or something like that."

Scott looked absolutely delighted with himself.

"What lights?" Asa was afraid this was totally a holiday cheer thing. Even though he'd absolutely forbidden any more holiday cheer. He'd done his part with the stupid Secret Santa, giving Scott his "small gift," though he had yet to receive his own. He'd even sent Scott an idea for Kenyon, a gift subscription to an audiobook service that he could use while working out or traveling.

He'd even endured that movie Beau had insisted they watch, though in the end, he'd enjoyed it more than he'd anticipated.

"It's a whole flotilla of lights. All the boat owners in this club decorate their yachts and sail around the harbor. I was told this was the absolute best vantage point."

"And let me guess, you thought of me," Asa said. Trying to be pleased. *Trying*.

"Nope." Scott looked so amused. "I thought of how you gotta stop trying to pretend you're some kind of Grinch when we both know better."

"The magic of the holiday spirit isn't going to change me, Scott."

"Oh, I bet it might. And honestly? I'm a betting man."

Asa knew it 'cause he'd lost a number of bets to him over the years. Silly bets, all of them, and for absolutely silly things, and it wasn't like this one wasn't silly, too.

But fine, if Scott wanted to have dinner while a whole bunch of lit-up boats floated past them, *fine*. He could do that.

Their appetizer had just arrived at the table, and he was dipping a piece of grilled pita bread into the bowl of lemon dill hummus they'd ordered when the first boat floated by.

It was decked from fore to aft in bright white twinkling lights, but that wasn't even remotely all. There were small lit green and red wreaths hung every few feet, and then Asa watched with an audible gasp as a monkey with a big red bow around its neck, created entirely from lights, began to jump through each wreath like it was a hoop and the boat was the center ring in a circus.

It was a breathtaking feat of lighting prowess and engineering and Asa watched it once, then twice, and then a third time, until he'd have to crane his neck to keep watching.

When he finally glanced back at Scott, he had his arms crossed over his chest and he was beaming.

"Too bad it's just holiday crap, right?" he asked, dipping a cucumber slice into the hummus and popping it into his mouth.

Asa stuck his tongue out. Not very mature of him but then Scott laughed and it didn't matter.

It was like they were twenty again, sneaking out with a six-pack, trying to find the best view of the river to toast to, just the two of them against the rest of the world.

He'd never wanted—or needed—anyone else.

"We didn't arrange what you'd get if you won the bet," Asa said.

"Oh, was there a bet?" Scott teased, when he knew perfectly well there'd been an unspoken bet. "If there was, I know exactly what I want to win."

"What?" Asa asked, expecting maybe to pay for this dinner. Or the next. Or maybe the next ten. He didn't mind. He had money—though Scott did, too—and he certainly didn't mind spending it on him.

"You. Tonight." Scott's gaze was very steady, very serious, and made Asa instantaneously hot under the collar—and hot a lot of other places, too.

"You already got me, though." Asa cleared his throat.

"Alright." Scott leaned forward. "You, absolutely at my mercy, with no complaints."

A thrill shot through Asa. A little dinner teasing shouldn't make him this hard, but he was as hard as he'd ever been, imagining it. Wondering how it would go. Would Scott take it easy on him? Would he make him beg? Plead? Scream?

"Is that what you want?" Asa heard how low and rough his voice was. And there was no way, from the satisfaction blooming across Scott's face, that he hadn't heard it too.

"More than anything," Scott said. "More than the next breath I'll take."

Asa shuddered, suddenly overwhelmed by the need he felt. By the love in Scott's eyes.

"Darlin'," Scott said, dropping his voice even lower, and leaning in, "you keep lookin' at me like that, we're gonna miss the next boat."

There was a part of Asa that wanted to miss *all* the boats.

But there was another part of him that liked sitting here like this, having dinner with Scott, and enjoying the lights floating by.

"And here comes another one," Scott said, drawing his attention outside. "Look at how cool this one looks."

It was decked out in bright red and white lights, with candy canes scattered along the hull, and in the middle, made entirely of lights, was a crew of elves baking cookies.

Or at least Asa was pretty sure that was what they were doing.

They finished up the hummus during the third boat—decorated with penguins, an igloo, and even a huge polar bear, opening his mouth and moving back and forth as the boat floated past.

"These rich folks have too much time on their hands," Scott said, shaking his head both in amazement and surprise.

"You're a rich folk too now," Asa reminded him as their entrees came to the table. Scott had gotten a steak with baked potato and broccoli, and Asa's own halibut with lemon wine sauce and risotto looked and smelled amazing. "Imagine what you'd be doing if you weren't coachin' football."

Scott shot him a look. "Yeah, what I was doin' before Beau called me. Fixin' up that old farmhouse I bought in my hometown. Gardening. Going to the high school games on Friday nights, and remembering why I loved to play. Why I loved to coach. It wasn't so bad, honestly."

Asa realized he'd never thought about it, not once. He'd been a football player, but he'd known, from almost the very beginning, that what he really wanted to be was a coach. He'd never considered doing anything else, though he'd once sworn to Scott that it wouldn't matter what he did. Who he coached. Even if it was the little kids' team down the street.

"Would've been better if you were there," Scott added. "But it was still nice."

It wasn't how Asa was made—because wasn't he meant to do this? He'd always believed he was—but he found himself saying, "I think it sounds nice."

Scott shot him a look full of disbelief.

"No, no, I actually mean it. I do," Asa said, and realized that he did.

"You're meant to do this, you're a coach these guys can trust and depend on," Scott said.

"Yes, but that doesn't mean I can't do anything else, ever," Asa pointed out. "What else is there? I don't know, I haven't thought about it, but I'm confident it wouldn't be that hard to figure out." He hesitated. "Especially if you were around."

Scott's hand reached over to Asa's and squeezed it for just a second, his heart in his eyes. "I'd say, no, I don't want you to give it up, but I'm done being noble, because all that got me was misery. And this way? This way gets me you."

Asa cleared his throat of the emotion that kept clogging it. "If this is some way to get me to accept holiday crap . . ."

Scott laughed. A deep belly laugh, like Asa was the funniest thing he'd ever heard.

That was a gift, too, like so many of Scott's others.

"Come on, you liked those penguins."

"And the candy canes, yes, and the elves. I did. More than I'm comfortable admitting to."

Scott's lips turned up into a knowing smirk. "Won't be the last time you admit *that* tonight," he said, and Asa was definitely just about ready for the date to come to an end. His pants couldn't get much tighter.

"And," he added, "you can stop looking like you're gonna ask to leave early. We're stayin', at least til the end of the holiday flotilla, so, darlin', you'd better sit back and enjoy every last ship."

"But—" Asa muttered.

"You promised: you at my mercy, with no complaints," Scott said smugly.

Asa knew that even under his unruffled calm, Scott was burning just the same way he was.

It wasn't that hard to spot, because he knew Scott.

Knew every expression, every glance, every flash in his eyes, and was beginning to recognize what they all meant.

"So, you're not gonna tell me your favorite boat?" Scott asked as they walked up to the elevator.

He asked it casually, like he hadn't been staring at Asa's mouth the whole cab ride back to his building.

Like he wasn't going to kiss Asa the moment they were alone in the elevator.

Asa hadn't ever considered the many nuances of sex, but he was beginning to appreciate—and also absolutely detest—the concept of delayed gratification.

He took a deep breath and told himself that it didn't matter how many more casual touches Scott gave him, how many times he'd "innocently" brush up against him, or touch his shoulder or his back or his hand, he was *not* going to pin him to the closest possible horizontal surface.

"I don't know why you care what my favorite boat was," Asa said, hearing the edge of frustration in his voice. How far Scott had pushed him. Anticipating just how much further he was going to push him.

"Oh, darlin', I care," Scott said.

"Alright, fine, the Santa one. You satisfied?"

Scott smirked as the elevator doors dinged open. "Not even remotely."

That was all the warning Asa got before *he* was the one who was pinned, and it wasn't a horizontal surface, it was the vertical wall of the elevator. But just like he'd predicted, Scott cupped his face in his palms, and then he was on him, kissing him fiercely.

Asa groaned as Scott's tongue stroked his own, really enjoying this sexually confident side of Scott. It pulled him right along, until he didn't even worry what was going to happen when they got into his apartment, he just wanted it. Didn't even matter what *it* was.

Scott's hands slid behind him and Asa felt his fingertips dig into his ass, yanking him hard against him.

It was the perfect amount of friction of his khaki-covered cock and yet not even remotely enough, at the very same time.

The elevator doors dinged open and Asa was a little surprised that when Scott moved to walk out of the elevator, he didn't just slide into a complete pile of mush on the floor.

"What, wait, what floor is this?" Asa said, realizing he was more than a little sluggish right now. Lust was crowding his thoughts right out.

"My floor," Scott said. "We're going to my place. Or I guess . . . the place Beau's lent me."

Scott reached for his hand and tugged him along, down the hallway, until they reached Beau's door and he punched his code in with trembling fingers.

Asa was expecting more bone-melting kisses immediately after they got inside, but instead, Scott just kept leading him, after they shed their shoes in the little entryway, down the hall, right towards the bedroom.

Scott let go of his hand and went to flip on a light in the corner of the room.

"We can stay here, if you want," Scott said softly, watching him, "or we can go back to your place. But there were some things I wanted to pick up first."

"Condoms." Asa's voice chose that moment to crack embarrassingly. "And lube."

Scott nodded. "Though the condoms are more of a formality. I'm assuming you've been spending all your time on sidelines and conference rooms, though it's okay if you haven't. I know I haven't been with anyone in a long time. But condoms . . . they'll be easier. Especially if . . ." Scott blew out a breath, and he was so keyed up, Asa felt like he was practically vibrating. "Especially if it's your first time."

"You know it is, and you know I haven't been with anyone else," Asa said. "Come over here. This isn't Beau's bed anyway. Beau's with Sebastian, he's been there with him for months now."

"Alright," Scott said and came over, wrapping Asa up in a tight hug. "God, I love you."

"I think you must," Asa said contemplatively. "How long, Scott?"

"Not as long as it's been for you," Scott teased.

"What did you tell me? It's not a competition."

"Eight years. Eight years, and some months and some kinda days." The corner of his mouth turned up. "I didn't keep track. Not exactly. Just knew . . . if it wasn't going to be with you, I didn't want anyone else."

Asa didn't answer in words. He just leaned in and kissed him.

It didn't take long for them to move to the bed, Asa shoving his hands up underneath Scott's t-shirt, groaning as he felt his chest and stomach pressed against his palms. Drifted lower, running his fingertips down Scott's hard length, still trapped in his jeans.

"Too . . . many . . . goddamned . . . clothes," Scott panted, after tearing his mouth off Asa's—and starting to yank Asa's polo off. Then he went to work on his belt and his khakis, stripping him naked.

"There," he said with satisfaction, kneeling in front of him, Asa squirming a little under the intensity of his gaze, "that's fucking perfect."

Asa raised an eyebrow. Aware that he wasn't exactly in a position to dictate, but . . . there was something so sweet about challenging Scott, pushing him *just* far enough.

"I was kinda hopin' for a little bit more," Asa said and spread his legs.

Scott swore, and then his hand was hot and heavy and right on his inner thigh, pulling him open even more. "I'm gonna make you feel so good, darlin'," he crooned, "so fucking good."

"Well, what are you waitin' for, then?" Asa asked.

But then he couldn't quite speak at all, because Scott's fingers were right there, pressing in, wet with lube, and Asa choked on his own breath. He'd experimented with this, with his own fingers, but it hadn't ever felt like this, had never been this intense, this amazing, before. Scott twisted his finger and Asa moaned.

His hand slid down his stomach and he cupped his own hard, leaking cock in his palm, giving himself an experimental tug as Scott's finger pushed deep.

"Yeah," Scott choked out, his cheeks flushed and his eyes burning bright with lust. "Oh, God, yes, please." Like he was the one being pleasured, even though Asa hadn't even laid a fingertip on him yet.

He was that worked up, because he was touching Asa, and Asa was touching himself.

"Like watching, huh?" Asa teased, and then wiggled on Scott's finger.

Scott didn't answer.

Instead, he glanced up, and his gaze burning into Asa, he slid a second finger in, twisting them both deep.

Asa keened as the pleasure hit him hard and fast, curling up inside him like a flame.

"That's right," Scott said, "show me you love it, darlin', show me how much you want it."

Oh, he wanted it. He wanted it *bad*.

He wanted to be so full of Scott he couldn't really breathe.

That had always been the fantasy that he'd reached for when he was tired or lonely or just too damn miserable without Scott. Scott pressing him down on the bed and filling him up, promising he'd never leave him again.

It had always made him come so hard he'd barely been able to walk after.

"Give me another one," Asa panted out.

Scott's surprise was smothered by determination, and after gathering more lube, he slowly stretched Asa out, going slow, but going deep, making sure he never forgot he was there, or what he was going to do, how hard he was gonna make him scream.

It felt damn good, too. So good that Asa had to let go of his cock, fisting his hands in the sheets, because he didn't want to come until Scott was all the way inside of him. He wanted it to last. To enjoy it.

"Come on," he begged, "I want you inside me."

Scott's fingers shook as he stripped the rest of his clothes off, exposing that big, beautiful body, and trembled as he ripped open the condom.

"Like this?" he asked, voice rough with desire and emotion as he positioned himself between Asa's legs. "I want to see you."

Asa nodded, past words. All he could do was feel.

Scott's calloused fingers on his knee, pressing into the tendon there, the stretch and the burn of his cock as it slipped in, the pressure relenting to a soft glide, the inescapable knowledge that Scott was sliding home.

"God, you feel . . ." Scott half cried, half sobbed, and Asa squeezed his eyes shut as he finished sliding in completely.

It was so much, an overwhelming awareness, but Asa never wanted to stop feeling it.

"Yes," he ground out. "*Yes.*"

When his eyelids flickered open, Scott was staring at him, complete wonder in his gaze.

"Please," was all Asa could say, but that was enough because Scott began to thrust then, gently at first, but then harder, faster, and Asa was lost.

He reached down, at the very last moment, and grasped his cock, pulling it in rhythm with Scott's thrusts, and then he was exploding into a million little pieces, his orgasm spinning out endlessly, as he pulsed into his fist, come dripping onto his chest.

Scott bellowed, hips stuttering, and then after half a dozen more gasps, it was over. Gloriously, perfectly over.

"Well," Asa said, still trying to catch his breath as Scott pulled out and fell to the bed next to him in a panting heap, "if all holiday cheer is like that, sign me up for Christmas every year."

There was no other way to describe it. Scott just *giggled*. He'd probably never admit it, but Asa knew the truth.

Asa knew all the truths now.

He loved this man, and he wasn't giving him up.

But more than that, too.

Because he knew Scott wasn't going to leave again. He was fighting this time, with every bit of strength he had, and maybe if the two of them held on to each other and gave it their all, it would be enough.

They could keep each other.

Chapter Eleven

Asa's first test came two days later.

Rudy Gonzalez, the owner of the Piranhas, had been fairly hands off when it came to the management of the team. It helped that most of what they'd done since the season had started was win.

They'd lost those two games to start the season, and then only one more, in week seven. And, even more, the Piranhas had found more than one way to win games. They'd had games they won with offense and defense and even special teams. Rudy wasn't stupid; he wasn't going to micromanage him when there was very little to improve on.

But that confidence in Asa and the system he wanted to implement had lost a little of its shine with the bad loss to Kansas City. Asa knew it from Rudy's comments after the game, when he'd said, "As long as we keep making money, I don't care what the record is," and when he got the email first thing this morning from Rudy's personal assistant, Taylor, who informed—didn't ask, just informed—him that he'd be having lunch with Rudy today.

The apprehension must have shown on Asa's face, even though he'd tried to hide it, because Scott had asked him as he'd stood up to head towards the owner's suite of offices on the top floor, if he was alright.

"It's just a lunch," Asa said, like he could convince himself of that particular fact. They were nine and four. There were four games left before the end of the season. If they even won half of those, they'd have won *ten* more games than the Piranhas had the year before. They were heading to the playoffs, the only factor left to be determined was what seed they'd be. Who they'd have to go and play.

It was an enormous achievement, and Asa wasn't going to let Rudy start voicing dire predictions, just because they'd lost one game. Even if that loss had been a brutal one.

"How often do you go to lunch with the owner?" Scott asked casually.

Asa made a face as he straightened his clothes. "Alright, you got me. Almost never. I'm sure he's got something to say about the last game, but it's fine. It's going to be fine."

Scott's gaze was warm, like a physical touch. He could tell, from the look alone, that Scott wished he could reach over and hug him, but it was the middle of the day, on a Wednesday. Staff was everywhere, and they'd certainly be surprised if they walked in and saw their head coach embracing the new special consultant to the head coach.

"I agree," Scott said, "you're gonna be fine. I just wanted to make sure you knew that."

Asa rolled his eyes. "I'm not that fragile, you know."

"Not fragile . . ." Scott hesitated and then caught his arm as Asa walked towards the door. Held his forearm in his hand for a split second, and maybe it wasn't quite enough, but it was still plenty. "Precious."

Asa didn't know what to say. But he felt it, the love in Scott's eyes. There was no denying it, he wanted this job, he wanted to *keep* this job, but what if everything fell apart? What if they just had this one perfect year, and that was it? Would he be able to do what he proclaimed to Scott he would be satisfied with, coaching the kids' team down the street from his farmhouse in Tennessee?

Nothing ever came guaranteed. But Asa didn't think he'd be entirely dissatisfied. He'd have a life. Football, in some form, and a life.

That thought was occupying the back part of his brain as he met with Rudy, and sat in the private dining room off his office. Made small talk. Rudy asked about how Scott was fitting in. Asa choked a bit on his bite of spring mix, but he recovered.

"Good, good," Asa said, after clearing his throat. "He's workin' with Micah Rose a lot, and of course Brett on re-envisioning the defensive scheme."

"You think it's gonna be better next week?" Rudy asked, leaning back in his chair.

Rudy had finally worked himself around to the point of the conversation.

Asa dismissed thoughts of evenings relaxing on the porch with Scott, curling up on the couch together to watch Sunday morning football games, and puttering around the kitchen, sniping at each other as they tried to make dinner—and focused.

"I do, I think it was actually better in the second half," Asa said, "but we were already too far behind to make a dent in their lead. Pax and the offense are comin' along, but they're not designed to come from two or three touchdowns back. I put this team together to be balanced, the defense not allowing more points than the offense could score."

Rudy made a noncommittal noise. The problem was that Asa *liked* Rudy. Had liked him from their first meeting in January.

They'd been aligned, nearly from the very beginning, on what they wanted for the Piranhas. A return to form. Shaping a new franchise quarterback. Bringing back old fans who'd gotten disillusioned and convincing new fans to join them.

They'd seen what the fans represented differently, of course. Rudy had seen dollar signs and a re-invigorated franchise willing to spend their hard-earned dollars. Asa had seen a team and a fanbase that could hold their heads high again.

"Seems like that didn't happen last week," Rudy said.

"We're going to have setbacks, especially in the first year of a program that's been totally overhauled from the year before," Asa pointed out. "We talked about this." They had. But then they'd come out of the gate strong, at least after those first two games. And he had a feeling Rudy had forgotten all about his warnings after the team had been so unexpectedly successful.

"I know, I know you said it. I know."

"Going into Arrowhead with the way the Chiefs have been playing was always going to be a challenge. I'd hoped we'd hang with them a bit better, but we'll get there."

"They're the playoff standard, Asa," Rudy reminded him, none too gently. "We can't just get there. Not if we want to have a chance in hell of winning this year."

"Rudy," Asa said gently, trying to keep his exasperation in check. "We're not going to win a Super Bowl this year. It's a great goal, of course, but we're still rebuilding. Pax needs more confidence. I'm still trying to find the right defensive staff. We're gonna get there, because I know we will, not just 'cause I promised you we would."

"Playoffs are where the money is, you know that. And season tickets."

"Last email the sales staff sent out, it seemed like they were up."

"They hiccuped this week. Stagnated." Rudy poured himself another glass of water. "I'm sure that doesn't have anything to do with getting blown out by the Chiefs."

"Of course not," Asa said. But he knew what Rudy suspected anyway.

He hadn't exactly made it a secret.

It was frustrating because he'd done everything he could to try to temper Rudy's expectations early. There'd been the fear after the first two games that everything was gonna be a disaster, but then the team had turned it around to an extent that now Rudy was gettin' crazy ideas in his head about winning a Super Bowl this year.

It wasn't going to happen.

Not like Asa wouldn't have *loved* that, but the Chiefs game had punctured that dream pretty thoroughly. They needed more work. They could use another offensive playmaker. A few more linebackers. Asa knew they weren't pressuring the opposing quarterback enough, and as a result, that was putting a lot more burden on the secondary—Sebastian and Micah, specifically. It was why the Chiefs had been able to pick them apart so easily.

"I just thought," Rudy said, "it was a good idea to check in, see how things are going. And they're going well. Mostly."

"Taking last week out of the equation, yes."

"And Scott's fitting in, that's good. I know you weren't happy about him coming here."

"He's helpin' with the load. And Beau too, of course."

"Lots of noise about Beau getting wooed for a head coaching job of his own next year. Maybe a small college."

"He's too young," Asa said. "Brilliant, but he still has a ways to go. He knows that. He's not going anywhere." He didn't add because Sebastian's contract was for another three years, and there didn't seem to be any push to trade him, not since he'd really begun to come into his own as a safety.

"Good, 'cause I'd hate to lose him." Rudy hesitated. "Hate to lose you, either, Asa, of course."

"Of course," Asa said dryly.

He left the owner's suite not feeling *better*, necessarily, because even though Rudy had veiled the threat more than he'd anticipated, it had still been there.

Rudy wanted to win at least one playoff game.

Asa wasn't dumb; he knew to have the best chance of doing that, they'd need to have a decent seeding, and the last four games of the season would absolutely determine that.

He walked back into his office, surprised to see that the door was closed, the light was off. Scott had mentioned he was going to try to fit a workout in after lunch and before practice, so he wasn't surprised to see it empty, but Scott had never locked it up before.

But when Asa turned the handle, it went easily, and then suddenly, as he went through the door, the lights flashed on and he was blinded.

Not by the lights.

Not by the sudden blaring noise, the Jackson 5 proclaiming they'd just seen Mommy kissing Santa Claus, but by the metric ton of glitter and fake snow falling all around him.

All *over* him.

What fucking fresh hell was this?

He bellowed and almost instantaneously his door was full of staff and players, but the person laughing the longest and loudest was Logan, and Asa knew, he *knew* who was responsible for the glitter cloud not only currently residing in his office but coating him in a thick layer of enforced holiday cheer.

Fucking holiday cheer.

He was trying not to hate it but everyone around him was making it damn difficult.

"Dad!" Beau wiggled his way through the throng of laughing players, almost all of them with their phones out, recording their glowering coach, currently covered in glitter and fake snow.

"I'm fine, I'm fine. Just . . ." Asa hesitated.

There were two ways he could play this.

The *pissed off, how fucking dare you, fire and brimstone* way. The *Grinch* way, a voice in his head that sounded suspiciously like Scott pointed out.

Or, he could laugh it off, like the harmless prank it was, and indulge in the joy it had brought to everyone else around him.

He knew what kind of coach he'd always wanted to be. He was tough, when the situation called for it, but he bent too, when he sensed that was what his guys needed.

It had been a very tough week of practice. Asa, Scott, Beau, and the rest of the coordinators had kept the players late every practice. Meetings had been longer than usual. Everyone had been forced to find a new gear.

But that kind of unrelenting pressure, it took a toll.

Asa relaxed his face into a smile. "I'm fine," he repeated. "Just a bit overwhelmed by the holiday spirit, I'm afraid."

The tone of the room relaxed another notch as Beau reached up and brushed red and green glitter and tufts of white snow off the top of his head. "I can see that," he said, amusement crinkling his features.

"Coach, you all good?" Dylan asked, having the nerve to walk in with a knowing grin on his face.

Maybe Logan had arranged this—and God help him, it seemed painfully obvious Logan had ended up his Secret Santa, because clearly fate did not have a sense of humor—but there was no way Dylan hadn't been with him every step of the way, from the planning to the execution.

"Yep," Asa told him, patting him on the back, depositing a healthy amount of glitter onto his t-shirt, "just someone tryin' to make sure I've got a decent dose of holiday cheer for this week's game. I gotta applaud them, nobody else would've tackled the impossible." The music had finally stopped blaring, not surprisingly coinciding with Dylan and Logan's arrival.

Dylan grinned. "'Course not."

There was another commotion at the doorway, and reluctantly, everyone stepped aside to let the new arrivals through: Scott, with a look of complete astonishment on his face, and a group of five, wearing shirts that proclaimed they were part of the best cleaning crew in Miami.

Asa raised an eyebrow as they approached. The leader shook his head, chuckling under his breath. "I didn't understand what the guy who hired us meant when he said we'd have our work cut out for us but I get it now."

"Wait," Scott said, mystified, "you were hired to come clean this up?"

"Yes, sir," the man said. "Booked with a huge tip, too, if we could be here exactly right now."

Asa chuckled. Only Logan would make a huge mess and then pay someone to clean it up.

"Well, don't let me stop you," Asa said.

The man glanced over at him, giving him a full head-to-toe perusal. "You need any cleanin', Coach?"

Asa laughed. "No, no, I'll brush off now though, get the worst of it off."

"Gonna take more than that." Scott chuckled under his breath.

"Nothin' else to see here," Logan proclaimed, shuffling everyone out of the office, leaving just Scott, Asa, and the cleaning crew, who had already pulled out several portable vacuums and were beginning to suck up all the holiday cheer.

"I'm sure I'll be cleaning glitter out of every nook and cranny for the next year," Asa said dryly as he approached his desk.

Scott's bright eyes proclaimed he'd be happy to find every last speck.

Sitting in the middle of his desk was a box. Plain brown cardboard. Asa gave it a suspicious glance, like it could be a snake—or one of those creepy Elf on a Shelf dolls.

There was a note next to the box, and on it, written in gold sparkling capital letters, was one phrase: "Keep your loved ones close during the holidays."

Asa glanced at the box again, not feeling even remotely less suspicious. "Loved ones"? Had someone guessed that he and Scott were involved? Did the mysterious gift leaver—almost certainly Logan, because this had to be another Secret Santa surprise—know? And *how* did they know?

Scott had said he thought Sebastian had guessed. He and Logan were close, so maybe Sebastian had confessed his suspicions to Logan. He just hoped that whoever he told wouldn't tell Beau.

That was on him, if he could figure out how to freaking do it, the right words to say.

"Well, you gonna open it?" Scott asked, jerking him out of his reverie.

The cleaning crew had flipped off their vacuums and were now working on the walls, wiping down the last bit of glitter.

Asa had to give Logan credit; at least he'd made sure Asa didn't have to work in all this.

"I'm almost afraid to. What if something worse pops out?"

"Worse than all that glitter?" Scott raised an eyebrow.

"Point taken," Asa said, amused. He turned to the head of the cleaning crew. "You guys contracted to clean up any more messes here today?"

The man shook his head. Asa scribbled down the name of the company on their shirts and made a note to have Kelly send them all game tickets. Even if Logan had paid them well, they deserved it for dealing with all of this crap.

It couldn't have been easy, even if they'd done it with smiles on their faces.

"Well, I think you're safe," Scott said.

Asa popped open the box and took a long second to read the colorful note nestled in the top of the box. "This is . . . well, I believe this is a 'date box.'"

"A date box?" Scott peered in, the warmth from his skin leaking into Asa.

"We're all done, Coach. Good luck next week, we're rootin' for you!" Asa glanced up as the cleaning crew departed, nearly as silently as they'd come.

"A date box," Asa said. "Like a *date* date box. Not a box full of sweet edible fruits."

"Ah." Scott put a hand on Asa's back, and it was miraculously even warmer. Asa wished they were not in his office, so he could put his hands a lot of other places too. Even though they had practice soon, and he should be focusing and not thinking about what they might do with a little privacy. "So Sebastian did figure it out."

"It seems likely," Asa said. "And that he told Logan."

"Oh, you think Logan's responsible for this?"

"I know so," Asa said, his tone wry.

"So Sebastian told Logan, but not his own boyfriend. Well, it seems when Beau finally does find out, we're not gonna be the only ones in trouble."

Asa chuckled, even as he felt the clock ticking. He should have already told his son. He knew it wasn't going to get easier, and yet he hadn't done it. The right words or not.

"Well, what kind of date is it?" Scott asked, leaning in a bit closer. "I like the idea of more dates."

"You'd better," Asa said, elbowing him.

Scott looked plenty pleased with himself.

"It's a holiday-themed date," Asa said. "Apparently we're going to make cookies and *decorate* them. Then"—he looked closer at the card, which described the contents of the box—"we're going to play holiday trivia, which I'm sure you'll excel at."

"Seems likely," Scott said with a faux seriousness. "I do love me some holiday trivia."

"We'll . . . we'll make time next week, alright?" Asa said. "I just gotta . . . we gotta turn things around."

"Your meeting with Rudy?"

"It was fine." Asa made a face, all too aware he was grimacing. "That's the best I can say about it."

"Then we're gonna win," Scott said confidently.

"And," he added, leaning down, his hair just brushing Asa's cheek. He swallowed hard. The temptation had never been stronger to say *fuck it* entirely and just kiss Scott right here in his office. "*And,* we're gonna have some fun doin' it. I was proud of you, that you didn't lose your shit about the glitter."

"It was what they expected," Asa said, trying for an easy, breezy tone, but failing, because no matter how many times he got close to Scott, he still wanted more than he could handle, "and I would hate to become predictable."

"Predictable?" He scoffed. "I'm lookin' forward to the day you don't keep me on my toes."

"No, you're not," Asa retorted.

"I think you've caught me, darlin'," Scott said, lowering his voice. "Red-handed."

Two practices left, Scott thought, before the team left for Chicago, and it still felt like the defense was a little wobblier than he'd have liked.

Asa's bright new idea, which Beau had seconded, was trying to get more immediate pressure on the other team's quarterback, which might give both Sebastian and Micah a break on having to cover every single pass play.

That required even more adjustment though, and Scott was tired. Practices had run long, and it felt like he'd barely gotten more than five or ten minutes alone with Asa since their date on Monday night. Everything and everyone was focused on the upcoming game—which he didn't even disagree with—he just missed his guy.

After so long without him, he wanted to spend as much time with him as he could.

"Hey," Beau said, approaching Scott, as he stood on the sideline. Players were beginning to jog onto the field to get ready for warmups, even though practice wasn't officially set to start for half an hour. It was a good sign, Scott knew, that the team was so dedicated and ready to work.

Didn't make winning any more of a guarantee but it certainly didn't hurt, either.

"Hey yourself," Scott said.

"I've been meaning to get you alone for a minute," Beau said. "Sebastian told me he thinks you're seeing someone. Is that true?"

Scott froze.

"Uh," he said. "Who'd I be seeing around here?"

It wasn't technically a lie.

"There's lots of guys around here that you might be interested in," Beau said, nudging him with a fierce grin. "You're not exactly old and washed up, you know. You still got it."

"Uh, thanks?" Scott hated this conversation. He understood why Asa kept putting off telling Beau—it wasn't going to be easy, and Beau was undoubtedly going to be pissed when he found out the truth—but Sebastian was *clearly* trying to push them if he was trying this tactic. Not telling Beau outright, but making him wonder. Giving him an opportunity to bring it up to Scott.

"I know a few older guys in town . . . maybe even a few *not* that much older that would kill for a date with the famous Scott Callaway."

God, now Beau was trying to set him up. Was he that pathetic?

He'd pined after a man for almost thirty years. He was absolutely, seriously pathetic. Even if he'd finally won the guy after all that time.

"Who you settin' up with a date?"

Oh shit.

Oh shit, oh shit, oh *shit*.

Could it get worse than Beau trying to set him up because he was too pathetic to get a man himself?

Yes, it could.

Because Micah, who had essentially introduced himself to the team by using a homophobic slur, had just overheard Beau suggesting that he could find him a date. A date that was definitely male.

"Uh . . ." The panic in Beau's eyes was unmistakable.

Scott found himself at a crossroads.

He could lie. He knew he could dredge up some kind of lie. Maybe Micah would believe it, maybe he wouldn't. It wouldn't be the first time that Scott had lied to stay in the closet, but it would be the first time he'd done it after promising to himself that he'd stop lying.

Or he could tell the truth.

You told yourself that you would, and what kind of person does that make you, turning tail the first time you've got a real test?

Scott stared at Micah, who stared back, a confused expression on his face. He'd probably never dreamt in a thousand years that Scott was queer, because he was big and tough and manly and was a famous football coach.

It makes me human. 'Cause I'm terrified as hell.

"It's alright, Beau, I got this," Scott said. Beau looked surprised, but gave him an encouraging pat on the shoulder before he turned away.

"Hey, we got a few minutes," Scott said to Micah, gesturing towards the bench. "Let's talk."

Micah shot him a suspicious look, but he sat down.

"I just wanted you to know that you heard what you thought you heard. I'm gay, and yes, Beau was trying to set me up on a date, but I really wish he wouldn't," Scott said, on the sideline of a football field, and the world didn't implode. He kept breathing, the sun kept shining, and he was still sitting here, just as much a part of the Piranhas organization as anyone else.

He'd worried about that part of it less, because the Piranhas had proven to be a surprisingly tolerant organization—but Micah Rose hadn't proven anything.

Beau had told him he'd claimed he wasn't homophobic.

But the insult he'd used made it difficult to think he was anything else.

Scott didn't know what he'd expected. Maybe for Micah to storm off. Maybe for him to repeat the insult, but he didn't say anything, just stared at the ground.

"What are you doin' helpin' me, then?" Micah said quietly. Not belligerently.

"You fucked up once. You're not *a* fuckup," Scott said.

"Not to hear Howard talk."

"Sebastian's got his own kind of baggage," Scott said. "We've all got our own journey, you know? Mine's different than his, and his is different from yours."

"I looked you up, you know?" Micah glanced up at him. "You're not out. You didn't have to tell me that. You could've . . ."

"What? Lied? Yeah, I could've. Done it before. Lots of times. 'Where's your girlfriend, Coach?' 'Oh, too busy for a girl-friend.' More times than I want to count, I lied. But I'm done with that now."

"Does it get easier?"

And suddenly, Scott had an idea why he'd tossed that insult at Beau.

Why he'd regretted it so much.

It sucked—no way around how *much* it sucked—to hate that part of yourself. A part of yourself that you couldn't deny or change or ignore.

Scott knew; he'd done it long enough.

"I don't know," Scott admitted, "ask me next time."

Micah looked floored. "You didn't . . . I'm not the first . . . Beau knows."

"A handful of people know. Beau. Sebastian. Coach. Some people from my hometown. You're not the first person I told, but you were probably the toughest."

It wasn't easy admitting that either, but Scott thought if someone had pulled him aside early in his career, and told him *their* truth, maybe it would've made it a little easier for him to stop swallowing his down.

Not easy, but easier.

He didn't know if his gut feeling about Micah and his sexu-ality was right, but if it was, maybe he could help.

Be a shoulder to lean on. A wall to pound on. An ear to listen.

"Huh," Micah said. "I'm actually . . . actually real glad you told me."

"Me too." Scott wasn't surprised to discover that he meant it.

Even if this had turned out far differently than it had, he still was glad he'd done it.

"You're the first guy who's come out to me, after I was a dickhead," Micah said with a gust of resignation. "You didn't have to."

"Trust that you'd do the right thing? Yeah, I did."

"But . . ."

"No," Scott said emphatically and put a hand on Micah's arm. Did it help he knew he wouldn't get punched for it? Sure it did. But it just felt good to tell someone, for once. "No. You don't get to do that. Sure, you fucked up. Said the wrong thing." Micah shot him a look. "Okay, you said a wrong *and* a fucked-up thing. You did. But do you know how many times I lied? To people I trusted? People I loved? How many mistakes I made? We're never stuck in those ruts, unless we choose to be stuck. We can always decide to try something else."

"It's that easy?" Micah's voice was full of disbelief.

"'Course it is. Not *easy*, mind you, but all you have to do is make the decision and stick to it. And I know you now, Micah, you've got that determination in spades. That stubbornness."

"You know, it's funny," Micah said. "People believe in you your whole fuckin' life when you've got talent. You're over-flowin' with people who believe in you. And then you struggle for the first time, and it's like . . . boom, all those people, they're just gone, like they were never even there."

Scott wished he was hearing this story for the first time.

The NFL was too eager to dismiss young men as talentless without ever giving them a real chance to get their feet underneath them.

"It's not right," Scott told him.

Micah shook his head. "And you're drownin' and you're *screaming* and nobody's listenin'."

It seemed the most right thing in the world for Scott to turn to Micah and hug him. Hard and tight. "I am," he said. "I'm always listening."

"Fuck," Micah said with feeling after Scott let him go. "You're a good guy, Callaway. I wanted to hate you, but I don't. I thought you were just another person being hard on me."

Scott laughed. "I am. That's not gonna stop. But I'm listening too. When it gets too hard."

"Well . . ." Micah hesitated. "If you're listening now . . . *God*, it shouldn't be so hard to say this, I never said this to anyone before, not anyone ever, but . . . I don't think I'm much different than you, actually."

"Yeah?" Scott had suspected. But he was honored—and maybe a little guilty that he was the one Micah had picked to come out to, because what had he ever done to deserve it?—that Micah would trust him with this.

The first person Micah had ever trusted with this.

"I mean, I been with girls. Lots of girls. I kept expectin' it to . . . I don't know . . . *feel* different?"

"Yeah," Scott said. He got that.

"And then I come here, and there's Sebastian Howard and he's so . . . *goddamn*, just . . . you get that?"

"Yep, I do," Scott said dryly. The first time he'd ever seen Asa. Every other time he'd ever seen Asa—it was a hit like that, right to the solar plexus. For a split second, every time Asa looked up at him, he couldn't quite breathe.

"Then I find out yeah, he's not interested. In fact, he thinks I'm a piece of shit."

"You were jealous of Beau." Scott didn't know why he was surprised. It made sense, the last puzzle piece falling into place and showing him the whole picture, finally.

"Fuck yeah, I really was. Not that I ever had a shot. Not that it makes it right. 'Cause it doesn't. I'm not *stupid*."

"Someday," Scott said, "you should tell Sebastian that. The truth."

Micah looked aghast and horrified at the idea. Scott understood what that was like, too. If someone had suggested, early on, that he tell Asa how he felt, he'd never have considered it.

For different reasons than Micah, but still.

"Seriously, hear me out. I think . . . I think maybe he might understand."

"Yeah, and then he's gonna feel fucking sorry for me," Micah said, dejected.

"Probably, yeah," Scott said, a smile creeping across his face.

"I feel like what I need is a fresh start, but how, 'cause this is supposed to be my start? How can I change it now?"

"I told you. We make our own fate, Micah. You got this. You make it one day at a time. One practice at a time. One game at a time."

Micah nodded, and there was a new resolution in his eyes that Scott hadn't seen before.

This was a good kid. Confused, maybe, and struggling, for sure, but Beau had been right. He wasn't bad.

"Come on," Scott said, standing up. "Let's get warmed up, and see if you can keep up with Tristan today."

"I got this," Micah said, and Scott believed him.

Chapter Twelve

If Asa had let himself consider it, he'd have told himself—and anyone else who asked—that he was absolutely not sneaking out of his room the night before the Bears game.

But after the walkthrough ended, Scott looked at him, on their ride up in the elevator, and the heat in his eyes had shifted his plans entirely.

He wasn't going to take a hot shower and lie in bed and scroll through the endless channels on the TV. And if he was going to, there was no reason not to do it with Scott lying next to him.

Beau would've called it a "total no-brainer."

"See you in the morning," Scott said, smirking a little as he exited on the floor under Asa's. This was a smaller hotel, and the team had taken over several floors. And naturally, because fate hated him, Scott was on the floor below his.

But that was alright. He was *allowed* to move around, right? He was allowed to take the elevator. Or maybe, Asa thought as he watched the elevator doors ding closed again, he could even take the stairs.

He dropped his bag in his room, tried unsuccessfully to fix his hair, not that Scott hadn't *just* seen it, or that he wouldn't be messing it up a whole lot more, and changed into sweatpants and a t-shirt.

The stairs were behind a door all the way at one end of the floor. He pushed open the door and froze, because those were definitely footsteps he was hearing.

You are the worst sneaky person ever, Scott would say to him. *The absolute worst.*

And Asa would retort that he should be glad he was bad at it or maybe he'd do it more often. A lie, because Asa wasn't built to sneak, which was almost definitely why he was shitty at it.

He was already halfway down the flight of stairs, so he couldn't exactly turn around and go back where he'd come from, and *God help him*, he was not going to just stand there and cower.

It was probably just staff, taking the stairs because it was faster with the team using the elevators.

But he rounded the corner and it was not someone from the hotel.

It was Kenyon, dressed nearly the same as him, in gray sweatpants, a black t-shirt, and feet slipped into black plastic slides with a designer logo printed on them.

"Uh," he said.

Asa gave him a frank stare. "Imagine seeing you here." He glanced down at his watch. Yep, it was definitely past curfew.

Beau and Sebastian, who'd had dinner with Asa and Scott, which felt like a weird pseudo-double date, even if Beau had had no idea what they were really doing, had barely slipped in before curfew hit. And after that, he and Scott had shared a beer at the bar while going over a last set of plays for the next day.

So Kenyon was out at least thirty minutes past when he was supposed to be in his room.

"Uh," Kenyon said.

"Where are you going?" Asa asked, nicely. Because while he took curfew seriously, these were also grown men, and he was absolutely, most definitely *not* their father.

"Out," Kenyon said, his jaw jutting out a stubborn angle.

"I see," Asa said. "Want to tell me where?"

Kenyon barely appeared to consider this. "Not particularly. You want to tell me where *you're* headed?" He gave Asa a long perusal from head to toe, saying, without speaking a word, that he knew they were both going to do the same thing.

Sneaking into someone's room.

Asa sighed. He could not tell Kenyon before he told his own son. And Scott still wasn't out to the team, though Asa was real proud that he'd come out to Micah.

But every person he came out to was Scott's choice. Asa didn't mind if people knew he liked men, he'd never really minded, but Scott was different.

"No," Asa said.

"It's totally Helen, isn't it? You guys have a vibe."

Asa internally rolled his eyes. "Aren't you what . . . I'm never quite sure what Beau means, but . . . pansexual, isn't that right?"

Kenyon's gaze narrowed. "Yes."

"Well, then, why assume it's a woman?" Asa said. "I do like Helen a lot, she routinely prevents me from murdering my own players. But no, I'm not sleeping with her."

"Let me guess," Kenyon said, "Beau doesn't know about this."

"No," Asa said, carefully. "And I'd like to keep it that way. At least for now. He deserves to hear it from me, don't you think?"

Kenyon considered this, and then nodded.

"You're really not going to tell me who it is?" He sounded frustrated.

Asa chuckled under his breath. "You're not going to be able to distract me. Who is it, Kenyon? Who am I gonna have to give the lecture to? You and who else?"

"Oh, that talk?" Kenyon laughed. But it was a little high-pitched, a little hysterical. "No, no need. It's not someone on the team. Uh . . . and to be honest, it's not like that. Not like . . . touchy-feely romance kind of feelings, you know? It's just . . ."

Kenyon trailed off and Asa raised an eyebrow. Apparently the point where he flinched was saying the word *sex* to his coach.

"Just sex, huh?" Asa said. 'Cause *he* could say it just fine. Could do it just fine too. Could be doing it right now if he hadn't run into Kenyon. "Must be real good if you're doin' it tonight, the night before a game."

Kenyon shifted uneasily from one foot to the other. "It's just a habit, you know? Keeps me focused. Keeps me relaxed. Just something to pass the time."

"Uh-huh," Asa said. Not believing it for a second. He was sure *Kenyon* believed it, or else he was trying to, but there was something uneasy in his gaze as he said it. Like he didn't quite buy it.

"The talk is completely unnecessary, I swear. We fuck and then it's over and . . ." Kenyon shrugged. "It just works."

"I have a feeling I wouldn't approve of whoever this is," Asa said. "You keep talkin' around it, like I wouldn't."

But he knew Kenyon wasn't going to give up the identity of whoever he kept seeing. Or kept fucking, to use his vernacular.

"Okay, probably not, but the only reason I didn't tell you—'cause I *would* have, if it was more—is 'cause it's nothing. I swear."

Asa looked at him sternly. "Are they staying outside of this hotel?"

AKA was he going *outside* the hotel during curfew? 'Cause he'd have to put a stop to it then.

"No," Kenyon said. "No . . . they're here."

Asa noticed he tripped over the pronoun usage. Probably not wanting to give Asa anymore clues as to who it was. But if they were here, in this hotel, it was someone on the team, or part of the staff that traveled with them.

It wasn't a huge list.

But for right now, Asa would keep his secret. And not just because Kenyon had essentially promised to keep his own.

God, he really needed to figure out a way to tell Beau.

Soon.

"Alright, well, don't stay out too late," Asa said. "Big game tomorrow."

"Yes, Coach," Kenyon said, and then he was gone, around the corner of the stairwell, like Asa had never seen him at all. It occurred to him then that Kenyon *was* good at being sneaky.

How long had he been doing this? It was clearly a long-standing arrangement.

It also occurred to Asa, as he exited the stairway on Scott's floor, that it wouldn't just be a player, or a member of the staff.

There was one other category of person that stayed with them, at the hotel: the small group of reporters assigned to follow the Piranhas.

Kenyon was right, Asa was really not going to like it if he found out he was sleeping with a reporter.

He knocked on Scott's door, and Scott opened it almost immediately, not looking surprised in the least to find Asa on the other side of it.

"You won't believe the weird conversation I just had," Asa said as he followed Scott into the bedroom. He tugged off his t-shirt, and for a split second, the Kenyon problem faded because seeing Scott shirtless was always a shock to his system.

Especially now, when he was allowed to touch.

Finally.

"You were sayin'?" Scott sounded amused as he sat on the bed.

"Ran into Kenyon on the stairwell. This 'sneakin' around' business . . ." Asa sighed. "I've got to quit it soon. I can't do it. I know you don't want to necessarily come out, but . . ."

"I know you've got to tell Beau, and after that . . ." Scott hesitated. "We can tell anyone you like."

"Wow." Asa knew he sounded surprised, but he couldn't help it. Scott had been so against this for so long, and they hadn't really discussed it when Scott had come to Miami. He'd sort of assumed that Scott's opinion of coming out hadn't really changed.

"I'd started it, actually, tellin' people in Alabama, where I was, after Washington let me go. I was ready to do it. And now I'm doubly ready."

Asa leaned into Scott's big body, felt the warmth and the steadiness of it. "I'm here with you, every step of the way, alright? If you go down, I'm going down with you."

"Yeah." Scott's voice cracked a bit on the end of the word, and if he held Asa a little tighter after, that was fair.

It was a lot.

"But I don't think anyone's goin' down," Asa added.

He felt Scott grin against his shoulder. "Weelllll . . ." he drawled. "I was kinda hopin' *someone* would be goin' down."

Asa couldn't help the laugh that bubbled out of him. "That how it is?"

"Yep." Scott shifted his grip, turning Asa until he was settled between his legs and he could see his eyes. "So you ran into Kenyon. Isn't it after curfew?"

"Oh, it is," Asa said. "And not just that, he was clearly on his way to do what I was."

"Spend some time goin' down?" Scott teased.

Asa shot him a look. "Exactly. He wouldn't tell me who the other person was, though I don't think it's a player. He claimed it was 'just sex' though, of course, he couldn't quite bring himself to say the word sex to his coach."

"Oh, wouldn't he be surprised by the unbuttoned Coach Dawson," Scott pointed out dryly.

Asa elbowed him in the side. Maybe he was older than the players he coached, but he didn't feel it. Especially when he was with Scott.

"I got the impression it wasn't a player, like I said, 'cause he's not real close to them, not the way I'd expect if they were . . . uh . . . fucking on the regular."

"And, there's the buttoned-up Coach Dawson I know and love," Scott inserted with a grin.

"You don't love that," Asa complained. "Nobody would." He was trying not to be a prude, but how long had it been since he'd been having regular sex? He couldn't remember. 'Cause it hadn't been during his marriage.

"Yes, I do. 'Cause I get to unbutton him, and that's *real* fun."

Asa rolled his eyes. "Anyway, I got the feeling it's worse than a regular player."

"Worse? What could possibly be worse than you givin' permission to your QB and your QB coach to carry on a love affair under everyone's noses?" Scott sounded incredulous. And yeah, it had been a little crazy to allow that, but what else was Asa supposed to do? Say no? Fire Davis? It would have been counterproductive. He'd made the right decision, he felt sure of it.

"Worse," Asa agreed. "Like a reporter."

"You think Kenyon's fucking a reporter?"

"I don't have any proof. But . . . if it's not a staff member, and it's not a player, and they're stayin' at this hotel . . ."

"Huh."

"I hope I'm wrong."

"It would sure explain why he wouldn't tell you who it was," Scott said wryly.

"I'm gonna trust him for now when he says it's not an issue."

Scott's gaze softened. "You're a good person, you know? Too trusting by half, but a good man. A good coach."

"Let's hope that tomorrow that's still true," Asa said with a sigh.

He couldn't say he wasn't worried about the game. He was.

But tonight . . . he would wrap himself up in Scott and try to forget about what was on the line tomorrow.

Everything.

Scott had debated with himself back and forth if he'd stay up in the booth for this next game or come down to the ground, to the sideline, and try to manage the new scheme with a more hands-on approach.

Brett would be there, of course, because he liked to stay on the sideline.

But it would be tougher to check in on how Micah was doing. How he was feeling.

"Guess I shouldn't be surprised you're slummin' it down here with us today," Beau said halfway through the second quarter.

Scott shrugged, watching the field as the Bears' quarterback dropped back, and feeling the pressure almost immediately, rolled out to his left, and not finding anyone open down field, threw the ball away.

"Felt good to switch it up," Scott said. He didn't like that little pulse of guilt he felt whenever he saw Beau now. Like he was lying to him, a man he considered practically his son.

Asa had said he'd tell him this week, but Scott wasn't stupid. He knew he was putting it off. Knew why, too.

"Looks like that was the right call," Beau said, nodding approvingly at the field as the Bears only got three yards on a third and five and were going to have to punt.

"Yep," Scott agreed.

The defense *was* holding up a lot better today. They'd allowed the Bears an early touchdown—their running back finding an unexpected seam and hitting it for fifty yards, which had freaked Asa out, but after that, the defense had calmed down and in a lot of football had only allowed a field goal after that, giving a little on early plays and then stiffening up, shutting the offense down the closer they moved to their end zone.

And the scheme? Working exactly as he hoped it might, the earlier pressure on the quarterback giving both Sebastian and the corners a bit of a breather.

Though Scott wasn't sure they needed it—finally Micah was playing with the confidence and the skill that he'd always been capable of.

Not every route he took was perfect, but he was executing at a much higher level, and Scott was feeling good about their chances in this game.

Except that the offense still kept stalling. They'd managed to move the ball and score a touchdown on one drive, but if they wanted to go ahead, they were going to have to do more than just settle for a field goal.

Scott knew if he glanced behind him, he'd see Davis and Pax on the bench, heads bent over a tablet, figuring out a way to convert third downs better.

In a few minutes, after the Bears punted, Pax would take the field again, and hopefully the Piranhas offense would find a new gear.

There was still six minutes left, plenty of time for a nice long drive that could put them in the lead going into the locker room for halftime.

Scott watched as Pax jogged out, followed by Kenyon, Tristan, Wade, and Logan and the offensive line.

"We gotta score this drive."

Scott felt Asa before he saw him, before he'd even spoken, really.

They'd always been attuned to each other, but it was different now, so much more intense.

Scott couldn't leave now, even if he was trying to be noble.

And he understood now, now that he was in the middle of it, what Asa was trying to build here. He'd seen some of it at Tennessee, but this was so much bigger, on such a broader stage, a stage everyone was watching. They wanted to know if a softer touch worked, if the freedom Asa had given his players led to wins. Led to championships.

With all those eyes came pressure, but he could be there for Asa, stand next to him, put his hand on his back, make sure he didn't falter. Make sure that he never fell.

They'd stumbled a little last week, but it wouldn't happen today.

"Pax is lookin' good," Scott pointed out.

Asa sighed. "He's just gotta make that third down more manageable. Get Kenyon goin'. He can't take it all on himself."

Scott shot him a look. "Yeah, don't know anyone else who likes to do that."

Slowly but surely, the offense was moving down the field.

They were across mid-field, then at the thirty-yard line, and then the fifteen. And then, the mother of all annoying penalties, Logan got called for holding, costing them the first down they'd just gotten *and* adding another ten yards to what they needed.

"That's a bullshit call, *bullshit*," Asa yelled, headset off, bouncing on his back, as he strode down the sideline to where the ref was doing his best to ignore his shouting.

Scott had done this so many times it felt natural now to position himself within easy reach of Asa. In case this temper flare grew, and he started to say stuff that might get him kicked out of the game.

It had happened, once or twice, when he'd been coaching in college, but it wasn't going to be a good look here—not when Asa hadn't explicitly told him what Rudy had said, but Scott could put the pieces together anyway. He wasn't on thin ice, because he'd created a miracle with this team, turning them around, already winning more than four times the number of games they'd won the year before. But Scott wasn't stupid, and Asa definitely wasn't, and that wasn't going to be enough.

Rudy had gotten a taste of success, and last week had been a rude awakening that maybe they weren't quite there yet.

A rude awakening for all of them.

Scott could see the burden all the players were suddenly struggling under, the realization that maybe they weren't as good as they'd believed they were.

But a ten-yard holding penalty was a tough thing to overcome, and while the offense made back fifteen of those yards, Asa ended up sending Dylan out to kick the field goal.

It wasn't what they'd really wanted, Scott knew that, but some points were always better than no points, and at least they went into the locker room at halftime tied and not down.

There's still time left, Asa thought to himself as the clock ticked down. Seven minutes left in the game.

They'd traded punts back and forth during the third quarter, neither team getting much of anywhere. *Still tied. Ten to ten.*

But now was the time to make the move. There was still time left, and what they needed was a nice long drive, and a touchdown. It wouldn't one hundred percent seal the win but it would get them damn close.

One bad loss was one thing. A second was inexcusable.

Asa couldn't even justify it to himself, never mind to Rudy.

And then there was the responsibility he had for his players. It was his job to put them in a position to win, to help them execute so they could come out on top.

Today? It had been a mixed bag. The defense was holding firm, unlike the week before, but the offense was struggling again. Not converting third downs. Getting stupid penalties that should've been preventable. Plays for a loss of yards. Plays that didn't go anywhere at all. And Pax looked comfortable in the pocket but frustrated on the sideline.

"Randy, you gotta dial up some good plays. We need a touchdown this drive," Asa instructed their passing coordinator. "Some down field stuff, to Tristan maybe?"

"Their pass rush is intense, not a lot of time for Pax to throw. Not a lot of time for that kinda deep play to develop," Randy told him. Which he knew, already, of course. He'd seen three quarters' worth of what Randy was describing.

"Well, *something*," Asa barked into his headset.

"We've got a few things up our sleeve," Randy promised.

The doctors had told him he needed to find a way, even in the most stressful of situations, not to let the anxiety get to him.

Asa had tried some slow breathing exercises, some mantras repeated in his head, but with the game on the line, watching Pax drive the offense down the field, honestly, there was no fucking way he could possibly contain the fear crawling up his body, threatening to strangle him.

He felt like he was right there, next to Pax, could feel the ball in his hands as Logan snapped it, feel the pocket collapsing in on itself as the defensive ends rushed in. Threw his arm back, made the throw, the ball zinging in between the corner and the safety, landing safely in Wade's outstretched hands for a solid fifteen-yard gain.

Every play felt like that, the field folding in on itself, until Asa felt like he could reach out and touch it, like he was *right* there, alongside his guys.

Randy had done as promised and was calling some of what he liked to call his special "wrinkle" plays. There was one where Kenyon took the snap directly from Logan, and tossed it to Pax, who threw long, hitting Carter Johnson for twenty-three yards.

He'd told Randy he wanted Kenyon more involved in the game, and he hoped that hadn't been a mistake, especially when continually pushing the run game was finally making a difference.

With the defenders having to hang back to watch for the run, Pax was finally getting that precious extra second to throw, which gave Tristan the same amount of time, and after a nice long drive of about seven minutes, Pax hit the rookie wide receiver on the ten-yard line, and he dodged the corner and rolled into the end zone.

"Yes!" Asa exclaimed pumping his fist as he watched Pax and Tristan and the rest of the offense celebrate in the end zone. He slapped a few hands, even more backs and wasn't surprised at all to see Scott approach out of the corner of his eye. They embraced, and it was brief, but Asa felt the impact of his touch everywhere.

"Great drive," Scott said. "Pax really brought it."

"Yeah. Now . . . defense has got to hold." Asa felt nervous. There were still thirty-four seconds left. The Bears didn't have any timeouts but it was going to be cutting it close. Closer than he preferred.

"They can do it," Scott said. "But kickoff first. You make sure the coverage teams know to not let anyone get behind them?"

Asa nodded. Roger, who ran special teams, knew how he felt about giving up a long return—or even worse, a touchdown.

"He knows." *He'd better know*, Asa thought, as Dylan set up to kick off.

With so little time left on the clock, this was going to be one of the few shots Chicago had left. And they needed a touchdown to tie.

Asa tried a few of those calming breaths, but they didn't work.

Nothing was going to work until he saw the clock hit zero, with the Piranhas still in the lead.

Not even the feel of Scott at his back. He wasn't touching him, but Asa could feel him anyway. Just standing there, in case he needed him.

After a hushed consultation with Roger, Asa watched as Dylan jogged onto the field, with the rest of the kickoff team.

The ball soared off Dylan's foot. He kicked it long and far, into the end zone, but Asa wasn't surprised, his heart beating faster as their returner caught it, but instead of taking a knee, he accelerated with the ball in his hands, missing the first tackler, then taking a good angle.

"Shit, shit, *shit*," Scott swore loudly, the rest of the sideline yelling as their returner crossed midfield and there was almost nobody left before he'd get a free and clear path to the opposite end zone.

It was the very last thing they'd needed to do—give up a freaking touchdown after *finally* scoring in the second half—but they'd done it, and now, Asa thought with frustration, they might be headed to overtime, instead of sealing this game with a win.

Asa sighed as the Bears' player crossed the line and started to celebrate.

"Well, that sucked," Scott said with a reluctant sigh. "I guess . . . I guess you're gonna be workin' with Roger this week on kickoff coverage."

"No shit," Asa said. It did suck. Just when he thought they'd pulled the win, they'd gotten sucker punched.

And he couldn't even blame anyone else. It was his team. His responsibility.

The Bears lined up to kick the extra point, but Asa was already looking down, searching through his tablet to find a killer opening play to start overtime with, so he missed it.

At least the beginning of it, and then he heard another triumphant yell, and then another, and that finally made him look up.

And instead of watching the extra point—the extra point that would have tied the game, and guaranteed they went into overtime—fly between the uprights, the Bears' holder was scrambling for the ball as it flopped across the turf.

"Bad snap! It was a bad snap!" Scott was yelling in his face, the widest grin he could remember plastered across it. "We fucking *won*."

They had.

Time had expired. Asa could see it on the clock. It read *00:00*.

Could see on the scoreboard that the Piranhas were ahead. Seventeen to sixteen.

And that, Asa thought, letting out a little of the anxiety he'd built up inside him over the last two and a half hours, was enough. It was going to have to be enough.

It wasn't enough.

It *was*, from the perspective that they'd needed the win and they'd gotten it.

But Asa couldn't deny it was an ugly win.

They'd almost not won at all.

In fact, now that Asa was sitting and thinking about it, on the plane ride home from Chicago, it was becoming clearer to him that they hadn't really won at all.

Yes, the official scorecard said the Piranhas had gotten the win.

But in the end, the Bears had actually done more to lose the game, by fumbling the snap for the extra point, than the Piranhas had actually done to win.

How many offensive drives had gone nowhere?

If they'd stopped the Bears from scoring that touchdown in the first quarter, things might've looked very different at the end of the game.

"You're frowning and you really shouldn't be," Scott said, dropping into the seat opposite his own. "We won."

Asa shot him a long-suffering look. "Did we? Why doesn't it feel that way, then?"

"Hey, it was a close game. Things swung our way. We got lucky. Sometimes that's what it takes."

"Luck isn't a skill. Luck isn't preparation or practice. Luck doesn't mean we executed our plan better. It just means it was . . ."

"Luck, that's what it means. And every playoff team? They get lucky once or twice. It's part of what sets teams apart." Scott stretched out his legs. "Count yourself *lucky* that you got lucky."

"Ha ha," Asa said, not very amused.

"Hey, there were lot of things that we did well, too."

"And some things we didn't," Asa retorted.

"'Course you're already thinkin' of those." Scott grinned. "Well, I'm sure you'll have a full list for us Monday morning. But you know what? Enjoy it tonight."

But as the plane fell silent around them, Asa found it difficult to do what Scott said, even though he wanted to.

Even when he tried his slow and steady breathing, it still felt like air was trapped in his lungs, anxiety pushing it down, keeping it away from where he really needed it.

Something, Asa thought to himself, *is gonna have to give.*

Chapter
Thirteen

It wasn't like Scott was particularly surprised.

He wasn't.

He knew Asa. A win like that was always going to sit uneasy with Asa.

Asa was the kind of coach—the kind of man, for that matter—who didn't like relying on luck. Who didn't like crediting it for any of his accomplishments.

He'd fully expected him to show up first thing Monday morning with a fire lit underneath him, determined, even more than the week before, that the next win they notched, they were sure as hell going to earn it.

Scott did not expect Asa to show up first thing Monday morning, ready to light a fire underneath everyone else's ass.

"This is unacceptable," Asa said, his fist on the conference table punctuating each and every word he said. He'd called for an all-hands-on-deck meeting, at eight in the morning, when the plane from Chicago had landed at two AM.

For the first time in at least a week, they'd fallen into their separate beds, though Asa had been knocking on his door starting at six thirty.

That should've been Scott's first indication that this was Asa on the warpath.

Scott considered raising his hand and pointing out that it was ludicrous to say winning was unacceptable.

But technically, he was new here. Not new to Asa, but new to the Piranhas, and the last thing he needed to do was piss Asa off even more, and as a result, create a living hell for the rest of the coaching staff. He wanted them to like him, not resent that he'd made everything worse.

"We're gonna sit here, for as long as it goddamn takes," Asa continued. "Til we figure out how to design a game plan that *works*. We don't rely on luck here. We don't rely on a bad snap. We certainly don't give up special teams touchdowns, not when we're in a position to win." Asa's glare met every single person at the table. Scott was surprised that Roger's hair didn't burst into spontaneous flames, Asa's ire was so pronounced.

"We're a better team than Chicago. We played better than they did, in every part of the game, and yet we were struggling to score, to take the lead. The defense played better, but we still gave up that long touchdown in the first quarter. We're better than that, but we can't seem to play better."

Scott heard the frustration boiling over in Asa's voice.

He knew if he could get on the field, if he could do more than just plan and talk and *watch*, then he'd do it. He'd put them all on his back and carry them to victory.

"We *have* played better," Beau spoke up, and Asa could hear the uneasiness in his voice. He was trying to bridge the gap—defend the coaching staff while also placating his clearly furious father.

Scott didn't envy him the tightrope line he was trying to walk.

"That's in the past," Asa said dismissively. "We're only talking about the Chicago game and the game next week. Where are we?"

"Tampa's coming here," Randy said uneasily.

"Alright. Tom Brady. The GOAT. You know what that means." Asa's voice was hard. Unrelenting.

This wasn't like him, but it also was.

There was a reason he'd gotten the reputation he had at Tennessee. He could be soft and lead with his heart, and Scott believed that was his default setting. But he was also driven to win, and frustrated by inadequacies, especially when he believed they stemmed from himself. He expected the very best out of everyone, and the most out of himself.

"It means," Asa answered his own question, "we work twice as hard. It means we work four times as hard. It means we're gonna sit here until someone tells me where we can start."

"We'll start with the offense." This time it was Davis who spoke up. "It was hard for me to convince Pax that he didn't need to be at this meeting, because he wanted to be. Wanted to take personal responsibility." Davis' mouth twisted.

But Asa didn't acknowledge that part of what Davis had said.

"Offense it is," Asa said. "Randy? Analysis?"

"It was a solid game plan," Randy started to say.

But Asa didn't let him even get more than five words out. "No, no, *no*," Asa said, banging his fist on the table again for emphasis. "An effective game plan would mean we wouldn't have to score a touchdown on the last drive of the game, and it wouldn't mean that we nearly lost because of a special teams disaster."

Randy looked surprised.

Obviously he had not worked with Asa before this. Or at least he'd never seen him in this particular mood.

Scott could count on one hand how many times he'd personally witnessed it.

"I . . . uh . . ." Randy stammered. "We need to reduce the number of stupid mistakes that stopped drives, obviously."

"Obviously," Asa repeated.

"We need to work on the receivers getting a touch more separation. And the only drive the field stretched out to give Pax the time he needed to throw more than ten yards was the last one of the game. We need to attack the run game earlier, be less complacent."

"Yes," Asa said. "Less complacent for sure. We can't always be thinking we'll get it next drive, because sometimes there *isn't* a next drive. Every single one we're runnin' . . . it needs to be planned and executed to maximize points. We're not doin' that now. I want to see a game plan for the Tampa game tonight, outlining fifteen drives that could legitimately result in points being scored."

"Fifteen?" Randy's voice squeaked. It was an enormous amount of work. And adding to that, everyone around the table knew that on average, an NFL team ran twelve offensive sets of plays per game, and usually Asa only wanted to see five or six total planned drives.

But he'd clearly decided that Randy wasn't calling the game right, during the game itself.

Scott knew part of this came down to a need to micromanage his staff to guarantee they did their jobs to Asa's own crazy-exacting standard. And the other part of this came down to the fury he wasn't doing a very good job of burying.

It was an ugly combination and it was making Scott uneasy.

He exchanged glances with Beau, who looked the same way Scott felt.

Asa was going to lead his way right into another heart attack if he didn't figure out how to calm down.

The meeting lasted another two hours.

Mostly it was a lack of answers and preparation, and every time a coach stammered out what they thought had happened, versus what they'd planned to happen, Scott could sense Asa grow more and more frustrated.

By the time they broke for lunch, Scott was genuinely worried.

"Come on," he heard Beau say as he approached his father who was packing up his laptop at the front of the room, "let's grab some lunch."

Scott watched as Asa lifted an eyebrow. "You analyzed every single play? You emailed me your notes on *every single play?*"

"No, because even you know that's not necessary," Beau said.

Asa shot his son a look. "You say that, but it sure seems necessary when I consider what happened yesterday."

"It was just . . ." Beau shrugged. "A freak thing."

"We scored thirty-eight points on the Condors. We gave up three in return. Where is that team? That's the team I want. That's the team I want here *every single fucking week,*" Asa said.

"That was after the bye . . ." But Beau didn't get the rest of his sentence out. Really, he should've known better.

"Yes, it was. Twice as much time to prepare. Which means," Asa said, pinning Beau with a look that Scott wished he wasn't quite so familiar with, "we've got to find the time to do twice as much work every single goddamn week."

Beau watched as Asa picked up his laptop and stomped out.

"Phew," Scott said, trying to break the tension as Beau turned to him, frustration etched on his features. "He's in a mood."

"I shouldn't be surprised," Beau said glumly. "Would've been nice though if he hadn't basically called out the lack of preparation before the last two games. Games I managed the prep on."

The thing was Beau was undeniably brilliant. But he was still young. He was still learning. He thought it was enough if you prepped once, twice, maybe. Asa prepped twice that much.

There was a reason he had the reputation he did.

And there was a reason he kept winning.

"You'll get there," Scott said. "He just hates winning because of luck. You know that."

"We might've won anyway. If they'd made the extra point, we'd have gone to overtime, and maybe we'd have pulled out the win, anyway."

"Maybe," Scott said. Personally he wouldn't stake his reputation on it. The team had been sluggish, especially offensively, all game. Could they have driven down the field and scored a touchdown in overtime? Sure. But he wasn't one hundred percent convinced.

"Hey"—Brett approached him as he was just leaving the conference room—"we could really use your help today." He sighed. "You really called it about the scheme, and you've helped Micah in a way I didn't think he could be helped. We . . . we're a little outmatched today, by all this, and you'd be a welcome addition."

The last thing Scott had expected was for Brett to ask him for help. Especially like this, essentially approaching with his metaphorical hat in his hands, admitting that he *needed* the help.

It also meant that if he went and assisted Brett and the other defensive coaches, he wouldn't be able to monitor Asa today.

Wouldn't be able to keep an eye on him and make sure he didn't lose the rest of his temper.

"Sure, I can do that," Scott said, deciding that it was the lesser of two evils to make sure that Brett and the defense wouldn't get torn to shreds again on Asa's exacting standards. He had a feeling Beau would be doing the same with the offense.

And special teams? God help Roger, but he was pretty sure Asa was going to be pretty hands on there, considering how the Bears game had ended.

Asa glanced down at his watch and realized with a start that it was six PM.

He'd been in his office working for hours, uninterrupted, probably because the rest of the staff was frantically trying to get about four times the usual amount of work together in about half the time.

He'd told them they'd need to send their game plans in by five, and as he looked in his empty inbox, his temper flared again.

Did they think just because he'd had a minor heart attack, that he'd been in the hospital, that Beau had taken point the last two weeks, that he wasn't really in charge? That he wouldn't light a blazing bonfire under their asses if he chose to?

That he wouldn't *fire* them?

Because he would.

He hadn't considered it before now because he knew they were capable of the high level of work he demanded.

That they could plan and execute exceptional game plans.

That they could make it possible for the Piranhas to win two games last year and ten and counting this year.

"Why am I surprised that you're still here?"

Asa glanced up, watching as Scott strolled in.

He looked tired, lines between his brows and bags under his eyes—*that's your fault,* Asa reminded himself, *you woke him up after not even five hours of sleep because you're insane*—but at the same time, Asa didn't want to look at anything else.

Today had sucked.

He'd known it would, he hated being a hard-ass. Except, of course, when he enjoyed the results of being such a hard-ass. And maybe next week, when Tampa Bay came to Miami, it would all feel worth it.

"You shouldn't be," Asa said bluntly. "Today was not a day to sit around and twiddle my thumbs. We're workin' here."

"Trust me," Scott said. "I know. I've been arguing with Brett for the last four hours."

"The game plan?"

"Should be on the way to your inbox," Scott said, sighing. But he didn't sit down. Instead, he propped a hip on the corner of Asa's desk. "Come on. It's way past five. You know the rules. It's time to get outta here."

Asa shot him a look. "Those rules were when we were winning."

"Like Beau said, we did, in fact, win yesterday," Scott said.

"Two more hours," Asa bargained.

"One hour." Scott paused. "And you won't argue with me, not a single fucking word, about where we go or what we do after we leave this office."

Scott's counter seemed suspiciously like a trap, but it was also Scott, and Asa knew he could trust him.

Would he like whatever he had planned? Probably not at first. But in the end, anything he and Scott did was good.

Better than good, usually.

"Fine," Asa said.

Scott raised an eyebrow. "Really? Promise me, Asa. Not a single word of argument."

"You're such a freaking stickler," Asa muttered. "Fine, fine, an hour of time for me to go through these game plans, and then I'll leave and not argue with you at all, even about where we're going."

"Good. I'm gonna go work out," Scott said. "Be ready in an hour."

"Sure thing," Asa said, and lo and behold, as Scott said, there was the email from Brett.

One from Randy, too.

He didn't even see Scott leave as he opened the first one.

But an hour later, just like he'd promised, he felt rather than heard Scott return.

He smelled like the lemon thyme soap stocked in the locker room showers, mixed with the undefinable scent that was Scott and Scott alone. It shouldn't have been enough to pull Asa's attention from the screen, from the notes he was making on Brett's defensive plan, but it was.

Then he glanced up and he wasn't ever going to get sick of this particular view. Scott in jeans and a green button-up shirt, with the sleeves rolled up and cuffed, exposing those mouthwatering forearms, corded with muscle.

Scott's gaze was amused. Knowing.

And it occurred to Asa, like a jolt of electricity, that he did this same thing to Scott, too. This breathing-too-hard, pulse-racing, mouth-dry, skin-tingling thing. Even with his totally normal, regular self, despite the polo shirt and pressed khaki pants that Beau was endlessly making fun of him for.

"You ready to go?" Scott asked.

Still amused, like he knew just how much Asa wanted to protest.

But what he didn't know was that Asa was ready to leave—the coaching staff had tried, but there were still so many holes left, ones even *he* could see—and the only thing he wanted to protest about was that no doubt Scott was going to take him to dinner, and instead, all he wanted was to drag Scott home by his collar and spend the next few hours working off all his (sexual) frustration.

"Yes," Asa said grumpily. Because Scott was going to want to wine and dine him, without even the wine part, and the romance was nice, but how long had they waited to fuck? It was a freaking miracle they weren't as bad as Tristan and Wade.

They exited the practice facility on the north side, and Scott only took them a few blocks, down the street. Asa was surprised to see him turn into the building he knew was Sebastian's—the building he supposed was Beau's now, too.

"I hear this place on the ground floor is good. Beau says the chicken is great," Scott said.

"Gettin' date ideas from my son now?" Asa knew he sounded grumpy as hell, and it would've served Scott right for turning around and leaving him right there—but he didn't. He only smiled and opened the door, gesturing inside.

It was a dark restaurant, modern fixtures interspersed with big groupings of potted palms.

"Like they're gonna fool us into thinking we're in South America and not Miami," Asa muttered under his breath.

Scott rolled his eyes. "You gonna be like this all through dinner?"

Asa settled down in the out-of-the-way table that the hostess had shown them to. "Yes, maybe. If I feel like it."

But Scott only laughed. "Well, I'll give you this. Nobody else can do a snit quite like Asa Dawson."

"I don't think that's a compliment."

"It's not," Scott retorted lightly. "Now look at your menu like a good boy, and maybe you'll get dessert, too."

Asa raised an eyebrow. "What's dessert?"

"I don't know, but whatever it is, it's back at my place," Scott said. "Or yours. I'm not that picky."

Asa picked up his menu. "It's not like I haven't made it *clear* I'm totally willing to skip dinner entirely. Head straight to dessert."

"Yeah."

When Asa glanced up, surprised at the serious edge to Scott's voice, he saw he was frowning. "That's what landed you in the goddamned hospital."

Asa muttered something about Scott being as bad a nurse as Beau, Scott shot him back a hot look, and then the waiter approached, so Asa couldn't say anything else.

He took their drink orders, Asa ordering a beer because it would make Scott frown, and also because he goddamn wanted one.

But Scott didn't say a word, and just got the same.

It was most annoying, Asa decided, after their food arrived, that it turned out Beau had been right. The chicken, rubbed with a flavorful spice mix, and then roasted til it was a perfect golden brown, was delicious served with an herb mustard dipping sauce.

Asa tipped the rest of his beer down his throat, setting it down with a hard click on the table.

They'd made harmless small talk the entire meal, and while he'd refrained from additional comments, he did consider ordering another beer.

But when the waiter arrived and Asa opened his mouth to do it, screw whatever Scott—and definitely screw whatever Beau thought—he talked right over him, asking for the check.

After he left with their empty plates and promise to get the check, Asa crossed his arms over his chest. "You're just as bad as Beau, you know? So fucking bossy."

"Pot, meet kettle, darlin'."

Asa told himself that he didn't feel a zing of arousal up his spine. No way. He was annoyed. He was frustrated. The game plans hadn't been as good as he'd demanded, even though he knew, *he knew*, he hadn't given the coaching staff enough time to make them as polished as they needed to be.

"Ugh," Asa complained.

The waiter arrived with the check. Scott pulled out his wallet and tucked a few bills inside the envelope.

"Come on," he said. "We're going."

"Where are we going? Dessert time?" Asa could hear the hopefulness in his voice.

Scott shot him another one of those chastising looks that really shouldn't have been as hot as they were. He stood, and gestured for Asa to do the same, and then they headed towards the door.

"No," he said, once they were outside. "I said *a good little boy*, and you weren't good, were you? You've been fucking impossible all day, and honestly, I'm sick of it."

"I'm annoyed and frustrated, and *rightfully* so," Asa insisted.

"Yeah, sort of," Scott said. "But I got an idea. Might snap you out of your head. Or pull your head out of your ass. Either one. Come on."

"Am I still not allowed to ask about the destination or convince you to change your mind?" Asa asked.

"Yes," Scott said, and seemed disinclined to say anything else. All Asa could do was trail after him, after he annoyingly did not turn in the direction of their building, but seemed to head back to . . . the practice facility?

No, *past* the practice facility.

He was heading straight towards the stadium, the east entrance, the one that the players and the staff used, as well as any VIP guests. It was the only entrance that was monitored twenty-four seven, and somehow Scott seemed to know that.

"What are you doing? Where are we going?"

Scott raised an eyebrow, and Asa rolled his eyes. "I'm not arguing, I'm asking."

"Well, stop asking," he said.

Scott approached the security guard, and was shocked to see he let both of them in with just a single nod.

Like he'd known Scott was coming.

How far in advance had he arranged this?

Asa wasn't sure he wanted to ask.

Or if he was allowed to.

Scott was on a mission and didn't hesitate, went right through the gate, and turned left, then right, then punched a code into a doorway—a code *Asa* didn't even know, thank you very much—and then after descending three flights of stairs, they were in a very narrow hallway.

"What on earth are you doing?" Asa demanded to know.

Scott didn't stop, so Asa made a frustrated noise and reached out, catching his shoulder with his hand.

Scott was stronger—Scott had always been stronger, which had, at first, been an annoyance, and then inexplicably, a turn-on—but Asa surprised him and had no issue pushing him against the wall.

Or maybe he just really likes it when you manhandle him around.

Because he certainly wasn't fighting it.

Asa reached up and kissed him, cradling his face in his palms. Each and every time they did this, it still felt like a miracle and a revelation.

Sighing into his mouth, Scott tugged him closer against him, and his tongue stroked Asa's, for a long moment, Asa's mind emptied out of anything except: *Scott* and *want* and *now.*

"You're tryin' to distract me," Scott said breathlessly, his mouth still so close to Asa's that it would be so easy to just kiss him again.

Distract him again.

"Is it workin'?"

Scott smiled, dopey and perfect. *God*, he loved him. It overwhelmed him, swamped him so completely it was amazing that he wasn't constantly drowning in it.

You weren't today; you were an insufferable asshole today.

He had been, a little.

And he wouldn't even regret it, if he got what he wanted out of the staff. Out of his team. They'd thank him for it, after.

"Asa, you gotta know, it *always* works for me. Always. Even when you're being a dick."

Nobody but Scott could make him feel so rotten about something that felt so necessary.

"Sorry," he muttered.

"Come on," Scott said. "You'll like this."

Scott was already moving further down the narrow corridor before Asa could pull him back into his arms. But Scott like this was determined, and Asa had a feeling that even though he claimed his distraction tactics always worked, they wouldn't work right now.

This was Scott on a mission.

Asa just didn't know what the purpose of the mission was.

Only that there had to be one.

Scott pushed open the door at the end of the corridor, and to Asa's surprise, he could smell the field right away.

It was turf, of course, because almost every NFL stadium was turf now. Even the field at Tennessee had switched over to turf, halfway through his tenure there, even though he'd fought it.

There was nothing like playing on grass. The way it smelled and felt and just *was*.

But even the turf had a distinctive smell, like they piped in the scent of fresh grass to fool everyone that what they were playing on was real.

It was dark on the field, almost every light off, and Asa followed Scott as he picked his way around the benches on the sideline and then headed right onto the field itself.

His destination suddenly made a hell of a lot more sense.

They'd done this, a handful of times, many, many years ago, back when they'd been players at Alabama.

So Asa wasn't surprised to see Scott stop at the center of the field, right at the fifty-yard line and flop down.

Asa didn't immediately follow him. "Come on," Scott said. "Come lie with me. Commune with the field."

"You know, shit like this is what gives me a weird reputation," Asa said. "And it's not even *me*."

"I know." Scott sounded entirely unrepentant.

Asa could fight it, but Scott had always been the kind of presence in his life that wasn't just easier to let in, but that he *wanted* to let in. Dropping down to the turf, he found himself lying right next to Scott a few moments later.

"See?" Scott said in a dreamy voice as he stared up at the sky. Faint outlines of the stars were visible—faint because the light pollution from downtown Miami was so strong—but Asa still felt himself caught by their power.

Finally, he'd had enough of them and he turned over, looked right at Scott. "What am I supposed to be taking from this?"

Scott chuckled under his breath. "You remember, I know you remember."

"Communing with the field, yes. Visualizing the next game. Knowing I'm going to bring my A game. All of that woo-woo shit."

"And calming the fuck down," Scott added.

Asa made a face.

"It would've been more fun to de-stress me in bed," Asa said. Hearing—and hating—just how petulant he sounded. Maybe he did need to calm the fuck down.

"But not as effective as this. I want you to just lie here and think of the Condors game, alright?"

"I can't think of what you'd do if I just rolled on top of you? Decided to hump you in the middle of the goddamn stadium?"

A rueful chuckle escaped out of Scott's mouth. "We can do that next."

"Is that supposed to be a reward for doing your woo-woo shit?"

"Yes."

"Alright, fine." Asa gave in because *one*, climbing on top of Scott sounded like an excellent reward, and *two*, it wasn't like he wanted to be so bitchy. He definitely didn't want to be so bitchy to Scott, even though he was a part of his staff and, as a necessity, needed to be included.

Beau, too.

And now that he was thinking about it, he'd probably add Randy and Brett to that list, as well, even though the latter continued to test his patience with not only his occasionally poor decisions but also his distrust of Scott.

But Scott had clearly spent the afternoon with the defensive coaches, helping him with their plan, because his fingerprints were all over what he'd read through.

"Just lie back, and think of . . ."

"England?" Asa teased.

Scott laughed. "If they're who you're playing in next week's game, sure. Just . . . visualize the moment. Think of those empty stands being full. Think of the team taking the field. Think of the defense sacking Brady. Think of Pax tossing a fifty-yard touchdown to Nicholson. The scoreboard at the end of the fourth quarter."

Asa let the deepness of Scott's voice, the care in it, lull him into a dream state. He closed his eyes and pictured every one of those things, and then more.

He imagined shaking the Tampa coach's hand. Imagined Scott's arm around his shoulders. Imagined the pride on Beau's face.

The email he'd get from Rudy. Seeing the stands fill with impassioned, committed fans.

Getting to settle in to Miami.

And all the time, every single day, there was one constant.

It was Scott.

He turned towards him, opening his eyes.

"Feel better?" Scott asked.

He did. He felt calmer. More resolved. More certain that they could do this.

But the thing he felt the most certain about?

It was the man next to him.

"Yeah." Asa realized his voice was rough. How long had they been lying here in silence?

He'd lost himself a little bit, but not entirely, because the truth was, he couldn't ever lose himself completely because right there, anchoring him in place, was Scott.

And even though during their seven years apart, that connection had stretched out, and grown dim with the distance, it had never left, and now it was snapping back into place, stronger and tougher, and even more resilient than before.

"You're welcome," Scott said softly. Knew, without the words, that Asa was grateful.

Asa reached down and took his hand, squeezing it. "I love you, even when I don't like you very much."

"What?" Scott sounded pseudo-shocked. "I'm so likeable, too!"

It felt so natural to curl into him, to lay his head on Scott's broad chest. "The most likeable," he agreed. "Call it a personality flaw that sometimes I can't appreciate it."

"And yet"—Scott's voice rumbled under his head—"I love you anyway."

His grip tightened on Asa's back. Like he never wanted to let him go.

But Asa already knew he wasn't going anywhere.

Scott's hand dipped lower, and then lower still, sliding right over his ass, and suddenly the pleasantly warm feeling inside him ratcheted up a few degrees.

"It's dark out here," he said softly, "though there are some cameras. I slipped the guard some money to flip the feed off, but I can't guarantee . . . if you didn't want everyone to find out in a blurry video of you humping me in the middle of the field."

"I usually try to *not* give Helen an aneurysm, because it seems the rest of the team is determined to do it, but I think I've got an idea."

It hurt to pull away from Scott, but it helped to know it was only temporary. He held out a hand to Scott to help him up, but when he was upright, Asa didn't let go. Just squeezed it as they made their way off the field, towards the doorway they'd come through initially.

The narrow hallway was dimly lit, lined with plain gray walls and scuffed linoleum, but Asa didn't see any of it because as soon as the door was closed behind them, Scott pressed him against one of the walls and murmured into his mouth, "Have I mentioned how much I love your ideas?"

He could feel Scott's thigh, hot and heavy between his legs and he gasped as Scott leaned in and kissed him. Hard and soft, all at the same time. Passionate yet loving. Sweet and also so dirty he had Asa panting into his mouth with how much he wanted him.

For a minute and then another it was enough just to rub against each other, their kisses growing wilder by the moment, but then

Scott's fingertips dug into his ass and Asa felt the blood in his veins heat to molten lava.

He slid his own hand down the front of Scott's jeans, and felt his sharp exhale like a physical touch against his own cock.

It was a wonder that he was allowed to do this now. That Scott *wanted* him to. Was desperate for just the brush of Asa's hand.

"Like that idea even more," Scott panted as Asa's fingers trembled, flicking the button of his jeans open and tugging down the zipper.

Scott's cock was heavy and hot in his palm, and he groaned, head hitting the ugly concrete wall behind them as Asa worked him.

"I was thinkin' about this," Scott murmured, low and rough. "All the time we were lying there, I was thinking about you touchin' me. Just like that. God, just like that."

"Just like that?" Asa murmured, tightening his grip.

Scott groaned. "Yeah."

"I was thinkin' about this too, well, actually *this*," Asa said, and it felt so right to drop to his knees, hand still working Scott's cock, as his tongue slicked up the fine hairs that trailed down his stomach.

He'd dreamt about this, the very first time he'd ever seen Scott this way. He'd wondered if the sheen of Gatorade coating him would taste sweet.

But the truth was, Scott's skin tasted so good—sweet *and* salty—without any Gatorade at all.

He couldn't get enough as his tongue ventured lower and then lower still, joining his hand.

"I wanna know all about your fantasies. Every single goddamn one." Scott's voice rasped over Asa's already-taut nerves and he moaned, reaching down and palming himself through his pants. He was so keyed up, he felt if he did more than just brush his hand across his painfully erect cock, he'd come.

"It isn't a fantasy," Asa said breathlessly, around licking Scott's cock up and down, like it was his favorite lollipop. "We were there, in that bathroom after the National Championship and you took your shirt off and I wanted to know what you tasted like."

Under his touch, Scott's balls tightened and that was all the warning that Asa got before Scott was shuddering and coming down his throat.

He'd known it could happen and he'd been prepared for it, but it was still a lot, swallowing his first load.

And somehow, impossibly, that made him even harder, until he didn't know if he could touch himself without exploding the exact same way.

"Jesus Christ," Scott groaned as Asa sucked the last bit of come out of him. "I can't even fucking believe you. You're . . . you're too good to be true. Am I dreaming right now?"

"No," Asa said, his voice scratchy as he finally let Scott's cock slip from between his lips. "No, 'cause I wouldn't be . . ." He palmed himself again, his whole body trembling at the contact.

"Darlin', you gonna keep touching yourself for me?"

Asa could do that. He could keep doing that. Scott's gaze on him as he fumbled with his zipper felt even better than a physical touch, anyway.

His fingers closed around his cock, the phantom taste of Scott still in his mouth, on his tongue, making him twitch with the pleasure of it, and then Scott said, "Tell me more."

"Tell you more?" Asa panted.

"You wanted to lick me."

Asa's hand stuttered. "Yeah, I wanted to lick you. And then, a few months later, we went to Dairy Queen. It was hot." He didn't even know if he was making any goddamn sense, but Scott's eyes were so intent on him, on everything he was doing, on every single word out of his mouth, maybe it didn't matter. "It was hot and you got an ice cream, and then I wanted you to lick *me*."

"Oh God," Scott groaned, like he remembered that evening. The heat in the air. The claustrophobic humidity. The sweat beading on his forehead. The ice cream dripping down his hand.

Asa was remembering it too, he was lost in it, his hand moving faster as his orgasm hit him hard, shuddering and letting himself be taken by the overwhelming pleasure.

"Well, shit," Scott said.

When Asa opened his eyes, Scott's were level with his own, and he was cleaning up the mess he'd made on the floor with a napkin.

"Did you grab that from the restaurant?" Asa found himself nearly giggling at the idea Scott hadn't just planned a way to calm his assholeness down, but to deal with the inevitable horniness when he did.

It was freaking adorable.

Scott shrugged, but he was smiling.

And so was Asa.

They ended up sitting next to each other, knees up and backs against the wall.

Maybe it wasn't the most atmospheric place, but Scott was there, so it was still the best place in the world, as far as Asa was concerned.

"Really, that was the beginning for you?" Scott asked softly. "That day we won the National Championship?"

Asa had thought about this a lot.

He'd considered if it had started before that, for him, and he just hadn't realized it. Hadn't realized what those feelings were, what they felt like, what they meant, until they'd turned sexual.

And then they'd been impossible to deny.

"Yeah," he said, finally. "Though I think . . . it might've started, in some way, before that. But that day, I wanted to kiss you."

"Me too," Scott confessed, with a wry grin. "Though that was true of most days. But definitely that day. It felt . . . way too close to the surface, and I was afraid I couldn't hide it."

"I thought you were smiling at me differently," Asa said. "I didn't think I'd ever seen that look on your face before."

"You probably hadn't." Scott ducked his head, a blush warming up his cheeks. "I . . . I couldn't control it. Not that day."

"Me either, apparently. I nearly pushed you against the bath-room counter and kissed you."

"Wish you had," Scott said softly. "But I get why you didn't."

"Wish I had the day you left, too, damn the consequences," Asa said. "But it's okay. I think . . . I think we appreciate this a lot more now than we would've then."

"And I wasn't ready," Scott admitted, regret tinging his voice.

Asa put an arm around Scott's shoulders. "You know, it doesn't matter when you're ready. I'm next to you, no matter what."

Scott's head dipped down, rested on Asa's shoulder. "You couldn't get rid of me now, even if you tried. I'm yours. I've . . ." He hesitated. "I've always been yours."

Chapter Fourteen

"I'm trying to figure out why we're actually doin' this," Scott said, as he stared at the contents of the bowl Asa was using to mix up the cookie dough.

Poorly. That he was using to mix up the cookie dough *poorly*.

They were cookies, they shouldn't have been hard, but Asa was having trouble following the directions. Maybe because Scott had refused to get dressed after their post-dinner handjobs, and was wearing *only* a frilly apron he'd dug out of the box.

"We're doing this because someone gave it to me, and it would be wasteful not to use it."

"Oh, is that what this is? I thought you just wanted to get an eyeful of me in only an apron."

Asa shot him a look. "That was your idea, not mine. Though I'm not exactly opposed to the view."

"Thought so," Scott said smugly, grinning. "My naked ass has won you over to the idea of Christmas spirit."

"I really don't think any of this is what Santa had in mind," Asa said dryly.

"No?" Scott teased. He sidled closer, and Asa had no issues letting the wooden spoon drop into the bowl and wrapping his arms around Scott's middle, embracing him. Leaning into the embrace.

Asa tipped his head back and Scott covered his mouth in a hot kiss. How was it that each and every time they did this, he got lost? They'd just gotten off in a fury of clothes flying and hands and mouths less than an hour before this.

He should be good. Satisfied, even.

But he wasn't.

He wanted more.

He wanted every single bit of Scott that he could get.

Scott groaned into his mouth, tilting his head for better access, and Asa found his hips stuttering, searching for friction, somehow, impossibly, finding himself grow harder again.

And then, catastrophe.

Absolute catastrophe.

"What the ever-living fuck."

It was cold water, dashed on his head.

Dashed on *both* of their heads.

Scott lifted his head off Asa's mouth slowly, cautiously.

They both knew that voice.

He'd be hearing that voice, in that betrayed, accusatory tone, forever.

He stepped away from Scott. One step back. And then another.

Beau made a disgusted noise and Asa's heart dropped to the floor. Scott was only wearing the apron, and it was impossible for his son to miss.

Or that they'd been kissing. Passionately.

"Beau," Asa said. He turned around. It was one of the hardest things he'd ever done, to face his son, now that he knew the truth, and not because he'd *told* him the truth, like he knew he should've done ages ago.

Utter confusion was written across Beau's features. Like he couldn't believe what he was seeing. Like he couldn't even compute the image in front of him.

Well, Asa supposed that answered the question he'd wondered, which was if Beau had guessed what was really going on.

He hadn't.

"I was knocking, and knocking . . ." he said, like he didn't even know how this had happened.

That made two of them.

Three of them, actually.

"I guess," Beau continued, voice and gaze hardening, "you didn't hear me 'cause you were *busy*."

"Beau . . ." But that was all Scott got out before Beau shot him a blistering look full of anger.

"No, you don't get to say a goddamn word," Beau said. "Not a *goddamned word*. Though maybe you should put some clothes on."

Asa just wanted to sink through the floor and die. And he was the one who was totally dressed. At least, he glanced down, he was *mostly* dressed. His t-shirt had come untucked from his sweatpants and he had a feeling his hair was rumpled, because Scott had had his fingers in it twice now.

"Beau, I'm real sorry you had to find out this way."

"Yeah, I just bet you are," Beau shot back. He crossed his arms over his chest. "So there's something to *find out*, then? This isn't just some random situation, where you accidentally fell into Scott's arms and his clothes flew off?"

Asa took a deep breath. "No."

"I didn't think so."

Asa thought of all the times Beau had been angry with him in the last twenty-five years. The list was actually not very long.

They'd always been close, had always operated on the same wavelength.

But of those half a dozen times Beau had been furious with him, he'd never looked like this before.

Like the Asa in front of him wasn't someone he recognized. Like he was a stranger.

Even when he and Lynn had sat him down and told him about the divorce, he'd never looked like this.

He'd told Scott a few weeks ago that Beau put him on a pedestal, that he'd never imagine that there'd be something this big that his father just wouldn't tell him.

The truth of that statement *ached*.

"I'm just gonna . . ." Scott waved towards Asa's bedroom. "Get some clothes. Give you two some space."

Beau rolled his eyes and didn't say a word, even when Scott slid past the pair of them.

"I'm so sorry, Beau, I should have told you a long time ago," Asa said, because it was true. He'd been a coward. And he wasn't usually cowardly.

Beau didn't say anything, just pursed his lips and looked away. Like he couldn't even look his father in the eye anymore.

The worst part of this was how justified Asa knew he was.

"I wanted you to be happy for us, when you found out, and maybe . . . maybe that was a pipe dream."

"Ya think?" Beau shook his head. "Sebastian told me he sensed some weird undercurrents between you two, and I told him he was *crazy*, I insisted on it, I promised him there was no way anything was going on, because all you were was friends."

"We *are* friends."

"That's not how I act with my friends," Beau retorted.

"Obviously not only friends now, but we were *just friends* for a long time." Asa knew how pathetic he sounded. How meager the excuses he kept grasping for were.

"I feel like nothing I knew was right," Beau said, damnably.

"Beau—" Asa tried again. Even though he already knew there was nothing he could say.

Nothing at all.

"Just tell me one thing," Beau interrupted. "How long has this been going on?"

"Before he left for Washington, before that. When we won the National Championship."

If Asa had thought Beau's gaze was cold before, it chilled him to the bone now.

"You mean *seven years ago?*"

Asa nodded. Miserable.

How could you be so happy and yet so completely devastated at the same time? He would have told himself it was impossible, but the two things warred inside with him.

He'd won the man he loved, possibly at the cost of the son he adored.

"That's why you didn't want him here. He what . . . went to Washington? Left you. And you were angry."

"Sort of like that," Asa said. Not sure how many details he should share. How many details Beau really wanted to know. Or if the nitty gritty of what had happened would actually make it worse.

Maybe he deserved that. Maybe he deserved it to be the worst it could be.

"And that's the truth of why you were pissed off."

Asa sighed, leaning a hip against the kitchen cabinets. He couldn't quite believe that only ten minutes ago, he'd been laughing with Scott, trying to make Christmas cookies. "Yeah. Things . . . well, they ended badly between us."

"And you never told me."

"There wasn't anything to tell you, Beau, back then. Nothing ever happened. I . . ."

Beau had been so bewildered and confused. Clearly pissed off, but the utter disorientation had been taking a backseat to the betrayal. The anger.

Now he lashed out with it.

"Nothing? You didn't know you were queer? You didn't know we were alike? I *came out* then, Dad, I got on the internet and told the world about me, and you just . . . sat back and said fucking *nothing*."

"I didn't say nothing," Asa said quietly. "I supported you, every way I knew how."

"Except telling me you got it. That you understood. That you were the *same*," Beau yelled. "All those fucking conversations about it and you never said! Not once! You did all this, with the team this year, and *you never said*. Not even to me. Not even when I wondered why you'd be this way."

"I'm this way, because it's who I am," Asa said.

It was the only defense he could offer.

The rest of it? Well, the rest of it was true.

Galling and painful, but *true*.

"You must've had a real good laugh at my expense, pulling one over on me, all these years," Beau said bitterly.

"No . . . never . . . we wanted . . ." Asa sighed. "I had this idea that I'd tell you and I'd tell you everything, and you'd be happy for us."

"One big happy family," Beau inserted sarcastically.

"I imagined telling you I loved Scott practically my whole life, and then, it was a miracle, because I fell in love with him," Asa said.

It was pitiful. But it was all he had.

"Well, keep imagining," Beau said. "This conversation is over."

He turned to leave, and Asa nearly went to stop him, but then Beau shot him a look, and it just . . . deflated him.

What if he never got over it? What if Beau spent the next twenty years, the next thirty years, hating him?

Asa gripped the edge of the counter, a nauseating wave of pain cresting through him.

"I didn't mean to listen."

Scott was back, dressed now in jeans and a t-shirt, and his expression was sober and sympathetic. Sympathy that Asa was pretty sure he didn't deserve.

He tugged Asa into his arms, and for a minute, Asa just let himself soak up the comfort that he knew, deep down, he wasn't worthy of.

"It's not a big apartment," Asa said, his voice muffled by the big, broad shoulder of Scott's.

"I'm sorry, Asa," he said finally.

Asa pulled away.

"Don't apologize to me," Asa said. "Apologize to Beau."

"I'm sure he'll take his pound of flesh outta me," Scott said regretfully.

"But you didn't tell him because I didn't."

He'd doomed not just his own relationship with his son—but Scott's too. He'd wiped away both of Beau's father figures with one misguided choice.

"No, but I could've pushed you harder about it. I could have done things different seven years ago, and then today wouldn't have ever happened."

"You can't keep apologizing for that," Asa said.

"Maybe not, but I can keep feelin' bad about it," Scott retorted.

"I did this," Asa said. "I did this, and I'm going to be paying for it."

"He'll get over it. He loves you. He wants you to be happy. He knew it, even though he didn't really *know*, when he called me and had me come to Miami. He knew you'd trust me, that I would help you. That I'd make you happy. Even if we were just friends. That's what he wanted, Asa. He's just feeling . . ."

"Betrayed and embarrassed? Pissed the fuck off?"

Scott's lips turned up into a bittersweet smile. "Yeah. All of those things."

"What if he doesn't ever want to listen? What if he won't forgive me?" Asa heard the despair in his voice.

"He's going to," Scott said. Asa wanted to know how he found that confidence. "He loves both of us. This is just a big shift. But he's going to find it in himself to forgive. You found it in yourself to forgive him."

"For what?"

Scott shot him a soft, chiding look. "For falling in love with your corner-slash-safety?"

Asa brushed that aside. "That wasn't something I needed to *forgive* him for. It was just love; I know how capricious it is. I guess I should've been surprised it didn't happen before it did.

And honestly, they tried to sneak around, bless their hearts, but they were terrible at it. I knew, probably before they even did."

"I don't think we were very subtle either," Scott retorted wryly. "Beau didn't see it because he didn't want to see it."

"Love never is," Asa said with a heavy sigh. "What am I gonna do?"

"Give him some time. Some space. I told you, he's gonna come around. Right now, he's probably crying and ranting and that's Sebastian's problem. But because he picked real good, Sebastian will listen and then he'll eventually tell him some hard truths."

"Like?"

"That you're his father. That he loves you. That he loves me. That he should be happy for us. Ultimately, that the only people whose business it is that we fell in love is ours."

Asa shot Scott a look. "I hope he saves that last bit until Beau's *really* calmed down."

Scott shrugged. "Sebastian's a real good straight shooter. I like him a lot. I like him for Beau. And hey, the silver lining in all this, Beau's angry boyfriend can't come punch you in the face for hurting him, 'cause you're his coach and he's not stupid."

"That's supposed to be the silver lining? Not getting punched in the face?"

"Did you want to get punched? In the face?"

Asa rolled his eyes. "Does anybody? Though it might actually hurt less."

Scott reached out and squeezed Asa's shoulder. "This'll be the worst of it. I know it's gonna get better."

Except Scott wasn't right.

The worst came the next morning—*early* the next morning—when after a mostly sleepless night, Asa was woken up by his phone blaring.

For one single moment, he thought it might be Beau, ready to talk, ready to listen.

But a single glance at the screen told him otherwise.

"Lynn," Asa answered with a sigh of resignation.

Of course Beau had called his mother.

Scott mumbled next to him, and Asa slid out of bed, as quietly as possible, heading into the living room.

"You there with Scott?" Lynn's voice was amused, and almost entirely free of judgement.

Of course she knew some of it—more than Beau, anyway.

He'd had to tell someone, in the aftermath of Scott's sudden departure, and it had felt natural to tell the one other person he'd trusted.

"Not right at this moment. It's really fucking early," Asa grumped as he opened up the sliding patio door. "In case you didn't realize."

"Oh, I did. Was up half the night, trying to reason with Beau."

"Oh." Asa felt the bottom drop out of his stomach again. And the worst of it was that he probably deserved it. He deserved Beau's anger and he deserved the frustration in his ex-wife's voice.

"Good news," she said, "he's not going to quit and go running off somewhere."

"Should I thank you for that?"

"Me, and definitely Sebastian. He's a good guy for our son."

"I know," Asa retorted dryly.

"I *am* disappointed that I had to find out that you finally did something about that long-burning crush of yours because Beau called me, pissed as hell that he'd caught the two of you kissing. And Scott! Only wearing an apron." She was chuckling now and Asa made a frustrated noise.

"It's the season, Lynn. We're busy."

"Not too busy to not *get busy*, apparently," she said lightly.

"I was going to tell you, you know? You and Beau, both, of course. Though you knew some of it already."

"Like I could ever forget you calling me in the middle of the night, crying, because he'd left."

"Not *only* because he left," Asa reminded her. "Because . . . well, you know why."

"And that's why I have to tell you first, that I'm really happy you found each other again. I'm assuming he apologized and groveled, etcetera, etcetera."

"Yes," Asa said. "Though not all of it was his fault, you know, I could have gone after him, I could have made him change his mind . . ."

"Spoken like a man in love," Lynn said mischievously.

"Yes, yes, but you knew that. You knew I loved him."

"Still fun to tease you about it."

"Lynn—it's not even six in the fucking morning."

"Yes, well, whose fault is that? You should have told Beau all about it when Scott first came to Miami, Asa. And you knew I thought you should've told him way back when, whenever it was that Scott left."

"I fucked it up. That what you want to hear?"

"Asa," Lynn chided. "Not at all. I wouldn't have spent half the night convincing Beau not to walk out and leave you if I thought you deserved any of this. Though you *still* should have told him."

"I know," Asa said. "Believe me, I know that."

"He's just shocked. Embarrassed. Feeling stupid that he was the last one to know."

"I don't think he was the *last* one to know," Asa said. "I haven't told my boss yet. Or any of the coaching staff. Or the rest of the team."

"So you're planning on doing that?"

"Beau was always the first step of the plan," Asa said wryly. "So yeah, eventually. This is still real new; we're still figuring things out . . ."

"He loves you, and you love him. Seems straightforward to me," Lynn said. Because she would think so. She'd always been so goddamned pragmatic. One of the things he'd loved about her.

It had taken him a long time to realize he'd loved her, but he wasn't in love with her. Maybe he never had been, but at the least she'd always been one of his best friends.

"Was there something else you needed?"

"Yes, actually . . ." Lynn's tone softened. "I wanted to say I'm happy for you, and also caution you to be understanding with Beau, Asa. He's hurt. He's prickly. He's going to lash out—even if he doesn't mean it."

"I know, I know all of that. I'm . . . I know I deserve it. You don't have to worry about what I'll say."

"I don't *worry* per se," Lynn hesitated. "I just think you both have your pride and sometimes you let that get in the way. Don't let it get the better of you this time. Eventually he's going to want to hear the whole story. Wait til he's ready."

"What if he's never ready?" Asa wasn't going to ask the question that had haunted his whole night—which might haunt his entire life—but it came out anyway.

Lynn sighed sympathetically. "I know why you're afraid, but, Asa, you have to know that won't happen. He's so hurt *because* he loves you. This didn't kill that vision of you in his head, it just dented it a little. And I trust, with time, it's going to get straightened out. But the time? That's going to be key. You can't rush him."

"Not even a little bit?"

He could hear her smile through the phone. "Alright, a little bit. We know he's stubborn too, and he'll be stubborn just because he can. But you'll know when the time is right, because you know him."

"Thank you," Asa said, and meant it. "For the advice and for . . . well, everything else."

"When I decided to move to New York, I told you I wanted you to be happy. That was all. I'm just glad you're doing something about it, finally."

"Me too." He'd have rather done it without costing him Beau's respect and his love, but if Lynn said that he'd get over it . . . she was usually right about these sorts of things.

When Asa opened the balcony sliding door and walked back into the living room, he saw the kitchen light was on.

Scott was standing at the sink, his back was to him, and he was filling up the coffee pot with water.

All he wore was a pair of those tight black boxer briefs that Asa imagined pulling off with his teeth.

Desire wasn't supposed to pull with those sharp claws. He'd never experienced want this potent before, and he didn't know how to deal with it.

Somehow, though, he didn't think Beau was going to want to hear that as an excuse.

"Hey, sorry, didn't mean to wake you," Asa said, leaning against the arched wall that led into the kitchen.

Scott glanced up at him. "It's all good," he said. "Though I don't think it was you. Thought I heard Lynn's voice."

"Yes."

"She yell at you?"

"About Beau? No, actually. Though she thought I should've told him ages ago."

Scott gave a noncommittal nod, as he poured the water into the coffee maker and hit start.

So noncommittal that it didn't matter what Scott didn't say, because he'd as good as said the words out loud.

"You think so too," Asa stated as he pulled down two mugs from the cupboard.

Scott shrugged. "I get why you didn't after I left. I sure as hell didn't want to talk about it, either. So I get why you didn't. But . . . now? If it was me, I'd have told him when he arranged for me to come to Miami."

"I know. I screwed it up," Asa said with a sigh. "It was just . . . so fucking much, you know? And what if it didn't work out? What if we didn't fix things?"

"Then he never had to know."

But the moment Scott said it, Asa realized just how shitty it was. Not that he was required to divulge every closely held secret to his adult son, but that he'd hoped that he wouldn't have to tell him *this* one.

"I fucked this up," Asa said, as the coffee finished percolating. "Maybe I'll get a chance to fix it."

"You will." Scott sounded certain. "I'm guessing Lynn told you to be patient."

"Yeah." Asa poured coffee. Took a sip and savored how strong it was. "The good news at least is I know he'll be professional."

"That is a certainty," Scott agreed, taking a drink of his own coffee. "He learned from the best, after all." He paused, after Asa made a face. "No, you don't get to do that, alright?"

"Do what?"

Scott set his coffee down and took Asa's from his hands. Put his palm on Asa's chest and wrapped the other arm around his waist, pulling him close. "Diminish yourself 'cause you didn't do the right thing, for once," Scott murmured.

In Scott's arms, skin to skin, it felt like everything would be better.

It would be so easy to let the comfort of him, and the love radiating out of every pore of his skin, chase all his worries away. It would be so much easier to shield the worst of it by hiding here.

Instead, they needed to go to work.

He'd need to face Beau, across the conference room table and on the practice field, and pretend nothing was wrong. He'd need to believe he hadn't completely destroyed his relationship with his son.

He sighed, and took one more moment of comfort, and then pulled back.

"I guess," Asa said, "it's time to go to work."

Scott didn't think he'd ever seen Asa more thrown.

When personal issues would have normally interfered with the regular work of the football team, Asa simply hadn't ever let them.

He'd gotten divorced, and nobody would've guessed.

Then he'd fallen in love, and until he'd told him, explicitly, Scott had never been entirely sure that he had.

After he'd left, Scott would guess that nothing outwardly had changed, because Beau had never suspected what really happened between them.

But today?

Asa was both quieter and also harsher. When he did speak up, it was like the situation pulled the words from him unwillingly. And he was even tougher on the staff and the players than usual. Even more so than yesterday.

He'd stood up in the meeting and, in a few clinical sentences, gave his assessment of the game plans. He'd adjusted them himself, he'd said, because that meant they were done right.

Scott hadn't missed Randy and Brett exchanging frustrated glances.

If Asa wasn't careful, his rough handling was going to result in losing staff when he needed to keep them the most.

And really, it wasn't like him. To be tough, yes, to be exacting, absolutely. The Monday morning meeting had been about that. But this was a different beast.

It was Beau sitting in his normal spot, his expression completely blank, not adding anything to the conversation unless someone asked him directly.

Scott inwardly sighed as practice began, because he knew he was going to need to talk to Asa about this.

He'd never been that kind of coach—and Scott *knew* he didn't have any intention of starting now, but he was doing this anyway.

Like he couldn't help himself.

Like he was trying to provoke a reaction out of his son. Any reaction at all.

Scott worried that he wouldn't like it when Beau finally broke.

"Yo, Callaway, you ready to get some good reps in?" Howard called out as he jogged onto the practice field for the team warmup. Micah was trailing behind Sebastian like a shadow, and at least that was something positive to focus on.

"I think the question is, are *you* ready?" Scott retorted.

Sebastian grinned and came closer, finally leaving Micah behind. He slapped Scott on the shoulder. "I have to say," he said, his mischievous expression turning solemn, "I did not expect Beau to come storming in last night, ranting about aprons and kissing and betrayal."

"Oh?" Scott asked, raising an eyebrow.

"Alright, I expected Coach to tell him, voluntarily, and *then* for him to start ranting about kissing and father figures and betrayal," Sebastian admitted.

"I think . . ." Scott hesitated. "The timeline just got moved up a little. And sincerely, I don't think either of us wanted to tell him that way."

"Your naked ass in an apron?" Sebastian raised an eyebrow. "I bet not."

"I'm not ever gonna live that down, right?"

"Never." Sebastian was smiling now.

"I had a feeling," Scott said with a resigned sigh. "But it was still worth it. Would've been *more* worth it if Beau hadn't interrupted."

"I bet." Sebastian chuckled. "I could get an apron; you gotta bet I'd look real good in one, too. I could whip up a meal . . . but maybe too soon."

"Beau would probably run screaming from the room." It felt good to laugh about it, actually. Especially when he'd felt so dragged down by Asa's understandably acute pain and self-loathing this morning.

It wasn't like he didn't regret the ability to tell Beau the *right* way about him and Asa, because he did, but he also trusted that Beau would come around.

"Yeah, the opposite situation I'm going for, you get me?" Sebastian said, winking.

"I do get you," Scott said dryly.

"I just came over to say . . . no hard feelings, alright? Beau's pissed, but I get that it's . . . complicated to come out. Not always easy. But you got a safe spot here, if you need it. If you want it."

"Thanks, that means a lot," Scott said. "I'm not sure you should be telling *me* this 'cause while I was worried before, I'm all in here."

"Ah, it's Coach."

"I'm not sure if *worried* is the right term. But I do know he agonized over what and when to tell Beau. And then . . ."

"He never got the chance."

"Yeah," Scott said.

"Huh, well, I just want to say . . . hang in there. You've got supporters here," Sebastian said, patting him on the back before he jogged over to join the defense.

He hadn't had to do that, but Scott appreciated it, deep down, because he'd never been sure that he *would* be accepted.

But here, he would be. And if he wasn't, for some bizarre reason, then he could go to a place where he was. He would carve out that spot, because he was done fitting himself into the available space—the next place he settled, it would fit around *him*.

He was just feeling resolved—*settled*, really, because he knew what he wanted, and that he was going to get it, and he *knew* Asa would be next to him, because there was no way he was losing him again—when Beau walked out of the tunnel from the locker room, onto the field. And instead of meeting his eyes, meeting Scott's friendly olive branch of a smile, Beau's glance slid right over him, like he didn't even fucking exist.

Well, shit.

Maybe it would take longer than he'd thought.

Maybe he'd underestimated how tough Beau's forgiveness was going to be to earn. Not just for Asa, but for himself, too.

Practice started. Asa was still veering wildly between silence and not-nearly-enough silence. He yelled at Sebastian, who brushed it off.

Spoke up to Pax a few minutes later, chastising him in a way that Scott hadn't heard him do once, not since he'd gotten there. And from the way Davis glanced over, concerned, Scott had a feeling he hadn't done it much before that, either.

"Again, *again*," Asa bellowed as the defense lined up against the second team offense, the line pushing against the backup offensive line. It was a push they should've gotten every time, and they weren't. It was why they were having such difficulty pressuring the opposing team's quarterback. Not enough push. "You guys gotta find another gear. An *NFL* gear," Asa muttered. It was low, but loud enough for nearly everyone on this side of the field to hear.

Brett glared, 'cause he was naturally protective of his guys and the effort they were expending. "They were *NFL* players couple a weeks ago," Brett muttered as he headed towards the bench. Where, Scott realized, Beau was sitting, with a tablet in front of him. His attention looked completely absorbed, but . . . well, this was Beau. He saw and *heard* everything. "Somehow now they ain't good enough? Bullshit," Brett continued to bitch as he passed right by Beau.

Brett had nearly made it past Beau when his arm shot out and he stopped Brett right in his tracks.

Beau was on the shorter side—maybe five ten on a good day—and slender. Brett was at least forty pounds overweight and had been a big guy before he'd started packing on the pounds. But Beau stopped him and didn't flinch.

"What the hell?" Brett said.

"He might be a real dick sometimes, but that man is your boss and your coach," Beau said softly. Enunciating each word clearly. "Some respect is in order."

"Not when he's goin' around talking shit," Brett blustered.

"He might be, and it might be *real* shit," Beau said. "But he's earned the right to do it. To expect the most out of us. That's why we're here, isn't it?"

And Scott knew, he *knew*, watching as Brett walked away, sulking, and Beau returned to his tablet, like nothing had ever happened, like they'd never exchanged words, that Beau would forgive.

It might be a bit of time coming, but Beau loved his father and respected him, with every ounce of his being.

He might resent that Asa hadn't told him about his queerness. Or who he'd fallen in love with. But that didn't mean he'd judge him for it.

At least not in the long run.

Scott let out his breath and the rest of the anxiety he'd been carrying around melted away.

Everything was going to be fine.

Just fine.

Chapter Fifteen

"I know," Asa said, as he stood in front of the gathered players and staff in the biggest ballroom of the hotel they always stayed at before home games, "that I've been hard on you this week. Extra hard. Which . . ." He smiled. "Maybe that seemed weird, since we bounced back in Chicago against the Bears, but here's the thing. I don't want us to win games because of happy accidents. Because of luck. I want us to win because we goddamn deserve it, because we played our fucking hearts out, because we outplayed the other team. That's how I want to win. We win that way? The sky's the limit. In a month we could be hosting playoff games here in our home stadium. But we won't, not if we don't hold the line."

The players erupted in a cacophony of whoops and cheers. They seemed focused. Ready. Everyone had settled down, after the first few rough days of the week.

Asa knew he could get intense. Over-focused, some people would call it.

He'd gotten that way, earlier this week. Scott had seen it and had helped him overcome it.

And then the thing with Beau had blown up all his carefully cultivated plans to dial back his intensity while keeping the players and the coaches locked in to the goal.

He hadn't even wanted to get up here and give a speech but he always did. He couldn't beg off because he'd felt sick to his stomach for the last few days. He couldn't delegate such an important task because he'd fucked up his relationship with his son and he wasn't talking to him.

Scott kept reassuring him that Beau was going to come around, but other than necessary conversations, they'd barely exchanged a handful of sentences.

And now, while every other person in the room seemingly hung on every word Asa was saying, Beau's gaze slid right over him, like he wasn't even up here speaking.

It sucked. It really sucked. But it really put everything in perspective, Asa thought. He knew what was most important now. Beau and Scott. Then football. He'd known it before, but he'd never believed it as strongly as he did now.

Still, he was the head coach of this football team and he'd committed to the season, to delivering a winning season to the people of Miami and the ownership. He wasn't going to let them down—not now.

"As always, great speech," Randy said, as he stepped down off the makeshift podium and eyed the group, wondering if he should mingle first.

"Thanks," Asa said, and because he knew he'd been hard on Randy—and Brett, too—he gave Randy a quick hug. "Appreciate you pullin' in such crazy hours this week, workin' as hard as you did."

"'Course," Randy said, smiling. "I think it'll be worth it."

"Me too," Asa agreed.

And because he'd started his apology tour, he found Brett, and smoothed things over with him. When he finished, he looked at his watch.

In twenty minutes it would be curfew, and the crowd would dissipate, heading to their rooms.

Where could he do the best good with what time they had left?

Genuinely, there was only one person he thought of. The only way to finish his apology tour.

The rest of the team was prepared.

But then there was Beau, sitting by himself, in the front row, eyes glued to his tablet.

Lynn—and Scott, too—had made him promise he wouldn't push Beau to accept an apology before he was ready.

He did not seem ready. But then he knew how stubborn Beau could be. He'd look stiff-necked and pissed off forever, if given half a chance.

I just want to explain. Except that Asa still wasn't sure he knew what he'd say.

Was there even a legitimate explanation that might soften him up? Asa wasn't sure.

He felt Scott come up behind him. "You sneakin' out again?" he asked, his warm breath close to Asa's ear. Goose bumps erupted on his arms. "'Cause I'm lookin' forward to it."

So was Asa, even though he shouldn't be. He should be feeling guilty til the end of time, but he just didn't.

Not even a little.

Making himself miserable wasn't going to make Beau forgive him any faster.

"You'd better be ready and waitin'," Asa said sternly. Turned just in time to see Scott's wide grin.

"How could I do anything else?"

"Besides," Asa added, before Scott walked away, "I wanted to tell you . . . I set up that meeting with Rudy, Christmas night."

"You're really gonna do it, then," Scott said, sounding surprised but not disappointed. Not afraid. There was a quiet resignation, an acceptance in his gray eyes.

It was that look that made Asa even more resolved.

He was going to tell Rudy about him and Scott, Scott right by his side when he did it. And it was going to be fine. More than fine, even. Rudy was gonna wave his hand and say, "Alright, it's not like I give a shit, as long as you keep winning, and we go to the playoffs."

But Scott, he had built this up in his head as a watershed moment, the opportunity someone was going to need to boot him right out of football.

He needed to see it for himself. Experience the validation of someone learning the truth and not caring.

"We're going to do it together, unless you've changed your mind," Asa said. "'Cause I know how you feel about it, and I could keep doin' things this way. But you said you never wanted to sneak around."

"I don't," Scott said. "Not anymore."

"Then we're on," Asa said.

Scott gave a sharp nod.

Asa headed over to where the offensive line was gathered. Joked with Logan, who told him that he'd better keep his eyes open for his surprise at the big Piranhas Christmas party, held this year the day *after* Christmas so that the players and coaches could spend the day with their loved ones.

After, Asa glanced around, wondering if Beau was still around, but he didn't see him. He'd left, apparently.

It shouldn't have made him feel worse, that they'd missed yet another opportunity to talk, but it did.

He rode up the elevator up to his floor, pulled his key out of his pocket and let himself into his room. This time he'd dropped a few discreet words into Kelly's ear about making sure he and Scott were close by. "Might be a few last-minute details we need to work out, night before the game," Asa had told her, trying to keep a serious face, because while there *might* be, it wasn't like that was the primary reason he was sneaking off to Scott's room in the middle of the night.

The truth was, he couldn't stay away.

And he supposed, next game, he wouldn't even need to tell Kelly the little white lie. After Rudy had been informed, they could tell anyone they wanted to. They could share a room without anyone blinking twice.

Well, Asa wasn't that naive.

There'd definitely be some talk.

There was nothing this team loved more than to gossip about who was sleepin' with who.

He waited ten minutes after curfew hit, and then after slipping into sweatpants and a t-shirt, sliding his feet into old, worn-out sneakers, he pocketed his room key and headed three doors down to Scott's room.

Scott answered the door before he could even get a second knock in, and greeted him with a hungry kiss, pressing him against the wall like he hadn't been able to wait a single additional second for him to show up.

"Hey," Scott said when he finally came up for air, "I wanted to show you something."

Flustered, Asa teased, "You know, you don't need to pretend it's not your dick."

Scott flushed. "It's actually *not* my dick. You know I was talkin' to Helen, trying to put together some kind of statement for the press?"

Asa nodded, because he knew Scott had been considering putting out a short, to-the-point statement about his sexuality. That it had been years and years coming.

He also knew he'd never been prouder.

"We finished it, I think," Scott said, rubbing his neck. Asa trailed after him, to where Scott's laptop was set up on the tiny desk opposite the bed. "I wanted you to read it, see what you thought."

"What I think isn't all that important," Asa said seriously, leaning over the screen. Scott's hand settled warm and heavy on his back. "What do *you* think about it?"

"I like it. I think . . . I thought I could avoid this, and then I thought, why would I? I hate what I did for all those years. If someone like me had come out twenty years ago, publicly, without flinching about it, maybe I'd have gone about everything differently."

Asa leaned into his touch. "You don't owe anyone anything, Scott."

"No, but the way I see it, I owe myself something. If I do it like this, I'll be able to hold my head high. And that . . ." Scott's voice was wry. "That matters."

Asa read through the few lines. It was sparse, which wasn't a surprise. The vehemence of it, though, took him by surprise.

"You're really gonna say the toxic masculinity still running rampant in the world of collegiate and professional football is what stopped you?"

Asa turned, in time to see Scott shrug. "It's the truth."

"Yeah, but it's . . ."

"Angry? Pissed off? Sorta." Scott looked vaguely embarrassed. "I guess I'm all of those things, still. Helen thought we should lean into it. Not sanitize it. And it felt right, but if you don't . . ."

"Scott." Asa laid a hand on his arm. "This is all you. What feels right to you."

"I know that. But you're part of me, too. You're part of this. Everyone's gonna know you and I, we're together. This colors you, too."

"Well," Asa pointed out dryly, "it's not like I haven't been actively trying to push down all these temples to toxic masculinity."

"You might've even inspired me a bit," Scott said. Leaning down and brushing a firm kiss across Asa's mouth. "A lot, actually."

If that's true, then why did I hide the truth from Beau? Was I really afraid? Was I makin' all these statements because it was easy when it wasn't me? When it didn't impact me directly?

Asa didn't know.

Because when he thought of everyone finding out the truth—that he was queer, and that he was with Scott—he didn't feel anything but joy. Joy for him, joy for Scott, joy that they could live together, finally, and stop being afraid of what the world might say.

But surely, if he hadn't been afraid, he would have figured out a way to tell Beau the truth?

A knock sounded on the door.

"Ugh," Scott said, pulling away. "I guess I better answer that."

"Do that, and then send them away ASAP," Asa teased.

But when Scott opened the door, he glanced back at Asa. "I don't think you're gonna want me to do that," he said seriously. Then opened the door wider and Asa caught a glimpse of Beau, the most emotion he'd seen on his face since he'd found out the truth, standing there.

He froze.

"I knocked on my dad's door and he wasn't in . . . so I figured the place he was most likely to be was here," Beau was saying. He didn't even sound upset about it. "Can I talk to him for a minute?"

"You think it's just gonna take a minute?" Scott asked.

Beau shrugged. "It's gonna take as long as it's gonna take."

"Alright," Scott said. Asa could see him lay a hand on Beau's shoulder and squeeze. "And we'll have our conversation soon, I imagine."

"I don't think you're gonna get out of it that easily," Beau teased.

Asa approached where they stood at the door.

"Come on," Beau said. "I think this probably deserves a beer. I have a six-pack in my room."

"You're gonna talk to me *and* actually gonna allow me to enjoy a beer?" Asa said with mock surprise. "Hell really has frozen over."

Beau rolled his eyes, and for the first time since he'd surprised him and Scott, the tightness in Asa's stomach began to loosen. Things really were going to be okay.

Beau wouldn't forgive him easily, but he *would* forgive him.

He wasn't going to gain the love of his life at the expense of the relationship with his son. *Thank God.*

The walk to Beau's room was quiet, and once they were inside, Asa took a seat in the chair in front of the desk and accepted the open beer when Beau handed it to him.

He didn't sit, he just stared at Asa.

Like he expected him to have grown a second head, or something.

Finally he spoke. "I keep lookin' at you and expecting you to be different. Look different."

"You know better than to believe that," Asa said.

"I do, and yet I keep doing it." Beau sighed. Then sat down on the edge of the bed. "Why didn't you tell me?"

"I didn't know how."

When Beau opened his mouth to question that, Asa held up a hand. "Just . . . let me finish this, okay? And then you can ask me anything you want, and I'll tell you the truth."

"Okay." Beau took a drink of his beer.

This was it. Now or never. It was funny, the moment had come, and Asa *still* didn't know what he was supposed to say. Usually he knew the right thing to say, the magical words that would unlock any given situation, but now? He felt stupid, like all his gifts had deserted him.

"I didn't know how I felt about Scott. I didn't know for a long time that I wasn't straight. I knew I loved him. I knew your mother and I had ended up better friends than a married couple. But I had no interest in dating or romance or any of that, I was only interested in football. And Scott, it turns out. Then we won the National Championship and . . . I'm gonna try to promise not to be too . . . what do y'all call it? *TMI?* But you wanted an answer and there's . . . well, there's some of that in there."

"It's alright. I can just bleach my brain, later," Beau said dryly.

"Remember when you walked into that bathroom where we were cleanin' up before the trophy presentation and all the interviews?"

Beau nodded.

"That was the first time I felt sexual attraction to Scott. I loved him before, but after that day, I loved him different. Maybe I always loved him different, and I didn't know. Didn't realize. I'm not sure. But after that day, it was undeniable."

"I've been thinkin' about that time, about that year," Beau admitted, "and you seemed different that year. Distracted. Not as dialed in as you usually were. I didn't realize it at the time, because I was pretty distracted myself, but now that I look back . . . I can see it."

"I should've told you, but I could barely admit it to myself. I was trying not to destroy a lifetime of friendship. I didn't know how Scott felt about me."

"Really?" Beau's grin was wry. "You didn't know he was in love with you? Even *I* knew that. It was pretty obvious."

"The irony," Asa muttered. "But no, I didn't. I had no idea. Months went by and it didn't go away, and then I thought, I really need to tell him. He should know. Maybe we'll stay friends, but he should know the truth of how I feel. So I told him. It was December. Right before Christmas."

"I remember that night, you convinced me to go to some stupid Christmas party, and were so insistent about it, and I came home and you were . . ." Beau paused, like he was searching for the right word. "You were diminished. Sad. I thought it was because Scott was going to leave, but it was more than that, wasn't it?"

"Yes and no," Asa said. "He wasn't ready. You're gonna have to talk to him about those details, because those are his to share. But he wasn't ready, and so he left. And that's . . . honestly, that's why I didn't tell you, Beau. Because it was all caught up in the pain of Scott leaving. I didn't think it was ever going to get fixed, and there wasn't going to be anyone else for me but him, so it seemed . . . almost pointless to share. And honestly, the only way I got through it, was to *not* talk about it."

"And when he came here, to Miami? You let me try to convince you to not be angry that he left. You could've just told me then." Beau sounded so frustrated.

Asa told himself he understood. That he felt the same. Why hadn't he said anything then?

Because he'd been so focused on trying to figure out how to get rid of him.

"I could have. I *should* have. I guess . . . I didn't know how to find the words. That's the only explanation I have. The only thing I can say, besides I'm sorry I didn't."

"You didn't want him here," Beau stated, rather than asked.

"I didn't. It . . . it hurt too much," Asa admitted carefully.

"You should've told me," Beau said. "'Cause I feel bad about that. Though not *too* bad 'cause clearly you two figured your shit out."

"We did." Asa couldn't help his smile. "I hope it doesn't bother you. I know I should've told you before, and I *am* sorry about that. I regret the way you found out so much, but you have to know, we're gettin' ready to tell Rudy, Scott is gonna come out and . . ."

Asa's speech was interrupted by an armful of Beau. "'Course I don't want you to give him up, you stupid man," he mumbled into Asa's shoulder as they embraced. "I'm happy as fuck for you two. So happy."

Asa swallowed down the lump in his throat. Beau was happy for him. He hadn't fucked this up beyond repair. It was more than he'd ever hoped for.

"Good. Good. I'm . . ." The lump couldn't be swallowed back anymore. He just hugged his son tight, and if a tear or two fell, he knew that Beau wouldn't ever judge him for it. And maybe if his own sleeve wasn't a hundred percent dry when they finally broke apart, then it was only them who'd know the truth.

"Jesus, though, Dad, he was wearing *only* an apron," Beau said, suddenly laughing as he wiped his eyes. "I think I'm gonna need more than brain bleach to destroy that particular vision."

Asa blushed. "Hey, it's not like I want to know what you and Sebastian get up to. I don't. But I definitely remember something goin' on in the steam room that one time. And you were both *naked*. No aprons in sight."

"True," Beau conceded. "But really, it's good. I can tell it's good for you. That he's good for you."

"He is. The best. I . . ." Asa felt another tear drip down his cheek. "I missed him so much."

"And now," Beau said, tugging him into another hug, "you don't need to anymore. Never again."

"Now, *that's* the kind of win I wanna see every goddamn time," Asa said, and the players around him cheered, chanting *Pir-an-has* in one continuous rhythm. "I wish I had more than one game ball to give out, 'cause y'all deserve it. Pax, you killed it today, I think you had more touchdowns than incompletions. It's a big deal when you out-throw the GOAT." He turned to where the defense was gathered. "And you pressured Brady *all* game. Gave Howard and Rose and the rest of the secondary a fighting chance. And special teams? I don't think I'm gonna forget that gorgeous fifty-seven-yard field goal, to put us up by twenty points, anytime soon. Perfect execution. You're doin' your jobs, and more than your jobs, and I think this ball, well, I think . . ."

But Asa didn't get the rest of the words out.

Instead, Beau jumped up on the table with him, and Sebastian reached up to steady the wobble of it before they both fell over. Asa, so distracted by the fact that Beau was up here, *with him*, he didn't even notice the ball was gone until after he'd plucked it right from his hands.

And then, he offered it back, with a grin on his face.

"And that's why," Beau said, raising his voice because the cheers had grown even louder, "this ball is yours, Coach. 'Cause you saw what we needed to do, and made sure we executed like we could. Nobody else could've done it."

Asa was shocked—and not much shocked him.

He wasn't sure he deserved this honor.

He'd been an asshole. He'd lied by omission to his son.

He hadn't been the kind of coach—or the kind of man—that his team deserved. But as he looked around, from Beau's warm gaze, to the players surrounding them, every single one of them looking like they not only approved of what Beau had done, but that they were all in, entirely committed, that they'd follow Asa into the depths of hell, if that was what it took.

You win people over by showing them the best version of themselves, Scott had said to him once.

He met Scott's eyes, across the expanse of the locker room, and he nodded, a smile growing on his face.

Asa took the ball, and lifted it over his head, and the cheers grew to a deafening roar.

You did this. For the first time, Asa let himself just feel it. Soak it all in.

He'd turned this group of misfits, who hadn't belonged anywhere else in the NFL, into a team.

Into a family.

It had been an awesome victory—not only so awesome, but so complete of a victory that Asa's butt had hit the seat, and to Scott's amusement, he'd been asleep before the plane even taxied down the runway.

It wasn't ever ideal to play on Christmas Eve, but at least, Scott thought as he tapped on the arm rest, they'd played early enough the team would be home with some hours before the night officially ended.

He and Asa had only vaguely talked about Christmas Day. Neither of them had been sure if Beau would feel like spending it with them, so they'd talked about grabbing Chinese takeout and Asa had suggested they might finish the Christmas cookies, barring any untimely interruptions from Beau.

It wasn't perfect, but they'd have each other, and Scott was learning that was always the most important thing.

And then, of course, Asa had set up the meeting with Rudy for Christmas night.

Tomorrow, after that was over, they'd finally be free. And that seemed like something worth celebrating, at least.

"Hey." Scott glanced over to see Beau drop into the seat next to his, keeping his voice lowered because Asa was still snoring away, head propped up against the side of the plane.

"Hey," Scott said. He'd hoped that Beau might reach out to him, the way he'd come to see Asa.

"Sebastian and I wondered if you and Dad wanted to come over tomorrow. We'll grab Chinese and see if we can drive him nuts with sappy Christmas movies."

"We'd love that," Scott said, and it hit him suddenly. He was part of a *we* now.

He'd never been part of a *we* before, not officially.

Maybe he wouldn't have been a fan of it, because he'd been alone so long, but with Asa, it just felt natural.

"Great." Beau smiled, like he really believed it would be.

"We've got a meeting with Rudy at seven, but I think we can find enough holiday movies to drive Asa around the bend before that," Scott said.

Beau raised an eyebrow. "Meeting with Rudy? Oh, *oh*, y'all are going to tell him, aren't you?"

Scott nodded.

"Makes sense," Beau said. "Dad wouldn't want to hide it."

Scott told himself this flare of frustration was unfair. He'd spent his life in the closet out of choice, after all, but it still sucked being reminded of that fact.

Would making the decision to stand up and walk out of it now erase all the shame he felt? Scott didn't know, but he hoped it might neutralize at least some of it.

"I don't either," Scott said firmly. "I would've done it, with or without Asa, but it . . . it helps that he wants to, too."

Beau's gaze softened. "I know this isn't easy for you, but things have changed."

"That's what Asa keeps tellin' me. And speaking of that . . ." Maybe Asa and Beau had made up, but Scott still had his own apologies to voice. "I should've told you. I couldn't, but I should have somehow."

"You mean, before I walked in on you making out with my dad, only wearing an apron?" Beau asked archly.

"Yes, definitely before that part."

"If it's any consolation," Beau said with a grin, "you look real good for fifty."

"Forty-eight, Jesus, you're trying to age me up two years. Maybe I did a lot of shit, but I still don't deserve that."

"Well, real good for forty-eight," Beau amended.

"Still, I'm sorry. I know your dad probably said this, but we didn't want you to find out that way."

"I'd imagine not," Beau said. "But . . . I don't know, it's not as big of a deal, to me anyway. I knew you had feelings. It was kinda obvious. It was just him that I didn't know about. And, if you'd had a choice, you'd have told me. I know that."

"What . . . you knew I had feelings for Asa?" This was news to Scott. And also a little sobering. Had he been that obvious?

Asa hadn't figured it out but then Asa was notorious for his blinders. He didn't see anything he didn't want to see. Just like Beau. At least *normally*.

"There was never anybody else. Just my dad. You hung out with him, just him. But then you left, and I thought, it all makes sense. If I'd been crushing on a friend for ages, and he never returned my feelings, if he was straight, even, I'd have eventually run as far away as I could." Beau shrugged. "Turns out I was wrong, and I was right, at the same time."

"Right enough," Scott said ruefully. "I had myself convinced that what we had was enough, that friendship could be enough, but it wasn't ever going to be that way."

"No shit," Beau said, chuckling.

"I knew it before, but from the moment I landed in Miami, I figured we'd either kill each other or . . . uh . . ." Scott hesitated. "That thing you're going to pretend we don't do."

Beau rolled his eyes. "That ship has sailed. Do I even want to ask what you were doing, wearing only an apron, making cookies?"

"It was one of those 'date bo', thingies . . . Asa got it from . . . a player? I don't know. But from somewhere, and he wanted to do it, and it made him smile, and you know how intense he was after the Bears game, so I figured, smiling was better than the alternative."

"Oh, I know what you're talkin' about," Beau said. "You got a date box? Logan likes to give those out. He gave me and Sebastian two or three. I know he gave Pax and Davis a whole bunch, and Dylan says their hall closet is still stacked full of them."

"It seemed . . . uh . . . not terrible?" Scott had liked the idea of it more than the execution of it, because God knew, neither of them knew how to bake anything, even with clear and precise instructions. But they'd been managing alright, at least it had seemed so, until Beau had interrupted.

"We liked them. Especially the conversation starters. Did you two do those?"

"Conversation starters?" That was something he'd never had trouble doing with Asa, so maybe he'd skipped right over those in the box. Probably he'd been too interested in the possibilities of the included apron.

"Yeah, it's like a card in the date box. Has a few questions. We thought we knew a lot about each other, but I think you're together long enough, you get stuck in a lot of the same conversations, you know? About day-to-day stuff. And it was nice to be pushed out of that comfort zone."

Scott made a mental note to look for the cards when they got back to Asa's condo.

"Not that you two probably need much help," Beau teased. "You're gonna automatically win the relationship goals contest, hands down. Nobody else has been friends for as long as you have. Not even close. And now nobody's gonna be sappier than you two, I can already tell."

"Thanks, I think?" Scott answered dryly.

Beau patted him on the arm as he stood. "I'm happy for you, really. I didn't want you to think I wasn't. This has been a long time coming."

Nobody knew that as much as Scott.

It was terrifying. Thrilling. Life-changing.

He was a cautious guy, maybe he should be hesitating now that reality was crashing in, colliding with a lifetime of fantasies, but instead of being scared, all he felt was exhilaration that finally, it was happening.

"We'll see you tomorrow."

"Noon-ish, I think? We could all use some sleep after this week," Beau said wryly.

"Works for us," Scott said.

And there was that *us* again.

He was still marveling over it, how lucky he'd gotten, how good it felt, when the plane started its descent.

Asa yawned and his eyes blinked slowly open.

"Hey, sleepyhead," Scott murmured. "You ready to go get some rest in a real bed?"

"Are you gonna be there?" Asa's voice was gravelly from sleep.

"Yes." Scott hesitated. "Always."

He knew he wasn't going anywhere; he'd said as much a handful of times, but he watched Asa's eyes as they softened, filled with love and affection. It was a look he was never going to get used to seeing, but also a look he was always going to crave.

Asa reached over and squeezed his hand. Briefly. Soon, *real soon*, he wouldn't have to move away. He could hold Scott's hand and not have to stop before someone saw.

"Best news I've had all day."

"Better than beating Tampa Bay forty-one to seven?" Scott asked archly.

"Better than that. Better than anything," Asa said, and Scott realized he really meant it.

He'd meant it before, seven years ago, when he'd said he'd coach the peewee team down the street, if it meant he could have Scott.

He hadn't believed him then.

But he did now.

A game ball. Winning the day. Being the last one standing at the end, hoisting the Lombardi Trophy, those were huge accomplishments.

But they didn't mean jack shit, Scott realized, if you weren't surrounded by people you loved, who loved you right back.

That was how he knew, no matter how their conversation with Rudy went, no matter how this season ended, they were going to be just fine.

Because they had each other.

Chapter Sixteen

"I am absolutely fucking stuffed." Sebastian leaned back against the love seat and groaned a little, patting his still-flat stomach.

"I told you, you shouldn't have eaten that last egg roll," Beau teased, his head propped on Sebastian's shoulder, his legs slung across his boyfriend's lap.

"I dare you to face down a hot, perfectly crisp egg roll and *not* eat it," Sebastian argued.

"This is . . ." Asa dropped his voice, tucking his head closer to Scott's ear. "This is weird, isn't it?"

Scott shot him a look. "How is it weird? We're celebrating Christmas with your son and his boyfriend. Isn't that what normal families do? Even families like ours? As for the takeout, did you actually want to cook? You should be glad that Beau didn't lose his shit over that big pile of beef and broccoli you ate."

"I mean . . . it's like a double date. *With my own son,*" Asa hissed.

Scott rolled his eyes. Asa was cute. Even when he was being annoying. "You should be worrying more about what movies *your son* is gonna make you watch, not that we're on a double date. It's *Christmas.* Families hang out together, that's what they do."

"I guess I don't have any reference for that."

"I know I went to holiday dinners at your house, before Lynn left. Semi-normal things, holiday dinners."

"Yes, well, it felt like half the team was at those. This is just . . . me and you . . . and them." Asa's gaze drifted pointedly to where Beau and Sebastian were cuddled up together very closely on the love seat.

It might have actually been more of a large *chair* than a love seat, now that Scott was looking at it.

"It's only weird if you make it weird. I actually think it's kinda neat," Scott said, putting his arm around Asa and tugging him closer. "Like I can do *this*, and nobody cares."

"Ew," Beau called out from across the room. "Hand check!"

Asa shot Scott a knowing look. "See?"

"He's happy about it," Scott reminded him. "About us. Would you rather him be icing us out, not teasing us about how freaking adorable we are?"

"I think . . ." Asa hesitated, like this was a truly heinous thing he was contemplating confessing. "I think I might not be a very good boyfriend."

Scott laughed then, so long and hard he couldn't hold it back. "Darlin', you could be an absolute shit boyfriend, and it wouldn't make a damn bit of difference."

"I don't think anyone thinks you're going to be good at this real-life thing, Dad," Beau chimed in. "Just sayin'."

"It's the effort that matters, Coach," Sebastian added.

"See?" Scott said. He leaned in and brushed a kiss across Asa's mouth. Ignoring the gagging noises that Beau was making.

"You'd better not whip out any aprons," Beau called out. "That's a step too far."

"I did bring something, but I'm sorry to say, it's not my best apron, ruffled or otherwise," Scott said and reached down, pulling a DVD case from the pile on the floor that he'd brought. "*Miracle on 34th Street*. It's a classic, and I don't think Asa's ever seen it."

"Asa is smart like that," Asa said dryly.

But Beau got up and plucked the DVD from Scott's fingers. "Where'd you get this?" he asked.

Scott shrugged. "I snuck out this morning to get coffee at the mini-mart and they had a whole bin full of them."

"Ooooh," Beau said, leaning over and considering the selection on the floor. "First this one, because it's a crime that my dad's never seen it, 'cause you're totally right, it's a classic for a reason. And then this one, and then *this* one." He gestured to two other brightly colored cases.

"*White Christmas*? Isn't that a musical?" Sebastian asked, and Asa groaned.

"Yes, and *another* classic," Beau retorted.

"Lots of classics around today," Sebastian said.

"Hey, watch it, bucko," Scott teased.

Sebastian chuckled. "It's a compliment?"

"I'm not sure it is," Asa said.

Beau put a hand on Asa's shoulder. "I know we can probably only fit these two in, 'cause I know you're heading over to Rudy's house, right? For a meeting tonight?"

Asa's eyes were bright. "Yes."

Beau's answering smile was even brighter. "I'm proud of you, you know."

"It's nothing, it's just . . ."

Scott knew Asa bluster when he heard it, and so did Beau, who just kept grinning. "Yeah, yeah, it is," Beau said, "and I can be proud of you if I want to."

"Well, nobody's gonna stop you, apparently," Asa said.

"Damn straight. Come on, babe," Beau said to Sebastian as he headed over to the giant TV setup on one side of the living room. "Help me figure out how the fuck this works. We have some classics to watch."

"Oh, I thought we were already doing that," Sebastian said with a laugh. "DVDs! I feel like we're back in the Stone Age."

"It's a big deal," Scott murmured to Asa as Beau and Sebastian figured out how to get the DVD to play. "And it's okay to think it is."

Asa glanced over at him. "Loving you isn't," he admitted. "Easiest thing I ever did."

After sitting through *Miracle on 34th Street* and *White Christmas,* Asa couldn't deny that he was at least a *little* bit glad to escape out of Sebastian's penthouse apartment.

"Thank God that's over," he said as they slid into the town car that Rudy had sent for them. "Though I thought some of the musical numbers were kinda fun. Especially the ones that had nothing to do with Christmas."

"How did you get this way?" Scott asked, curious. "Did you come out of the womb unimpressed by holidays?"

Asa shrugged. He supposed he'd never been particularly interested in them. But then Lynn and he had divorced, and it had been so much easier to focus on his job. On football. And then Scott had left, right in the middle of December.

He hadn't felt much like celebrating that year.

Or any year after, if he was being honest.

"Is it 'cause I left in December?" Scott sounded genuinely concerned that was the reason.

"It's not *not* the reason," Asa said honestly as the car headed towards Rudy's big South Beach compound where they were having the meeting.

"Kinda seems like it is," Scott said.

"Honestly, before that year, I didn't care one way or the other. It just seemed like . . . a lot of work, you know? All that forced merriment."

"It's not always forced, you know," Scott pointed out dryly.

"I know, I know, but that year . . . you know the one. Everyone was so goddamned happy, and I was so miserable. I tried to put on a face for Beau, but I think he saw right through me, and for once, I didn't even care." Asa sighed. "So yeah, after that, I just pretended it wasn't happening. Better for everyone."

"Now that is a lie," Scott drawled out softly. "It wasn't better for you. You had family. You had people there for you. Before *and* after."

He knew who Scott was referring to.

"Except that Lynn and I were never really a couple, not in the ways that mattered. We had Beau, and that tied us together. Then she was gone, and you were there, and things were good—but *God*," Asa said under his breath, "they could've been so much better. I know that now. We could've been a real family."

"Like we were today?"

Asa thought about it for a long moment. He'd asked Scott earlier if it was weird. It felt like he'd just gotten used to watching Beau with Sebastian, and now he had to mentally adjust to being free to show his feelings for Scott in front of his son.

But once he'd gotten over the momentary weirdness, he could . . . well, the truth was, he'd really enjoyed himself. Even with the takeout. Even with the holiday movies.

It had felt . . . solid. *Real*. A real fucking life.

Not just something he went through the motions to do, when he wasn't lost in football.

"Exactly like today," Asa said softly. He tucked his hand into Scott's and didn't move it as they drove closer to Rudy's gigantic mansion.

Ten minutes later, they were climbing out and walking down the path to the front door, lined with palm trees, sprinkled with ropes and ropes of multicolor lights.

"You ready for this?" Asa said, turning to Scott.

There was a calm, prepared expression on his face. No panic. No fear lurking in his gray eyes. There was only resolve. Excitement.

"Yeah, I really think I am," Scott said, and raised a hand, knocking on the door.

To Asa's surprise, Rudy answered the door. "Come in, come in," he said, pushing it open wider. "We always give staff the holidays off, so it's just us, and they get some much-needed time off."

"Thanks for taking the time to see us," Asa said, as Rudy led them from the enormous foyer, topped with the biggest wrought iron chandelier he'd ever seen, down a hallway to a much smaller room, lined in mahogany wood paneling.

This room he'd been in before; Asa knew it was Rudy's office. He'd sat in here, as Rudy had offered him the job with the Piranhas.

Rudy gestured towards a trio of chairs arranged by a large, ornately carved fireplace—though Asa couldn't figure out *when* in Miami Rudy would ever need a freaking fireplace—and they took their seats.

"First, I just want to say, fantastic team win. I know I sent the email, but this was great. A great comeback. Ticket sales are going steady, and it looks like the playoffs might actually come through Miami."

"That's the hope," Asa said. "Though . . . I wouldn't be surprised if we're heading further west, if we make it deep enough in."

"The Riptide," Rudy said, leaning back in his chair and steepling his fingers. "They do look like the team to beat this year. Too bad we couldn't have sent them our quarterbacks coach as a backup, had him learn all their secrets, then bring him back." Rudy had a teasing glint in his eye but Asa was not one hundred percent convinced he was joking. Rudy was . . . well, every really rich person he'd ever met was odd, but Rudy could be *very* odd.

"I don't think that was ever going to happen," Asa said firmly. "Davis is here to stay."

"Oh?"

Asa decided this was as good of a time as any to tell Rudy the *other* secret he was holding close to his chest. "He's not going anywhere because Paxton isn't going anywhere."

For a second Rudy just stared at him, dark eyes confused in his tanned face. "No," he finally said, "no, you are not telling me that . . ."

There was no point in prevaricating. "Yes," Asa said crisply. "Yes. They're together."

"You really think that's a good idea?" Rudy asked and then continued, with a wave of his hand. "Of course you do. You know best when it comes to the players. So, Pax and Davis, huh? Well, that's going to be a big shock when it comes out."

"No doubt," Asa said, "but Helen thinks we can manage it alright. Maybe during the off-season? She's got some plans up her sleeve, and I wouldn't bet against her."

"Me either," Rudy said ruefully. "Wait a minute, how many people know about them?"

"Me, and Scott, obviously," Asa said. "Beau. And well . . . maybe a few other players? They're being circumspect, just like I asked them to be."

"Well, that's something. I'm sure when the news does come out, it'll be Heath Harris and Sam Crawford all over again." Rudy's eyes gleamed, no doubt thinking of all the ways he could make money off it. Asa found he didn't even mind that attitude, because as long as Rudy saw it as a positive and continued to allow Asa to make the personnel decisions, he could keep building the culture he wanted. "Is that what you wanted to tell me about? Pax and Davis?"

"There's something else," Asa hedged.

Rudy raised an eyebrow, then stood, heading over to a selection of bottles on a bookshelf. "Anyone want a drink? I feel like I'm going to need one to hear whatever's next. Asa? Scott?"

"I'm good," Scott said firmly, and Asa shook his head. He wanted to keep his wits about him, because while Rudy was generally pretty easygoing about his team, wanting only to win and to make a lot of money, he was going to ask for a lot from him today.

"Alright," Rudy said, pouring himself a few inches of whiskey from a bottle and settling back down in the chair opposite them. "So what other news have you brought me? Must've been important, you said it was."

"It is," Asa said calmly. He'd primed the pump with the Pax and Davis news. Rudy hadn't freaked out.

But this? Well, this was big.

But before he could figure out exactly where to start, Scott jumped in.

"Sir, first, I just want to say thank you for this opportunity."

"Of course," Rudy said, lifting his glass in a quick toast. "We're glad to have you."

"I'm gay," Scott said, "and I'm in love with him." He glanced over at Asa, and shrugged a little like . . . *sorry, couldn't wait anymore. You were taking too long to get to the point.*

That was Scott for you. Always ready to drill down to the bare facts. But then, could he blame him? He'd been waiting to come out forever, and now he'd done it.

Asa sighed. Resigned. Proud. Hoping that Rudy continued to have *only* that flabbergasted expression on his face and nothing else that was worse.

"Is this true?" Rudy glanced from Scott to Asa. "And honestly, I think I've made it clear I don't really care what sexuality people are, as long as they do their jobs, but that's what you came to tell me, isn't it? You're together, too."

"Yes," Asa said wryly.

Rudy slumped back into his chair and took a long drink. "Fuck me sideways," he said.

"You look surprised."

"You would be too, if your football team had this perennial habit of pairing off," Rudy said.

"Believe me, nobody is more surprised than me," Asa said. "I . . . I did not think I even wanted him here."

"We all heard that message loud and clear." Rudy sounded amused. "But probably you heard it the loudest." He gestured with his glass towards Scott.

"This is true," Scott agreed.

Rudy sighed. "There's no precedent for this. I'm assuming you want to keep him around now, now that you're both . . ." He gestured between them.

"That's the plan," Asa said.

He felt Scott's astonishment even though he never looked away from Rudy.

Sure they hadn't talked about it, explicitly, but they'd said *forever*, hadn't they? Did Scott really think he was going to send him back to Alabama?

"Well. *Well*." Rudy hesitated. "And I don't suppose you want to follow in Paxton and Davis' footsteps and be circumspect about it."

"Not particularly," Asa said. "We came here for your blessing, though, because it's your team, sir."

It hurt to beg like this, to lay the possibility of their future here, at Rudy's feet, but he was a fair man, at least. All he really wanted was to make money.

And if this didn't actively *lose* him money . . .

"I can't see that it makes a difference to me, one way or the other," Rudy finally said. "If it doesn't affect your work, same as it didn't affect the players on the field, then you can do whatever you want." A glimmer of a smile emerged on his face. "You told Helen yet?"

"She knows about me," Scott said. "We've been working on a statement to the press about my sexuality."

"And you?" Rudy said, turning to Asa. "You going to make a statement too?"

"Wasn't planning on it." Asa hesitated. "I was just planning on living my life the way I saw fit."

Rudy nodded in approval. "Alright, then. You know how I feel about this team. It's a business to me. And we're in business to make money. As long as you keep winning, I don't foresee an issue . . . if you don't . . . well, we'll cross that bridge when we come to it though I have to say, based on this year, I'm not particularly concerned. But I appreciate you coming to me, and keeping me informed, even though you know I trust your judgment." He paused. "Even in this."

"That means a lot," Asa said. He'd known that for Rudy, the money always came first. Rudy had told him himself, and now he'd repeated it. He'd have to remember that, because the thing was, being in charge was all great when things were optimistic, but when they weren't, there was nobody to take the fall but him. And now it wasn't just him and Beau, it was him and Beau and Scott. And that pressure that had always followed him around, since the beginning, wrenched a little tighter. But, Asa reminded himself, there were plenty of ways—more ways than just this, anyway—that Scott alleviated that pressure. Made it easier. Made it so much more bearable. It wasn't just him anymore. It was him *and* Scott. It was *us*.

"Now we'd better be going, get out of your hair and let you enjoy Christmas with your family," Asa continued. They stood, and Rudy shook Scott's hand, and then Asa's.

He was showing them out when he said, "And, Asa, I fully expect we'll want to work on an extension in the off-season. Think about where you want to open negotiations."

Asa supposed he shouldn't have been very surprised. He'd taken a team with two wins and they already had eleven and the season wasn't even over yet. They were heading to the playoffs. They might even get home field advantage. Rudy was a smart businessman and would want to make sure he locked him down for the foreseeable future.

"Gotta get you tied up," Rudy added with a grin, "before you win Coach of the Year and then you get really expensive."

The car was still waiting for them outside, and they climbed in, and this time, Asa didn't feel any compunction, even though the window separator was down, and the driver could easily see them in his rearview mirror, at taking Scott's hand and lifting it to his lips, kissing his knuckles one at a time.

"Proud of you," Asa said quietly.

"Felt good," Scott agreed.

The look in his eyes said it all.

Forever.

Scott managed to wait, to hold in his inevitable question, until they were back at Asa's apartment. Asa was puttering around the kitchen, warming up some hot cocoa and piling it high with marshmallows, apparently deciding that Christmas meant a day off from his diet.

Scott leaned against the counter and watched as Asa popped a marshmallow in his mouth, and then another.

"So, were you going to tell me about these plans to keep me around?" he asked with amusement.

"I was, actually, but trust you to ruin the surprise," Asa grumbled. He fumbled in his pocket and then pulled out a creased envelope. "Here," he said, handing Scott the envelope. "Merry Christmas from your Secret Santa."

Scott grinned at him as he opened the envelope and pulled out several pieces of paper, and he peered closer at the writing on them.

It was an employment contract. A contract with the Miami Piranhas. His title—special consultant to the head coach—was filled in already. There was his name. And it was for three years, which was usually the default, with an option to pick up two more. The salary was fair, and reasonable, more than he'd been getting paid at Washington, and right there, at the bottom, was Asa's signature.

All he had to do was sign it and it would be real.

Scott glanced up, suddenly aware his throat was getting tight, emotion overwhelming him.

"It's not forever," Asa said, coming over and putting his arms around him, crumpling the papers between them, "but I thought it might look a little weird to state that on an official HR document."

Scott tipped his head close to Asa's. "A little," he said, choking back his tears. "Just a little."

"I had them draw this up almost a week ago," Asa said seriously, "after the night you took me to the stadium. I don't want to do this without you. I should have called you the moment I got this job, I *wanted* to, but I was so goddamned afraid. Afraid that you might say no again, that you might . . ."

"Trust me," Scott interrupted, more sure of this than anything in his whole life, "there was no way I could've said no to you again. It was hard enough the one time. You called, I would've come. Immediately."

"You did." Asa pressed his mouth to Scott's. Then annoyingly, pulled back. "Well, I guess Beau called."

"No," Scott said, reaching up and cupping Asa's face in his palm, "no, you called me. Maybe you didn't dial the phone and say the words. But it was you, pulling me here."

"I guess we don't have to give Beau credit," Asa said with a watery laugh.

Scott set the papers on the counter. He'd sign them after. But right now . . . what he needed was something that had been humming under his skin all fucking day. He needed Asa, as close as he could get him, in every single way that mattered.

"Come on," Scott said, and kissed Asa.

Asa groaned into his mouth and they stumbled backwards, heading straight towards the bedroom. Maybe this white-hot wanting would cool in time, but Scott didn't think it would.

He'd desired Asa for so long without having him, that every single time felt like a miracle.

And Asa? He was blown away, each time he touched him, by the fire burning under his skin, that he only unleashed for him.

Asa pulled off his shirt and had him pushed down on the bed before Scott could even take a breath or *think*.

"Hey, hey," he said, reaching up, pushing back Asa's hair, messy from his own hands. "Wait a second, there's something . . . I hoped

. . ." He swallowed hard. It had always been tough asking for this, but something about Asa and the love in his eyes made it easier. Unstuck the words. "I want you inside me, okay? Is that okay?"

"I want whatever you want," Asa vowed, and leaned down, kissing him soft and sweet.

But it didn't stay soft and sweet.

Scott could already feel desire rising in him, his cock growing harder as their kiss grew deeper, more intense.

"God, I want you," Scott growled as Asa took a step back and pulled his shirt off.

It was so easy for the Asa of the past to blur with the Asa of now. Scott saw a dozen different Asas, each one handsome and each one tempting beyond belief, and then they all blurred together, becoming the one who was stripping naked now.

With the gray hair at his temples, and the lines between his dark brows, and the brightness of his blue eyes never diminished—Scott wanted him more, now, than he'd ever wanted him before.

"Take off your clothes," Asa said steadily, as Scott's blood pumped harder, faster, the heat rising in him until he felt flushed.

Before this, Asa had seemed content enough to let Scott take the lead.

But this was an Asa in charge. An Asa that Scott was *very* familiar with, but not in the bedroom.

It shouldn't have been so unexpected that it was such a goddamn turn-on—because nearly everything about Asa was a turn-on, and he'd certainly gotten worked up just watching Asa in in-charge work-mode, before—but it was something else to watch him like this, now, as he lifted up his shirt and pulled it off.

Those blue eyes narrowed and grew resolved, and Scott discovered his fingers were trembling so hard he could barely get his jeans off.

Asa leaned in and kissed him, hard and deep, and Scott got lost in it, moaning into his mouth even as he knew Asa was distracting him. Rearranging him to his own purpose.

When Asa finally lifted his mouth, Scott looked down, dazed and aroused, as his man, his lover, his fucking *everything*, sank to his knees.

"I'm never gonna get tired of this," Asa said, right before his tongue licked a stripe right up his cock, pleasure shooting through him.

"Trust me," Scott panted, as he dug his fingers into the comforter, "I'm not either."

"Good, 'cause we're gonna do this a lot, a *lot*," Asa said, and Scott could only groan in agreement as Asa nudged his legs apart further.

He was so sensitive that he nearly gasped out loud when Asa circled his hole with a wet thumb as he took his cock a little deeper into his mouth, sucking hard enough that Scott saw stars.

He wanted to keep his eyes glued on Asa, to experience every single bit of this incredible experience, but it was too much, like staring right into the sun, and eventually he couldn't look anymore. He could only feel, as Asa worked one finger inside him, then another, turning him inside out with the pressure and the pleasure.

"God, look at you like this," Asa said, hushed as he brushed against the spot inside Scott that made him shake with the intensity of it. "You're so fucking gorgeous."

"It's you," Scott moaned, feeling wrung out already. If Asa didn't get inside him soon, if he kept talking to him like this, kept coaxing the pleasure out of him like there was an unlimited well of it, he was going to lose his mind.

"Imagined you like this," Asa said roughly. "So many fucking times."

Scott lost his fight with control and pressed down harder on Asa's fingers, the feeling of them lighting him from the inside out. "God, please," he begged.

As a general rule, he didn't beg.

But he'd beg for Asa, every single goddamn time.

He felt the loss of him, the warmth of him, the instant he was gone, and he reached out, blindly grabbed Asa's arm. "What are you doing?" he asked, hearing the desperation in his own voice.

"Condom?" Asa said, unsteadily.

"No, no, just *please*," Scott said. And then Asa was next to him, surrounding him, and he was sliding inside him, and it was the best thing he'd ever felt in his whole life.

Like he was finally home.

Like he could finally breathe.

"Love you, love you, *love you*," he chanted as Asa began to thrust.

It wasn't anonymous anymore, it wasn't just two bodies passing in the night, exchanging pleasure, but nothing else. This was so much more than that, it felt more real, more immediate than Scott had ever felt before.

And he wanted more.

So much more.

Asa gripped his knee, each finger leaving an indelible print against his skin—but it was more than that, too. It felt like he was leaving irrefutable marks deeper than that, deep in a place that nobody had ever touched before.

He'd known he loved Asa. That couldn't be new.

But it was something else to share the love, to exchange it back and forth, to let it grow and breathe and become a real life *together*.

Then Asa thrust harder and those thoughts were chased away by all the pleasure mounting inside him, as Asa reached down and stroked a palm over Scott's cock. He was so close, so ready to explode but he didn't want to do it without his man.

His partner.

His lover for life.

Asa groaned, the feedback of Scott's own pleasure circling back into him, and that was it, they exploded together. Scott gripped Asa's shoulders and buried his face in his chest.

When it was finally over, the last bit of ecstasy wrung out of them, Asa collapsed on his chest.

For a long time neither of them said anything. Scott just stroked Asa's hair, while the warmth of Asa's palms soaked into his chest.

"So," Asa finally said, raising his head and looking Scott straight in the eye, "that's what sex is really about."

He was so wrung out and relaxed it was hard to feel true shock, but he felt the reverberation of it. "You're saying . . . come on, you've had good sex before."

"I guess," Asa said, not seemingly convinced of this fact. "Like something was missing, almost. It was fine, it was fun, I enjoyed it. But this . . . it's like burning up alive."

"For me too," Scott admitted.

Asa shot him a chastising look. "You don't have to say that, I know you hooked up with other guys, I wouldn't have expected you to do anything else."

"Yeah, but . . ." Scott hesitated. "I love *you*. And it's different. It's just different now. Like it means something, and that makes it so much better."

"Yeah," Asa said, and his eyes were glowing again. All that love banked in them.

"We should . . ." Scott gestured.

Asa nodded, and it was a loss to feel him slip out of Scott's body, but Scott wasn't disappointed. Because he knew it would happen again. That they'd do this again and again and it would somehow, impossibly, be better every single time.

Scott had just gotten out of the shower and was toweling off, the lights turned down low in the bedroom, Asa already lounging in bed, having dried off first, when it occurred to him.

He detoured to the dark kitchen, grabbed the contract from the counter and was waving it resolutely when he walked into the bedroom.

"What is that? Oh, your contract. Well, you want to sign it? Or is this a negotiation for more money?" Asa's grin was knowing. "'Cause I think you had more leverage fifteen minutes ago."

"It's not a negotiation . . ." Scott set it on the bed. And dropped to one knee. "It's a proposal. I have only one change I want you to make to this. My name. It needs to change."

"Did I write it wrong? Did HR get it wrong?" Asa was peering down at the paper, and it was like he'd totally missed the point.

Which, this was Asa. It happened. He could get so hyper-focused on one thing that he missed everything else.

"No," Scott said steadily.

He'd never really thought about proposing before. Truthfully, he'd never really thought about marriage. Because if it was going to be anyone, it was going to be Asa, and that had been an impossibility forever—and then a chance he'd squandered through his own stupidity.

But now, he could do something about it.

Asa finally glanced up, in the middle of telling him all about how the name was right, they'd even spelled his middle name correctly, and he went dead silent. Right in the middle of his rambling sentence.

"Asa," Scott said, "I don't want to do this without you. Not a single goddamn day. Not any longer. I want to stand next to you, and behind you, and be the push you need to keep moving. I want to share a life with you. And the best way I can think to do all of that, and so much more, is to marry you."

Asa seemed shocked into silence.

For a single, horrible moment, Scott wondered if he'd made a mistake. If he'd pushed too hard, too fast.

But how could he have? They'd been dancing around this for nearly *thirty* years.

If they weren't going to do it now, it was never going to happen.

"Was there a question in there, or just an assumption?" Asa spoke up, and his voice was teasing and his eyes were soft. So soft. Scott had never seen him look at him that way before, even though they'd been looking at each other for so many years.

"A question. Asa Dawson, will you marry me?" Scott asked.

"New Year's Eve," Asa said instantly. Like he couldn't wait another moment, either. "'Cause I don't want to spend another year without you."

Scott didn't know who was crying, whose tears he felt as they embraced, as they kissed, but maybe . . . it was both of them.

Together.

The way it was always meant to be.

CHAPTER
SEVENTEEN

"I think Logan has outdone himself with . . . all this." Asa glanced around the cafeteria, which was festooned with swags of red and green and gold balloons arranged to look like holly. And interspersed every five or so feet was a massive and ornate arrangement of what had to be mistletoe. At least that was what Asa assumed, considering that Tristan and Wade had spent what seemed to be at least fifteen minutes so far under one or another.

There were Christmas trees, decorated with glittery fish ornaments, all over the room, and a corner where fake snow sprinkled down from the ceiling. There were trays of punch and hot cocoa topped with snowmen marshmallows, and more Christmas cookies than even a whole football team could eat.

A band played Christmas classics in the opposite corner from the snow, and some of the married players had brought their families, their kids rotating through Logan's red velvet-covered lap.

'Cause, who else could've been Santa but Logan?

"He does seem to love the holidays," Scott said dryly as he handed Asa a cup of punch. "Or impromptu make-out sessions. It's hard to say which takes priority."

Asa's eyes drifted up. He felt like he'd spent the first half hour of the party making sure he didn't accidentally end up under a clump of weeds that meant he needed to be kissed.

The only person he was interested in kissing was Scott. Ever.

They'd told Beau and Sebastian about the wedding, but they were hoping to keep it to just family. Beau and Sebastian, of course, and Lynn was going to fly in, and there were a few old friends from Alabama, from their old player days, who had been thrilled to hear, *one*, that they'd gotten together, and *two*, that they were getting married.

Rudy had also RSVPed yes, and Helen, when he'd told her, had actually hugged him, and had to wipe a few tears from her eyes before she got down to business.

"So," she'd asked, "when are you going to tell everyone? *How* are you going to tell everyone?"

"Well, Scott's made his announcement." It had gone out this morning, buried in the post-Christmas haze, though there'd already been a lot of positive response to it. "I don't want to make it official or make an announcement, too. I just want . . ." Asa had stopped, frustrated. He didn't really know what he wanted. Only that when the right moment presented itself, he'd take it.

"You'll know it when you see it," Helen had said, patting him on the shoulder. "Alright, you're free to do whatever. I'm sure I'll know the moment the reporters start metaphorically beating down my door, wanting the big story."

"There's no big story," Asa said. "It's just . . . a little story. A story about two guys. Two football coaches who were best friends and just happened to fall in love."

Helen's eyes had twinkled. "Two *famous* guys," she'd said, "and *famous* football coaches."

"But still just two guys," Asa retorted.

They were just two guys now. Two guys who had, not surprisingly, worn red and green. Asa had, reluctantly, put on a sweater in a muted shade of evergreen in deference to the holiday atmosphere, though it was hardly the ugly Christmas sweater that so many other players and staff members had donned.

Scott was in red, in a maroon polo from when he'd coached at Alabama, and *damn*, did he not fill it out just as well now as he had all those years ago.

Tristan and Wade, apparently taking a gulp of fresh air, approached. "Hey, Coach, and well, *Coach*, now, I guess," Tristan said, grinning, "merry Christmas. And congrats on coming out."

Somehow the news had leaked that Asa was offering Scott a full-time position on the staff, and considering the number of players and coaches who'd not only come up to congratulate and offer their support after his coming out statement, but had brought up his new position, Asa figured he'd done good.

Not that he'd ever doubted that Scott would earn his place, or that he'd *already* earned it, but it was especially gratifying to see (and hear) that he wasn't the only one who believed in him.

"Thanks, Tristan," Scott said.

Tristan had taken the ugly sweater theme to an extreme. His was bright white, trimmed with feathers at the cuffs, and had a fully bejeweled image of Mariah Carey from her famous Christmas album emblazoned across the front.

Asa remembered when December would hit and that album and George Michael were all he could get Beau to listen to.

Wade's sweater was slightly more subtle, which was not saying much, because the entire front was a huge tree, complete with blinking lights and actual ornaments hanging off it. *Let's Get Lit,* it proclaimed.

"Coach, I think you forgot your sweater," Tristan said.

Asa eyed his rookie wide receiver. When they'd drafted him, several staff members went out of their way to tell him he was taking a major risk on the guy, because he'd come from such a small college. Hadn't had much competition. Of course, at the time, they hadn't realized he'd turn into an incredible player, who also happened to be an utter pain in the ass.

Or that he'd become such an invaluable member of his team.

Or that he'd look at Tristan and Wade and the love they clearly shared, and think, *I hope they know just how lucky they are.*

They knew, Asa thought wryly, and they liked to remind themselves of it every chance they got.

"Ugly Christmas sweaters aren't really my kinda thing," Asa pointed out.

"You should be lucky he agreed to wear *that*," Scott teased. Clearly amused that the players were giving him shit.

"What did your Secret Santa get you, Coach?" Wade asked respectfully, after shooting his boyfriend a dirty look. Honestly, the two of them balanced each other out well. Even Asa, at his most bitter and regretful, had seen that.

He could see flashes of him and Scott in the pair, now. And he was pretty much afraid that between the two of them, he was the Tristan in their relationship.

"So far, just an office full of glitter," Asa said dryly. "But hopefully something better, soon."

"Kelly got me a dildo with flashing lights!" Tristan said with clear excitement. "And it plays 'God Rest Ye Merry Gentlemen'!"

Wade hustled him away after that, because apparently even the mention of the dildo was enough to necessitate the need for a heavy dose of mistletoe.

Scott was laughing.

Still laughing.

"It turns out, you were not either kidding *or* exaggerating," he said, when he could finally breathe.

"Do I ever?" Asa asked.

"No, but you can be real dramatic when you feel like it. Like with all this Scrooge business."

"I'm not a Scrooge," Asa protested.

"You kinda are," Scott teased. "But it's alright. I love you anyway. Scrooge bits and all."

"Come on," Asa said, changing the subject, because the truth was, he was feeling rather un-Scrooge-like, and if he didn't distract himself from how fucking edible Scott looked in that old polo shirt, so tight across the chest and the biceps, maybe he might even veer wildly right out of his comfort zone and find some mistletoe of their own. "Let's get some cookies."

"You actually want to eat a Christmas cookie?" Scott said, but he followed Asa over the table full of goodies.

"It's a cookie that Beau isn't prying out of my mouth before I can enjoy it," Asa said. "So *yes*."

The sugar cookie was only crumbs in his mouth, currently being washed down with another glass of punch, when Beau approached, Sebastian in tow.

"I thought you'd be in and out of here in under twenty minutes," Beau said. "Congrats on swallowing more than your usual dose of holiday cheer."

"That isn't all he's probably swallowin'," Sebastian muttered behind him, quietly, but definitely loud enough for everyone around to hear.

Asa flushed bright red. Would he have actually cared if he *hadn't* been?

"Sebastian!" Beau cried. "My brain! You can't do that to me again."

"Don't worry, babe," Sebastian said, slinging an arm around him, "I promise, I'll do everything I can to make sure you're thinking of *nothing at all*, later."

It was Beau's turn to flush, and he pulled Sebastian off. To do what . . . Asa decided he'd really rather not know.

Asa turned to Scott. "I think I really have become a matchmaker. What happened to football coaching?"

"I think you missed your real calling," Scott said, chuckling. "But now you've self-corrected."

"I guess it's only fair, considering I finally gave myself the best guy," Asa said, gazing at Scott with all the emotions swirling inside him. He wasn't really trying to hide it anymore. There was no reason to.

And wasn't that a fucking beautiful thing?

Almost as beautiful as Scott in that shirt.

Or Scott in the ruffled apron.

Or Scott in absolutely nothing at all, lounging on his bed like he didn't belong anyplace else.

"Yeah?" The corner of Scott's mouth quirked up.

"Yeah," Asa said. "And I'm gonna marry him, too. He's never gettin' rid of me now."

"Can't wait," Scott said and his eyes filled with love.

Asa glanced up because he couldn't quite help himself. Surely they would've accidentally stopped under a sprig of mistletoe by now? There was so much of it, Logan must have bought out the entire greater Miami area supply.

But the space above them was shockingly empty.

Scott grinned, following his eyes. "Oh, don't worry about that," he said. "I'm sure we'll find some."

"If you end up with mistletoe-printed briefs, like Dylan was bragging about, I will absolutely make you sleep on the couch."

"No, you won't," Scott said knowingly. Smugly. Because he knew just how much Asa liked sleeping next to him.

Asa smacked him on the arm. "You don't know everything, you know."

"About you? Yeah, I do. Especially how you scream when I do that thing with my tongue . . ."

Asa flushed. "You're gonna be the death of me, you know. I'm wearing a *sweater* here, and it's fucking Florida. Don't make me sweat through it."

"You could always take it off," Scott said, raising an eyebrow. "I wouldn't argue with that."

Asa supposed he should have been expecting it.

After all, his first Secret Santa "gift" had been an office chock-full of glitter, and a date box that included a ruffled apron Scott insisted on wearing without a single scrap of clothing underneath.

Of course, Logan couldn't have foretold that, or that Beau would show up and interrupt their cookie baking.

But the moment Logan hopped down from the large, ornate gold "chair" he'd been using as Santa, and headed over to the stage, Asa felt his apprehension grow.

"Do you think it's possible that Tristan arranged this?" he whispered in Scott's ear.

"Logan playing Santa? I don't think so . . . I think you'd have had to wrestle the honor right out of his hands."

"No, *no*, that *Logan* got me as a Secret Santa," Asa hissed.

Scott shrugged, but Asa could see that he was laughing.

"The biggest fan of Christmas getting the world's *least* fan of Christmas for Secret Santa? I don't know, that seems like serendipity to me."

"If something happens, save me," Asa said.

"Nope, darlin', you're on your own with this one. You faced the SEC on a regular basis, I think you can deal with a lineman dressed up as Santa Claus."

But then Logan, amongst cheers, hopped up on the stage occupied by the band, and grabbed the microphone that the lead singer tossed him.

"Merry Christmas!" he bellowed.

"I don't think he really needed that microphone," Asa muttered.

Scott was still laughing.

"I'm thrilled you came and joined us today for the big Piranhas Christmas party. It's been a freaking incredible holiday season—a freaking amazing *season*—and this is just the topper."

Asa's apprehension spiked. What was going to happen? What was Logan going to make him do, under the guise of Secret fucking Santa?

It was his worst nightmare, come to real life.

"Coach," Logan said, beckoning to him. The crowd parted in front of him, like he didn't *own* their asses any other day of the year. "You wanna come up here with me?"

"Not particularly," Asa said, but Scott gave him a little shove.

Traitor, Asa thought, and shot him a look that promised a whole lot of retribution later as he walked towards the stage.

How bad could it be? After all, even after Logan had doused his office in glitter, he'd hired a crew to come and clean it up.

"How're you doin', Coach?" Logan asked after he'd climbed onto the stage next to him. "Feelin' very merry?"

"Can't complain," Asa said. He wasn't quite to the point of feeling *merry*, especially with whatever Logan was no doubt about to drop on his head, but he wasn't about to say that in front of a bunch of his players and kids, all decked out in their ugly Christmas sweater glory. "It's been a . . . nice time."

He caught Scott's gaze, and he was grinning, miming that he needed to smile, too. Asa tacked one on, even though it probably looked more like a grimace.

Maybe he *was* Scrooge. And wasn't that fucking depressing?

"We noticed that you weren't wearing an ugly Christmas sweater . . ." Logan said, and Asa nearly sighed with relief. He could accept an ugly Christmas sweater. There was nothing wrong with owning one, because it would just sit in the back corner of his closet, gathering dust, and not offending anyone. "So we got you something else to wear . . .

"Though," Logan added as he pulled out a jersey from behind his back, "you might not want to actually *wear* this."

He spread it out, and it was one of the Piranhas' away jerseys . . . white with aqua-blue trim, and the fighting Caribe on the front corner. The number was fifty-five, the number he'd worn while playing at Alabama, and above the number, the jersey was emblazoned with a single name: Coach.

And covering almost every inch of the white background were signatures.

Asa peered closer and felt emotion suddenly clog his throat.

These were his team's signatures.

"Every single one of us," Logan said softly, voice no longer booming. "We thought you deserved one, because we wouldn't be here, we wouldn't be anything like we are, without you. You're one of us."

"I . . ." Asa found he could barely speak as Logan passed him the jersey. "This means a whole lot to me," he said. *An understatement.* "I think it's safe to say . . . I wouldn't be here without you, either."

Logan pulled him into a big, tight hug, and when they were embracing, he murmured, "And it's not just the wins, either, Coach, it's everything."

He knew. He *knew.*

There was only one thing to say: "Just a man, Logan, just a man."

"But the best man," Logan said with the biggest smile on his face as he pulled back. "And the best goddamned coach in the NFL."

There was nothing Scott loved as much as seeing Asa get the kind of love and credit he deserved.

Of course, nobody could possibly love or appreciate him as much as Scott did, but he wasn't stingy; he hoped that Asa would get as much as he could handle.

When he returned to where Scott was standing, his fingers carefully gripping the jersey, Scott could see his eyes were bright with unshed tears.

"You good?" he asked.

"I'm . . ." Asa shook his head, almost in disbelief. "I'm so good. Better than good. I didn't think this could happen for me."

"Be a respected and adored head coach in the NFL? Sure you did."

"No, so goddamned happy, Scott," Asa said. "That I could have *both*. Love and this. A family. A football family." He hesitated. "And *you*."

"I don't think it's always gonna be easy," Scott said. "But sometimes the tough things are worth doing."

"Worth more," Asa agreed.

"Come on," Scott said, gesturing towards a table. "Set that down. There's something I want to do."

"What?" Asa said, carefully setting the jersey down.

Scott extended a hand. "Dance with me," he said.

Asa didn't hesitate. Everyone was watching them—Scott wasn't stupid, they probably all suspected or flat-out *knew* at this point, depending on if Sebastian had actually managed to keep his mouth shut after Beau had found out the truth—but even though Asa had to realize that, he didn't hesitate. He took Scott's hand, and it felt natural, settling into each other's arms, and into a two-step rhythm to the song the band was playing.

"Hey, look," Asa said, gesturing up at the ceiling. And like it had been scripted, there was one of Logan's enormous bunches of mistletoe. "I think we'd better."

"Don't have to ask me twice," Scott said, and dipping him low, kissed him firmly.

EPILOGUE

"You nervous?" Beau asked Asa as they stood in the tunnel.

"About gettin' married?" Asa was surprised. Why would Beau even ask him that? Sure, he hadn't been on board with their relationship at the very beginning, but he knew now just how much they meant to each other—and if he didn't know the entire extent of it, he was beginning to. "To Scott? No way. Not in a million years. I feel like I've been waitin' my whole life to marry that man."

"I mean, you've only been dating for like a few weeks," Beau teased. "That's pretty quick to get married."

Asa rolled his eyes. "A few weeks and thirty years. That's all. It doesn't feel quick at all. Feels like we really took our time. Found our way back to each other, and finally, *finally,* made it right."

"You told me once, that the right man will always fight for you. How did you know that?" Beau asked, leaning against the tunnel wall. The opposite tunnel wall that they'd sat against the other night, when Asa had told Scott about the very first time he'd realized that he might not just be a friend.

"I knew it, 'cause I wanted to fight for Scott, and I wished . . . *God*, I wished, that he'd have fought for me."

"But he didn't," Beau said, frowning.

"Not at first. But you think it was easy for him to come here," Asa said, "and face me? Face what he'd done? Face my anger?

Stand in front of me, loving me, and thinking that I might never forgive him? Never mind playing defense in the SEC, and being a football coach, that's the toughest thing anyone could ever do. Face someone you love who might never give you the time of day ever again. So yeah, he fought. For me. And for himself."

Beau smiled. "I'm real happy for you, Dad, really. And glad you're doing this."

"Even though it's too quick?" Asa teased.

"You're right, it wasn't. Not even a little." Beau pulled him into a tight hug. "You ready?"

"Never been readier in my whole damn life," Asa said, and taking Beau's arm, they walked out onto the field.

When Asa had said he didn't want to spend another year not being with Scott, he hadn't imagined that it would be so hard to find a place to get married on New Year's Eve.

Probably because he'd never really ever thought about the logistics of getting married.

But it turned out that six days before the day you wanted to get married was not the best time to start planning a wedding.

They couldn't find a venue. They couldn't find an officiant.

Until Kelly had stepped into his office one morning and said she'd solved all their problems.

And, Asa decided, as he and Beau walked to the 50-yard line, where Scott waited for him, resplendent in a black tux, with an iridescent gray bowtie, Sebastian standing next to him, their friends and family gathered around, there was nowhere more appropriate to get married than on a football field.

The one thing they'd told Sebastian, after he'd gotten his officiating license online, was that they didn't want a traditional wedding. They didn't want the traditional kind of vows. They wanted to say their own, and then just be married.

Neither of them had ever put much stock in what was normal, and this night, when they promised each other that they were going to stick by each other, through thick and thin, and always have each other's backs, and love each other for the rest of their lives? Didn't seem like a good time to start.

Scott's eyes never left his as they walked down the middle of the field and came to stop right on the fifty-yard line.

A glow surrounded him, not just because of their friends and family, holding votive candles in their hands, but the love that seemed to surround him like a halo.

"Fancy seeing you here," Scott murmured under his breath as he took Asa's hands and squeezed them.

"Wanna get married tonight?" Asa asked, and the glow from Scott's gray eyes in the dim light was all the answer he'd ever need.

"Ladies and gentlemen, we're gathered here today to celebrate two men," Sebastian said, his voice carrying without a microphone. "Two wonderful men—honorable, noble men, who've set their reputations on the line for us, and for each other—who've asked you here today to witness their vows as they declare their love."

Asa only had eyes for Scott. He could barely look away as the candlelight reflected in his gaze. But he knew there were people he cared about there. He'd told Beau to keep it small, but there were more here than he'd anticipated, and he had a feeling that if he asked, Beau would tell him that he couldn't keep them away.

Tristan and Wade, holding hands. Dylan and Logan. Pax and Davis, not touching, but surrounded by an air of undeniable intimacy, anyway. Lynn and Kelly. Rudy. So many people who they'd touched in their journey, who'd made this ending possible.

"They've asked you here today," Sebastian continued, "to hear their vows to each other." He turned to Scott first. "Scott, your vows first."

Scott's grip on Asa's hands tightened, but his voice was steady. Like a rock. Just like the rock he'd always been for Asa. Through anything, he'd always had his back.

Now he had his heart, too.

"When we first met," Scott said, "I told myself it was some kind of cosmic joke, falling for the worst possible person I could. Not just someone on the football team with me. Not just someone who accepted who I was, but didn't seem interested himself. But a friend. A best friend. A friend I never wanted to give up. We stuck by each other, through anything, and I thought, so many times, this is gonna get better. It's gonna get easier. But I never got over you, and it never did. Every single morning, I woke up and I thought, *I love Asa*. And it felt miraculous, and a little crazy, when one morning I woke up and thought, *I think Asa might love me too*. Then it wasn't just me thinkin' that, it was you tellin' me that, and I'll never be proud that I didn't fight for us, the first time, but then I came here, to Miami, and I knew I'd fight for you now."

Asa had known it. How could he not know it? Scott Callaway had never given up on anything without a fight. Maybe that's why he'd been so angry that Scott was coming. Because he'd known he wouldn't want anything else but *this*, the moment Scott started fighting for him. It couldn't be a fair fight. Not even close. And Asa had never been more relieved that Scott fought dirty.

"And I'm gonna fight for you," Scott said, "every single day for the rest of our lives. Right next to you. Behind you. In the booth at the top of the stadium. Wherever that fight takes me, takes us, you've got me. I love you. If I wake up in the morning, I'm going to love you. That's all there is to it."

He'd expected to cry. He'd expected to feel a flood of emotions, hearing Scott's vows. Because even though Scott wasn't much of a talker—especially about his emotions, there was always a rawness to his confessions when he did. And nothing else would ever have the power of Scott promising, Scott *vowing*, to wake up loving him every morning.

"Asa?" Sebastian said.

Asa cleared his throat. Wiped a tear away. Hung on to Scott's gaze, because that was the only sanity in an insane world. "I'm sorry," he said, "that I didn't love you the way you loved me, right away. I'm sorry we wasted some years. But I'm not sorry, too, because we ended up here, with the people we have in our lives today, and honestly, I wouldn't change a thing. I know how much you mean to me, what it feels like to have you in my life now, because I didn't. Because you were gone. I understand the power of it now, how goddamn important you are, and how much I want to fight for you too, because I know what it feels like to lose you. And I won't lose you, ever again. You go, I'm gonna follow."

Scott's smile could've lit the whole stadium. "You've never been a follower. Not once in your whole life."

"Except I've always followed you," Asa swore. "Always wanted to rush out to do the next craziest thing with you, sneak out, raise hell, become a coach, everything I ever did, the person I most wanted to do it with was you. You tell me I can do that for the rest of our lives? Nothin' else will do, nothing else but you. Just you. You and me."

"Together," Scott said, and their heads tipped together, drawn tight like two magnets.

"I now pronounce you husband and husband," Sebastian said. Or at least Asa assumed he must've said it, because Scott was kissing him and it was so sweet, so goddamn perfect, Sebastian could've said anything, and he wouldn't have heard.

Or cared.

Because he had everything he needed, right here, right now.

Forever.

Intrigued by Kenyon's mystery hookup? Find out more in his book (and the last in the Piranhas series!), *Playing Deep.*

Want to read more about Beau's reaction to Asa and Scott (in the apron)? About the rest of the Piranhas' reaction? Download a bonus scene here.

INTERESTED IN READING MORE OF
BETH'S BOOKS?

CHECK OUT A FULL LIST OF TILES
BY SCANNING THE QR CODE
OR VISITING HER WEBSITE

WWW.BETHBOLDEN.COM/BOOKLIST

WANT TO FOLLOW BETH?

MAKE SURE YOU NEVER
MISS A RELEASE?

SCAN THE QR CODE BELOW
OR VISIT HER WEBSITE
FOR A SOCIAL MEDIA LIST,
NEWSLETTER SIGNUP,
AND SO MUCH MORE!

WWW.BETHBOLDEN.COM/ABOUT